Praise for...

# The Scavengers

This epic tale slowly unfolds, revealing flawed characters, some seeking the way, while others are bound to repeat the mistakes of their ancestors. *The Scavengers* is full of symbolism, adventure and religious metaphor. A perceptive allegory replete with love, honor, treachery and spiritual profundity.

**- Phil Boatwright, Preview Online**

With characters so well described I could visualize the bottoms of their boots, Parker has created his own realm. It is full of mythology, destruction and deconstruction. Dialogue flows easily and with each twist and turn I found myself wanting more and more.

**- Paige Crutcher, Examiner.com**

*The Scavengers* is a fast paced, fantasy thriller with real life characters and an epic story of good and evil. Mike Parker's first book of fiction is not to be missed.

**- Chris Coppernoll, Author**
**"Providence: Once Upon a Second Chance"**

"This is an amazing novel. From the outset it is gripping and tense. I cannot imagine an America after such an apocalyptic event - this book tells me just that. If you like suspense, action, and thrills then this is for you. The best book I have read in years."

**- GP Taylor, #1 New York Times Best Selling Author**
**"Mariah Mundi: The Midas Box"**

# The SCAVENGERS

Book I of the Tyrfingr Chronicles

# THE SCAVENGERS

Book I of the Tyrfingr Chronicles

# Mike Parker

WordCrafts

Published by WordCrafts Press
Tullahoma, TN 37388
www.wordcrafts.net

# For Paula

# PROLOGUE

*America - The day after tomorrow*

**"In America tonight,** despite allegations of a cover-up, the government denies there is any danger of Puhl-Lichter striking the earth. In a press conference earlier today White House press secretary, Jill Grossman, told reporters the comet would indeed pass between the earth and the moon tonight, but aside from a spectacular meteor shower, some unusual tide activity, and perhaps a few hours of communications disruption, Puhl-Lichter will have little effect on life as we know it on earth.

"The government's assurances have not convinced the followers of the Reverend Paul Samuelson to abandon their occupation of Carlsbad Caverns, however. It is estimated that several hundred of the fundamentalist preacher's flock are holed up in the famed caverns awaiting the destruction of the earth. In a prepared statement, Samuelson promised to surrender to any authority figure still alive after sunrise tomorrow."

Taylor turned on cue toward Camera Two. The red eye on Camera One winked out.

"In The World tonight - fiery protests erupt over the proposed Middle-East peace treaty. For more on that story, here's world news correspondent, Roxanne Cameron."

"And...out."

Taylor heard the director's cue through his earphone. Cameron's report would last exactly one minute, fifty-five seconds before the camera would again be turned on him. Instinctively, he checked himself out on the monitor.

Hair...*in place*. Teeth...*no spinach*. Eyes...*no dark circles*.

*Never let 'em see you sweat,* he thought.

But J. Ransom Taylor was sweating tonight, and it wasn't the hot studio lights, nor the dismal news that had him in a lather. He had long ago learned the secret of reading the news without getting emotionally involved with it.

Tonight he was sweating because he was worried about Kim.

Slim, petite, prim and proper, but with smoldering green eyes that seemed to burn into his soul, Kim had been a beauty queen and a model before 'retiring' to teach pre-school. They met at a fund-raiser for Multiple Sclerosis and he had been trapped by her eyes.

They had married in three weeks time and by the end of the first month she was already dragging him to church. At first he had resisted. He didn't like Christians, he had told her. Didn't like Jews or Muslims or Buddhists for that matter. He just didn't think anyone could possibly have all the truth. He wasn't even sure Truth existed. At least, that's what he said. But he inevitably succumbed to her eyes. He always did.

He was surprised to find how much he liked the church - liked the pastor, liked the quirky little community of believers, even liked those musty old hymns. They reminded him of his childhood.

"On in Five...Four...Three..." The director's voice shook him from his reverie. A quick glance at the teleprompter and he was back in character. A hand signal flashed from the news director and Camera Two winked back to life.

"Today was a scorcher. Will the heat wave continue through the weekend? Meteorologist Ken Bartholomew has the five-day forecast, right after this."

Taylor flashed an easy smile until the red light perched atop the lens dimmed to announce he was off the air. The studio clock showed 10:17. Five minutes for weather; four-thirty for sports; a minute and a half commercial break; light news team banter and roll credits over a sweet human interest story about a dog rescued from a drain pipe by a volunteer fireman, and he could finally leave.

The candy-apple red '68 Mustang flew down 4th Street toward St. Mary's Hospital. Taylor cursed the red lights that blocked his way. He cursed the gas gauge that rested comfortably on "E."

Kim always told him "E" stood for "Empty." He always replied that "E" stood for "Enough."

Today he feared she was right and cursed himself for not stopping to fill the tank on his way to work. He cursed the news director for holding him up two minutes longer than he had to with some innocuous chitchat about a company volleyball tournament.

And he cursed that infernal comet that threatened to outshine the moon.

Most of all he cursed himself for going to the station at all. Oh, Kim had said it was okay. The baby wasn't due for another two weeks, she said. She'd be fine, she said.

Taylor ran his fingers through his wavy brown hair, still stiff with setting gel for the camera, gunned the engine impatiently while cursing the light again, and cursed himself again for wasting what little gas he had left. It would be par for the course if he managed to run out of gas on the way to the hospital.

Kim's water had broken somewhere between the Texas Tech women's basketball scores, and the dog story; and he hadn't found out until the newscast was over.

Green light; and the Mustang's tires left a ten-foot reminder of where they had once rested.

The Mustang coughed and choked before wheezing its last gasp of gas fumes, then coasted to a laconic stop on the outskirts of the hospital parking lot. Taylor leapt from the restored classic, not bothering to even lock the doors, and ran the last forty yards to the emergency room entrance.

"Maternity," he sputtered to the nurse through the four-inch round hole in the glass.

She pointed down the hall with her pen. A half-amused grin curled the corners of her mouth, but never touched her eyes. She had seen that same frantic look on too many almost-fathers' faces for the humor to reach further. She shook her head, let out a sigh and returned to the endless pile of paperwork before her.

Taylor forgot her as soon as he received directions. He took off at a half-trot, trying to follow the yellow line on the floor but without success. Yellow merged with green, then with red, separated back into yellow and merged back with green - a labyrinth of wards too complex for any but Theseus to decipher.

"Might have guessed it would be all the way on the other side of the hospital," he muttered, cursing himself once more as he turned into the Geriatrics Ward.

They had taken Lamaze at this hospital. They had visited the birthing center at this hospital. Kim's OB/GYN had her office in the clinic across the street from this hospital. So, why couldn't he remember where the Maternity Ward was located!?

Finally a heavy-set black woman in a happy green smock populated by little blue men in red hats came into view, and he hurried to catch her before she got away.

"Maternity?" he begged.

The nurse paused long enough to peer over her glasses at the frantic newscaster.

"You're J. Ransom Taylor," she said, in a manner that said she was not impressed at all. "I watch you on the news when I get the chance. You're not bad, but I gotta tell you, honey, that Chad Henderson you got doing the sports, he is fine. Umm, hmm, hmm."

She motioned him to follow as she wound her way through the corridors. She stopped briefly to look at him as if the light suddenly dawned on her.

"You're Kim Taylor's husband. Why, she's been waiting for you. I tell you, she is just the sweetest thing."

"Is she all right? Has the baby come yet? I'm not too late am I?"

"Tush," she said, waving her hand as if to brush his worries away. She started off again at a nonchalant waddle. "First babies don't come that fast. You got some waiting to do yet. Might as well get comfortable. It's likely you'll be here for a while.

"Kim's fine. We've got a monitor on her and the baby's heartbeat is just fine. Her contractions were a good five minutes apart, last I checked, but she's only dilated to four. She wouldn't even be here yet if her water hadn't broke."

As she finished her speech the pair rounded a corner, and she ushered him into one of the hospital's beautifully appointed birthing rooms that looked more like the bridal suite at a posh hotel than a delivery room - rich, polished mahogany furniture, delicate floral wallpaper, a state of the art entertainment center, and a spare bed in case dad needed a place to crash. The local hospitals were competing for the baby business, even promising valet parking and a candlelight dinner for the new parents.

*Nothing like the old days when fathers had to pace in the*

*waiting room*, Taylor mused.

Kim lay on the bed, alternately watching a black and white rerun of "I Love Lucy" on the television and the black and green squiggly lines on the baby's heart rate monitor.

She looked up at Taylor and smiled, a dimple appearing on her right cheek. With a leap he was at her bedside, shaking with relief that he had not missed the birth of their first child.

John Knox ran the calculations again. Blinking behind his glasses, he tried to deny his conclusion. He pushed the specs back up on his nose and ran the figures through the Cray CX1 Supercomputer one more time.

*Unbelievable.*

He shook his head.

*They were wrong. They had been wrong all along. They were using outdated information. Possibly even erroneous information.*

Knox stood, walked to the window, ripped off his glasses and polished them with the tail of his untucked shirt.

*It is erroneous information. It has to be erroneous information.*

He settled his glasses back into place, returned to the Cray and ran the calculations a third time, just to be sure.

*Impossible, yet unmistakable. These figures can only apply to Puhl-Lichter. The official version is close, so close. No layman would ever notice. The vast majority of professional mathematicians and astronomers would never know the difference.*

*You could run the official figures through a computer a dozen times and still come up with the wrong conclusion. After all, computer geeks don't question the input data. But 'garbage in, garbage out' as the saying goes. These figures are obviously wrong.*

Knox jerked the sweat-flecked spectacles from his face, mopped his brow with the back of his hand, then pushed the glasses back into place, startled at the sudden clarity as the world once again snapped into place.

He could no longer argue with the results. Puhl-Lichter wasn't going to pass between the earth and the moon. Puhl-Lichter was going to *hit* the earth.

And *they* knew it. *They* had known it all along.

Knox was afraid he was going to be sick, or soil himself. He had to tell somebody. There wasn't much time, but maybe people could get to a shelter...Or something.

*Why hadn't they told the truth, warned the people? Millions... billions could die. Would die!*

He reached for the phone, then let it drop as the truth set in. *He* was going to die. Today. In about four hours and twenty-seven... no... twenty-six minutes, if his calculations were correct. There was no place to hide. Not for him. Not for anybody.

In order to survive the impact of a comet the size of Puhl-Lichter you would have to be a hundred feet underground, and be prepared to stay there for years, decades, maybe even a century. No one could plan for that contingency.

He wasn't sure how long he sat there, staring at nothing. Numb. The footsteps in the doorway roused him from his stupor. He pushed his glasses back up on his nose and looked a silent question at his project manager, Dr. Lawrence Wilkes.

"Yes. It's going to hit the earth," Wilkes answered the look.

He walked to Knox's work station and nodded at the calculations.

"This is very good work, John. Very good. You always were one of the best. You never accepted the facts as presented. You always wanted to know for yourself."

Wilkes ambled across the room and slid down to sit next

to his young protégé.

"It will probably splinter when it enters the atmosphere," he said as if talking were a catharsis for him.

"Parts of it will likely strike the Atlantic, producing tidal waves that make the 2004 Indian Ocean tsunami look like it was made by a toddler splashing the bathtub by comparison. Depending on how much the atmosphere slows it down, portions with likely fall all across North America, principally in the south, with Georgia, Texas and Mexico the most likely candidates.

"Smaller bits will continue to fall in its wake for days after, striking the Pacific, China, India, Africa. There is a sizable chuck that will likely smack down somewhere in France. Serves them right. I never much cared for the French."

"Not that it matters," Wilkes rubbed his hands together as if to shake the chalk dust from them after a lecture in his college classroom. He shook his head slowly at the old habit that had refused to die when he left academia.

"There likely won't be much of anyone left alive anywhere on earth by that time. The atmosphere will become super-heated when the comet hits, spawning tornadoes, cyclones and waterspouts all over the world.

"Its collision with the earth will produce earthquakes, of course; volcanic eruptions and tsunamis will follow for months after. Millions of tons of debris will be thrown into the air, blocking out the sun's rays, ushering in a new ice age that could last decades - or centuries."

Wilkes checked his watch, a ridiculously expensive, and not particularly attractive, Rolex that had been a gift from the institution for his thirty years of service.

"I'm sorry, John. In roughly three and a half hours, civilization as we know it will cease to exist, and there is not a damn thing anyone can do about it. Nothing anyone could have done to prevent it. Puhl-Lichter is just too damned big."

"Does the President know?" Knox asked.

"Of course he knows," Wilkes snorted. "He's known for months. Members of the UN Security Council have been briefed. Every head of state in the free world and some in the not-so-free world are privy to the information you just discovered."

"Then why? Why not tell the people? Maybe they could have done something. They don't know this is their last day on earth..."

"What good would it do? There's no place to hide. Oh, there are a few security bunkers for some of the higher up muckity-mucks and their families.

"The military may have a few places that can weather the storm for a few years, if it's not as bad as I think it will be. But announce it to the world? Do you think anyone would take the view of *Eat, drink, and be merry for tomorrow we die?* Do you seriously think life would just go on as usual? It would be Bedlam; or worse."

Wilkes stood, shoved his hands into his pockets, and strolled across the room and looked out the window.

"Come here, John," he commanded. "Take a look. See that? A woman and a man, holding hands, sharing a quiet lunch, discussing their future, perhaps making sweet love-talk. Scenes just like that are happening all over the world right now, right at this very minute. Pretty peaceful, huh? Let them have these last few moments. It's better this way, don't you think?"

Knox crossed to the window, and watched as the young man, who appeared to be barely out of his teens, handed the woman a daisy. The chorus of an old song drifted through his mind.

*"I'll give you a daisy a day, dear. I'll give you a daisy a day. I'll love you until the rivers run still. And the four winds we know blow away."*

Knox nodded. The four winds were about to blow away.

He glanced at his watch, took a deep breath and ran his fingers through his hair. He suddenly wished he had taken the time to try hang gliding. It might have been fun. He reached again for the phone.

"What are you doing, John?" the elder scientist asked.

"I thought I might call my mom," Knox replied. "Just to tell her I love her."

The labor had been intense. Kim couldn't stop sweating, her pixie-cut, auburn hair matted against her forehead. She slept fitfully during the moments between contractions, but she was near exhaustion.

Taylor was exhausted just being in the same room with her. He sweated too, and this time he didn't care who saw. Not for the first time he thanked God he was not a woman; and at the same time wished with all his might that he could be allowed to bare the pain his wife was enduring, if only it would somehow ease hers.

At last Dr. Jocelyn White sauntered into the room, smiling as if this were the most natural thing in the world. She was a small woman. The gray in her hair and the lines around her eyes placed her well past her middle years, but she exuded more energy than Taylor could have mustered in his college days.

He heard she had been recalled to active duty during the Third Gulf War, and she had been no spring chicken even then. Taylor had shaken his head at that news. This was one tough bird.

You could never tell her age from the quixotic sparkle in her eye. If he hadn't seen the date on her diploma from Vanderbilt Medical School, he would never have believed it.

Garbed in an unflattering shade he could only describe

as puke green, Dr. White rolled a stool to the base of Kim's bed and peered between her thighs as she snapped on a pair of latex gloves. A quick examination, and she grinned up at Taylor.

"Dilated to 10, 100% effaced. We're going to have a baby," she announced.

Taylor could have kissed her. Instead he stammered, "Now?"

Dr. White nodded as the nurse tied her gown. She leaned over Kim and whispered something into her ear that made Kim laugh. Taylor wondered what was so funny, but knew better than to ask. There were some things that women shared, that men were not privy to. He accepted that. It was only a mild irritation. But it would have helped if they shared their woman stuff when he was not in the same room.

Taylor backed out of the way and watched, fascinated at the process. He had seen the films during Lamaze class; been a little disgusted with them if the truth be known. Birth was all about blood, sweat and tears. It was not a pretty sight.

Until today.

Until it was his child being born.

Until it was his wife sweating, straining, pushing the new life out of her own body.

Today it was incredible. Indescribable. Beautiful.

Everything ground down to slow motion, like a grainy, black-and-white 8mm film clip. The head...the shoulders...the tummy...the feet. Then it was over. And it was beautiful.

"We have a man-child," Dr. White exulted, as if this was the first time she had ever delivered a baby in her life. She flashed a triumphant, yet somehow coy, smile toward Taylor.

"Would Dad like to cut the cord?"

Taylor stood dumbfounded, as if his feet had suddenly grown roots and burrowed into the floor. It never occurred to him he might be allowed to do that. It had never been discussed. What if he did it wrong? What if he hurt the baby?

What if he hurt Kim?

Man-child? He had a son?! It was a boy!

He stumbled forward.

"You bet he would," he said as he grabbed the surgical scissors, a stupid grin splitting his face in two.

Guided by the watchful eyes of the obstetrician, Taylor administered the cut that divided mother from son. Dr. White gently laid the softly crying infant on Kim's chest, smiling congratulations.

"What are you going to call him?" she asked.

Kim looked triumphantly, fiercely at her husband, and announced with more strength than she could possibly have left, "James Ransom Taylor, the Second."

Taylor felt his heart fill to bursting. He didn't think he could ever be any happier if he lived for eternity. He leaned over the bed to embrace his wife, and for the first time, he looked into the eyes of his son. They were bright, prescient, knowing. They looked just like Kim's eyes. He would have sworn his son smiled at him.

The light grew bright; unbearably bright. The air crackled and hissed; took on the pressure of an impending thunderstorm, and in the twinkle of an eye J. Ransom Taylor, still embracing his family, found himself smiling back into the eyes of his Creator.

# A LEGEND OF TYRFINGR

**In the time** before the Time of Madness there lived a great king whose name was Svarlym. Valiant in battle and wise in government, he fought for many years to rid his kingdom of evil and at last he drove all those who practiced darkness to the frozen wastelands far to the north.

All but two.

Dvalinn and Durin, twin brothers who were dark and shrunken, but powerful in the black arts, remained hidden in the rocks they called home.

King Svarlym trapped the brothers within their den and would have killed them, but Dvalinn offered to forge the king a great sword with a golden hilt that would never miss a stroke, would never rust, and could cut through stone and iron as easily as through cloth. Though Svarlym was known to be both wise and good, the thought of such power beguiled his mind. He agreed to spare the brothers' lives in exchange for this marvelous sword.

Long did the twins labor at their forge, crafting the mighty sword they called…TYRFINGR. It shone like the sun and gleamed like fire. King Svarlym laughed loud and long as he swung it in a wide arc above his head. Surely the hand that wielded Tyrfingr was the hand that would rule the world.

Dvalinn and Durin laughed loud and long, too, as they told the king of the curse they had forged into the great sword. Tyrfingr would be the cause of three great evils and it must take a life every time it was drawn from its sheath. The first life it was destined to take, Dvalinn cackled, was King Svarlym's own.

The king tried to slay Dvalinn and Durin, but the dark brothers escaped into the rocks. Too late King Svarlym realized the foolishness of his lust for power. Raising the great sword high over his head, Svarlym cried with a loud voice, "Though my life is forfeit, no other evil shall come from my folly, for no other hand shall draw Tyrfingr forth."

King Svarlym's mighty heart burst as he drove the shining blade of Tyrfingr deep into the stone, where it remains to this day.

*- From the Hervararkvida. Recorded in the Regius Codex and kept safe among the forbidden works in the Great Library of Omaha.*

# CHAPTER 1

*Many Centuries after The Great Burning*

**It was late** before Alwyn finally stumbled back to his cubicle in the Library. It was a small, non-descript room with barren, white plastered walls, furnished simply with a bed shoved against one wall, and a desk and chair against the other. Like all the rooms in the Library, there was no door. A heavy, deep blue tapestry edged in golden embroidery, provided a modicum of privacy.

He shed his sodden, brown wool cloak onto the floor and let it lay where it fell, then dropped onto his bed to wrestle with his boots. The first slid off reluctantly, but the other refused to cooperate.

Weariness clung to him like a cockle-burr. Fatigue streaked his hazel eyes with red, and the cold numbed his fingers to near useless stubs. He almost gave up the fight when his foot suddenly popped loose. He looked at the worn leather boot in his hand with mild surprise, trying to remember why it was there, then dropped it to the floor beside its mate.

Alwyn sat staring at the lone candle flickering on his desk, letting the weariness wash over him as the warmth from the fire, laid by a compassionate steward, leached the cold from his body. He tried not to think, but thoughts came unbidden anyway. He desperately wanted sleep, but there was too much information, supposition, and insinuation fighting for his attention.

He began to consciously slow his breathing, to let his surroundings blur. It was a trick of concentration he had learned in the Amarillo Waste.

A dull glint of candlelight reflecting off of a polished surface on his desk distracted him, breaking his concentration. It wasn't much, but it was enough to draw his attention for a moment. He scanned through the collection of mementos that populated his desk for the source of the glimmer. Then he saw it - the burnished steel of a marriage knife - *his* marriage knife. The memories came crashing back with a force that burgled his breath.

*Catharine!*

Alwyn forced himself to his feet and staggered forward languidly, as if in a dream, toward his desk. Gently, reverently, he picked up the dagger with the three red cords twined about its hilt, unconsciously rubbing the trio of scars on his chest.

He didn't remember returning to his bed. He didn't remember lying down upon it. He didn't remember drifting into sleep.

The air was crisp and clean, cold to the point of searing Alwyn's lungs, but in his dream he was the only one who seemed to be bothered by it. He tried to will his body to stop shivering. It refused to comply. He breathed slowly through his nose and let his surroundings blur. It was a trick he had learned from Jon, his closest friend among the Amarillo Nomes, soon to be his brother-in-law. His nervousness wrestled with his self-will and his artificially induced calm evaporated like the morning mist under the onslaught of the rising sun.

Suddenly she was there, looking more radiant than that sun rising over the plateau, and thoughts of the cold were banished from his mind. His body no longer shivered, though his mouth went dry and he knew a stupid grin was working its way across his face.

*Catharine.*

*Liberty on high, she's beautiful!*

Catharine walked exactly three paces in front of Theodora, her mother, who walked exactly three paces in front of old Sara, the oldest woman in the clan, who walked exactly three paces in front of Brianna, his mother. They were followed by the married women, some with babes in arms, who were followed in turn by the maidens.

There was no trace of nervousness on Catharine's face; no indication that she was affected by the cold - though, as custom dictated, she was barefooted. There was no hesitation in her walk.

Catharine moved with the grace of a wild pony; confident, exuberant, free. Her raven black hair, bound loosely at the shoulders with a simple white ribbon, fell below her waist and glistened like obsidian in the sunlight, rippling on every hint of a breeze. Her emerald green, almond-shaped eyes glowed with an inner fire above her high cheekbones; her coppery skin shone like burnished gold beneath the fireball of the rising sun.

In a heartbeat Catharine was standing before Alwyn, and the cold truly did vanish. Her smile, at once shy and bold, warmed him thoroughly. She smelled of sunshine and wildflowers. Radiant in an unadorned, pure white, linen wedding dress that left her shoulders bare, gathered about her tiny waist, and fell to within a hand's breadth of the ground, she took his breath away

Catherine was barely one day past her sixteenth naming

day. Neither honor nor tradition required her to marry before her eighteenth. But she had chosen him, an outlander, and demanded the ceremony be performed not one day later than was permitted, as was her right.

That day was today.

Theodora and old Sara took their places on either side of the girl. Theodora stood staring at Alwyn for what seemed an eternity, as if weighing and measuring his character to the last degree. Alwyn was tempted to lick his lips, and would have if he could have worked any moisture onto his tongue.

Apparently finally satisfied with what she saw, Theodora suddenly turned toward the gathering of women at her back and nodded.

Brianna stepped forward bearing a small, highly polished wooden box, ornately carved with twisting knots and fanciful animals. Blonde-haired, blue-eyed and fair skinned, Alwyn's mother stood out from her dark-eyed, ruddy-skinned Nomish counterparts, though her knowledge of the customs and traditions of the Amarillo Nomes allowed her to blend comfortably into their society. She knelt once before Catharine, twice before Theodora, and three times before old Sara, then opened the box.

The oldest woman in the clan reached into the box and drew out a dagger. Its blade was slightly curved and, like the box, delicately decorated with twisting knots and fanciful animals; its hilt was twined with three red cords. She nodded approvingly at the workmanship, then nodded to the men who stood silently behind Alwyn.

Pepin, Catharine's father, stepped forward on one side while Malcolme, Alwyn's father, took his place on the other. At another nod from the old woman the two men grasped Alwyn's lightweight linen shirt and ripped it down the front, exposing his chest.

Old Sara stepped forward, placed the point of the razor sharp blade of the dagger just above Alwyn's heart and pressed until it pierced the flesh. With a slow, practiced hand she drew the blade down three finger lengths as she recited the ancient marriage ritual of the Amarillo Nomes.

"It is written: Where there is life there is pain; but where pain is shared by two, the pain is cut in half. This will be a mark of remembrance for the pain that has been."

Theodora, called Dora by the womenfolk and close family, now stepped forward, took the knife from the old woman's hand, and placed its point slightly to the right of the wound which was now leaking blood down Alwyn's chest and onto his belly. For a long moment she searched his face, looking for any sign of hesitation. Finding none, she allowed herself a brief grin of satisfaction, and then pressed the blade through his skin, making a duplicate incision.

"It is written: Where there is life there is pain; but where pain is shared by two, the pain is cut in half. This will be a mark of remembrance for the pain that shall be."

Theodora stood for another moment before pulling the dagger from Alwyn's chest. He experienced an odd, sweet ache of sadness as it was withdrawn, like a long forgotten lover's kiss.

Catharine took her place before him in all her radiant beauty. She tangled his thoughts and threatened to wrest his concentration away from the ceremony. He stood still, immobile, awaiting the final stroke that would rend his flesh and seal their union.

Catharine smiled sweetly as she raised the dagger to his heart. A petite creature, she placed the knife point on his chest barely at her eye level, between his two bleeding wounds.

"It is written," she intoned, "Where there is life there is pain; but where pain is shared by two, the pain is cut in half. This will be a mark of remembrance for the pain that now is."

The dagger entered his flesh, piercing, burning, slicing easily the ritual three fingers; but instead of drawing the knife out, Catharine began to push the blade deeper into his chest.

The blood which had trickled from the first two incisions began to flow freely from the third wound.

In shock Alwyn tried to back away, but found himself held fast on either side by the iron grip of Pepin and Malcolme. Catharine's sweet smile degenerated into a rictus snarl as she began to decompose before his eyes.

Up the plateau he could see a war party of the White Sands Nomes advancing, cutting down everyone in their path. None of the Amarillo Nomes turned to run; none tried to fight. All stood smiling ruthlessly at him as they were slaughtered before his eyes.

"Why did you leave me, my darling," the cadaver that had once been his bride spat as she pressed the dagger deeper into his flesh. "Was your precious collection so important? You knew my time was near to deliver our child, but you couldn't wait, could you? You needed to find out what lay buried in that mound across the border in the White Sands, though you knew it was forbidden, didn't you?"

Still the warriors advanced, hacking their way toward him with their thick-bladed machetes. He could hear them coming from behind him; saw them murder young and old, women and children, without pity; limbs and heads severed, soaking the landscape with blood.

He wanted to beg the people to run, to fight, to beg for mercy; anything but to accept this senseless slaughter. But the people only stood and smiled at him as they died, and the dagger in his chest cut off all sound from his throat.

He watched in horror as an ax severed his mother's head from her body; felt his father release his grip, and saw Malcolme's bloodied body fall at his feet.

"We are all dead now, my darling. All dead, because of you," Catharine whispered as she twisted the knife, trying to wedge it between his ribs. "Because you violated the ancient burial site of the kings of the White Sands Nomes, we are dead. And it is all your fault."

The putrid, rotting figure that moments before had been his beautiful Catharine, prepared for the final push that would end his life; and then hesitated. She gradually began to withdraw the blade from his chest, a hairbreadth at a time, until only the point continued to pierce his flesh. With the same measured precision that she had used to slice a furrow three fingers long down his chest, Catharine gently pull the blade from his flesh.

"No. You will not die, my darling. You will live. But your pain - pain which should have been halved - will now be doubled."

The figure that he could no longer recognize as Catharine dropped the dagger with the three red cords twined about its hilt into the dust at his feet, turned and walked away.

She stopped once to look back at him. "Why *did* you leave me, my darling?" Catharine asked sadly, then turned and walked unhindered through the rising tide of howling White Sands warriors, before crumbling into dust, and blowing away.

"Catharine!" Alwyn cried out, just before a blow to the side of his head crumpled him to the ground.

Alwyn rolled from his bed, landing on his hands and knees. Slowly the cold stone floor of the Library cubicle he called home lured him back to his senses. He shook his head to clear away the images. They weren't real. It didn't happen that way. It did *not* happen that way.

His marriage ceremony was a sweet memory. He and Catharine had enjoyed life as husband and wife. She had been pregnant with their first child before...

Alwyn took a deep breath to steady his emotions. He

forced himself to his feet, stumbled to the water basin and poured icy water from the pitcher into the bowl. Plunging his hands beneath the surface Alwyn splashed his face and scrubbed away the tears.

It was a hard dream. LaFranc would say it was just his mind dealing with the uncertainties of the past and the chaos of the present triggered by some spicy flat bread, topped with sausages and covered with cheese.

LaFranc could be annoying at times.

Weariness tugged Alwyn back to his bed like a half-sleeping lover. His face was still wet and his hands were still icy. He was asleep by the time he closed his eyes. The dreams reasserted themselves.

Alwyn lay prone just below the crest of the hill. Low-crawling on his elbows and knees he worked his way up until he could peer down into the valley beneath. He was on sacred ground; at least it was sacred to the White Sands Nomes. On the other side of the hill lay the legendary burial mounds of the Loch-Lann, the ancient kings of the Nomes.

The Annals of the Four Masters, reputed to have been written in the fourth century of the Common Era, claimed the huge stone chamber-mounds were exactly 286 hands high with entrance passages more than 90 hands long. The riches of the kings were listed in detail in the Annals: golden masks, crafted in the likeness of the dead kings, gemstones, exotic wood furnishings, aromatic incenses, precious metals of steel and silver. But more important to Alwyn was the enigmatic ring-and-spiral artwork that decorated the mounds' iron-bound doors.

Still more exciting, the inscriptions on those doors appeared to be written in Ancient American, though he could not be sure until he had a closer look. Malcolme, his father, had spent his lifetime deciphering the maddeningly simple yet infinitely complex script, and Alwyn had inherited his obsession. He was fascinated by the genius of the Ancient Americans in developing a written language using less than fifty characters which could be rearranged to create individual words. This written language bore not even the slightest resemblance to Modern American script.

Few outside the Guild of the Librarians and court scribes could read Modern American. This written language was composed of more than 5000 unique symbols, one for each word, and was primarily used for official government documents. Malcolme believed it was the ability of the Ancients to pass on their knowledge through their written language that allowed them to create the mythical marvels attributed to them. He had even theorized publicly that the Ancient Americans had all known how to read and write, though his colleagues scoffed at his belief in universal literacy.

Most common folk outside the Library, and many Guild members within its walls, considered the marvels of the Ancients to be folk tales at best. Reading and writing was far to complex a task to be bothered with when there was a crop to bring in. Besides, such a skill was too important to be left to the common people.

The Loch-Lann mounds were not guarded, yet Alwyn felt a twinge that told him something was not right. Collections could be dangerous expeditions, and although he was not yet seventeen years from his Naming Day, this feeling had already saved his life more than once. He had learned to trust it. He motioned his older brother, Burtyn, to stay where he was, and inched his way back down.

"Guards?" Burtyn whispered.

Alwyn shook his head.

"Then what are we waiting for? This is the chance of a lifetime. Think of it, Alwyn. We will see things no American has ever seen before. Ancient weapons, steel and precious stones. There may even be books in there, Alwyn. Books from before the Great Burning. We'll be famous. Maybe even more famous than Father."

Alwyn pressed his finger to his lips, and tried to stifle his older brother's enthusiasm. Burtyn was good, better than Alwyn, nearly as good as Malcolme. But Burtyn was reckless; impetuous; prone to taking shortcuts when the long way around would be more prudent. Burtyn had no patience for the long way around. He had almost gotten them both killed on more than one occasion, but he seemed to have a charmed life, often claiming that Liberty loved him best.

It had been Burtyn's hunch to explore south of the Grande River Valley for the mounds, when all evidence pointed north. Now that he had been proved right Burtyn wanted to exploit his good fortune.

*Books from before the Burning?*

Alwyn felt a thrill rush through him that threatened to overwhelm his common sense, but he squelched the thought before it could gain a foothold on his reason.

"We both agreed," Alwyn whispered, "that if we found anything we would ride back to camp and consult Malcolme. This is his collection, not ours. Besides, something is not right."

"What?" Burtyn demanded.

"I don't know." Alwyn pursed his lips, trying to put his finger on what was troubling him. "Something. A feeling. We should go. Now."

Burtyn's laughter was tinged with scorn. He had little use for Alwyn's *feelings*, but he raised his hands in acquiescence.

"Go get the horses saddled," he said. "I've got a pebble in my boot I want to get out, and then I'll join you."

Alwyn gave his brother a knowing look and raised a warning finger.

"Don't do nothin' dumb," he quoted Strom Maxwell, a friend from their years in Omaha.

Strom had been a scalawag and a trouble-maker, but he had a quick wit and easy grin, and the uncanny ability to get out of trouble as easily as he got into it. Strom and the two brothers had been all but inseparable. *Don't do nothin' dumb*, had been Strom's favorite saying, though he rarely followed his own advice.

Neither did Burtyn.

Alwyn waited for his impetuous brother to acknowledge the warning. Burtyn nodded, and Alwyn scrabbled down the hill as quietly as he could and rapidly started saddling their mounts, beginning with Burtyn's chestnut pony.

Alwyn lost himself in the work, thinking about how proud Malcolme would be. Perhaps Malcolme would even let him work on the translation of the doors...*I'm not so bad with Ancient American glyphs*...if it did truly turn out to be Ancient American glyphs.

Alwyn had barely finished saddling the first horse when he was jolted from his reverie by the sound of pounding footsteps. Without a word, Burtyn ran past him, leapt into the saddle and spurred his pony to a gallop.

Alwyn stood stunned for a moment, watching Burtyn ride away. When he turned back toward the mound, the hilltop was lined with warriors of the White Sands Nomes, resplendent in paint and feathers.

He thought he should run, but his feet seemed planted in the earth. The warriors approached, laughing mirthlessly, mercilessly; some swinging their long swords at nothing, others hacking the wind with their wicked, double-edged battle-axes.

Alwyn looked back long enough to see his older brother disappearing over the hill and cursed him by all he considered holy. His thoughts went at once to Catharine. She was great with child; their first child; his child.

She was near her time. She had begged him not to go on this collection. She said she had a very bad feeling about it. She sensed something bad would happen. He had laughed at her. After all, he told her, Burtyn would be with him. What could possibly go wrong?

"Catharine," he cried out just before a blow to the side of his head crumpled him to the ground.

Alwyn groaned on his bed, thrashed and moaned, clawed his way to momentary consciousness before sinking back into the nightmare.

Alwyn lost track of the days that had past since the White Sands Nomes captured him. He knew from the change of the seasons that it had been more than a year, but beyond that, one day was pretty much like any other. He was a slave…less than a dog…less than a pig. He slept with the animals; ate with the animals; and on more than one occasion, he wondered if he was to be butchered and eaten, like the animals.

He was beaten worse than an animal, though as time passed the beatings became less frequent, and were administered with diminished enthusiasm. They were now delivered more as an afterthought than as intentional punishment.

His work consisted of the most menial of tasks — he dug the latrine pits and cleaned the chamber pots for the Nomish priests. He slopped the pigs, gathered dried horse dung for the cook fires, and fetched water from great distances.

In the beginning he lived in fear for his life; now he

would have welcomed death. Except for the burning hatred that turned his heart into a cold, hard lump in his chest. Hatred for the White Sands Nomes. Hatred for Burtyn for leaving him to this fate. Hatred for himself, for choosing to go on that Liberty-forsaken collection in the first place.

He rarely thought of the horror of seeing his parents' heads displayed on pikes at the entrance to the high priest's tent anymore. They had died quickly. For that he was grateful.

He had overheard talk among the priests that there had been a raid of retribution on the Amarillo Nomes for the sacrilege his brother had committed, thought he never learned how many had died in that raid - other than his parents. It was clear, however, that whatever bond had once connected the two Nomish clans was irreparably severed — as severed as his parents' heads.

The White Sands Nomes migrated north immediately after the raid. They settled near the foothills of the Central Highlands, near the haunted lands of the fabled *Fair Folk*. Perhaps they feared reprisal; perhaps they had merely exhausted their land and required new pasture for their herds and flocks.

There wasn't much to recommend the White Sands Waste to begin with, to Alwyn's way of thinking, but the Nomes had lived there for longer than the oldest among them could remember.

Leaving their homeland had not been easy, and most of the Nomes blamed him. The blows had come hard and frequent on the journey north, a journey that took the better part of the warm season. The mood shift was palpable when the clan arrived at their new home. Game was plentiful, water was abundant, the soil was fertile, though Alwyn found it hard digging in the granite-laced soil to construct the high priest's latrine pit.

By nightfall Alwyn was always more than exhausted.

Stumbling to his place in the makeshift stable, he fought the pigs for his evening slop, and tried to find some dry, unlittered hay to lie down upon.

He usually slept like the dead until first light, but for some reason, on this night, Alwyn awoke in the pitch black of the pre-dawn, disquieted by a presence he had never felt before. He lay still with his eyes wide open, allowing them time to adjust to the darkness before scanning the area for the source of his disturbance.

Alwyn gave a start as a figure in the darkness moved toward him. It appeared human, fully mature and perfectly formed as a man, though small, almost childlike in stature. It seemed to radiate light, or perhaps to reflect what little starlight was present - he wasn't sure which. It was clothed in a shirt and breeches woven of a gossamer-like material that rippled and fluttered with the slightest breeze.

It was the creature's eyes that captured Alwyn's full attention, convincing him this was not a dream. They were large; too large for the face. Except for the deep black pupils, they seemed to be completely white, perhaps tinged with the palest of blue where color should have been in any human eye. Whether blue or white, those eyes seemed to bore into his mind.

The face - it was a man's face, Alwyn was sure - seemed accustomed to smiling from the lines around its mouth and eyes, yet it bore a scowl of outrage, though not directed at Alwyn. Alwyn sensed compassion emanating from the creature, or man, washing over him.

Oddly, he felt no fear, only curiosity.

The creature moved swiftly forward and with surprising strength for one so small, lifted Alwyn to his feet. A knife severed his bonds, and a water skin was thrust into his hands.

Silently the creature beckoned for Alwyn to follow, and with stealthy, measured steps led Alwyn through the sleeping camp, past the outpost guards, and farther up into the highlands. Weakened from his ordeal, Alwyn could not manage much speed, but the creature seemed to know exactly how far he could travel before succumbing to exhaustion. A granite outcropping gave way to a hidden cave, and before the sun rose, Alwyn was tucked safely inside.

For the next several days the strange little creature cared for Alwyn, visiting him only by night, bringing him food and water, and clothing made from the same gossamer-like material the creature wore. Alwyn had never seen its like before. It was light yet remarkably sturdy, and provided more warmth than he had known during his captivity. On the final night, the creature brought an even greater treasure - a map.

The creature had never spoken to Alwyn, nor had Alwyn discovered how to communicate with it. It had always just seemed to know what Alwyn needed, and was happy to provide it, if it could.

On that last night, with the map in hand, a pack filled with food and a skin filled with water, just before he left the cave to try to make his way back to his people, Alwyn had tried to speak to the creature.

"Who are you?"

Alwyn spoke slowly, enunciating each word distinctly, as if to a dimwitted child.

"What do you want? Why did you help me?"

The creature smiled, revealing a mouthful of small, white, even teeth. It stood straight, proud, with unfeigned dignity, and though no words were spoken, Alwyn *heard* the words form in his mind.

*"I am Glenferrin, who sits at the feet of Timoth. One day, if The One wills it, we shall meet again, Alwyn, son of Malcolme, Scavenger. One day."*

✠

Alwyn threw his arm over his eyes in a vain attempt to shut out the night visions, but to no avail. The dream shifted, but continued unabated.

It had taken Alwyn months to make his way back to the camp of the Amarillo Nomes, traveling a wide, circuitous route to avoid any scout from the White Sands Nomes. When he finally arrived, there was nothing to indicate there had ever been a settlement there. The clan had migrated, and there was no way to tell which way they had gone, or where they would end up.

Instinctively he knew searching was futile. They were simply gone. Catharine was gone. His child was gone.

*Catharine!*

Alwyn made his way up to the ridge, the highest point for miles around. He would be able to see any sign of a settlement from that vantage point.

Once at the top he scanned the horizon, hoping against hope that he would see what he knew would not be there. He found nothing.

He felt dead inside. He felt nothing; not even the hatred that had kept him alive during his days of slavery with the White Sands Nomes. He sat wearily on an outcropping of rock and began to chew absently on a piece of dried meat Glenferrin had provided for his journey.

Too much emotion clouded his thoughts, and he needed to think. His friend, Jon, had once taught him how to center his thoughts in the Nomish manner. He began to consciously slow his breathing, to let his surroundings blur, but a dull glint of sunlight reflecting off of a polished surface in the dirt at the edge of his vision distracted him.

It wasn't much, just a glimmer, but it was enough to

draw his attention for a moment. The source of the reflected sunlight, he saw, was the burnished steel of a knife.

He moved as if in a dream, gently brushing the soil away and pulled the dagger from the dirt. Its blade was slightly curved, and delicately decorated with twisting knots and fanciful animals; three soiled red cords twining about its hilt - a marriage knife marked with two unique runes to identify the couple it sealed in wedlock — his marriage knife.

He unconsciously rubbed the scar on his chest; three bold, straight lines, three fingers in length, immediately over his heart. And the memories came crashing back with a force that stole his breath.

Weeping, he recited the final lines of his wedding vows; "It is written: Two are better than one, because they have good success from their labor. If one falls the other will lift him up; but woe to the one who falls alone. Where two lie down together there is warmth; but who can be warm alone? One can overpower him who is alone; but two can withstand the onslaught of the enemy. A cord of three strands is not easily torn apart."

Alwyn woke to find sunlight streaming through the windows of his cubicle. He still clutched the dagger with the three red cords twined about its hilt tightly in his grip, and his face was wet with tears.

# CHAPTER 2

**Glenferrin paced back** and forth across his room, his mood alternating between fury and consternation. He had been careful. It was impossible that anyone could have found out.

*Impossible!*

And yet somehow they had found out.

*It shouldn't be that important.*

He plopped down onto his bed and dropped his head into his hands. But it was that important. He knew it was that important.

He took a deep breath to steady himself, and began to quote aloud from The Pol, "*We have not been given the spirit of fear, but of a sound mind.* All very well for The Pol to say. He never had to deal with the pig-headedness of the Twenty-Four."

A soft, "Ahem," from the doorway snapped him out of his reverie and back to his senses. He had been so wrapped up in his thoughts that he didn't hear the knock at his door; had been unaware of the young woman who was now standing at the foot of his bed, smiling sweetly at him. His frustration melted the moment he saw his betrothed. She took his breath away. She always did.

Gwendelyre was tall for a maiden, almost as tall as Glenferrin, nearly ten hands. Her pure white hair fell gracefully to her slim waist, held away from her heart-shaped face by a finely wrought headband of gold braid. Her large eyes were a startling shade of pale emerald – unusual among the Fair Folk. Most had little eye color, and those who did had eyes tinged with blue, or sometimes brown.

Her garment, of the same pale, shimmery material worn by all the Folk, did little to conceal the sweet curves of her body. Her delicate arms and shapely legs were accentuated by the finest of downy white hair.

"Muttering to yourself in the ancient tongue does no good," Gwendelyre chided him playfully. She swayed toward him in that way that always made his mouth go dry. In the back of his mind he wondered if all women practiced that walk.

"No one understands it," Gwendelyre continued. "As the Pol says, *Is it not better to speak fewer words in a language that the people can understand?*"

Lyre's laughter, a sound which usually enchanted him - had enchanted him since he was a child - now chafed his already frayed nerves.

"It is the language of The One, to be used in the service of The One," he snapped more harshly than he intended and immediately regretted. "It is not to be made light of."

Gwendelyre laughed her delicate, tinkling laugh again as she dropped lightly on the bed beside him. If she caught the solemnity of his mood she didn't show it.

"But you are the one who is always telling me, *When I am one of the Twenty-Four, I will speak The Words plainly, so that all may hear and understand.*"

Glenferrin raised his eyes to meet hers for a brief moment, and then lowered them again, shaking his head slowly.

"I was a fool," was all he said.

"Glenferrin, a fool?" she laughed, wrapping her milky white arms around his shoulders. "The youngest man to ever sit at the feet of one of the Twenty-Four, a fool? A man wise enough to choose me for his future bride, a fool? I think not. Now, come. Tell me what it is that has your spirit in such an uproar."

Glenferrin did not raise his head this time, but merely shook it sadly.

"I was a fool."

Gwendelyre's perpetual good humor began to wear thinner than her gossamer gown.

"You are acting the fool," she snapped.

She rose from his bedside, folded her arms beneath her breasts and tapped her foot, much like his mother had done when, as a child, he was acting particularly petulant.

"And if you don't quit this nonsense and tell me what is wrong I shall drag you before old Timoth myself and see what he has to say about it."

"Timoth knows what is wrong." Glenferrin raised his eyes to meet hers in a resigned stare. "The Twenty-Four know what is wrong. And you won't have to drag me before anyone. I have been summoned."

Lyre's sudden burst of anger turned to dark foreboding.

"Glenferrin, what have you done? You haven't gone Outside again? Not after your last escapade. The Twenty-Four put a seal on that opening. To break the seal is to break the will of the Twenty-Four. It just isn't done. And besides, they commanded you to not go. Tell me you didn't go."

Glenferrin shook his head, but never took his gaze from the misty green eyes of his beloved. A wry smile creased his lips.

"The Twenty-Four are meeting even now," he said. "And it is quite possible that this time they may actually want me to make one more trip Outside. Permanently."

Gwendelyre stared at him, dumbfounded. She shook her

head in disbelief, silently mouthing, "No," as the reality of the situation sank in. At last she threw herself into Glenferrin's arms and wept.

"Oh, Glenferrin," she sobbed. "How could you?"

"How could I not, my beloved?" he answered, stroking her hair. "The men who dwell Outside *are* men. Only different. I've seen them. They have wives and children. They laugh and weep. If you cut them they bleed, just as we do. They live and die, and have no one to tell them of The One. They deserve to know the Truth, even if the Twenty-Four does forbid it."

Lyre pulled herself from Glenferrin's embrace. Scrubbing tears from her face she rounded on him.

"You *are* a fool," she cried. "If the Twenty-Four say they are not men, then they are not men. Who are you to say otherwise? The Twenty-Four say they are bloodthirsty giants who kill and destroy for the love of destruction; that their skin has been burned dark from the wrath of the One; that they are cursed to walk on the surface where there is violence and pestilence. It is said they eat flesh and drink blood. You've seen them yourself, Glenferrin. Is it not so?"

Gwendelyre dropped to her knees before Glenferrin, grasping his thighs and laying her head in his lap.

"Glenferrin, my beloved, my betrothed, go to old Timoth. Confess your sins. Beg forgiveness. He will intercede with the Twenty-Four. There will be penance, of course, but..."

"Beg forgiveness? For what?" Glenferrin took her face in his hands and raised it to look into her eyes. "My Beloved, I've done nothing to beg forgiveness for. I know the edict. The edict is wrong. I violated it willfully and I would do so again. I'll not repent, for I have done nothing worthy of repentance. And if that means exile - or death - then so be it. I shall embrace whatever punishment the Twenty-Four mete out - for the love of The One, and for His children who remain Outside."

# CHAPTER 3

**The youth stood** without movement, a sinewy statue facing west. The breeze ruffling his flowing, sandy blond hair was the only betrayal of life. Sharp-eyed, he had spotted his prey, a long-eared hare, more than a hundred paces away. It was an impossible shot for the short bows common to his people, the Amarillo Nomes.

Impossible was not a word in the youth's vocabulary.

Slowly, with inscrutable discipline, he raised the contraption to his shoulder. He made no sudden movement that might startle his prey. Without taking his eyes from the oblivious hare, he laid a bolt into the groove and fitted the nock into the drawn and locked string. There was no tension in his arms or his shoulders. He was free to concentrate on his target. He sighted down the shaft of the short quarrel, aligning the notch on the animal.

He ceased thinking, becoming one with the weapon, just as his Uncle Jon had taught him. His breathing slowed, became almost imperceptible. His surroundings faded, became a blur on the edge of his vision. There was only the quarrel, the trigger, and the hare.

His right hand found the release mechanism. A slight touch and the quarrel flew; silent, swift, deadly.

The hare leaped once, and then lay still.

Franklyn allowed a brief grin to turn up the corners of his mouth. His invention had worked. This one at least had worked. He was better known among his people for his spectacular failures.

As a child he had displayed an insatiable curiosity about everything. He had worn out his elders with endless questions.

*Why was the sky blue and the grass green?*

*Why did smaller fish taste better than larger fish?*

*Why did women watch the children until they were six years from their naming day, and then the men assume the training of the boys?*

*Why did the owls hunt at night and sleep during the day?*

Most adults had simply thrown up their hands after hearing *Why?* more times than they could count. His grandparents had not. They had raised the boy to seek knowledge, and he had not disappointed them.

Of course there was that time one of his inventions had nearly burned the Long House down to the ground, but that was long past and nearly forgotten. At least it was only spoken of in jest now during feast days.

Some of his inventions *had* worked.

*This* invention had worked.

He turned to face the man standing behind him. Jon, the boy's uncle, stood silent, betraying no emotion.

"It worked," Franklyn said.

The older man nodded, not taking his clear, gray eyes from the spot where the hare had fallen. Clad in leather shirt and breeches, stained in irregular patterns in the colors of the earth, Jon would be hard to see from one hundred paces. He would not be seen from much closer if he did not wish it.

"A hundred paces."

Again the nod.

"There is not a man in the clan who could match that shot. Not at that range," Franklyn continued.

It was not a boast. Not really. Well, perhaps a small boast. Yet Franklyn knew he spoke the simple truth. The short bows of his people would barely reach one hundred paces, and even the best among them was not effective at more than forty paces.

Franklyn knew of the fabled long bow that the old men said could kill at a hundred paces, but what good were they? You could not shoot one on horseback while riding at full gallop, and none of his people would consider fighting on foot. It would be a dishonor.

Jon's eyes lowered. He studied the ground for a moment before raising them to meet his nephew's gaze. He spoke seldom; an attribute that lent great weight to his words when he did choose to speak.

"A remarkable shot," he acknowledged. "A remarkable weapon."

Franklyn's crystal blue eyes shone bright with pride at the rare complement, but then turned hot and fevered. His earlier triumphant grin transformed into a rictus snarl.

"It can still only kill one man at a time," he spat.

Jon reached out and placed his hand on the boy's shoulder. He moved close to Franklyn's side, speaking softly, but with the authority of experience and of family. It was an old argument; one that held the frustration of familiarity.

"Let it go, Franklyn. They have migrated. We have migrated. It has been fifteen years. You never knew them. Give it up."

Franklyn turned from his uncle, tried to shake his hand from his shoulder, found himself firmly gripped, and finally left off struggling.

He gazed at the spot where the hare had fallen, then let his eyes drop to his newest invention. It had worked. The smile returned, though it did not touch his eyes.

"Their blood still runs in my veins," he answered. "The blood does not forget. Perhaps you may forget. Perhaps Dora and Pepin may forget. Perhaps the whole clan of the Amarillo Nomes may forget. I do not forget. I will not forget."

When he turned back to face his uncle the smile was gone.

"One day I will be Raek; clan chief of the Amarillo Nomes. On that day I will discover the hiding place of the White Sands Nomes. On that day there will be a reckoning. I do not forget. I do not forgive. One day."

Jon loosed his grip on the boy he had raised as his own. He turned once more to look on the place where the hare had fallen.

"Perhaps. But this is not that day. It is written, '*Love those who love you. Hate those that hate you,*'" Jon quoted. "There can be no honor in hating those who do not even know you."

"They *will* know me."

Jon nodded slightly, still staring west. He had had this discussion with his nephew before. He was sure they would have it many times again. He put it from his mind. The corners of his mouth turned up, almost imperceptibly.

"A remarkable shot."

This time Franklyn's grin was genuine. Praise from his uncle was hard won, and rare. He wanted to savor it.

The moment was broken by the pounding hooves of an approaching rider. As one, man and boy turned to face the intruder. Even at a distance, Franklyn recognized Baldwyn, cup-bearer to Pepin, Raek of the Amarillo Nomes; his grandfather.

Baldwyn rode at a dead gallop until he was within paces of the pair, then reined in brutally, his mount almost sitting on its haunches, blowing hard, foam flecking its mouth. Baldwyn leaped from the saddle and ran to Jon. His face, framed by a shaggy main of jet black hair, was flushed from exertion, white with worry.

"Pepin has been hurt," Baldwyn said bluntly. The

menfolk of the Amarillo Nomes were not known for subtlety. "He is feverish; at times barely lucid. He calls for you both."

"How?"

The question erupted from man and boy at once.

"Boar hunt," Baldwyn replied, breathing hard from his long ride. "Pepin's spear snapped. The boar died, impaled, but not before it gored Pepin in his thigh. The wound did not appear serious at first. I've seen him take worse. Much worse. Pepin laughed it off and said Dora would sew it up for him. But there must have been some kind of poison on the boar's tusks. By the time we returned to camp the fever was already upon him. He could not sit in the saddle unaided.

"He fights it. He is strong. The healers bled him and cleansed the wound, but the infection returned. Red streaks running from the wound turned first green and then black. And the stench; it is like the smell of death. This wound is beyond their power to heal. Pepin sweats. He thrashes about on his bed. He talks incessantly about the past as if it were today. He burns. He calls for you. Come."

Jon nodded. If he were shaken by the news he did not show it. There was work to do, and Jon was not known for letting his emotions impair his actions.

Franklyn, on the other hand, stood slack-jawed. He had always thought his grandfather indestructible; a rock; a fortress. Pepin had never even been sick. The possibility that he might die shook the boy to his core.

A nudge from his uncle brought Franklyn back to the moment. He clamped his mouth shut and moved toward the horses, his cheeks burning with shame for his unmanly display. He did not want Jon or Baldwyn to see. There would be time enough for mourning when the old chief actually died. *If* he died.

*It is written, 'Let the dead bury the dead,'* Franklyn quoted to himself. *But he is not dead yet. No, he will not die.*

Franklyn saddled both his and his uncle's horses

silently, with deft fingers that were used to the task. He poured water from his flask into his hand and let Baldwyn's mount drink. The ride to find them had been hard. This horse would not be ready to run again that day.

Jon and Baldwyn stayed where they were, talking in quiet tones, waiting for Franklyn to bring the horses. He might be the next Raek of the Amarillo Nomes, but he was not Raek yet. It had only been fifteen years since his naming day. It would be another year before he became a man, took a bride, and joined the men in the Long House. It would be five more years after that before he could claim the title of Raek, and even then he would have no real authority until the current Raek, Pepin, his grandfather, died.

For now he served.

It is written, '*Let him who would lead know first how to serve. And he who would be first among all, let him be servant of all.*'

Franklyn led the horses to where the men waited and impatiently leaped into the saddle. Jon took what appeared to Franklyn to be an inordinate amount of time examining the site. It was their custom to leave the land as they found it. He would leave no sign that they had ever been there. No overturned rock; no half-eaten fruit; no charred wood.

Once Jon was satisfied with the condition of their campsite, he mounted his big, red stallion and galloped west for a hundred paces. Leaning over in the saddle he plucked Franklyn's hare from the ground, still impaled on the short quarrel.

"It is a long ride," he said simply when he returned. "There will be no time to hunt."

He pulled his knife from his belt and quickly dressed the hare. He cut a plug of sod from the earth, buried the entrails, and replaced the plug. He took one more quick scan of the area and allowed himself a brief smile. Few could tell anyone had been there in years. None who could would know *who* had been there. He turned the stallion east and without another word began the long journey home.

It took nearly two full days to reach the settlement. They rode silently, steadily until it was too dark to continue without risking their horses stepping in a hole and breaking a leg, and rose before the sun cleared the horizon.

The hare, cooked hastily over the small fire Jon allowed at the end of the first day, was the trio's only meat during that time. Hard biscuits made days before and cheese, washed down with cold water, made up the difference.

Though Franklyn's stomach rumbled in rebellion, no complaint passed between his lips. Worry for his grandfather washed any thought of grumbling from his mind.

The settlement was unnaturally quiet as they rode in. Children that normally would be running rambunctiously across the village green - chasing hoops, throwing balls, getting under foot - were nowhere to be seen.

Womenfolk hung laundry silently on lines strung on poles erected for that purpose, nodding to neighbors, but saying nothing. Their eyes followed the three men as they rode wearily past, a slight lowering of the eyelids their only acknowledgment of the position Jon held in the settlement. Their eyes lowered more deeply for Baldwyn, the Raek's cupbearer.

None lowered their eyes for Franklyn. The boy who would be Raek was still just a boy, after all. Yet a curious look from a number of the goodwives unsettled Franklyn. He felt weighed and measured, like a bolt of cloth or a sack of corn. He had the uncomfortable feeling that they were considering what kind of chief he would be - or perhaps more likely, what kind of husband he would be.

He would, after all, be Raek, and he would need to choose a wife within the year. Whose daughter he chose for wife would elevate the girl's family's position in the hierarchy of the clan. If she produced a daughter, her family would rise even higher.

Yes, there was more behind their gazes than sympathy for his grandfather.

Franklyn ground his teeth and refused to look back.

*Pepin is not dead yet. May the Mother send that he is not dead yet.*

There was nothing to distinguish Pepin's home from any other daub-and-wattle hut in the settlement. Although the old chief was by far the richest man in the clan, his power and authority among his people was not reflected by any exterior flaunting of wealth.

Pepin was a man of simple tastes, quiet wisdom, and an iron will. His father had sat close to the door in the Long House, marking him as a man of importance. Pepin, himself, had proved to be adept at the hunt and meticulous in trade.

It was his marriage to Theodora, eldest daughter of the revered Raek, Peiter and Evlyn, that elevated him to the position of Raek when Peiter died. He proved more than equal to the task. He led his people to a good land where they were free from want, and free from the incessant border skirmishes with their warlike cousins from the White Sands that had plagued their clan for generations.

The Amarillo Nomes grew prosperous under his rule, but no one could say they had grown fat or lazy. Pepin held to the old ways. Everyone had a place in the community and was expected to fulfill it. Those who refused were declared unclean, banished from the clan, and not spoken of again.

*I wonder what life will be like without him.*

The thought skittered across Franklyn's mind, but before he had time to squash it, a surreptitious cough freed him from his reverie.

Jon and Baldwyn were already on the ground, waiting for him to dismount. Embarrassed, he jumped down, threw the reins to a waiting groom and followed the two older men inside his grandfather's home.

The room was dimly lit but hot; sweltering after the chill outside. The stench of impending death hung like a curtain in the air. The old Raek lay unconscious on his bed with the Healer and the Holy Man conversing in hushed tones on one side, and Dora, Franklyn's grandmother, on the other.

The old woman held her husband's hand, her face a dichotomous mask of loving devotion and fierce determination, as if by sheer force of will she could hold the infection at bay.

She shifted her crystal blue eyes briefly toward the newcomers and then resumed her vigil, watching over the only man she had ever loved — the only man she ever felt was worthy of her love.

Jon approached the Healer, whispered a low question, then nodded, thin-lipped, at the reply. He looked a question at the Holy Man and was answered with a shrug and a slight shake of the head. To this man he bowed slightly at the waist, arms raised with palms faced out. The Holy Man bowed slightly and returned his salute in acknowledgment.

There was a hard look in Jon's eye when he rejoined his nephew and Baldwyn; a set to his jaw that said he would not speak. There was no need. It was obvious that the old chief would die, and there was nothing healing or the Mother could do to stop it.

Franklyn choked on the realization. He clenched his teeth hard, biting the inside of his cheek to hold back the tears. He would not weep. Weeping was womanish. Worse, it was childish. He was not yet a man, would not be for another year. But he was no child. And he was no woman. He would not weep.

Slowly, deliberately, he moved to the bedside, knelt

beside his grandmother and took her hand in his. Neither spoke, but Franklyn felt the raw determination in the grasp of her hand. Her hair may have been pure white, the flesh of her face lined to mark the passing of the years, but there was nothing of frailty in the old woman.

Franklyn concentrated his thoughts on the unconscious Raek, adding his determination to his grandmother's, willing Pepin back to health.

It is written, *'Where there is life, there is hope.' He will not die.*

Franklyn was unsure how long he knelt by Pepin's side. He may have dozed; he wasn't sure. He became aware of Jon's presence at his side. He wondered briefly what had become of Baldwyn, but the thought skittered away like sunlight on the surface of the water when he dropped a pebble into it. Baldwyn was not important. Pepin still lived.

The light filtering through the doorway startled him by casting its beams on the west wall. It was morning. Pepin had passed a night of fever-induced dreams, tossing and crying out, murmuring and drifting into periods of fitful sleep. But he lived. He still lived.

Dora startled Franklyn further by rising from her vigil. Her piercing blue eyes - eyes he had inherited - were underscored by dark circles, her cheeks sunken. She had not taken food in five days; had not slept in two. She beckoned Franklyn with those eyes. He shook his head, intent on keeping vigil at his grandfather's side. Dora laid a hand on his shoulder and the look she gave him brooked no argument. He dutifully rose and followed her to the door, away from earshot.

Dora stood silent for a long moment, casting a brief glance back at her husband, and then stared hard at

Franklyn, weighing him more completely than any of the village goodwives had.

Her eyes were hard - *hawk's eyes*, he thought - the determination, if possible, even more fierce than before. Standing nearly twelve hands, she was easily as tall as most men in the clan. Her posture eliminated the possibility of argument. She leaned forward and croaked a whisper into his ear.

"Know ye the whereabouts of Massad?"

Franklyn hissed at the name, lifted two fingers to his lips and spat to ward off evil. He jerk back and looked around to make sure no one else had heard the forbidden name.

"Grandmother…"

"Know ye how to find the Samildanach?"

Dora's eyes never left his face. If anything they grew harder, holding him like a bird transfixed by the lidless gaze of a serpent.

Franklyn swallowed a hard knot in his throat — and nodded. Everyone in the village knew where the old wizard could be found, at least on the days when he cursed. Few had cause or courage enough to seek him out, and those who did had enough sense to keep silent about it.

Dora studied him for a long moment, nodded back, and let out a sigh of exhausted resignation, suddenly looking her age and more.

"Go to him," she breathed. "Seek his cures…or else your grandfather dies."

# CHAPTER 4

**Alwyn strode briskly** toward the Capitol Building. He had kept the Adam waiting for a long time. He knew that Julian would not hold it against him; at least he would never admit it. But there were those who served under Julian that thought any delay was a slight to both the man, and to the office he held. Those men were not known for leniency...or gentleness.

The day was fine, though brisk. A few high wispy, white clouds drifted by, riding on a gentle current that seemed at odds with the stiff breeze that blew across the ground and carried more than a hint of moisture as it prowled through the streets. Alwyn paid little attention to the weather, concentrating instead on the urgent summons that called him from his cubicle in the Library.

Julian was his best friend; had been since childhood. They had grown up together; fought together, cavorted together, gotten into and out of trouble together. Julian had even taken Alwyn's twin sister, Alycia, as the second of the four wives he was required by law to have.

But Julian was also the Adam, arguably the most powerful man in the United States of America; more powerful than the electors of the ten United States and certainly more powerful than the President, whom everyone knew was little more than a figurehead.

Alwyn gingerly sidestepped the joints in the variegated, gray granite paving stones that had been laid generations before to prevent the street becoming a quagmire during the rainy season.

"Step on a crack, you'll break your mother's back," he quoted aloud from an obscure saying he had discovered during a collection on the far side of the Central Highlands.

He was positive there was more to the incantation. Surely to effect a curse of that magnitude would require more than simply stepping on a crack, but the remains of the fragment of paper it was written on had crumbled to dust before he could translate more.

*Not that it matters*, he mused.

A wry grin played around the corners of Alwyn's mouth, though few would be able to tell through the pure white mustaches that grew far down over his upper lip and disappeared into his equally snowy beard. His mother was already dead; had been for more than fifteen years. And he hadn't needed an incantation to cause her death. Or his father's.

Alwyn blew out his mustaches and shook the images from his mind, like so much dust on a polishing cloth, letting the motes spin in the sudden breeze and drift silently into the corners of his thoughts. As paving stones gave way to solid granite courtyard he paused for a moment, blinking to adjust his eyes to the shadow cast by the imposing edifice before him.

The Capitol Building.

Alwyn nodded appreciatively at its majestic domes and massive columns, the granite steps leading up to the portico, the larger than life sculptures of past Adams strategically placed to catch the light at different hours of the day, their shadows stretching far down the steps as if to extend the reach of their influence far beyond their physical limitations. This was a place of dignity and gravitas. He inclined his head in silent acknowledgment of the power represented here, then raised his eyes to meet the statues' frozen stares with an odd mixture of awe and satisfaction.

He allowed his imagination to drift back to that ancient race that had spawned the modern Americans. For all the grandeur of this place, it paled in comparison to the tales of the incredible technology the Ancient Americans must have possessed.

Before the Great Burning.

Before the Time of Madness.

The smallest of the Holy Medallions depicted a building like this. The general consensus of the Guild of the Librarians was that the engraving represented a holy place - a temple, or shrine - to what no one knew, though hypotheses abounded and every librarian worth his ink had an opinion on the subject.

Smit Mikalsson, Alwyn's grandfather, had been one of the few with the stature and experience to formulate a theory and forge a general consensus among the most learned of the librarians. Perhaps the most renowned scavenger of his day, Smit believed the engraving on the Holy Medallion to be a depiction of the mythical Capitol Building, a holy place of power where ordinary men assumed the mantle of gods, creating law and dispensing justice. It was said in tales told late at night around campfires and in hushed tones, that even women had made the treacherous journey up that sacred hill and achieved immortality.

Of course, Smit gave little credence to such stories. The Ancient Americans, he knew from his research, were a highly evolved race; far too intelligent to allow women a place among the rulers of the earth — not like the savage Nomes of the plains and the barren wastelands south of the Central Highlands.

Nomish kings, *Raeks* they called them, were all raised to

their office through the maternal line. It was rumored among the learned men, and Alwyn knew it to be true, that the Nomes made no important decisions without the blessings of their women.

"But then," Smit had declared, "the Nomes are barbarians. What could you expect from such a barbaric race?"

Although the Capitol Building figured prominently in the collective mythology of all the United States, its existence could not be corroborated independently by any of the ancient texts. It was a problem that perplexed Smit, and every other librarian in the Guild.

No mention of the building existed in any document dating back more than three hundred years, and all reputable librarians agreed that the Ancient American civilization ceased to exist more than nine hundred years past, perhaps as much as twelve hundred years. Indeed, there were no reliable written records dating back more than seven hundred years. No one really knew why; a catastrophe of some sort, that had always been referred to as The Great Burning.

Perhaps the Capitol Building of the Ancient Americans was only a fable. Still, it was a magnificent hypothesis.

The Capitol Building had been the center of life in Ancient America, Alwyn's grandfather had surmised. It was a place of commerce; a place where great men exchanged great ideas; a place where rulers planned war and made peace; a place where mortal men communed with their gods. The building was a worthy tribute to both the Ancient Americans and the gods they served — strong, wise, just. Whether the Capitol Building had ever really existed or not, surely Omaha should have such a building, he had argued to anyone who would listen.

And the people had listened. They enthusiastically embraced the construction of a new Capitol Building, even though the cost in taxes was exorbitant. The prestige it brought was worth it.

It had taken forty-three dry seasons to complete. Smit had died that year, as the last stone was laid. It was the same year Alwyn was born.

*Smit Mikalsson was an extraordinary man*, Alwyn mused.

At least all the texts said so. Alwyn's own father had told him so.

*I wish I had known him.*

Alwyn allowed himself a moment of pride while standing there in the shadow of the massive stone structure. No other United State had a Capitol Building. Oh, there were governor's mansions in the ten United States, each gaudy or austere depending on the taste of the house that held tenuous rule at any given moment. And the North Iowans had a White House, where the President of the United States resided. But it was almost universally accepted that the White House, as a building, was less than a myth, much more ephemeral than the Capitol Building, for no engravings had ever been found to substantiate the few historical references made to it.

Alwyn, along with the vast majority of librarians, believed the White House to be more of a symbolic ideal - a reference to presidential power created by the Federalists to justify the existence of their figurehead office - rather than a physical structure. Still, the North Iowans clung tenaciously to their traditions, and even convened their Congress there.

Alwyn shivered as a sudden gust of wind whip-cracked around the corner of the Capitol Building and wormed its way down his thin woolen shirt, compelling him to tug his cloak more tightly around him and settle his bald head deep within the folds of his hood. He eyed the sky. It had been clear when he left the library; the only clouds in the bright blue sky had been the fluffy white kind that children saw fantastical animals in.

There was nothing friendly or whimsical about the clouds now piling up on top of each other in north. They were dark and angry, gathering like a Canadian horde, aching to burst across the border and wreak havoc on the unsuspecting Americans.

*Blue*, he noted. *The first of the season.*

It came early this year, unexpected. And it would hit soon; perhaps within the hour, two at most. Temperatures would plummet rapidly, and those who had not already put by their stock of winter wood would have a shivery night of it. The thought alone was enough to drive another shiver up Alwyn's back. He didn't much like cold weather. It made his joints ache. He wasn't looking forward to the long walk back to the Library in that weather.

He shook himself from his reverie and forced himself to concentrate on the situation at hand. Julian was waiting, and he was dawdling. With a deep sigh he awkwardly began his ascent of the thirteen steps that led from the cobblestone street up to the courtyard of the Capitol Building.

He stifled a curse at the pain in his leg that started as a pinprick then detonated into a cascade of mini-explosions. His right knee was acting up again. It always did when the weather changed. He could almost hear it creak, as if bone were rubbing against bone with no grease to lubricate the joint. He rubbed it for a moment, then continued to hobble, stiff-legged, up the granite steps.

*Thirteen*, he pondered.

He knew there must have been something significant to the Ancient Americans about the number. It occurred much too frequently in the old texts and engravings to be mere coincidence. The Sons of Liberty, the priestly caste of the United States of America, insisted that thirteen was a holy number, and Alwyn had been forced to concede their point. Thirteen was, after all, represented on the most holy medallions, and cropped up with uncanny frequency in ancient mythology.

Still, it did not seem to refer to any attribute of God that

Alwyn could decipher. Not like the holy numbers five and two.

There were, of course, the Five Faces of God. There were five days in a week; five weeks in a month; five months in a season; two seasons, summer and winter, in a year; a two-week Candlemas celebration to commemorate the shortest day of the year, and hence the end of the winter season; and a two-week sun festival to commemorate the longest day of the year, and hence the end of the summer season.

Just like there were five fingers on a hand, and two hands on a body, the world was based on five and two. Nothing could be more obvious.

But thirteen?

Some of his research even indicated thirteen to be an evil number, a harbinger of bad luck. He couldn't puzzle it out. He would someday. That's what scavengers did. They solved puzzles.

But not today. Today he had a summons from the Adam. Alwyn sighed, rubbed his knee, and continued his ascent.

The temperature dropped perceptibly when Alwyn passed from bright sunlight into shadow as he crossed beneath the granite archways, into the hall of the Capitol Building and entered the Seat of Liberty. A soldier of middle rank, puffed up by the authority of his position, stepped lightly from behind a heavy, ironwood desk to intercept him.

It was only a mild irritation. In the old days no one would have dared to even think of stopping him. In the old days there had been free access to the Capitol Building. Old men and young women, families with their children, young lovers and eager merchants had roamed its sacred grounds without hindrance.

But these were not the old days. Attempts had been made on the Adam's life, and the Libertarian Guards were taking no chances.

The soldier wore unadorned leather armor over his red woolen shirt, the sleeves cut short between the elbow and shoulder, guaranteeing uninhibited freedom of movement. As was custom in the Capitol Building he wore no sword, but the dagger strapped to his hip marked him as a member of the elite, Libertarian Guard.

Alwyn had no doubt it was as every bit as functional as it was ceremonial. He noted that the young man's hand rested comfortably on the dagger's ornately carved hilt. This man was hand-picked from his childhood, trained with deadly precision to dispatch the living into the embrace of Hel instantly, with or without weapons, and without remorse.

The Libertarians were noted for their unwavering loyalty to the Adam. Duty was their life; honor their only code. They had no family but their brothers in the Guard. Alwyn had no doubt that this young man knew how to employ the tools of his trade to good advantage, nor did he doubt the soldier's willingness to do so.

"May I see your summons?"

The soldier asked politely enough, but Alwyn knew it was not a request. The cool glint in the guard's eyes said he hoped the summons would not be in order.

Alwyn studied the young man for only a moment before fishing into his voluminous sleeve pocket to retrieve the small vellum scroll that gave him free access to the Adam. No sense causing a fuss, and possibly getting himself killed in the process.

*Still young*, he thought, *but deadly; dangerous; puffed up by his position; looking for an excuse to use his knife. Doesn't recognize me. No reason he should. Perhaps it won't go too hard on him.*

"You're new here, aren't you," Alwyn said. He gave a slight smile as he handed the scroll to the guard. "I haven't seen you before."

The guard ignored Alwyn's attempt at polite

conversation.

"Wait here."

He pointed to a gray square of granite on the floor in front of his desk, indicating where he expected to find Alwyn when he returned. He waited a moment to acknowledge Alwyn's assent, then he turned on his heal and disappeared into the corridors that led to the greatest power in the United States; perhaps in the world.

The sardonic smile never left Alwyn's face as he spread his arms in acquiescence. He planted himself on the exact spot the young Libertarian pointed to, then folded his hands inside his sleeves to wait and watch the scene unfold.

It happened much the same whenever there was a new guard assigned to the Capitol Building. The knock on the door, the inquiry, the pained look on the general's face, the tongue lashing for not recognizing the Adam's confidant, the threats of transfer to the Canadian front minus some very significant body parts if it ever happened again, the white-faced young Libertarian Guard ushering Alwyn into the Adam's office.

Once inside Alwyn turned to face the man responsible for all the uproar.

"Do you have to do that, every time?" Alwyn tsk'ed.

Strom Maxwell wrapped Alwyn in bear hug, lifting him from the ground as he burst out laughing.

"Of course I do. Cooped up here in Omaha with nobody to fight with except Julian? I'd go postal if I didn't at least get to chew someone out from time to time. It's good for them. Keeps them from getting too cocky. Besides, he won't bother stopping you next time you see fit to drop by for a friendly visit."

Alwyn shrugged with open palms, amused at Strom's choice of metaphors. The phrase, *go postal*, came from the famed, York Codex, a remarkable find of a collection of forty-eight bookrolls dating back some seven hundred years.

The bookrolls had been placed inside sealed earthenware jars and stored in a series of caves in the State of York. They had been accidentally discovered some seventy years before, when a young shepherd boy, throwing rocks to drive a wolf from his flocks, heard something shatter and went to investigate.

The York Codex was generally accepted as the work of a renegade sect of Ancient Americans who regarded the written word as sacred, many of whom gave up their lives during the Time of Madness to preserve the writings. That renegade sect eventually evolved into the Guild of the Librarians, and their more adventurous brothers, the Scavengers.

Most of the bookrolls crumbled to dust before they could be translated, and several others were only vaguely legible. Alwyn's grandfather had been on the team that had translated the Codex from its original Ancient American.

The knowledge of the dead language had passed from father to son, and now Alwyn was one of the few men in America with the ability to translate the strange, ancient glyphs.

Not that it was a particularly lucrative aptitude. There just weren't that many Ancient American relics around that needed translating.

*Going postal,* as near as he had been able to determine from the texts, meant dying of boredom.

"He was just doing his job," Alwyn offered. "I doubt anyone told him any different. It wasn't that much of a bother. Besides, these are dangerous times. What if I'm really a spy for the Calif of Orange, with a vial of poison to assassinate the Adam? You can't be too careful these days."

"The day I can't trust you, is the day I fall on my own sword."

The voice rang out with conviction, and Alwyn did not doubt that it spoke the simple truth. Julian never lied. Rising from behind a massive desk made from the precious wood of the rare and beautiful oak tree, the Adam moved confidently across the floor toward him.

Alwyn waited, as was both custom and law, until Julian stood directly in front of him. He then bowed low at the waist, hands covering his heart, and intoned formally, "Give me Liberty, or give me death. I regret I have but one life to give."

"This nation was conceived by Liberty. Life, Liberty, and the pursuit of happiness be to you and to your posterity," the Adam responded with equal formality.

Julian lifted the holy medallion that hung from a heavy chain about his neck and offered it to Alwyn. Alwyn received it into his cupped hands, raised it to his lips and kissed the Face of God.

The ritual over, the two friends embraced with a laugh, and thumped each other three times on the back in the manner of men.

"Walked all the way from the Library, I see," Strom chided. "I sent a carriage."

"My feet are good enough," Alwyn replied. "I don't like being carried around by people I don't know. Never can tell where you might end up. Besides, this is still Omaha, and I am still a free man. I come and go as I choose. Even the Adam can't compel obedience from free men... although the Sons of Liberty do try."

Alwyn had a stubborn streak. He truly didn't like to be ordered to do anything. A simple request from his oldest friend and he would move heaven and earth to comply; but an Adamic Command? Now that was a different matter. He would come; the ten Governors and the President himself would come for an Adamic Command. The Calif of Orange and the Emperor of Canada would come, albeit kicking and screaming, for an Adamic Command. But Alwyn would come in his own good time and Julian knew it, or should have.

Strom chuckled as if he knew the reply was coming. He enjoyed the game. Julian laughed out loud as well, but his piercing, crystal blue eyes flashed with an inner irritation. He did not issue commands lightly. The summons was important. Alwyn must have known it was important for him to issue an Adamic Command to his friend. He could have at least pretended to hurry, if only to observe protocol.

"The Sons of Liberty spread the blessings of Liberty throughout the United States and even into heathen lands," Julian answered as he picked up a silver pitcher that beaded condensation. "It is good work that they do; necessary work. Citrus?" he offered. "Over ice?"

Alwyn raised a single eyebrow and made a conscious effort to keep his mouth from dropping open. In a month, perhaps sooner with that Blue blowing in from the north, ice would be plentiful. But it had been a hot summer. Ice was hard to come by this time of year in Omaha.

He knew he shouldn't be surprised. The Capitol Building was one of the few structures in all of Omaha that had its own ice well. Comprised of three chambers, the well was sunk sixty hands deep and lined in laced brickwork. Blocks of ice were cut from the frozen lakes surrounding Omaha during the dead of winter, packed in straw and layered in the chambers to be used throughout the year.

Mostly the ice was used to preserve fresh meat and fish. Only the very wealthy crushed it to cool their drinks, and even they did it only on special occasions to impress their fellows with such ostentation.

The juice of the citrus was almost as rare a treat as ice. With the delicate political climate between the Adam, the President, and the Calif, it was nearly impossible to procure. Citrus was only produced in the Califate of Orange, and transporting it across the Gulf of Orange, over the Central Highlands, and through the White Sands Waste was risky business at best.

The Sons of Liberty had been agitating for a holy war against the Califorangians for generations. The President hated the Calif, claiming the land was originally a United State and must rejoin the Union.

The Adam had his own issues with the Califate because they refused the worship of Liberty, preferring allegiance to their own strange amalgamation of gods. The Calif, for his part, remained an enigma wrapped in a mystery. He lived in a walled city and gave audience to no *foreign devils*, as the Califorangians termed anyone not born in their nation.

All communication was conducted through ministers who were extremely polite, but extremely unyielding. As a result, little of the golden liquid managed to make it to market in Omaha, or any other United State for that matter. Any that did was almost always the result of enterprising smugglers, and cost the world besides.

Alwyn cast a furtive glance at Strom Maxwell, sensing his presence behind the citrus. Prior to his service as the Adam's General of the Armies, Strom had made a fortune in commerce by knowing when to look and when to leap, and not all of his enterprises had the official stamp of approval.

A smile played over Strom's lips before he schooled his face to back to an unreadable mask. Just because he served the Adam didn't mean he had given up his other business interests.

"Over ice," Alwyn murmured.

He shook his head. Rank did indeed have its privileges. He accepted the chilled goblet of citrus, swirling it lightly, admiring the rich, golden color, and savored the tangy, sweet flavor that preceded the sharp bite of fermentation. He sat down and settling comfortably into a richly brocaded settee.

"I've noticed the Sons get a bit zealous when they find someone who doesn't embrace Liberty in the same way they do. Those who don't repent of their heresies fast enough sometimes find themselves dancing in the air...or worse. Are you putting on weight?"

The question sounded innocent enough. Alwyn

studiously regarded the contents of his cup as Julian grimaced at the slight pudge around his waist.

"The food is good here at the Capitol Building," he replied. "The chief cook believes it is a point of honor to never serve the same dish twice. He is a Highlander, and you know how touchy they are about their honor. He gets offended if I don't finish everything on my plate every night. I would discharge him...except the food is too good, and if I did he would probably kill himself - or me - to satisfy his code of honor."

Julian laughed, "It's not like the old days when I could hunt or fish or carouse at will. I don't get out much anymore, not without half a dozen of the Libertarian guards dogging my every step. But at least I still have my hair. And we are, after all, one nation under God, with Liberty for all.

"The Sons of Liberty have held back the darkness for a thousand years, Alwyn. They paid dearly to preserve what civilization was left after the Great Burning. The Law of Liberty was the only thing that held this country together and kept it from sliding back into the anarchy of the Time of Madness. If the Sons are overly zealous at times, it is with a holy zeal. Few are punished who don't deserve it."

Alwyn nodded a quick touché, mentally contrasting the Adam's full head of thick brown hair with his own premature tonsure. He began losing his hair before his sixteenth naming day, and his friends made great sport of it. To add insult to the injury, his once jet black beard had turned snow white by the time he reached twenty-four, contrasting oddly with the still dark fringe of hair that wreathed his head like a crown of thorns.

*Not yet thirty-two and I look like an old man*, he thought ruefully.

"I still have my hair," Alwyn replied, surreptitiously rubbing the top of his head. "I keep it in a bag under my pillow. I'm sure the Ancient Americans had the ability to restore lost hair; some pill or lotion or incantation. Eventually I'll unearth it and I'll be a rich man."

Setting his cup on a richly polished side table that glowed the color of honey, Alwyn barked a quick laugh.

"But you didn't *invite* me to the Seat of Liberty just to taunt me about my hairline. And I didn't come just to argue with you about the excesses of the Sons of Liberty. So, what's on your mind?"

Julian downed what was left of his citrus in a single gulp, placed the ornately engraved silver goblet on the edge of his desk, turned away, then walked stiffly back to his chair. He held the chair's back in both hands, drumming the soft leather inlay with his fingers, his lips pressed tightly together. It was a nervous habit. Abruptly he pulled the chair out and sat, steepling his fingers, gazing over them at his friend.

Alwyn knew the signs. It was bad news. Julian was a master manipulator. He preferred the almost conspiratorial nature of winning influential people to his point of view through his wit and charm, sitting side by side with them while sharing a drink.

His desk was a symbol of power and authority. He only resorted to speaking from behind his desk when he felt he needed all the weight of authority it projected. When Julian sat behind his desk, it was very bad news indeed.

Alwyn picked up his cup, took another sip of citrus and allowed the pungent taste of the liquor to linger on his tongue while he waited with thinly veiled impatience.

"Willam Norman," the Adam finally announced.

Alwyn waited for more, but it seemed the Adam had expended his vocabulary on the subject.

"Willam Norman?" Alwyn repeated. He stared at his friend with bemused, slack-jawed incredulity. "You issued an Adamic Command to me because of Willam Norman?" Alwyn settled back into the settee and bit back an unamused chuckle. "And what has our beloved President done this time that has you in such a lather? Declared war on Canada, again? Provoked the Calif into breaking the border treaty, again?"

Alwyn rose to his feet and began to pace, his irritation growing as he walked. He waved his arms to emphasize his point, threatening to slosh his citrus on the floor. It was a trait he had inherited from his mother. Tie her hands behind her back and she would not be able to speak, Alwyn's father had always laughed.

"Or perhaps it's something worse," Alwyn continued his tirade. "Perhaps he is advocating a tax on the tithe collected by the Sons of Liberty, and we all know the tithe is holy, only to be used by the Sons."

"For Kennedy's sake, Julian," Alwyn slapped his hands down on the Adam's desk and stared full in his face, allowing the full brunt of his frustration boil to the surface. "Send Willam an official envoy and threaten to excommunicate him. Threaten to excommunicate any one who follows him. He'll stop for that. Whatever he's doing that's irritating you so badly, he'll stop for that."

His venom spent, Alwyn sauntered back to his chair, slumped down, took another long draught of citrus and waited for the explosion he was sure was to come.

The Adam might be his friend, but he was still the Adam, the First Man in all of the United States. Alwyn was pretty sure he had overstepped his bounds, but he couldn't understand why Julian allowed the President to upset him so. It wasn't as if Willam posed a threat to his power.

Willam Norman was the President of the United States of America, but everyone knew the title was more honorary than effectual. The United States was, in reality, anything but united. Each United State was little more than a loose confederation of city-states, ruled jointly by a Governor and an Elector, and none really controlled the territory it claimed; few controlled more than the capitol city of their state.

The mayors of the lesser cities in each state pledged

loyalty to their Governor, and each provided a levy of soldiers to serve in the state militia. The Governor provided military leadership and protection from brigands to the outlying provinces. He was responsible for keeping the roads in good repair, and patrolled those roads to insure decent citizens could travel in relative safety.

The Elector of each state handled all the civil issues including an intricate system of courts, sanitation and the collection of taxes. As long as everyone within the state knew their place, order generally prevailed.

Order was less prevalent between the states, however. No Governor would consent to a military presence from another state, except a small retinue to accompany visiting dignitaries. And the monetary exchange from state to state was so complicated that few merchants bothered to cross borders to do business. Those who did so successfully became wealthy. Those who did so unsuccessfully became paupers.

The unity of the states had always been tenuous at best, but even after nearly a millennium the memory of the nation that had existed before the Burning was seared into the consciousness of the citizens, and none could bear to see it dissolved. Thus the United States of America lived on, if in name more than in practice.

The true unifying force in the nation was the Faith - the worship of the God of Five Faces, the God of the United States of America whose name is Liberty.

Excommunication was the sole prerogative of the Adam, and was a penalty so severe that it had only been administered six times in the past two hundred years. It involved depriving the victim of his tongue, his eyes, and his hands, so he could no longer speak heresy, no longer lust with his eyes, and no longer feed himself on the bread of ambition. His ears were left whole, so he could hear the words of Liberty and repent before he died.

No American would risk being cut off from the blessings

of Liberty, and few had a cause so dear they would risk the harshness of excommunication. Julian knew that. Willam Norman knew that. Everyone knew that. Even so, Alwyn found his palms starting to sweat as he waited for Julian to reply.

"Willam has declared himself emperor," the Adam replied softly. "Emperor of the United States of America, the blessed one of Liberty, and above the Law and the Adam."

Alwyn burst out laughing.

"Willam? Emperor? Of the United States of America? Absurd."

The laughter was met was stony stares from his two friends, and soon died an unnatural death. Alwyn sat up in his chair, alternating looks between Strom and Julian.

"You're serious."

Slight nods from the general confirmed Julian's pronouncement. The Adam merely stared at him over steepled fingers.

Alwyn fell back against the chair, sloshing the chilled citrus over his hand. Unconsciously he wiped it on his cloak.

"Emperor," he mused aloud. "Americans don't have emperors; don't have nobles, aristocrats, lords or any such nonsense. We have electors, governors, senators, mayors, even presidents. But not emperors. Liberty on high, who does Willam think we are, Canadians? Kings and emperors are all well and good for Canadians, but we're Americans. We don't have emperors. Willam knows that. Every child in America knows that."

He looked up from his mutterings to find his friends studying him.

"When? Has he demanded fealty from the governors? Surely he can't believe any would throw their support behind him."

At a quick glance from the Adam, Strom became animated. He was accustomed to speaking for the Adam. He had the remarkable and rare ability to tell a tale straight, fast and accurately, while at the same time managing to keep his audience completely in the dark. His talent for revealing volumes of minutia without revealing anything of any real importance had more than once kept the Adam in power.

Alwyn knew he would leave nothing out of this report. They had known each other far too long.

Strom handed him a leather packet, sealed with Willam's own Presidential seal. The wax had been broken, of course. Julian had already seen what lay within. Alwyn slipped the contents from the pouch as Strom assumed a lecturing posture and began pacing.

"Willam has made no secret of his desire for a more unified United States," Strom explained. "He's been yammering on about it to anyone who would listen for years. He fears a renewed Canadian invasion from the North, he hates the Calif of Orange in the West and he mistrusts the Nomes in the South. His answer to everything is a strong federal government, under his leadership, of course."

Alwyn only half listened to his friend. His attention was on the contents of the packet, his eyes traveling from Julian to Strom, back to Julian, then back to the items before him. Strom continued as if he has Alwyn's full attention.

"Oh, there will be resistance from the electors, of course. None of the governors will willingly give up any of the territory they claim to control, and none will allow taxation by a federal power if they can help it. But Willam is a hero to the people. To hear the stories, he stopped the Canadians at the Battle of Thousand Lakes single-handedly."

By now Alwyn had stopped listening altogether. His whole concentration was on the small vellum scroll that he had taken from the packet. The words were written with studious precision, the characters painstakingly copied. Unmistakably Ancient American glyphs, but...

"Where did he get this?" Alwyn demanded.

Strom continued over Alwyn's question. "And if push comes to shove, Willam can be…shall we say…convincing. He has the army of North Iowa at his command, not to mention his private Republican Guard. He pays them out of his personal fortune, and they are loyal to him to the death. He has a large enough military force behind him to force the issue in a number of states."

Alwyn waved away Strom's explanation. Political intrigue, even of this magnitude, did not interest him. He was more interested in the scroll with the strange script.

"But where did he get this," Alwyn asked again.

"Willam claims Burtyn discovered the original manuscript, and made this copy," Julian answered.

Alwyn's eyes widened slightly at the mention of his brother, now a renegade scavenger, but he said nothing. He had not seen his brother in years - *not since he left me to die in the the Amarillo Waste* - and the mention of Burtyn's name left a bitter taste in Alwyn's mouth.

"Burtyn says this is but a fragment," Julian continued. "He says there is more. Much more. Alwyn, Willam must be mad. He claims freedom from all earthly authority; that he is subject to Liberty alone. He claims not only supreme political power, but supreme spiritual power as well."

"As Emperor of the United States, Willam has declared himself the true representative of God on earth, and he demands that I swear fealty to him. He has confiscated church property in North Iowa, and demanded the Sons of Liberty who minister there swear allegiance to him. Any who refused he has exiled or imprisoned — or executed in public and in excruciatingly painful ways."

"I can see why you are upset," Alwyn said. "But I still don't understand what this has to do with me?"

"Willam wants to legitimize his claim of Divine Right," Strom answered for the Adam. "His messenger said any questions we might have would be answered by that scroll.

Unfortunately, the scroll is written in Ancient American. You are one of perhaps a dozen people this side of the Central Highlands who can translate it."

"I need to know what is in this fragment that it could stir someone, even someone as ambitious as Willam, to commit blasphemy," Julian said.

Alwyn whistled through his teeth. No wonder Julian was agitated. He moved to the window to take advantage of the brighter light. He fished inside his sleeves and produced a hard leather case from one of his many interior pockets.

Casting an embarrassed look at his friends, Alwyn opened the case and unfolded his oculars. The odd contraption of wire and glass that fit over his ears and rested on his nose made him look like a four-eyed monster from a children's story, and he refused to wear them except when he was studying privately. Without them he got tremendous headaches when he tried to read for too long. With them on, everything appeared magically enlarged. Today his vanity would have to wait.

As the glyphs jumped into bright relief on the scroll, Alwyn's breath caught in his throat.

"It's archaic, even for Ancient American," he finally managed to stammer through his excitement. "In fact it's not Ancient American at all, but a dialect that died out shortly after the Burning. It's called, *Angleesh,* and it is quite similar to Ancient American, but there are some striking differences," he explained, more to himself than to the Adam.

"For one thing Angleesh has only twenty-six distinct glyphs which are arbitrarily arranged to produce different thoughts, and a number of additional markings to indicate pauses in thought. Now, it is obvious that the original was damaged."

Alwyn motioned his friends over to point out the anomalies.

"See these glyphs?"

He pointed out squiggly lines that were equally incomprehensible to both Julian and Strom.

"They appear to have been cut off half way up. And this; this is wrong. This is all wrong. Burtyn has them wrong. This should be a jot, not a tittle."

"This is all fascinating, Alwyn," Julian muttered. "But I don't know a jot from a tittle, and I didn't summon you for a lesson in Scavengry. Just tell me what it says."

Duly chastised, Alwyn nodded and peered though his oculars, comparing the glyphs to notes from another small scroll he produced from yet another hidden pocket.

He began to speak as he translated, "*The apparition of The God is upon me; The God has required…*no, that's wrong."

Alwyn ran his finger through his scroll, looking for a reference point.

"*Anointed.* That word should be translated, *anointed. The God has anointed me to proclaim…*" Alwyn stopped, looked at his friend, and took the name of God in vain.

"Liberty," he swore.

"By the Fifth Face. Julian, Strom, if this is real, if Burtyn really does have the original manuscript…I don't know how he did it. He couldn't have found it. It's impossible. It's only a myth. He can't possibly have found…" Alwyn's voice trailed off into silence.

Julian's face grew hard has he listened to the translation.

He knew the Prophesies of the Pendraig.

They all did.

It was said He would come again, in mankind's darkest hour. He would proclaim Liberty when Tyrfingr was pulled from the stone, and the one true Son of Liberty would return to judge the quick and the dead.

All nations would gather to fight against the Son, but they would not prevail. The world would be plunged into a time of destruction not known since the Burning; the blood of men would run as high as a horse's bridle before it was over. Then He would reign for a thousand years of peace, and those who followed the Son would reign with him, enjoying the wealth of the nations.

"Julian," Alwyn swallowed. "Willam has just declared himself to be the Son of God. If he truly has pulled Tyrfingr from the Stone..."

"If Willam possessed Tyrfingr, he wouldn't send a cryptic note, with a veiled threat," Strom snorted. "Tyrfingr has the power to level cities, to cause mountains to burn with fire, and to turn men into weeping babes. With Tyrfingr in his possession, Willam would have marched his army to Omaha, crushing any resistance he encountered, and set himself up as God on earth. No, Willam doesn't have Tyrfingr. He is ambitious but he is not insane."

"Tyrfingr is a myth!" Julian exploded, smashing his fist against the unyielding surface of his oak desktop. "A tale mothers use to frighten their children."

He paused long enough to regain his composure, then turned to face Alwyn.

"But apparently this mysterious text is not?"

Julian raised an eyebrow at Alwyn for confirmation. Alwyn shrugged, pulled his oculars from his face, carefully folded them, returned them to their hard leather case and made them disappear within the sleeves of his robe.

"Without seeing the original it is impossible to say," he said. "The syntax, the poetic structure, even the power of the words...Burtyn might be able to forge them. But the formal, archaic style? It smacks of authenticity. I've never seen anything like it. I doubt Burtyn could concoct it on his own."

"Whether this text is real or a fraud, Willam will use it to his advantage," Strom interrupted. "Few citizens other than government officials and town scribes can read. The people believe if it is written it must be true. And that is especially true for anything from antiquity. Burtyn will translate this manuscript - probably already has translated it - to prove that Willam is the one true Son of Liberty. The only real question is why Willam hasn't already made this revelation public."

Julian nodded. "Willam is cunning and ruthless, but he is also a pragmatist. He doesn't want a civil war if he can avoid it, although I'm sure he would be quite willing to fight one if it comes to it. He would much rather convince, or intimidate me into accepting some under position, perhaps as his Vicar."

Julian barked a mirthless laugh. "Me, the Vicar of God on earth. That, gentlemen, is totally unacceptable. There is only one Adam, only one Nation under God, and only one God - the God of Five Faces, the God of the United States. We have no need of any bastard son of God."

Julian was seething, but already a plan was formulating in his head. He stalked back to his desk and sat. Planting his elbows on the desktop and steepling his fingers, he stared straight at Alwyn.

"That's why we must obtain this wondrous text, the whole manuscript, and have it *properly* translated - so the people will know the truth."

"And just how do you intend to manage that," Alwyn asked. "You can't expect to just march into North Iowa and demand the manuscript. It is against all treaties and traditions, not to mention your own law, to send an army from one state into another. And even if you did, Willam is too strong. It would take the combined armies of six states to challenge Willam in North Iowa. He has the power to crush any army you could muster before you made it across the Great River Mis."

"True. But he would have to accept an official delegation from the Adam," Strom mused, "if the delegation could make it to White House without being regrettably wiped out by 'bandits.' A small contingent of say, a dozen hand-picked men who knew the terrain, who knew how to survive in a hostile environment, behind enemy lines…"

"Led by the legendary General Strom Maxwell," Julian finished. "Pick your men, Strom. You must leave at first light. It will take you a month to get there, even if the weather holds, and we don't have time to waste."

Strom nodded and started for the door.

"And make room for two more."

Strom stopped in mid-stride and rounded on the Adam.

"Who?" he demanded.

"Strom, you are a cunning warrior, a daring strategist, and an implacable enemy, but you are no negotiator. I'm sending, Sencha, my personal ambassador along with you."

"No," Strom answered. "I don't take stragglers."

"Yes," the Adam replied. "He has skills you lack."

Julian stared his old friend in the eye, and surreptitiously rubbed his left arm.

"Strom, just get him there alive. And I promise I'll never ask anything of you again."

Strom stammered, and then nodded his assent. He knew Julian was right. He could have a silver tongue when he wanted to, but more often than not, and generally at the worst time possible, he was blunt and tactless. He could get to Willam, but he would never be able to obtain the manuscript.

He hated being reminded of how Julian had once saved his life, injuring his left arm in the process. But he doubted Julian would never ask anything of him again. He had used that ploy too many times in the past when the two didn't see eye to eye.

"Who is the second?" he growled.

"Alwyn," Julian replied.

"What!" Alwyn was taken by complete surprise.

"No!" Strom shouted.

"Yes!" Julian shouted back. Staring down both men, Julian rose to the full stature of the authority of his office.

"No outside power or authority can deprive any citizen of any United State of their property. You won't have sufficient force to compel it, and I doubt even you can manage to steal it and make it out alive — not that I could possible condone such an action anyway."

Julian turned to face Alwyn. "But there is Guild courtesy among scavengers, is there not? Nothing written may be hidden, isn't that right? Knowledge must be available to all who ask?"

Alwyn nodded, though it irked him to do so. Guild business was, after all, Guild business. He didn't like it that outsiders knew of the Guild's codes.

"Alwyn, you are the foremost authority on Ancient American languages this side of the Central Highlands. You may be the only man in the ten United States that can determine whether or not this manuscript is authentic. And you are certainly the only man Burtyn would allow to examine the original, Guild etiquette or not. Alwyn, you have to go. You have to somehow obtain that manuscript and bring it back to Omaha, where it can be studied and translated by trusted librarians. The fate of civilization as we know it rests on it."

"I'm not a soldier, and I'm not a politician," Alwyn sputtered. "I'm a scavenger, for Kennedy's sake."

"Which is precisely my point," Julian shot back.

The Adam walked around his desk and planted himself in front of Alwyn, laying his hands on his friend's shoulders. His voice took on that mellifluous tone that charmed both nobles and ordinary citizens, as if he understood you completely, and wanted only what was best for you.

"Alwyn, this manuscript, if it exists, could be the key to unlocking life before the Great Burning," he reasoned. "Think of it. It's what you have searched for your whole life, a glimpse into life before. The wisdom of the Ancients, Alwyn. It can't be left in the hands of incompetents and frauds who would twist it to their own ends. I believe peace or civil war, maybe even world war, rests on this manuscript. It is too important to leave in the hands of any lesser man. Will you go?"

# CHAPTER 5

**The storm that** was threatening when Alwyn arrived at the Capitol Building chose the moment he exited to erupt in full fury. Already a fine dusting of wet, gritty ice crystals obscured the cracks in the cobblestone that he had flippantly used for cursing earlier. He cursed in earnest now.

The wind bit sharp, whipping his cloak into a frenzied ensign behind him. Alwyn grasped his cowl with one hand and pulled it tighter about his head. His other hand fought a losing battle to keep his cloak closed about his throat.

The sky, a deep blue-gray that obliterated the sun, matched his mood. The soggy snow was a cold and clutching lover that embraced him with clammy fingers, soaking through his wool coat and obscuring his vision. The Library was an hour's journey by foot under normal conditions. Under normal conditions he wouldn't have minded the walk. These were not normal conditions.

In this weather it would be well past dark before he reached the welcoming fire of the Library. He cursed himself for a fool for refusing Strom's offer of a coach, but he needed time to think, and he did his best thinking when he walked alone. Even if that walk included the cold, the wet and the wind.

What was Julian thinking, sending him to White House?

*I'm a scavenger, not a spy.*

It wasn't the danger that bothered him. He was accustomed to danger. He had risked his life and various limbs on more than one occasion as he ventured into inhospitable territory searching for his little bits of antiquity. He undertook his expeditions, *his collections*, for the thrill of discovery. He dug for knowledge, for truth, for those small fragments of civilization that had survived the Time of Madness, for anything that gave a hint of the glory that had once been the United States of America.

But he did not risk his life for politics. *Never* for politics.

*Burtyn.*

Alwyn ground his teeth until he was afraid they would pop in his jaw.

*Liberty on high, why did it have to be Burtyn? Anyone but Burtyn.*

He scanned the sky for an answer, but was rewarded only by the wet kiss of the snow on his face, and the icy fingers of the wind down his back. When he returned his gaze to the horizon he was genuinely surprised to see the Never-Dimming Flame that marked the entrance of the Library. It burned cheerfully, as if the Blue Norther that howled around it was an inconvenience too insignificant to notice.

Alwyn passed the orange-red flame, and mounted the final expanse of wood that led to the welcoming warmth of the Library, crossing it quickly, if painfully. His right knee was starting to act up again. It always creaked and groaned in damp, cold weather, as if bone rubbed against bone.

He cursed mentally.

*Too many miles.*

Rubbing his aching knee, he limped across the drawbridge, a relic of a distant past when it was more functional than ornamental. Unlike the Capitol Building there were no guards with puffed up pride guarding the entrance to the Library. The massive, iron-bound wooden door that blocked immediate passage within was ingeniously counterbalanced, allowing it to be opened with minimal effort.

Doors were frowned upon in the Library. The only ones allowed were the ones on exterior walls, and they were only tolerated to keep out the weather. Locks were strictly prohibited.

Alwyn pushed past without giving the obstruction a passing thought, and blinked as his eyes adjusted to the brightness of the interior after the gloom of the storm.

He instinctively sought out the welcoming warmth of the fire roaring in the massive fireplace of the Library's common room. Ripping off his sodden cloak, Alwyn threw it across the back of one of the simple, ladder-back chairs that were scattered about the room. He backed up to the fire pit that was large enough to roast a whole ox, raised the back of his robe above his thighs and let the flames lick the chill from his bones.

Dispersed among the tables were clumps of men — students and professors; scribes and scavengers. Most talked softly, though adamantly, arguing some point in some obscure text. Alwyn knew them all by sight if not by name. There were no strangers here.

Alwyn couldn't suppress a grin as he watched toothless elder Gaithyr gesticulating wildly, plunging his right forefinger into the palm of his left hand, while an equally animated and equally aged colleague, Holm, shook his head in disagreement while he quaffed a mug full of something brown and steamy.

Scrolls scattered across tables were being read aloud, though in hushed tones, by young apprentices under the close scrutiny of instructors.

The ability to read, although held in high esteem by the people, was a skill learned only by government officials and academics. Few outside of those callings had the time or inclination to master the complex system of symbols that comprised the written language of the Americans.

Alwyn allowed his eyes to roam about the room until they settled on a lone man in a corner, absorbed with his quill and ink - Paval LaFranc, the Chief Librarian.

Alwyn studied the older man's precise motions, his deft touch. Twice his age, and nearly twice his size, LaFranc moved with a grace and poise that was startling. *Dip, scratch, scratch, scratch. Sand. Lift the page gently. Pour the sand back into the box. Blow lightly. Examine the page and then repeat the process.* Paval LaFranc never varied. Alwyn smiled in spite of his mood.

He crossed to LaFranc's table, drew a chair under him and sat down, waiting for the older man to acknowledge his presence. LaFranc never tolerated interruption when he was writing. Ink and paper were too valuable, too scarce to risk a mistake. His rages were legendary, even when directed toward someone he liked, like Alwyn.

The scratching continued for a few moments more. Alwyn noticed a flicker of a sandy-red eyebrow. LaFranc knew he was there.

Alwyn waited.

At last LaFranc closed his sandbox, wiped the quill unceremoniously on his sleeve, and made both implements of his trade disappear somewhere inside the voluminous folds of his robe. He raised his piercing gaze to Alwyn and smiled. The creases around his emerald green eyes, deepening with the effort, were the one concession to his age.

"I need to talk," Alwyn said.

"So talk," LaFranc replied.

"Not here."

LaFranc's smile disappeared. There were few secrets in the Library. Knowledge was too valuable. Too much had already been lost to allow any revelation, however small or personal, to be hoarded. That was why in their wisdom, the Founding Fathers had decreed there would be no doors in the Library; no locks to keep knowledge hidden. What was learned by one must be available to all.

LaFranc nodded.

"Where?"

"My cubicle."

The older man rose to his feet and gathered his papers. He was making a copy of Girard's *History of Life in America Before the Burning*. Written three centuries after the event, most librarians dismissed it as flights of fancy, full of children's tales of flying machines, creatures with huge feet, weapons that could destroy whole villages in the blink of an eye, and enormous dragons at the end of the world waiting to gobble up sailors who ventured too far.

LaFranc had his own doubts about the author's objectivity and scholarship. But it was a book, an old book, and it had survived when most had perished during the Time of Madness. There were only three known copies of *History of Life in America Before the Burning*; one in White House, one in Atlantis, and this copy – the Library's copy.

It was old, and the vellum - cured animal skin scraped thin - that it was written on was beginning to disintegrate. The words must be preserved, LaFranc insisted, whether they spoke the truth or a lie.

He had worked on the massive volume for the better part of the year. With luck, he would finish before Candlemas. He placed both the original text and his copy together in a leather satchel, and followed Alwyn out of the common room.

The pair made their way through the labyrinthine hallways to the Cubicles, the living quarters of the Library's inhabitants. The cold stone corridors echoed a dull ring in response to their footfalls. Neither spoke.

Rounding the final turn, Alwyn pushed aside the heavy, maroon drapes that afforded a modicum of privacy, and held them back for his friend to enter. LaFranc walked in with a grace belying his bulk and sat on the lone stool in Alwyn's cubicle laying his precious satchel across his lap.

Coals, carefully laid by one the legion of stewards who tended to all the mundane tasks that the inhabitants of the huge structure took for granted, burned cheerfully in the firebox, warding off the chill that seemed to seep perpetually through the thick stone walls of the Library. Alwyn touched a matchwick to the coals and lit an oil lamp, adjusting its wick to produce a startling brightness in the modest cubicle. He blew out the matchwick and laid it aside.

The big librarian folded his arms and waited in silence as Alwyn stalked back to the doorway and poked his head back into the corridors, scanning both ways to ensure their privacy. If LaFranc was impatient, he didn't show it. He reached into a pouch at his side, pulled out a wad of shredded leaf that reminded Alwyn of the rich, aromatic dirt of the Kanetuck Wilderness, and shoved it into his mouth. He chewed slowly, obviously relishing both the taste and the mild euphoria the juices produced.

Alwyn shook his head; a nasty habit to his way of thinking. He offered his friend a spitting jar, specially designed for the purpose and LaFranc expectorated a prodigious amount of rank, brown spittle. Working the wad into the left side of his jaw, LaFranc once again commanded, "So talk."

Alwyn poked his head back through the drapes one more time, ascertained the halls were empty, took a deep breath, and began.

He paced. He fumed. He railed. He left nothing out. By the time he finished recounting his meeting with the Adam he was exhausted. He collapsed onto his cot, breathing heavily through his mouth, and lay staring at the ceiling.

LaFranc waited a moment more in silence. When he was sure his former pupil had nothing left to say, he casually spit the spent wad of leaf into the jar and assumed his accustomed role as lecturer, educator and counselor.

"You are angry."

It was not a question. Alwyn remained silent but eyed him suspiciously. When LaFranc stated the obvious there was always something not so obvious behind it.

"At who?" LaFranc persisted.

Alwyn blinked. The older man smiled and began ticking off observations on his fingers. Alwyn always hated it when he did that. He hated it even more when LaFranc was right, which he generally was.

"You are angry at Julian for commanding you to go on an errand you would give your back teeth to pursue under any other circumstances."

LaFranc ticked off another finger.

"You are angry at Strom Maxwell for providing the necessary means to accomplish this errand."

A third finger fell.

"You are angry at Burtyn for finding this wondrous, mythical manuscript before you did."

Alwyn began to sputter, but LaFranc merely continued, his eyes twinkling. He touch a fourth finger.

"And you are angry at yourself, because…?"

"Because I am no spy." Alwyn shouted, before remembering he was trying to be unobtrusive.

He jumped from his cot and peered into the hallway again. Once more he returned to face LaFranc.

"I am no spy," he repeated in a voice pitched low enough to not penetrate the heavy cloth hanging over the doorway. There was heat in his tone that belied the softness of his voice. "And I am not afraid."

"So who said you were afraid," LaFranc prodded innocently. "I don't remember saying anything about you being afraid."

"I am a *scavenger*," Alwyn wanted to shake his finger

under LaFranc's nose, but that would have been shockingly disrespectful. "I've spent my life collecting fragments of the past, trying to make sense of a history that simply stops seven hundred years ago. I've risked my life more times than I can count to obtain those relics of the past, and I would do it again. But I am not a spy, and I don't relish losing my head in Willam's court over a forged document that Burtyn has supposedly discovered."

"Burtyn is good," LaFranc replied. "Perhaps not as good as you; perhaps just as good. He is, after all, your father's son. What's to say he hasn't discovered a new book?"

"A book from before the Time of Madness? From before the Great Burning? Impossible," Alwyn scoffed. "No one has ever discovered a book from before. Fragments...bits and pieces, perhaps. But a whole book? No. It is not possible."

"And I am hearing these words coming out of your mouth?" LaFranc replied. "Impossible? It is not only possible, but inevitable. Why should it not be so? You said yourself the glyphs were authentic, even antiquated. Angleesh, you said? Is Burtyn so clever as to create such a book in a written language that few even know exist?"

"Yes. No. Of course not. I don't know," Alwyn fumed. He paced like a Canadian snow tiger, growling as if ready to take off someone's leg below the knee.

LaFranc had succinctly articulated the argument that had tickled the back of Alwyn's mind on his long walk back from the Capitol. The syntax was too complex, too elegant for Burtyn to forge. *Hel embrace him.* It was too complex for *him* to forge, and *he* was good; better than Burtyn, and that was Liberty's own truth.

This book, if it existed, would be the greatest discovery of the Common Era. A book from before the Burning. He couldn't simply ignore it.

Alwyn paced the length of his cubicle, contemplating his options as LaFranc shoved another wad of leaf into his mouth

– chewing and waiting, a wry smile creasing his lips.

Alwyn began ticking off observations in his head. He struggled to keep from ticking them off on his fingers. Only a stubborn resistance to LaFranc's presence prevented him from doing so. Julian, his friend, had asked him to go. Julian, the Adam, had commanded him to go.

*A book from before the Great Burning.*

"I'll go," he declared, the decision made in an instant. "But I'll not be a stooge nor a spy. It is the book that is important. Whether it confers power on Willam or the Adam, it must be found and translated. I'll request; - no, I'll demand professional courtesy. Guild law requires that all discoveries be made available to any scavenger who asks. Even Burtyn would not refuse a formal request from a fellow Guild Scavenger."

LaFranc nodded, and raised the spitting jar to his mouth. He studied it for a moment, perhaps seeking some mystic answer to an unspoken riddle, before spitting the leaf juice into it. He wasn't so sure Burtyn's loyalty to the Guild extended that far.

# CHAPTER 6

**With the decision** made, Alwyn felt the pressure band that had been constricting his chest suddenly relax. He blew out a deep breath that he was only vaguely aware of holding. Before he could draw another, his breath caught in his throat. He looked into the eyes of Strom Maxwell.

LaFranc turned to see what had given his younger friend such a start, but merely grunted in disgust at the soldier's presence. He spat the spent wad of leaf into the jar.

"You do not knock."

LaFranc's statement was laced with contempt.

"There is no door," Strom replied, the hint of a smile lurking around the corners of his eyes.

"You are a boor."

LaFranc spit again into the jar, more from disgust than any lingering effects of the juice of the leaf. He did not approve of Strom Maxwell. He did not approve of Strom's involvement in the Canadian slave trade. He did not approve of Strom's dubious relationship with the confidants of the Calif of Orange. He did not approve of Strom's legendary love of gambling, his extravagant parties, nor his seemingly insatiable appetite for keeping company with the opposite sex. And he most certainly did not approve of Strom's notoriously touchy sense of honor that, if rumors were to be credited, had left more men dead in the street, run through by the steel at his side, than could be counted on two hands.

At this particular moment, what he most disapproved of was Strom's complete disregard for common courtesy.

"This is the Library."

LaFranc rose to his full stature and assumed his lecturing position; a stance that inspired fear and awe in his students, but produced only mild amusement from Strom.

"It is a building without doors; and a building without doors requires a unique protocol. The lowest servant to the highest senator would knock before entering a cubicle not his own. You do not knock. You are worse than an infidel. You are a boor."

LaFranc turned from Maxwell as if the matter were settled, and sat back down on his stool.

Strom sauntered further into the cubicle, the enigmatic grin never leaving his face. He really liked the old librarian despite his occasional tirades, but he had never understood LaFranc's need for what Strom referred to derisively as *protocol and etiquette.* He held to few social conventions, and those were mainly the ones that dealt with self-preservation. Knocking on someone's door, particularly when there was no door to knock on, was not one of them.

"I've walked into Alwyn's cubicle for more than ten years without knocking," he replied. "I'll lie in the embrace of Hel before I start knocking now, just because you happen to think it polite."

LaFranc and Strom stared at each other without blinking, as if the first to blink would lose the argument. Alwyn broke the silence.

"How long have you been here," he asked.

"Long enough," Strom replied as he plopped down onto Alwyn's cot, "to hear things discussed that could, and quite frankly should, get tongues cut out in less civilized surroundings."

The room grew silent for an awkward moment as the two friends eyed each other. Strom was the first to break eye contact. He turned his attention to the collection of antiquities that populated Alwyn's desk; mementos of his many journeys into strange lands. Several new ones had been added since his last visit. He mentally cataloged the new ones, filing them in his memory for future reference.

A small, flat stone at the edge of the desk he hadn't noticed before caught his eye and he rose to examine it. It was etched in the likeness of the Great Stone Wall in Atlantis, with mythical beasts, half horse, half man, carrying swords as if for war, but sheathed as if the battle were already won.

Strom had seen the Wall once, as a lad. The images carved there were ten times larger than a man and over eight hundred hands high up on the Stone Wall. Faint, worn by time, and in places indistinguishable, the images were still awe-inspiring. It was no wonder pilgrims came to the Wall to worship. It was, indeed, holy ground.

"Please be careful with that," Alwyn sighed. "It was a gift from the Governor of Atlantis."

"Oh."

Strom carelessly replaced the stone. He had little respect for, Powyl Mac, the Governor of Atlantis. Mac was a firebrand in his disapproval of the slave trade. Although the practice of slavery was protected by law in all the United States, the Atlantian Guards had forcibly *liberated* Strom's last shipment.

The Governor of Atlantis had cost him a great deal of time, money and effort. Strom would find a way to repay the Governor's kindness, but that would have to wait for another day.

Strom began absently fiddling with the other memorabilia on the desk while Alwyn fidgeted nervously, waiting for one of his precious mementos to break under Strom's careless handling.

"I'm sure you have some reason, other than trying to irritate Master LaFranc, for being here," he said, removing a dull and pitted pewter mug from Strom's fingers and replacing it on the desk. He had found that mug on a collection at the foot of the Central Highlands, just before a spring cloudburst caused a flash flood that washed the entire area clean. He had barely made it to high ground with his life and the mug.

"Just a friendly social call," Strom replied. "But I admit I am a bit curious. Are you seriously considering this fool's errand Julian insists upon sending you on?"

"You were there, Strom," Alwyn eyed him sideways. "Julian made his wishes quite clear, and his reasons make perfect sense. Besides, Julian is the Adam. He has commanded me to go."

Strom chuckled like an uncle indulging a favorite nephew.

"A command you are just as likely to wave away like fly-specked dessert. As I recall your words to the Adam, *This is still the United States of America, and no citizen can be compelled to obey.* Since when have you ever obeyed a command you didn't agree with? I've never known you to take anyone's authority seriously unless it suited you."

Alwyn nodded.

"I know. You're right. I'm not the acquiescing type. But Julian is my friend, Strom; one of the few I have. A command I can ignore. But he *asked* me to go, as a friend. I have never let a friend down yet."

"Alwyn," Strom began slowly, not meeting Alwyn's eyes, "do you consider me to be a friend?"

"You know I do."

"Then as your *friend* let me say, there is a first time for all things."

Alwyn barked a startled laugh.

"You're suggesting I turn down Julian's request? Why?"

The soldier locked eyes with the scavenger, and stared at him hard.

"You don't want any part of this mission, Alwyn, believe me."

Alwyn caught a glimmer of something he had never seen in Strom's eyes before, and it shook him.

"You're afraid," Alwyn sucked in his breathe, startled by the sudden revelation. "Liberty on high, Strom, you're afraid. I've seen you face down Canadians, Highlanders, lynch mobs and cuckolded husbands wielding pickaxes, all without so much as a quiver. I've never seen you show more than a modicum of caution, much less fear. Hel embrace me, what's this all about?"

Strom lowered his eyes and began doodling on the dusty desk. With one finger he drew a wide arc, then raised his eyes, examining first Alwyn's face and then LaFranc's, seeking any sign of recognition. If either saw anything in his obscure doodle it failed to register on their faces. Strom wiped the desk clean, dusted his hands on his trousers, and turned his back on his friends.

"The Stewards are getting lax. You should have them dust more often."

He took a deep breath.

"Join me for a drink."

Strom turned back to Alwyn and gave a look that took in LaFranc as well.

"Regardless of what the Founding Fathers intended for the Library, trust me when I say there is knowledge that was not meant to be shared freely. I know a public house that affords more privacy than the doorless cubicles of this Library."

He leaned in, and spoke in a voice pitched to carry no more than the inches between them.

"And what I have to say requires privacy."

Alwyn exchanged a bewildered look with LaFranc, and

then nodded. Strom rose and began leading the others out when his eyes fell on an artifact that looked curiously out of place among the dozens of dust-covered antiques in Alwyn's collection.

It was a dagger. Its blade was slightly curved, gleaming and delicately decorated with twisting knots and fanciful animals. Its hilt, a lustrous, polished wood so dark it was almost black, was twined about with three red cords. Set on a stand in a back corner of the shelf, it was half-hidden from view; clearly visible only from the pillow of Alwyn's bed.

Strom picked the dagger up with uncharacteristic gentleness. A quick test proved the steel blade remained honed to razor sharpness. Strom's thumb went into his mouth as he sucked the blood from the neat slice.

Few men had ever seen such a knife. Fewer still would recognize it as a ceremonial marriage dagger of the Amarillo Nomes.

"Put it back," Alwyn whispered. "Please."

"She's gone, Alwyn," Strom replied. "The Nomes have moved to Liberty knows where. When they move, they leave no trace that they were ever there, and there is no way of knowing where they will end up. Finding them again is next to impossible. You know that. Let her go."

"I can't."

"Alwyn, it's been sixteen years."

"She was pregnant when I was captured. Did you know that?" Alwyn eyed the dagger, but seemed focused on another time; another place. "I have a son, or a daughter. Somewhere."

"Alwyn…"

"I can't give up, Strom. She's my wife. I love her. And I will find her. If it takes the rest of this life and into the next."

Strom placed the dagger back in its holder and turned to face his friend, laying his hand on Alwyn's shoulder.

"Perhaps," he breathed. "But are you prepared for the

very real possibility that Catharine is no longer waiting for you? As far as she knows, you are dead, or worse. She may have remarried. Or, Liberty forbid, she may be dead herself."

Alwyn's hands gripped the front of Strom's shirt and forced him against the wall with a barely controlled fury that for once took the soldier by surprise.

"She's alive, and I will find her."

Alwyn's tone was deadly calm, but his hands were shaking visibly. He forced his fingers to relax their grip on Strom's shirt, but his eyes maintained their intensity.

"Catharine is the only woman I have ever loved, Strom, and I will find her and our child. Or I will die trying."

Back out in the weather, Alwyn's mood degenerated into an internal mirror of the winter storm that enveloped him. His cloak, still sodden from his journey back from the Capitol, afforded little warmth, it was better than nothing at all. The snow, which only a short while ago had been fat, fluffy flakes, was now sharp, stinging pellets of ice, driven horizontally by the relentless north wind. The angry blue clouds of the afternoon had conquered the sky by nightfall, obliterating the moon.

A grim-faced but determined young apprentice - Alwyn thought he could be no more than ten years from his Naming Day - attended the Never-Dimming Flame. Its fire battled valiantly to provide what little visibility there was, but even it cast only a small circle of illumination.

A bulky figure sat atop Strom's waiting carriage, swathed in deep furs. At a signal from Strom he leapt down, opened the carriage door and dropped a step stool to the ground. This time Alwyn gladly accepted Strom's offer of a ride. He was in no mood to walk anywhere.

The carriage was non-descript, without sigil or crest to identify its owner or employer, black inside and out, the kind that plied its trade throughout the city, but generally catered to the needs of the burgeoning merchant class. It was not the kind normally associated with transporting personages of the stature of generals and librarians. Other than being out on a night that was unfit for swine, it would attract little attention. Strom had made the arrangements and Alwyn assumed he had his reasons.

At least the carriage was fitted with an iron warming chamber which was filled with hot coals. It was not enough to keep the cabin comfortable, but it did manage to to take the edge off the cold. Small comfort, to Alwyn's way of thinking. The darkness and the silence in the cabin matched his mood, but the cold he could do without.

Alwyn thought about settling his cloak over the warming chamber, allowing the warmed air to funnel up and around his body, and be trapped inside his cloak. *But that would be rude,* he suppressed a wry chuckle. His mother had indoctrinated him on proper manners, and even now, more than fifteen years after her death, he could not escape her voice in his head.

No one spoke as the carriage jostled over a road that was equal parts frozen mud and cobblestone. LaFranc continued to glare at Strom, and Strom continued regarding the old man with his sardonic smile. Alwyn merely pulled his cloak tighter and stared moodily out the window, wishing to Liberty he was back in his cubicle in the Library, hunched over an obscure manuscript with no one to make him feel guilty or obligated.

The ride was a long one, made even longer by the growing storm. The cab driver seemed ambivalent to the cold; an occasional clucking to keep his horse at a slow, steady plod was the only indication that he was a living being. Nor could he be induced by LaFranc's chiding to make the horse go any faster. *A careless step in this weather could break a horse's leg,* the driver explained. *That would be bad business, not to mention making for a long walk back home.*

The carriage finally came to a stop, jarring Alwyn from his drowse. Chilly as it was, the interior of the coach was balmy compared to the gust of wind that slapped his face when the door opened.

Stepping out in front of a rundown building with no windows, Alwyn was sure there was some kind of mistake. Swirling snow and darkness all but obliterated any recognizable landmarks, but Alwyn was certain this was not a section of Omaha that one should walk in unarmed, even in the best of weather. If you fell victim to a cut-purse on a night like this, chances were no one would find your body 'til the first thaw.

The sign above the door, swinging drunkenly in the wind, bore the snow-encrusted image of a harp and clover, marking it as a tavern. Alwyn was sure it was one he had never visited before, and left to his own devices never would again.

Strom climbed out of the carriage after Alwyn. He tossed the driver a silver ring.

"For dragging you out on such a night as this," Strom shouted to be heard above the roar of the storm. "And another for the inconvenience of waiting until we return."

The driver caught the rings in a gloved hand and made them disappear somewhere beneath his cloak. A curt nod indicated he would be waiting when they were ready to leave.

If Strom's extravagance with his money surprised his companions, neither showed it. LaFranc followed Strom into the snow, spitting onto the ground and leaving an unsightly brown wad of spent leaf beside his footprint. Alwyn may have been reluctant to leave the relative warmth of the carriage, but though he had his doubts about the wisdom of Strom's selection for their meeting place, he was the first to reach the door of the seedy looking public house. He was tired, raw-nerved and in no mood to stand out in the cold any longer than was necessary.

He pushed open the door to reveal an odd scene of revelry mingled with boredom that bordered on anarchy. Fires roared in two massive fireplaces in the common room, building the heat to just shy of stifling. The stale aroma of old wine and unwashed bodies permeated the atmosphere. Tables were crowded with men who had the hard look of those who had gambled with fate and won...so far; men who knew that their next gamble might be their last.

At one end of the room three men were playing music, badly. One beat incessantly on a series of upright drums, while another strummed out something that resembled a melody on a ten-stringed instrument, and yet another was wrenching what sounded like cat yowling from an odd looking collection of pipes. He blew into a reed to fill a sort of bladder, while simultaneously forcing the air from the bladder through the pipes.

Some might have called the sound *haunting* or *mournful*. To Alwyn it sounded like shrieks from a haunted graveyard.

A woman wearing far too few clothes, and who seemed far too young to be allowed onto the premises, was dancing provocatively on a table in front of the players, but no one paid her much attention. Men diced, laughing or groaning loudly as fortune smiled or frowned upon them. Others stared silently into their cups, looking for answers to questions they were not sure they wanted to ask.

Two burly fellows in the middle of the room had apparently let the wine go to their heads and began pummeling each other with their fists. At a nod from the stout man behind the bar, the biggest man Alwyn had ever seen sauntered up behind the two pugilists. He cracked both on the head with a thick cudgel before they even knew he was there.

The giant grabbed each man by his collar, dragged them through the crowded room, and casually tossed them out into the snow. Perhaps they would wake up and find their way home. Perhaps they would freeze to death in the elements. It did not appear to make any difference to anyone there.

LaFranc snorted his disapproval as Strom tossed the half-dressed young dancer a silver ring. A familiar smile played across her face, making her look much wiser than her apparent years, and she made the ring disappear. Alwyn couldn't imagine where. There didn't seem to be enough material to hold the ring in place.

Barmaids wove their own peculiar dance through the crowded room, supplying its occupants with dark brown ale, hot spiced wine or harder liquor as they required. They retrieved empty mugs as they were drained and danced back to the bar to start the cycle again. They seemed adept at avoiding attempted pinches and pats as they passed by their half-drunk clientele.

Raucous laughter and coarse jesting competed with the music for dominance. Alwyn shook his head in disbelief.

*This is more private than the Library?*

Strom brushed past him and made his way to the bar. Alwyn saw him motion to the short, fat, balding man of middle years who had only moments before ordered his giant to crack a couple of skulls. A glint of gold passed from Strom to the man and soon Alwyn, LaFranc and Strom were ushered to a table in the middle of the room.

The three men who had recently occupied those seats were now standing by the door, flanked by two burly peacekeepers. They glared at the newcomers, but they had their coats on and were donning their cloaks and hats. None seemed willing to argue with the steel at the peacekeepers' sides. The giant sat peacefully in his chair beside the door.

A plump barmaid with porcelain skin and auburn hair wiped the table with her apron, flashed a familiar smile at Strom and gave him a saucy wink before hurrying back to the bar to fetch drinks for the three. Her hair, which was tied tightly with a ribbon high on the back of her head, flowed down her back, reminding Alwyn of a wild pony's tail.

"Friend of yours?" Alwyn asked.

"We've met," Strom answered.

"You come here often?"

"As business requires."

"And what business would the Adam's Commanding General have to conduct in this den of thieves?" LaFranc demanded loudly enough to be heard over the din.

"I serve the Adam as the Adam requires," Strom replied. "But I take no pay for my service. Call it a debt I owe. Beyond my service to the Adam, I am a man of business, with wide and varying interests..."

"Slaves." LaFranc snorted.

"Yes, slaves," Strom snapped back. "Who do you think digs the black rock that fuels the furnaces that heat the water for your bath, Master LaFranc? You couldn't pay enough if free men mined the rock. Who do you think digs the salt from the mines beneath Omaha City? The cost to season your soup would be exorbitant without slave labor. And don't get me started on the road, viaducts and sewage troughs. Beside, they're only Canadians. It's not as if they have a soul.

"But I trade in much more than slaves, Master LaFranc. I bring in grain from the Great Plains for the city's granaries. Do you think the farms of Omaha produce enough grain to make bread for all the inhabitants of Omaha City? If there is no bread, there will be riots in the street. It's happened before, remember? I was only a boy the last time, but as I recall the mob reached the Library moat. Lucky you had that drawbridge, hmmm? The last Adam didn't fare so well. His head rested on a pike for a month at the entrance of the Capitol Building.

Strom's normally low-pitched voice began to rise with his pique.

"Your precious ink and paper - paper that is only

produced in the Kanetuck wilderness, Master LaFranc? It's scarce, hard to trade for, and expensive. No one outside the Paper Guild even knows what your precious paper is made from. And they will kill - have killed - to preserve that secret. I bring it in.

"You have a taste for citrus, don't you, Master LaFranc? With relations between the Calif and the President at an all time low, it is almost impossible to obtain. And transporting it across the Central Highlands? Suicidal. The Highlanders have an uncompromising sense of propriety. Few know their customs. They are easy to offend, and once offended they are savage. They'll take off your head and shrink it to the size of a turnip to decorate their tents. I bring it in. *I bring it in.* So have a little respect, old man."

LaFranc glared at Strom. He reached into the pouch he kept ready at his side and pulled out a prodigious wad of leaf and stuffed it into his mouth, chewing vigorously. He glared and fumed and spat a brown stain onto the sawdust floor, but he said nothing more.

"I even trade Canadian slaves with the Southlanders for that leaf you enjoy chewing so much, Master LaFranc," Strom added as a final dig.

LaFranc looked like he was ready to swallow the wad of leaf in his mouth before Alwyn cried, "Peace!"

LaFranc hesitated a moment before nodding, and Strom leaned back in his chair, an easy grin once more appearing on his face. The saucy barmaid appeared at that moment, distributing mulled wine among the three men. Strom supplied a quick swat to her ample backside and tossed a silver ring her way. She graced him with another surreptitious wink, then she was gone, tending the needs of her other customers.

Alwyn wrapped his hands around his mug, relishing the warmth of the hot liquid inside as it radiated from from the mug into his fingers. He inhaled the rich, spicy aroma, as he swirled the wine around in the mug. He stared into his cup as if trying to divine the future, but nothing was clear. He took a small mouthful of the golden liquid and rolled it around his tongue, relishing its sharp bite, then swallowed, allowing the heady drink to warm him all the way down to his toes. He looked up from his cup and met Strom's eyes.

"What is this all about, Strom? What is so important that we couldn't talk about it in the Library, but we can safely discuss in public?"

Strom leaned forward resting his chin on the back of his interlaced fingers.

"We are indeed in the middle of a den of thieves," he said with unfeigned seriousness. "Everyone here has both legitimate and, shall we say, ambiguous, business interests. Deals are made here that cannot be made in more formal settings. Politics gets in the way of progress. The Elector of the Southlands may have slapped an embargo on Iowan silk in retaliation for Iowa raising the import duties on Southlander cheese. But the fact is, Iowans like Southlander cheese; and Southlanders like Iowan silk. Neither Elector will back down for fear of losing face. That's where these *gentlemen* come in."

Strom waved his hand across the room, taking in its inhabitants in a single swipe.

"These men make the deals that provide the goods to the people. The government turns a blind eye, the people get the goods they want, and everybody's honor remains intact. Unless someone gets careless or excessively greedy. Then that someone ends up on the wrong side of a dagger, or finds themselves dancing in the air from the end of a rope."

Strom fixed Alwyn with a stare that took in LaFranc as well.

"Everyone here has business to conduct. Everyone here makes it a point to *not* listen to anyone else's conversation. It could be dangerous. It could get you killed."

Alwyn took another long draught of his hot, mulled

wine and swallowed hard. LaFranc spit. Both nodded as understanding dawned. A sardonic smile to play around the corners of Strom's mouth.

"So you see, my friends," he pronounced, "we may speak our most intimate secrets here, without fear of compromise. But keep your voices low just the same."

"Alright," Alwyn responded, meeting his friend stare for stare. He might understand the need for circumspection, but he was tired, irritated, still chilled to the bone and in no mood for polite conversation. "We're here. Talk."

Now it was Strom's turn to stare into his mug. He took a large swig and let the liquor warm his insides before he began.

"Julian is the Adam," he began. "And he is my friend. But more than that, he is a true man of God; a man of integrity, honor and duty. He is also a man of power, vision, intelligence and great ability. He holds both his power and his convictions tightly, and it is unlikely he would willingly relinquish either.

"Willam is equally a man of vision, ability and conviction, though he holds to his own code of honor. He has intelligence mixed with cunning, and a ruthlessness forged in battle. He does not lightly suffer fools, and he considers anyone who disagrees with him to be a fool.

"Unfortunately, both men have the same vision — a reconstructed, truly united, United States of America, with themselves as the undisputed head."

LaFranc and Alwyn listened impatiently. Nothing Strom had said shed any light on the situation.

"Old news, Strom," Alwyn muttered. He stared sulkily at his near empty mug, and cast a furtive glance around the room, hoping to make eye contact with their saucy serving maid.

"Julian has the superior claim because he *is* the Adam," Strom continued as if he had not been interrupted. "As President, Willam may claim the power of life and death; but

Julian, the Adam, claims not only power over life and death, but ultimately over eternal life or eternal damnation. Willam himself was forced to kneel in the snow for three days to win release from excommunication, after the Highlander debacle, remember?"

Alwyn stifled a yawn behind his fist. This was all common knowledge. Strom was droning on and on, and it was getting late. Alwyn finally spied the serving maid with the quick smile and the twinkle in her eye. She was slapping a hand away while sparing a wink at a rather large, rough looking fellow in the far corner.

Alwyn started to raise his hand to hale her when Strom snapped, "Pay attention, Alwyn. This is important."

Strom's stare brooked no argument, and Alwyn cast one last, longing look at his empty mug, sighed and acquiesced.

"This scrap of a manuscript puts a new wrinkle in the balance of power," Strom continued. "To Willam's way of thinking, there is one God and only one God: Liberty, the God of Five Faces, the God of the United States of America. The gods of other nation are, by definition, false gods who should be trampled under foot.

"Willam believes, since there are not many gods, but only one God, there should not be many nations, but only one; The United States of America. Canada, the Califate of Orange, the Confederation of the Southlands, to Willam's mind they must all bow the knee to the United States. And of course, there can be only one ruler over that nation — himself.

"If this manuscript exists, then Tyrfingr must also exist, and Willam with stop at nothing to pull it from the stone, to prove he is the One foretold. Truth be told, if he holds Tyrfingr, no one could doubt the legitimacy of Willam's claim of spiritual authority over the Adam. Not even the Adam."

"Old news, Strom," Alwyn snorted, fighting boredom and still wishing for another cup of something hot, and preferably strongly alcoholic. He saw no need to keep the irritation from his voice, but he did manage to keep his volume in check.

"Tell me something I don't know. Something made you drag me out of my nice warm cubicle on this Liberty-forsaken night, to this Liberty-forsaken hole of a public house. If you are trying to frighten me out of going by telling me some fishwife's bedtime story, you are making a bad job of it."

But even through his frustration something tickled the back of Alwyn's mind, and the thought made his eyes burn with his peculiar passion.

*What if it's not a fishwife's tale? What if the fragment really is from the time before? What if a whole book really does exist? No, it's not possible. Tyrfingr is a myth…but…*

"Besides, Julian has asked me to go. And this fragment, if it is not a fake, may be the most significant historical document of all time."

For a moment the seedy surroundings of the tavern faded from Alwyn's view as he contemplated the possibilities. His eyes took on a faraway look and he caressed his empty mug absently.

"Think of it," he murmured to no one in particular. "If this manuscript really exists, it is something actually written before the Great Burning. That would be something to see."

Strom licked his lips, drained his mug, and flicked his eyes around the raucous room. He leaned forward slightly, almost imperceptibly, and spoke in slow, measured tones pitched to draw Alwyn back from his reverie. Alwyn and LaFranc had to lean in to catch his words.

"Oh, it exists, all right," Strom whispered. "And Tyrfingr exists, too. But, Alwyn, it was not meant for human eyes."

Alwyn would have laughed out loud had the look on Strom's face not been so intense. For a moment no one spoke, but merely stared at each other.

LaFranc nodded, drained his cup, and raised his hand

for a refill. The saucy, dark eyed serving girl was nowhere to be found, but a tall, thin, blonde girl with full lips and twinkling blue eyes appeared, replacing their empty mugs with ones filled with steaming mulled wine. After tossing a familiar glance at Strom, along with a surreptitiously blown kiss, she danced away.

"What?" Strom demanded as his companions stared at him with blank expressions. "A man has needs."

LaFranc 'harrumphed' loudly, quaffed half of his mug with one draught and reached for his leaf pouch.

"I seem to recall legends of this relic from the past you speak of," LaFranc had assumed his lecturing posture. "There are a few obscure references in volumes so old and musty that few, other than full librarians, are even allowed access to them."

At this revelation Alwyn raised an eyebrow. Knowledge that was not accessible to all? It was strictly forbidden.

"Do not raise your eyebrow at me, young master Alwyn Malcolmesson," LaFranc scolded. "These are documents much too fragile for any but the most skillful to touch."

"And which contain knowledge much too dangerous to make public," Strom added.

Alwyn stared holes in both of his friends.

"Does everyone know of these secret treasures except me?"

The plumb barmaid with the porcelain skin and auburn hair danced past, deposited a fresh round of drinks on the table, though their mugs were not yet empty, and skittered away without so much as a wink this time. She seemed to have caught the mood of the table.

"Alwyn, those musty old volumes are not important," Strom said. "This manuscript is. What Burtyn has somehow managed to scavenge is a fragment of a *grimoire*, a book of ancient magic. It belongs to the Fairies."

Strom waited for the inevitable ridicule that would

come, and on any other night Alwyn would have obliged. But fishwives' tales were coming true tonight, and Alwyn was pretty sure the Fair Folk were more than tales told around campfires. He was pretty sure he had met one once, a long time ago. Alwyn merely waited for more information. Strom would have to look elsewhere for ridicule.

"Everyone thinks the Fair Folk are a legend, made up to frighten children," Strom sounded more defensive than he wished. "You've heard the stories around the fireplace as a child – how the Fair Folk live underground and only come out at night. They come for bad little boys and girls who don't eat their greens. *If you don't go to sleep the Fairies will get you.*"

Strom stopped, took a long draught of the hot, spiced wine, wiping his mouth with the back of his hand. When he continued there was no hint of defensiveness in his voice.

"Alwyn, the stories are true. Some of them are true." Strom's eyes took on a far off look, as if lost in a distant memory.

"They exist," he whispered as if to himself. Then more forcefully to Alwyn and LaFranc, "The Fair Folk exist. They live underground, away from the light, because they are evil. They come to the surface only at night. They practice human sacrifice. Their rituals require them to eat flesh and drink blood. They believe it makes them one with their god."

Strom shook himself back to the present.

"I don't know how Burtyn managed to obtain this fragment. I suspect he stole it. I do know that the Fairies will stop at nothing to get that fragment back. It is holy to them, and civil war between Julian and Willam would be a blessing compared to the hell they would unleash on the earth. Tyrfingr, the legendary Sword in the Stone, is indeed a weapon of great power, Alwyn. But it was not meant to be wielded by human hands. Death and damnation have always surrounded it. If you persist in this quest, you are not only risking your life. You are risking your immortal soul."

# CHAPTER 7

**Julian sat rigidly** behind his desk. The sound of his fingers drumming the arm of his chair reverberated off the walls and filled the silent vacuum of the room. Strom and Alwyn had left hours ago and night had long since fallen, as deep and silent as the snow that piled up against the granite walls of the Capitol Building. The oil lamps that illumined the room burned low; the fire in the massive stone hearth had long since burned down to a few glowing embers, crusted over by gray ash. Still he sat, brooding.

*Willam…the Bastard.*

It was both title and invective — for though the late president, Occam, formally acknowledged the boy as his own, he had never bothered with the formality of marrying the child's mother.

*Why couldn't the Bastard have just died at Thousand Lakes?*

For the hundredth time his eyes fell on the small vellum scroll that was the focal point of his irritation. He unrolled it for the hundredth time, and for the hundredth time cursed the fact that he could not decipher the Ancient American glyphs it contained. That he knew Alwyn spoke true did not help. He flung the scroll back onto his desk and began massaging his temples. The left side of his head was beginning to pound. It was a bad sign.

He had been prone to incapacitating headaches from his youth; blinding headaches that might last for hours, sometimes days. He could always tell when one was coming - the dull thud, thud, thud in the left side of his brain that seemed to mirror his heartbeat, that seemed loud enough that everyone else in the room should hear it; the shimmering lights that danced before his eyes, that started as pinpricks, then expanded to fill his entire vision; the suddenly clarity of vision and heightened senses just before his world caved in and he was sucked into a vacuum of pain, pain that was exacerbated by the slightest light or sound. The pain rendered him senseless, useless, helpless.

Nothing but sleep eased the agony, yet sleep was hard to come by when his head felt as if it were splitting open at the seams. There were concoctions that could knock him out, and at times he had availed himself of their sweet oblivion.

Oddly enough the headaches had stopped the same year he took Scylla to be the first of the four wives he was required by law to have. He had been free of their tyranny for years. But now they were back and for no good reason that he could fathom. They were not frequent. Not yet. But when they hit, they hit with a vengeance, making up for lost time.

This was going to be a bad one, and he did not have the time for it. He smashed his fist into the desktop. Hel take him, he did not have time for it!

*How to deal with Willam…the Bastard?*

*I should have crushed him before Thousand Lakes,* he mused. *He was at his weakest then. The electors in The Ohios and Dakota were both clamoring for Willam's head on a platter. Too ambitious, they claimed. Wanted authority to raise troops from their states, they said. Wanted to tax their citizens to pay for it, they said. They wouldn't stand for it, they said.*

*The Bastard! I should have crushed him then.*

But he hadn't crushed him then, and Willam was proven right at the Battle of Thousand Lakes. He had needed every soldier he had recruited in The Ohios and Dakota to turn back the Canadian onslaught, and had nearly gotten himself killed in the process. No one could claim Willam was a coward, Julian grudgingly admitted to himself. And there was ample reason to credit him with being a bona fide military genius.

After Thousand Lakes Willam had risen from being merely the old president's bastard to full fledged hero in the eyes of the common people. Even the electors in The Ohios and Dakota were forced to hold their peace because of Willam's rabid personal popularity with the people. It had stoked the fires of ambition that Occam had been planted in the boy's youth.

*I should have crushed him then.*

Julian swept the scroll to the floor in irritation.

"That bad, my love?"

Julian looked up slowly to lock eyes with Alycia, his first-wife. He had been so engrossed in this latest threat to his Adamic authority that he had not heard her enter. There were few men who had unhindered access to his private study; and none of them would consider entering unannounced.

Alycia was the only woman granted such access, and she never allowed herself to be announced. Julian trusted her implicitly, and hid nothing from her.

*Age and guile always defeats youth and beauty*, she quoted her mother, the one concession she made to her relationship with Alwyn. Julian would smile, for though she possessed the wisdom of age beyond her years, and was well versed in guile, she was also a stunning beauty who had never lost the dew of youth.

"That bad," Julian acknowledged.

She was the second woman Julian had taken as wife. Alycia beguiled him, thrilled him, enchanted him. He had formally elevated her to the honored position of first-wife, relegating Scylla, the first woman he had wed, to under-wife.

The slight to Scylla's family - one of the wealthiest in Omaha - had not gone unnoticed, and the social rumblings his actions caused nearly required force to be quelled.

Once again Strom Maxwell, through his uncanny combination of political astuteness and military prowess had proven an invaluable ally. The situation was resolved without bloodshed, and Scylla's family even gained in social stature with the appointment of her father to a prestigious governmental post that required little, paid much and kept him out of state for the better part of every year.

Alycia glided across the floor and settled behind his chair, rubbing his temples with her soft, pampered fingers.

"Talk to me, my love," she coaxed. "I am but a woman, but sometimes talking things out, even to a woman, helps."

Julian smiled in spite of the hammer pounding behind his eyes. *Just a woman? Ah, no, my love. You are much more than just a woman.*

"A master stroke by my old friend, Willam the Bastard," he said at last, pointing to the scroll on the floor.

Alycia looked askance at the innocuous looking scroll, as if half expecting it to transform into a six-legged serpent from the Amarillo Waste. She bent to pick it up, spilling her waist-length honey-golden hair over her shoulder, then peered coyly through it to her husband. Neither her startling, sapphire blue eyes nor her generous display of cleavage captured her husband's attention. He sat unseeing, with the heels of his hands pressed against his eyes.

She gave him an unnoticed, wry smile, mildly chagrined that her carefully executed feminine wiles had gone unnoticed, then turned her gaze back to the scroll. She studied it, turned it first upside down, then right side up, then laughed in sweet, bell-like tones.

"It's gibberish," she smiled. "This is a master stroke?"

Julian snatched the scroll from the hands of the still snickering woman and threw it violently to the desk. Alycia did not appear the least bit impressed by either the writing on the scroll or her husband's tantrum.

"This *gibberish* is Ancient American," Julian chided, "and according to your brother, the dialect is peculiar; formal; steeped in an authority not commonly found in Ancient American writing."

At the mention her brother, Alycia stopped laughing. Her voice carried an edge that could cut marble whenever she spoke of Alwyn.

"And how is my dear, twin *brother*?" she spat. The gentleness with which she had resumed caressing his temples belied the venom in her voice.

"He is fine, I suppose," Julian replied, already regretting mentioning Alwyn's name. The tiny flecks of light were beginning to dance before his eyes. It was going to be *very* bad. "He is a bit frustrated with this scroll, though."

*Liberty send that he chokes on it*, Alycia thought. Aloud she said, "And just what is it about this ridiculous scroll with its gibberish writing that frustrates my illustrious brother so?"

Julian felt the tension begin to loosen just a little as Alycia's fingers worked their way down to his neck. She had magic in those fingers. He barked a wry laugh.

"Probably that Burtyn found it before he did."

Alycia permitted herself a surreptitious smile, and began kneading his shoulders with her small, practiced fingers.

"Yes, that would put him in a snit."

She stopped her ministrations long enough to lean over and retrieve the scroll. Few had ever seen Ancient American script. By virtue of her parentage, she had had the opportunity on more than one occasion. Not that she ever had any interest in learning to decipher the cryptic mess. She had more important things to do than follow her parents and two brothers on their Liberty-forsaken collections. She was far more interested in the future than the past. Besides, she hated getting dirty, and they were always digging in the dirt.

Alycia studied the precise characters. Even though she had little interest in their meaning, she admired the artistic simplicity of the intersecting lines and graceful curves that were so different from the picto-graphic writing of Modern American. Unlike the vast majority of citizens, common or noble, she could read, though apart from official government documents there was little use for that talent. Still, she could not decipher this ancient, cryptic message.

"What does it say," she demanded.

"According to Alwyn, it says, *The apparition of The God is upon me; The God has anointed me to proclaim... Liberty,*" Julian answered.

Alycia resumed massaging Julian's neck. She stood behind him, silent, her full, rosebud lips pursed. Her hands never paused in their work, but the import of Julian's words sank in.

"Willam has declared himself to be Adam," she whispered. "More than Adam; God on earth, or perhaps the Son of God?"

Julian nodded, and immediately wished he hadn't. Though the tension in his neck had lessened, the pinpricks before his eyes had started their macabre dance, joining together and growing larger. When he moved his head it felt like his brain was shaking loose and banging against the sides of his skull. Yes, it was definitely going to be a very, very bad one.

"Willam relies on a document, this document, that is ancient...beyond ancient...lending the weight of ages to his claim," Alycia continued, barely aware she was speaking aloud. "The common people place great faith in ancient customs *and* the written word, and this document appeals to both. Few can read, and almost none can decipher the ancient script. But it is the very antiquity of this document that will appeal to their need for an ancient authority in their lives."

Again Julian nodded, then bit back a whimper. Any movement now would only compound the pain that was piling up in his brain like a thunderhead on a hot summer afternoon. When it broke, it would be with a white hot fury.

"A master stroke, indeed, my husband."

Alycia bent low, nestling Julian's head between her breasts and wrapping her arms around his chest. She nibbled his earlobe as she whispered, "How will you counter it?"

"How, indeed?" he replied, devoutly wishing her wifely ministrations had come at a more opportune time. The mounting pressure drove any thought of physical pleasure out of his mind. Pressing the heels of his hands against his eyes did nothing to shut out the growing light that threatened to engulf his world.

"Talk to me, my love," Julian said through teeth gritted against the pain. "Give me your thoughts on this matter. The sound of your voice helps me to think. Talk to me."

Alycia allowed her hands to roam back up to Julian's temples, and she ran her fingers absently in tiny circles.

"Perhaps this scroll can be shown to be a fraud, a forgery, a complete fabrication," she suggested. "Burtyn has been known to be less than scrupulous in the past. You could simply denounce it as a clever, but misguided hoax."

"Perhaps," Julian agreed. "But Alwyn was shaken when he saw the script. The style, the syntax, the very power of the words - it was too...*real*...to be a fabrication. Perhaps Burtyn did change a word or two to make it appear more favorable to Willam. I don't know. I can't read the Liberty cursed thing. But without the original to compare this fragment to there is no way to properly translate it. There is no way to tell whether it has been tampered with or not."

Julian felt his mouth going dry, tasted the familiar metallic tang in the back of his throat.

*Washington and Kennedy, this is going to be a bad one.*

The thought passed into oblivion almost as soon as it appeared, relegated to a remote corner in the back of his mind. He had no time to give to his own discomfort.

"And to denounce it as a fraud would be to acknowledge that it exists," he continued. "Rumor would build on rumor until rumor was accepted as truth. Willam would be hailed as the fulfillment of ancient prophecy – the One true Son of Liberty who is to return in the time of America's greatest need, riding a white horse and carrying his great sword, *Justice,* on his back."

Julian reached up and took Alycia by the wrist, pulling her hand to his lips, kissing it gently on the palm.

"There would be civil war such as has not been known since the Time of Madness. It is not a pleasant thought, my love."

Alycia moved from behind her husband and knelt in front of him. There was fire burning behind her sapphire eyes that could have rivals the depths of Hel, and venom in her voice as she grasped his knees with fierce fingers.

"You are Adam."

She might have shouted for all the force she put behind the words, though Julian knew she spoke in her normal, measured tones. Yet her words echoed in his ears, a sudden gong, ringing wildly, uncontrollably, swept into a crescendo by the blood swirling in his ears.

"Willam swore fealty to *you* when he ascended to the Presidency, in accordance with the Donation of Constantine. He acted as your groom for three days as custom demanded. Write to him with your own hand. Remind him of his obligation – the same obligation every President for the past 700 years has accepted.

"Tell him the fragment is a fraud, and that you do not accept its authority. Demand that he come to Omaha, without his army, and prostrate himself before you in repentance. Tell him that obedience will result in forgiveness, but refusal invites excommunication both to him and to all who follow him. Tell him," she seethed. "Seal it with the Adamic Seal."

"And you think he'll obey?" Julian barked a mirthless laugh.

His first-wife was bathed in a corona that blotted out all detail; a corona not caused by the delicate light behind her, but by the blinding light in his own brain. He could not see the rictus snarl that marred the delicate lines of her face.

"Of course not," Alycia snapped. "Do you think me a fool?"

There was no sympathy in her voice or demeanor. Gone was the considerate counselor, the gentle masseuse, the loving wife. The woman before him could have been carved from marble. There was a dangerous flash in Alycia's eyes that would have cut the laughter from Julian's throat had he been able to see it beyond the waxing light that engulfed everything. The laughter faded of itself. He did not miss it. He truly wanted her advice, desired her wisdom, needed the soothing sound of her voice as a buttress against the pain, but he had never heard this kind of quiet fury in her voice before.

"Tell me, my love. What is your real plan," Julian asked.

Alycia's lips drew back in a triumphant grin, revealing her perfectly spaced, perfectly white teeth.

"Write the letter, my love." Once again her voice was honey and rosewater. "Let your advisors know that you have written it, and let them know what is in it. You are Adam. You are kind. You are long-suffering and forgiving to those who have gone astray; even to your enemies, if they will only repent."

The brilliant, white lights suddenly faded, leaving behind a familiar crisp clarity. It was as if his head were in a vacuum, with nothing to filter sight nor sound.

"Tell me more, my love."

"Willam has not merely gone astray," Alycia lowered her lips to croon in his ear, as if what she was about to say was a secret too dangerous for even the flagstones in the floor to overhear. "Willam is not simply an enemy. Willam is a cancer. Cancer cannot be forgiven, only excised. Call for the H'ashasine, my husband. Excise the cancer."

Julian stared at his wife for a long, long moment. Of his four wives, she was the only one he loved. He kept nothing from her, either personally or professionally. He shared with her his deepest fears and loftiest ambitions. Today he wasn't sure he knew her at all. This woman before him now was not flesh and blood, but marble — cold and impenetrable, beautiful beyond words.

He could see everything clearly now; too clearly. His hearing was accentuated. He thought he could hear his wife's breathing, the staccato beating of her heart. He could almost see the plan behind her eyes.

*"Call for the H'ashasine…Excise the cancer."*

"My love," he whispered at last as the crashing pain obliterated all thought, "it shall be done."

Julian gained his feet, though unsteadily, the pain driving thought from his mind. That he had lost consciousness he was certain, but he had no idea how long he had lain on the floor. He saw neither Alycia standing at the side table, nor the packet of powder she stirred into his goblet of chilled citrus. He staggered to the armless divan before the marble fireplace and lowered himself to sit. He barely noticed when Alycia raised the cup to his lips, stroking his throat to encourage him to drink.

"Sleep, my love," Alycia purred, knowing her husband would be incapacitated for the better part of two days. The finely crushed henbane she had added to his drink would see to that, and the headache he would have when he awoke would seem a blessed relief compared to the one he had now. Her smile held no warmth; her ministrations no wifely concern.

She continued caressing Julian's temples until the creases in his forehead relaxed, and his breathing evened, proving the henbane's effect.

"Sleep well," she crooned, then rose and sauntered back to his desk with a feminine sway that would have made his mouth go dry if he had been even vaguely aware.

Though paper and ink were scarce, there was no shortage of these luxury items in Julian's office. Alycia retrieved a leaf of the precious commodity from a drawer in Julian's massive oaken desk, casually sat in his chair, and picked up Willam's scroll.

She pulled the stopper from the inkwell, taking care to not let a drip of the purple-black liquid fall, picked up the quill that lay beside it and dipped its nib into the well. Carefully, with practiced, deliberate fingers, she scratched the strange glyphs onto the paper, stopping frequently to compare, making sure they were identical.

Satisfied, she sanded her copy, stoppered the inkwell and laid the quill back in its tray. She scrutinized her hands to make sure there was no telltale drip of ink on her milky white skin; no marring of her brightly lacquered nails. Stealing another look at her drugged, sleeping husband, Alycia smiled once more, sweetly, to herself.

"Sleep well," she murmured again.

There was a hint of emotion in her voice that had nothing to do with affection. Rolling the copied glyphs into a tight scroll, Alycia left Julian to his troubled dreams.

# CHAPTER 8

**The knock sounded** again from outside his cubicle, insistent knuckles rapping in repetitive sets of three. It was that persistent knocking that had roused Alwyn from his dreams.

"Come," he mumbled grumpily as he stumbled to the wash basin, flexing his fingers in an effort to work the stiffness from his knuckles. He poured icy water from the unadorned, porcelain pitcher into the basin, scooped it up with his hands and scrubbed the sleep from his eyes.

Toweling his face dry, Alwyn blew out a quick shiver and turned. LaFranc stood behind him. His mentor was dressed in traveling clothes, a quarterstaff in is grasp, a claymore strapped to his back. Alwyn raised an eyebrow at the massive, two-handed sword that reared over his teacher's shoulder, more surprise by the weapon than LaFranc's garb. He knew the older man was a blademaster, though few, even among the blademasters still carried the unwieldy sword. It had been popular with the giant Canadians three centuries before, but American warriors had never taken a fancy to it, preferring the more versatile, less cumbersome short sword.

LaFranc was famed for using the ancient sword as a teaching tool in the practice field.

*Balance*, LaFranc always said. *Cold steel, cool head, fire in your eyes, but above all, balance.*

Alwyn had never known him to carry any weapon inside the halls of the Library.

"Expecting trouble," Alwyn asked, turning his attention back to the icy water in the basin. He splashed his face again and rubbed the last vestiges of his dreams from his mind.

"Expect the worst," the big librarian replied with a shrug, "and all your surprises are pleasant ones. General Maxwell will guard your front. He is a good man, though I would not tell him so and I would deny it if you did. He knows his job. Though he will guard your front, you will need someone to guard your back. I am not so bad with a sword."

Alwyn nodded. He dipped his chew stick into a cruse of pulverized salt and soda, then rubbed the salted stick across his teeth and gums. He slurped up a mouthful of water, swished and spat. Patting the towel against his dripping face, Alwyn said, "Thank you, Paval, but are you sure you want to be part of this? It could be nasty business before it is over. A man could lose his head in this kind of venture, or worse."

LaFranc nodded solemnly, without hesitation, as Alwyn dressed. There was a liquid fire behind his clear, green eyes that Alwyn had never seen before; a slight crease at the corners of his mouth that hinted at amusement, like a farm child promised a holiday from the drudgery of the field.

"Indeed, a man might loose his head on a venture like this," LaFranc repeated as he reached into his ever-present pouch of leaf for a fresh chew. He held the aromatic, shredded leaf in a wad between his fingers, half-forgotten in his enthusiasm. "But men have lost their heads for lesser prizes — gold; women; kingdoms. I have spent my life in this Library; dedicated my life to the preservation of the written word, the knowledge of the ages. But this...a book from before the Burning...this is the discovery of a lifetime; of more than a lifetime. This could well be the defining moment of the age."

Alwyn smiled as his friend and mentor allowed a sheepish grin to play across his face. LaFranc shoved the leaf into his mouth as if that settled the matter.

Alwyn stamped his feet to settle them in his boots. He threw traveling clothes into a pack with nonchalant efficiency. Unlike LaFranc who rarely left the Library, and then only under protest, Alwyn frequently embarked on collections. He knew what items he needed for travel, and what items to leave behind. He was ready in moments.

Shouldering his pack, Alwyn headed for the door.

"Let's go, Paval. Strom will be chewing saddle leather by now. He always was one for an early start."

LaFranc eyed his young protégé with mild disapproval, and spat into Alwyn's fireplace, watching the brown liquid sizzle and pop on the hot coals.

"You go unarmed?" he clucked, a teacher reprimanding a dimwitted pupil for an obvious error. Then, more gently, he said, "Alwyn, this will be more dangerous than a collection in the Central Highlands or on the Canadian border. Some form of self-defense would be advisable, don't you think?"

When Alwyn turned to face the older man there was no hint of illusion about him. He spoke quietly, but with the force of conviction and reality.

"Paval, you and I, along with Strom and his band of twelve hand-picked men, and Julian's ambassador, whoever he is, are getting ready to walk into the middle of White House, where Willam commands his elite Republican Guard, not to mention the combined armies of Dakota, North Iowa, and The Ohios. Do you really think there is any weapon I could take that would make any difference at all?"

"There may be more to fight than Willam on this venture," LaFranc snorted, poking the younger man in the forehead with his finger. "Have you learned nothing?"

Alwyn stood for a moment, half-angry, half-chastened. He hated it when LaFranc did that. It always gave him a headache. He turned back to his desk and snatched up his marriage knife. He turned back to the older man with the blade held at eye level.

"Will this serve?" he choked out.

LaFranc's green eyes widened.

"It will serve," he whispered, then said nothing more.

"It is small enough to conceal," Alwyn continued as if to himself. "It is razor sharp and perfectly balanced. It can cut a man's throat, or cut out his tongue as the need may be. And it will serve as a passport of sorts should the need arise to return to the land of the Nomes."

"We should go now, Alwyn," LaFranc urged.

Alwyn nodded, made the dagger disappear somewhere within the folds of his cloak, snatched up his pack, and turned to join his companion. Before they reached the opening of his cubicle he hesitated once more.

"Paval, I believe this manuscript truly exists, or I wouldn't be going on this fool's errand. But the other...the Tyrfingr. What if it also exists? What if Burtyn really has found it? What if he has already pulled Tyrfingr from the Stone?"

Paval LaFranc threw back his head and roared with laughter.

"If Burtyn had already pulled Tyrfingr from the Stone, we wouldn't have to worry about the manuscript," he replied. "Life as we know it would cease to exist."

Strom Maxwell was indeed ready to chew saddle leather. By the time Alwyn and LaFranc reached the courtyard of the Capitol Building the sun stood a full hand above the horizon, and reflected cheerfully on the blanket of snow that had covered the ground during the night. It blazed less brightly than Strom's clear, brown eyes. Alwyn wisely decided against the jovial greeting he had planned and instead strode directly to the two saddled, but riderless horses that were obviously meant for him and LaFranc.

It took less than a moment for him to stow his belongs in the empty saddlebags and launch himself into the saddle of the silver dapple. It was unusually short for a horse, standing perhaps thirteen hands high. It had huge forelocks hiding its eyes, a coarse, heavy mane, a thick winter coat and its tail brushed the ground.

Alwyn had ridden this breed before, and liked it. They were hardy, bore the cold well, and could tolt smoothly, almost as fast as most horses could gallop. And they could keep it up for hours.

Alwyn patted the pony's neck and bent low to whisper a few words a few words in its ear.

"I shall call you Homyr, in honor of the great poet," he said. "It is said he was blind, and with all this hair before your eyes I cannot imagine how you are able to see, either. Perhaps both you and the blind poet see better than we."

LaFranc was more meticulous, taking the time to check all the cinches himself. Then he added a few moments more familiarizing himself with the horse. It was taller than than Strom's gray mare; much taller than Alwyn's sturdy little mount, and black as midnight with a white star marking its forehead.

That Strom sat smoldering did not seem to disturb LaFranc in the least. When at last he was satisfied with both the animal and the tack, LaFranc mounted his big stallion with ease. He flashed a brief grin at Alwyn, and then nodded to Strom.

Strom nodded back, his shaggy brown hair dancing about his face in the wind.

"I have named my pony, Homyr," Alwyn, proud of his wit, announced in a voice pitched low enough to not carry beyond their circle of three. "What will you call yours?"

"I call him horse," LaFranc replied, "for that is what he is. I do not name animals," he added. "When you give something a name, you give it a soul. There might come a time when I will have to eat this horse in order to survive. If that time comes, I do not want to know his name."

Strom turned his mount toward the east, and without a word led the party at a fast trot out of the city. Alwyn fell into line behind him with LaFranc bringing up the rear. Life was beginning to stir and Strom obviously wanted to be beyond the walls and into the countryside as quickly as possible.

The city gates stood wide, dutifully opened at sunrise by the watchmen. Except for a scrawny, slat-ribbed, yellow cur that barked once before retreating back into an alley, they cleared the city walls without exciting much notice. To anyone who cared to observe them, they were simply travelers going about their business.

The three companions rode in silence for the rest of the morning through the gently rolling plains of the United State of Omaha. Alwyn allowed himself a moment to turn in the saddle and study the city that had been his home...and at the three sets of tracks that pointed straight at them if anyone wished to follow

The famed granite Walls of Omaha gleamed white in the rising sun. Those walls had been erected generations before Alwyn was born and tripled the size of the city. The security offered by those walls made Omaha an enviable trading destination. Commerce flourished and the city became a center for the arts, culture, politics and worship in the United States. Alwyn could still remember LaFranc lecturing him about the importance of those walls when he was still an apprentice.

The deep, rumbling tones of the bell in the Waterhalle, the tallest tower in the city, peeled four times, informing Omaha's citizens that it was time to start the day. Most cities worth their salt and fire had a central bell tower that served as the regulator of civil activity. People rose by the bell, ate by the bell, conducted business by the bell and went to bed by the bell. The bell kept order. Alwyn couldn't help feeling he was abandoning any order his life might have had.

*Nothing for it,* he thought and turned back toward the horizon.

The road ran straight as an arrow through land as flat as a griddle, punctuated by farm houses and occasional copses of pine trees. The plains would give way to rolling hills before the day was over, Alwyn knew, but for now the snow-covered ground seemed an endless sea of flat, lifeless white.

The sun, glowing bravely as it climbed in the sky, gave but an illusion of heat. The wind continued unabated, stiff and crisp, whipping cloaks about riders and horses, changing direction abruptly, dying, then gusting suddenly with an icy blast that carried the threat of more sleet and snow.

Alwyn gripped his brown, woolen cloak tighter about his shoulders. He was not a fan of cold weather. The Blue Norther of the night before might be a memory, but the clouds that were piling up on his left looked like they were eager for a repeat performance. If he knew anything about the weather, those clouds would obliterate the sun long before it set. Then it would be *Katie bar the door.*

Katie, as near as Alwyn had been able to surmise from his research, was a mythical goddess of great power who had been worshiped by the Southlanders before the Time of Madness. She was often depicted in ancient lore as a rustic farmer's wife, dressed in stout woolens, with a hard face and little compassion.

It was said she had the power to either unleash or corral fate. It was said that after a particular run of unfortunate events, the Southlanders would pray for Katie to bar the door of the barn where she kept calamity.

*Foolish prayer. What good would it do for Katie to bar the door after the damage had already been done? Surely there is more to the prayer. I will discover it one day.*

The growl in Alwyn's stomach shook him from his reverie, reminding him that he had eaten nothing since the night before, and most of what he had eaten then consisted of hot, mulled wine and a bowl of stale nuts served by the saucy blonde serving girl at Strom's tavern. He thought fondly of warm porridge and hot tea, but settled for a hunk of cold bread and white cheese that was common traveler's fare. He ate while he rode and washed it down with icy water from his waterflask, bound close to his horse to keep the water inside from freezing.

He was still licking the last crumbs from his gloved fingers when Strom turned in his saddle and motioned him forward.

Alwyn spurred his horse along side his friend, but continued to ride in silence. Strom had not said a word the entire morning. He would talk when he was ready, and not before. Alwyn was content to wait. He had plenty of his own thoughts to keep him occupied.

"Don't do nuthin' dumb," Strom muttered at last, half to himself.

He cast a furtive glance at Alwyn who was trying hard to cover his smile with the hand that held the reins while holding his cloak shut with the other. Strom turned his eyes back on the road ahead.

"Do you know what soldiers call that phrase?"

Alwyn gave him a blank stare.

"Maxwell's Rule 14," Strom elucidated. "*There are fourteen rules,* I've always said. *You can forget the first thirteen if you just remember Rule 14. Don't do nuthin' dumb.* And look at me now, running off to White House to beard the lion in his den."

Strom chuckled. "Ah, well. Better to burn out than to rust away, eh, my friend."

Alwyn smiled and nodded. Still he waited. He knew his

friend hadn't beckoned him forward just to make small talk.

"Julian wants me to look after you."

"I can look after myself."

"No doubt. No doubt at all."

Silence separated the two companions for another long stretch. Alwyn eyed the sky and unconsciously pulled his cloak tighter about his shoulders. The clouds gathering in the north had begun to obscure the sun, and what little warmth it had provided was quickly dwindling. Strom didn't seem to notice the wind that cut like a scythe. Bare-headed, his shoulder length, brown hair whipped unfettered about his face. He paid it little mind. He had ridden through worse; much worse.

Strom Maxwell was not a big man; a couple of fingers shorter than Alwyn, with no body fat to hold in the heat. His cloak flapped around him like a sail, but he was oblivious to it. He had been a soldier long enough to know when to ignore such insignificant discomforts as heat and cold. He was intent on scanning the horizon for any movement that might appear the least bit out of the ordinary. Everything else was of secondary importance.

"Alwyn," Strom began slowly, picking his words with the utmost care, the way he would navigate a trail in Canadian territory when he suspected an ambush. "You don't belong on this mission."

Alwyn laughed at his comrade.

"I may not be a seasoned veteran of a dozen campaigns, but I'm pretty good in a fight. And after all, I really can read Ancient American."

"I'm serious, Alwyn. I don't doubt your courage, your loyalty to Julian or your professional curiosity about this grimoire," Strom's mouth twisted on the word. "But this is not one of your collections, and it is certainly not just a simple, diplomatic mission. This could be – probably will be - the matchwick that lights the fuse of civil war. And that's the *best* we can hope for, even if this grimoire is a forgery."

For once Strom's eyes left the horizon and he focused his complete attention on his friend, willing him to obey.

"You can still back out, Alwyn. Do it. Go back to the Library. Tell Julian you had a change of heart. Tell him your research discovered the fragment was forgery. Tell him anything, but go back now."

Alwyn gave his friend a sidelong look and shook his head.

"I can't go back, Strom. You know that. This is too important."

The silence thickened again as the clouds continued to roil, building an ominous castle in the air. Soon the drawbridge would be lowered and the storm would unleash its fury. Alwyn prayed to Liberty they would be safely ensconced in a nice warm inn by then.

Strom let out a deep sigh that mimicked the wind, and turned his attention back on the road ahead. He scratched at his short-cropped beard with a gloved hand, then absent-mindedly fished inside his coat and produced a small scroll. He looked at it for a moment as if wrestling with his own thoughts before deciding to hand it to Alwyn.

Alwyn eyed the scroll suspiciously before taking it. He unrolled it and began to read. Strom's eyes never left the road. He could have been discussing the weather for all the emotion in his voice.

"Just a routine report from one of my…sources," he said. "Not much to it, really. A report on the grain crop in Atlantis; some subtle troop movements in Canada; and Ricard, remember him? Ricard is going to be a father again…for the seventh time, may he finally be blessed with a son. And then there is that report of evidence of a settlement of the Amarillo Nomes on the coast of the Gulf of Texas. It's not conclusive. Might be a mistake. Then again…"

Strom turned in the saddle and looked a stunned Alwyn

full in the face.

"Still want to go to White House?"

# CHAPTER 9

**Homyr, Alwyn's silver** dapple pony, kept plodding on impassively, as if the world had not just imploded on the man riding him. For long moments Alwyn wasn't sure he even drew a breath. His chest constricted; his throat tighten; he felt like he had been kicked in the gut. His vision blurred from a filmy liquid that covered his eyes and threatened to leak down his face.

Through an act of sheer will he forced himself to fill his lungs. *In through the nose, out through the mouth. Again. Again.* He choked on the frigid air, sputtered, wiped his eyes with a gloved fist, and after what seemed an hour, but was probably only a few minutes, was able to gain a modicum of control over his emotions.

He looked a hard question at Strom, who was still riding at his side, straight, but relaxed in the saddle. If Strom took any notice of Alwyn's emotional state he did not reveal it. His eyes never left the horizon; never ceased scanning for danger. He was at home in this element. Yet he knew the unasked question behind Alwyn's eyes.

"How long have I known; and why didn't I tell you earlier?"

Strom's tone was conversational, but flat. He could have

been discussing the price of tea in The Ohios, or the purchase of a new slave girl from the Central Highlands.

"Truth is, I've heard rumors of a Nomish settlement along the Texas Gulf coast for months, but nothing of substance. Nothing reliable."

Strom took his eyes from the horizon long enough to shoot Alwyn a quick, knowing glance.

"I didn't want you running off half-cocked on the basis of some unfounded rumor. You've done it before, Alwyn, you know you have; so don't look at me that way. No offense, but unless it disrupts business, the whereabouts of a band of thieving Nomes is of little use to me. I've kept my informants looking on your behalf, not mine."

Strom turned his full attention back to scanning the horizon. Alwyn never had figured out how the man could be so focused on one thing, while carrying on a completely different conversation.

"This time the information is from a reliable source, confirmed by another," Strom continued. "Bad for business, you know, what with them being situated on the Gulf of Texas coast and all. Could disrupt shipments from my people in the Califate of Orange. I'd hate to have to develop an alternate route through the Central Highlands. You know what sticklers for protocol they are. But that's business. The fact of the matter is, dealing with the Highlanders would be preferable to negotiating some kind of truce with that twit who serves as Governor of Atlantis. The man is insufferable. Yes, it would appear the price of citrus is definitely going to hit an all time high before the spring thaw."

Strom looked Alwyn full in the face.

"Go, Alwyn. She is your wife. You have a child. Go."

"But Julian..."

"Julian be damned, Alwyn," Strom shot back. There was heat in his voice, and Alwyn thought he even caught a quiver. "I don't want your blood on my hands or your immortal soul on my conscience. You have an excuse that even the Adam will understand. Take it. Go. Please."

The emotions swirling in Alwyn's brain threatened to overflow into his eyes. He choked them back, forcing them to submit to his will.

*Catharine.*

"I...I'll think about it," he stammered.

Strom eyed him intently for a moment longer, then nodded and reached his hand out for the scroll. Alwyn surrendered it like he was surrendering a part of his soul. Strom tucked it back away inside his cloak, then continued as if it had never existed.

"I would appreciate it if you didn't mention this report to anyone. More than a few lives would be in jeopardy if the wrong people knew what you have just learned."

Alwyn nodded, then allowed his horse to fall back into single file between the warrior and the Chief Librarian. The trio rode in silence for several more hours at the same ground-crunching gait, pausing only briefly to spell the horses and to relieve themselves. No more words were spoken. Each man rode alone with his thoughts.

The sun, obscured by increasingly threatening clouds finally gave up trying to warm the planet, and began its descent toward the horizon. As if to underscore the drabness of Alwyn's mood, it began to sleet.

Strom pointed to a copse of evergreen trees on a low rise.

"There," he said. "They will meet us there."

He looked once more at Alwyn, searching for an answer on his friend's face.

Alwyn shook his head, wretchedness etched across his face.

"I've waited fifteen years, Strom. I can wait another month."

As if needing to explain he added, "Julian is the Adam, and he is my friend. I gave him my word, Strom."

Strom nodded once, gravely. Alwyn understood he would not bring it up again.

Alwyn nodded to himself. *I have promises to keep,* he quoted to himself from an obscure manuscript Malcolme had discovered on a collection in the Kanetuck Wilderness. *And miles to go before I sleep. And miles to go before I sleep.*

Daylight gave way to darkness, sleet gave way to freezing rain and freezing rain turned to snow before the travelers reached the designated rendezvous site. A challenge from an unseen watcher halted the three men momentarily until Strom gave the appropriate response.

A small mountain of a man emerged from the woods shaking a layer of snow from his cloak as he approached. A quick fist to his chest and the man-mountain spoke.

"He's in there General, and he's fit to chew saddle leather. Keeps demanding to know why we're out here in the woods instead of some fine inn. No doubt he's used to the finest ale and serving wenches on the side. I tells him, *We waits for the General. Them's my orders and Binnie Tuk obeys his orders,* I says. That's what I told him, General. But he's fit to chew saddle leather, I tell you what."

Tuk drew a breath, then pointed his still nocked crossbow at Alwyn and LaFranc.

"Brought your own personal entourage, did you General?"

Alwyn had a sneaking suspicion that Binnie Tuk would like nothing better than to skewer the pair of them.

"Tuk, this is Alwyn. His life is more important than mine. Understand? You don't need to know more."

Binnie Tuk thumped his fist against his chest once more in acknowledgment and flashed Alwyn a grin that appeared reserved for his long lost brother.

"The big one with the paring knife strapped to his back is called LaFranc." As if he couldn't resist, Strom added, "His life is less important than mine."

LaFranc snorted. Alwyn tried to hide a weak grin. Binnie Tuk merely nodded, absorbing this bit of information and filing it for future reference.

"Take me to him," Strom ordered.

Once more Tuk struck his chest with his fist, and turning on his heel, waded deeper into the evergreens through snow that reached halfway to his knees. Within minutes he was pulling aside a make-shift doorway of pine boughs, and ducking inside the tangle of roots and underbrush. Strom, Alwyn and finally LaFranc followed and soon found themselves in a hollowed-out shelter that was surprisingly warm.

Tuk waited for the others to pass by, then replaced the branches over the opening.

"Is he not coming in," Alwyn asked the general.

"Tuk is a soldier to the soul, Alwyn," Strom replied. "He'll see to the horses, and then he'll stand guard."

"He'll freeze to death," Alwyn muttered.

"Not Binnie Tuk," Strom said. "He's a hard man."

The fire that burned low in one corner of the dugout shelter provided enough light to rob Alwyn of his night vision, and it was several moments before he became aware of his surroundings.

The floor was bare, hard-packed earth. This was obviously not the first time it had been used. Ten paces across and five paces deep, the dugout could shelter a dozen men if necessary. The roof, however, extended no more than eight hands from the floor, requiring all but the shortest to crouch low.

A slight movement caught Alwyn's eye and he became aware of another figure crouched before the tiny fire. Alwyn studied the face of the man as he moved graciously aside, offering to share what little warmth the fire afforded to the newcomers.

*Black eyes*, Alwyn thought and shivered.

Alwyn didn't think those eyes missed much.

*No, those eyes saw everything; filed and cataloged everything; weighed everything.*

Alwyn disliked the man instantly.

Abruptly the figure rose, though not to his full height. The enclave might provide shelter from the elements, but it was too shallow to allow a man to stand up straight.

"I am Sencha," a mellifluous voice announced. There was a hint of irritation in the voice, but only a hint, as if the accommodations were only a trifle below the aristocratic standards the man was accustomed to. "Give me Liberty or give me death."

With hands to heart the man bowed fractionally toward Strom. Alwyn and LaFranc he ignored altogether.

"I am Maxwell," Strom replied formally, hands to heart, nodding almost imperceptibly. "I regret I have but one life to give."

The two men stood stooped in the cramped enclave, neither bowing lower than the other; each waiting for the other to acknowledge their superior rank; eyes locked.

"This is foolishness," LaFranc snorted, and both men turned to stare at him in disbelief.

The Chief Librarian ignored them both. In his realm at the Library, LaFranc exercised complete authority. He did not recognize classes, castes, or rank - other than his own — and he found the power-jockeying that went on among the elite tiresome and boorish. He unrolled his bedroll near the fire, laid down upon it and turned his face from the men.

"You both know why we are here. This is no place for misplaced pride. Maxwell is the Adam's general. Sencha is the Adam's ambassador. They are equals in their fields. Here, on the road to White House, Maxwell must be first among equals. Once in White House that distinction must revert to Sencha."

As if that settled the matter LaFranc snorted once more, and drifted off to sleep.

# CHAPTER 10

**The First Lady** Madeline sat cross-legged on the huge four-poster bed, absently sipping at a cup of hot, spicy tea; studiously *not* watching her husband pace back and forth across his bedroom. She appeared to be enthralled with the austere stone walls of her husband's chamber - all grays and muted greens with embossed depictions of iconic war horses. A larger than life-size, painted portrait of her as a much younger woman, hanging over the mantle of his massive stone fireplace, was the only other decoration in the room.

Madeline, *Maddye* as he called her, cast a furtive glance at her still pacing husband. He would want her advice, she knew...soon...but not yet. She suppressed a grin, blew across the surface of the steaming, aromatic liquid, took another sip and waited.

The man she watched was an imposing figure. Easily a hand taller than most men, Willam Norman was broad-shouldered, powerfully built and ruggedly handsome, with sandy blond hair cropped short on the sides but with a jaunty tousle on top, and eyes so blue they were almost black. When he smiled he looked startlingly young and innocent.

He seldom smiled.

At twenty-nine years from his naming day he was the

youngest man ever to be elected President; elected by acclamation when Occam, the last president — his father, so they said - died.

He grappled with the position he considered both his right and his destiny. He would bend it to his will. He would bend the Governors of the United States to his will. And he was smart. Smart enough to surround himself with advisors who were at least as smart as he — and who were completed devoted to him.

*Smart enough to have married me,* Maddye allowed a slight smile to turn up the corners of her full, ruby red lips.

*Soon,* she thought as Willam's eyes fell on his desk where he kept his private correspondence.

It was an extraordinary piece of furniture, Willam's desk. Maddye had admired it ever since they were wed. Iron-hard redwood, polished to a gleaming luster, the desk boasted stacked, sliding drawers ingeniously built into the pedestals that supported the surface. There were cubbyholes, hidden compartments and locking storage spaces built into an upright extension that rose from the back of the desk.

But even more amazing was the system of interlinked wooden slates that somehow rolled up into the top of the desk and disappeared when Willam was working, but that could be pulled down to completely enclose the work surface, and locked to keep curious servants, *or wives*, she thought wryly, from seeing what they should not.

*Genius!*

She knew, though she never asked, that the desk was filled with bits of information from across the country. Willam paid handsomely for information, and he had no lack of informants. They could be found in the capitol cities of every United State, and even in the courts of the Calif of Orange and the King of Canada.

Even so, the reports he had received recently from Omaha were vague and contradictory. His mounting frustration revealed itself in the twitch around his mouth.

Maddye waited, blowing absently over her cup of tea.

*Soon.*

"What *is* he up to?"

Willam's musing was almost too low for Maddye to hear. She strained to listen harder, without seeming to listen at all. She sipped her tea and watched.

Once again Willam paced. He reminded Maddye of a caged mountain lion she had once seen in a traveling menagerie when she was a girl. It had paced the limited confines of its cage, breathing heavily, desperately. Six steps in one direction before its path was cut off by heavy iron bars, the lion would turn and pace another six to the other side, turn and begin the ritual again. Over and over, incessant, hopeless, yet somehow undefeated.

She dismissed the image almost as soon as it appeared. Willam's gait was not the angry stalking of a caged lion. That analogy was all wrong. Willam paced like a wolf — slow, lumbering, purposeful - a pace that spoke of controlled, confident power. Willam was a man of action. He did his best thinking while he was moving, and he was thinking now. He was thinking hard.

Methodically he weighed and eliminated his old adversary's options, ticking them off one by one on his fingers.

"Is he capitulating without a fight," he wondered aloud. "Unlikely," he answered himself. "Julian is many things, but a coward is not one of them."

Maddye sipped her tea and frowned. It had grown tepid. She wished it were hot or cold. She could not abide anything lukewarm. She swallowed anyway. It would not be lady-like to spit it out.

She smiled inwardly at her husband's verbal sparring. He once explained to her that thinking required the use of all his senses. Movement was action, he told her, and action helped him to think. If he verbalized what he was thinking, then he used his hearing as well as his reason, and it made the process of decision-making twice as efficient.

She thought it a boyish concept, but said nothing, only smiled demurely as if he had just imparted to her the wisdom of the ages. She believed women lost most of their power when they spoke at the wrong time. As Saryh, her old Nomish nurse had been fond of saying, *A word fitly spoken was like a golden apple in a silver bowl.* The trick was knowing when to speak, and when to be silent.

If the truth be told, Willam did seem to come to the right conclusion most of the time, she admitted to herself — even without her help.

Willam reached the foot of the bed, turned on his heel and stalked back toward his desk, exactly seven paces.

"Perhaps he has decided to accept my claim of supreme authority."

He snorted a harsh laugh.

"Perhaps pigs fly and the sun rises in the west. No, Julian has been Adam too long to even consider sharing power with another, not even if Liberty Himself commanded it."

Willam stopped in his tracks.

"War?"

He turned to his wife.

"Could he be considering war?"

Maddye gave him one of her practiced looks that said such things were too complex for her, a mere woman, to fathom. He shook his head and resumed his slow, lumbering pace.

"Unlikely. If Julian wanted to start a war, he would not bother with a delegation. He would send an army, a big one, and make damned sure I knew it was coming. So what *is* he up to?"

The President of the United States turned back to his wife, ready to ask her help - she was sure of it — but the words stuck in his throat. Instead his eyes raked her, drinking the sight of her in. There was little in the world that could distract Willam Norman. But Maddye knew she was one, and relished the knowledge of the power she wielded.

She set the teacup on the nightstand and stretched with a mock yawn of indifference, causing the bodice of her thin linen gown to pull tight across her breasts, and enjoyed the effect she knew she was having on her husband. She smiled a secret smile and settled back into the pillows of her husband's bed, allowing her waist-length mane of deep auburn hair to spill carelessly around her. Her gown had fallen askew, revealing a milky white, bare shoulder.

"What is it you want," she breathed a demure double entendre.

It was a game she played with herself. Yes, she knew the effect she had on men. But she also knew her husband was a man of power, a man who would not allow his personal drives to rule him. She wondered how long she could hold him before he broke free of his physical desire and turned his thoughts back to affairs of state.

A slow grin split Willam's face. He stood at the foot of his bed, drinking in the sight of her, appreciating the perfection of her body, the curve of her face, the scent of her perfumed hair. Of all the women he had had, and he had had more than his share, it was Maddye that boiled his blood and muddled his thoughts. She was beautiful beyond measure. But more than that, she seemed to know him in ways that no other woman ever had. It was as if she could read his thoughts. And she was at the very least as ambitious has he.

He moved with the brutal grace of a timber wolf to the the side of his bed, bent low and kissed Maddye full on the mouth. Pulling his lips away he whispered in her ear, "I know what you are doing, you little minx." His rich laugh was deep in his throat. "And you *know* what I want. But business before pleasure. Pleasure will come soon enough."

Willam rose, stalked back to his desk and snatched up a

scrap of vellum that tried to curl back into a tiny scroll. It was a message that had been delivered by pigeon that morning. It was this message that had him in such a lather.

He strode purposefully back to the bed and threw himself on it beside his wife. He tossed the source of his frustrations onto her lap, and as if satisfied that the problem was longer his, laced his fingers behind his head, crossed his bare feet at the ankles and lay back on his pillow, gazing at the ornately carved ceiling.

"What you do make of that," he asked.

Maddye snatched the scrap of vellum greedily, no longer content to play the nonchalant temptress, and pored over its contents. Political intrigue was mother's milk to the auburn-haired beauty. She recognized early in life that knowledge was power. She cajoled her first husband, Stephyn II of North Iowa, who had died tragically defending her honor, into teaching her to read. If there were a clue in the message that would help to make her husband Emperor, and more importantly, make her Empress, of the United States, she would find it.

There was little to puzzle out from the vellum, and Maddye's brow creased into a frown.

*A delegation. Twelve. Perhaps more.*

That was all. She spun the information around in her mind, pondering, as she searched the scrap in vain for any hidden glyphs. Five words written plainly, in American. *Strange that it should not be in code,* she thought. Still, to anyone other than Willam the message would mean nothing, so perhaps it was not so strange…*and yet.*

"It makes no sense," she murmured aloud.

Willam burst into laughter. It felt good to have someone to share his confusion with.

Maddye reddened, mentally cursing her slip of the tongue. Then she silently cursed her inability to control the flush that brightened her cheeks and throat when she was even slightly embarrassed. She hadn't intended to so easily reveal her lack of insight, and certainly not to her husband.

"What I meant to say," she recovered quickly, "was that we should not have expected Julian to react like an ordinary man. He is clever, our Adam. Still, less than twenty men? That is indeed a puzzle."

Eying the scroll once more, her mind seized on the riddle, her momentary embarrassment forgotten. Sliding off the bed, Maddye began to pace across the floor, barely aware of the cold seeping through the flagstones into her bare feet. It took her eleven paces to reach Willam's desk.

"*Twelve. Perhaps more.* What are you up to, my dear Julian?"

Tapping her finger against her lips, Maddye paced while Willam watched appreciatively. Her hips rolled in the manner of women that he found charming, and her breasts, swaying provocatively beneath the thin linen gown, would be a huge distraction of he allowed himself to study them too closely. She stalked like a wildcat in a cage - slowly, gracefully, dangerously. Her pace spoke of cunning, intelligence, power and feminine ruthlessness. Willam was grateful this woman was on his side.

Maddye stopped pacing.

"The answer does not lie in the numbers," she whispered, as if to herself. She turned back to her husband and repeated the revelation aloud to him.

"The answer lies not in the number, but the names," she declared. "Discover who they are, and you will discover their mission."

Willam gave her a sardonic smile and clapped in a manner that could only be called sarcastic; a dangerous gesture for anyone one other than him.

"Well and good, my love. I had come to the same conclusion myself. But how are these *names* to be procured? If the names were known, they would have been included in the message."

Now it was Maddye's turn to display a sardonic smile.

"There are ways," she purred, dropping the scroll onto Willam's desk, a trinket forgotten.

"Give me the time, and I will give you the names. In the meantime, we should prepare for guests, don't you think?"

"I think," Willam replied in a low growl, "that you should come to bed."

# CHAPTER 11

**Somewhere in the** middle of the night the storm abated. Dark clouds surrendered to the morning sun which hung a half-a-hand above the eastern horizon, a brilliant ornament on a Candlemas tree, bright yet cold, refusing to shed more than light.

The day started early and cold, with barely enough time to add lukewarm water to the pasty, oat porridge that Binnie Tuk produced from his saddlebag before Strom had them in the saddle and on the road. They ate while they rode, stopping only long enough to rest the horses, sop out the tin cups that held their gruel, relieve themselves and mount up again.

Strom had lead the party off the snow-crusted road - if the wagon ruts that stretched straight as far as the eye could see could be called a road - before the sun was full up, and struck out cross-country. Riders attracted attention, and attention was one thing Strom did not want.

*He who gets there first with the most men, wins.*

It was Maxwell's Rule 7. Strom definitely didn't have the most men.

*When you can't get there first with the most men, make damned sure you get there undetected.*

That was Maxwell's Rule 8.

Strom stood in his stirrups to survey the landscape. He sniffed the air, grunted and spat as if he had a bad taste in his mouth. They could all feel it. The air was taking on an ominous feel; close and heavy like an impending storm.

By early afternoon those blue-black clouds resumed their assault on the sky, piling up like a horde of Canadian demons in the north. The clouds matched Strom's mood as he rode out ahead of the column, which now numbered five.

He had seen this weather pattern once before as a boy. Wave upon wave of snow interrupted by brief interludes of cold, deceptive sunshine, interspersed with ice storms that turn the landscape into a glittering, blinding, deathtrap.

The power and unbridled fury that was evident in the roiling cloud bank mirrored the turmoil in his soul. Though it lay camouflaged behind his soldier's eyes, it was no less dangerous for its containment. Strom rarely showed emotion beyond that frequent enigmatic smile that crept across his face. Except on the field of battle, and that emotion could only be described as…joy.

Strom was in a deadly mood, though few beyond his closest associates would recognize it. Those who knew him well enough to read his eyes, knew well enough to leave him be.

"Don't do nothin' dumb," he muttered under his breath.

His creed. Maxwell's Rule 14. *There are fourteen rules,* he was fond of quoting himself. *You can forget the first thirteen if you just remember Rule 14 – Don't do nothin' dumb.*

Yet he was here, doing the dumbest thing he had ever done.

*Julian will get me killed for real and true this time,* he thought, and not for the first time. *Not bad enough he has to get me killed, now he has to go and get Alwyn all mixed up in this mess with all his talk of ancient manuscripts.*

*And Alwyn. Fool scavenger never would listen to reason, Hel take him. He never was one to listen to reason. Don't suppose I should have expected him to start listening now, but I had to try.*

*No sense in getting us both killed.*

*It's all Julian's fault, Hel take him for real and true. Him and his damned, precious Medallion, and the Sons of Liberty too. Never should have let him save my life. Then I wouldn't owe him anything.*

Strom barked a harsh laugh in spite of his black mood. *'Course, then I'd be dead.*

Once again he scanned the horizon for some sign of the scout. They should be close now.

Stray pellets of ice hitchhiked on the blast of frigid air that whipped his cloak into a flapping banner. The wind carried the promise of an icy night, and cajoled him into tugging the cloak tighter around his shoulders. With luck the storm would hold off until sundown. By then they would have made camp.

Strom eyed the sky. He didn't much believe in luck.

"Yes, it is definitely going to get nasty," he told himself, and spat again. The spittle splattered on a rock and turned to ice before it could dribble to the ground.

The sound of hooves crunching through the snow to the hard-packed ground beneath broke Strom's concentration. A glance over his shoulder was all it took to drive his black mood into a throbbing headache. Sencha, the Adam's ambassador, trotted his horse up beside Strom, then reined it in to walk in unison.

Strom spat again and muttered something about a perfectly good bad mood gone sour, then greeted the Adam's ambassador with a nod that was low enough for protocol, but not one finger lower.

*Diplomat to the core,* Strom thought. *A master compromiser.*

He eyed Sencha surreptitiously and shivered in spite of himself. The man had black eyes, dead eyes, eyes that never smiled, even when his lips did; eyes that stared through you to your very soul; eyes that could read your thoughts; eyes that saw the lie behind your own eyes.

Sencha made Strom nervous. Strom didn't like people who made him nervous.

He nodded once more, a bit deeper this time, then went back to scanning the horizon, still searching for his scout. It was as good an excuse as any to turn his attention from Sencha.

If his lack of cordiality offended the ambassador, Sencha displayed no outward sign of it. He seemed content to ride silently by Strom's side. A hand taller than Strom, Sencha was the epitome of the enigmatic aristocrat. His jet-black hair was closely cropped in the fashion of the day. His angular face was shaved smooth, an observation that rankled Strom. Any man who could put a cold razor to his face without the aid of soap and hot water, and didn't manage to slit his own throat was just a bit to elegant for his taste.

Sencha rode on, untroubled, as if the mission he was on was of little consequence to him, or anyone else for that matter.

*He rides well,* Strom admitted to himself, gritting his teeth and hating the man all the more for his skill. It didn't help that Sencha's steed was a magnificent animal, jet black from mane to hooves, as if bred to match Sencha's hair and eyes. Broad-chested and obviously spirited, it took a master horseman to command that beast.

Abruptly Sencha pointed toward a copse on the horizon and asked in a voice that was oiled to prevent any words from sticking, "Pardon, General, but is that perhaps the man your have been seeking?"

Strom's gaze followed Sencha's outstretched finger and registered the faint glimmer of a mirror reflecting the last rays of sunlight that managed to peek through the gathering clouds. Nonchalantly, without answering, he bent over and spat.

Grunting what could have been an assent, Strom turned

the column of mounted men toward the flash. He made no effort to acknowledge the signal. That his scout had signaled was evidence that he saw the approaching riders and recognized them.

Sencha turned his mount in time with Strom, and seemed content to ride along side him in silence, two old friends out for a morning ride, nothing more. Strom gave him a furtive look, trying to get inside his head, trying to find some hint of what made the man tick.

If Sencha noticed Strom's glance, he gave not the slightest hint. Strom was certain he noticed. That fact made him all the more nervous. He abandoned his surreptitious scrutiny of the man beside him, and focused his attention back on the copse of pine trees.

The horizon cut the warmthless sun in half before they arrived. Still, the Adam's ambassador was content to remain silent. He had not uttered a syllable since pointing out the signal that Strom had somehow managed to miss, and Strom was beginning to understand the man's power – he talked little when there was nothing to say. He observed everything, and forgot nothing.

*A dangerous man,* Strom acknowledged to himself. He determined to say very little in the man's presence.

Once inside the copse, Sencha cast an experienced eye around the site and gave a slight nod of approval.

"Your men are well trained, General," he offered at last, throwing Strom off balance with his sudden loquaciousness. "This is a good site. Easily defensible; good cover from the elements; excellent sight lines to prevent ambush. My compliments to your man."

Strom eyed Sencha briefly, weighing, evaluating this new revelation.

"Your pardon, Ambassador, but I am surprised a man of your...position...would know, or care, what makes a good military site."

Sencha allowed a slight grin to turn up the corners of his lips, though it never touched his eyes.

"You would be surprised at what a man of my…position…knows or cares about, General."

Strom nodded a mental touché, spat, and pointed toward a diminutive figure crossing the campsite.

"As for paying compliments to *my man*, well, you can do that yourself," he said. "Graumet! Get over here. The ambassador has something to say to you."

Obediently scampering across the open ground, Mol Graumet planted herself squarely in front of Sencha. Fists to hips and looking up expectantly, Mol allowed the cowl of her cloak to drop back revealing piercing, sapphire eyes peering from her smooth, oval face. Her delicate features were framed by a mass of chestnut brown hair. Her full lips were pursed into a perfect bow, as if ready for a kiss - or to unleash a tongue-lashing. A dull red scarf swathing her neck was the only outward sign of feminine vanity.

Sencha's jaw dropped for a moment before he recovered from his surprise at seeing the young woman dressed in Forrester garb standing before him. Strom hid a victorious grin behind his gloved hand at finally having caught the ambassador off guard.

"Well if you are going to say something, spit it out," Mol demanded of the man on the black horse. "This isn't a picnic, and I've got work to do."

Sencha's eyes flashed daggers at Strom, then his easy grin crept back across his face. Strom wasn't sure that grin had never left.

"My compliments, young lady…"

"Graumet," the woman corrected. "Just Graumet. Or Mol, if you simply must be familiar, but I'm not that young and I've never been mistaken for a lady."

"Indeed. Well then, my compliments…Graumet…on selecting a most remarkable site to make camp."

Mol waited a moment longer to make sure Sencha was finished, then nodded curtly.

"Uh huh." She turned a derisive look on Strom, her sapphire eyes flashing blue fire. "You called me over here for that? Your pardon, Strom, but I've got *important* things to attend to."

Without another word, or the customary fist to chest, Mol Graumet turned on her heel and disappeared into the trees. Strom was pretty sure he heard something about, *Men!* followed by some choice invectives floating behind her.

Strom didn't need to see Sencha's eyes to know they burned hot.

"You brought a *woman* on this mission, General? Have you gone mad?"

This time Strom did not even try to hide his amusement. Instead he threw back his head and laughed.

"Ambassador, Mol Graumet is half-Highlander and half-Canadian...and oh, yes, she is *all* woman. Believe me when I tell you she would cut out your liver and serve it to you raw for breakfast if she heard you call her, *a woman,* with that inflection in your voice.

"Oh, yes, she's half-breed all right - outcast from both societies. She made her living thieving and smuggling hwana into Canada. That is, until she got caught relieving Canadian soldiers of their pay without delivering the promised goods up at Thousand Lakes. I cut her down before she choked to death. After she tracked down and settled her account with those Canadians, she tracked me down. Now I can't seem to get rid of her.

"She's a pretty little thing, though she is a bit touchy about the scar the rope left around her neck. She usually keeps it covered with a scarf even in hot weather. I wouldn't mention that to her if I were you."

Sencha looked dubious, but Strom continued.

"Mol knows more about how to live off the land than

any scout you've ever known or heard of. In the woods or in the city, you won't see her unless she wants you to. She knows what makes a campsite, a battle site or safe site in the city. She can sniff out information like a bloodhound sniffs out the scent of a runaway slave.

"Men talk to pretty, young women. Something about fluttering eyelashes, a hint of cleavage and a flash of thigh that makes a man want to prove how important he is; how much he knows that others don't.

"Mol can be pretty when she wants to. As a matter of fact, she has to work at it to not be pretty. And she knows how to put scraps of information together so it makes sense.

"She owes allegiance to no army, but Mol Graumet is a soldier to the core, Ambassador. One of the best you are ever likely to see. Don't make the mistake of underestimating her. She will outlive us both."

"I see," was all the reply Sencha gave before turning his mount toward the center of the camp. He no longer looked offended; that infernal, infuriating aristocratic demeanor once again firmly in place. Strom doubted he would see it slip again.

"There is one more thing that is troubling me, Ambassador," Strom called out at the man's retreating back. "You are right, of course, about the benefits of this site. It is indeed easily defensible and it provides good cover. But you mentioned excellent sightlines to prevent ambush. You are right again, of course. But, why would you think of the possibility of ambush? This mission left in secret. Nobody knows we're here."

Sencha reined his mount to a halt, turned and flashed that condescending smile with his perfect white teeth back at Strom.

"Oh, my dear General. Don't you know? There is no such thing as a *secret*. Somebody knows. Somebody always knows. And if somebody knows, then the wrong person can know. After all, General, everyone has a price. Even you. Why else would you be here?"

With a smile that never reached his eyes, Sencha trotted off at a casual, unhurried pace toward the center of camp.

Strom sat his mount stiff-backed, and grunted. Yes, he knew that. Of course he knew that. Any soldier worth his fire and salt knew that. It just rankled that a civilian court popinjay would know that, *Hel take him for real and true.*

*And Hel take Julian, too.*

Loyalty was a high price, indeed.

Strom entrusted Binnie Tuk with charge of Alwyn and LaFranc, then proceeded with his customary inspection of the camp. He did not intend to be long, but he wanted to know everything was in place.

Mol Graumet was good, better than good, the best second-in-command he had ever had, but he trusted his eyes and his instincts more than he trusted any man. Or woman. He would see to the security of the camp himself, and he would not relax until he did. He probably would not relax even after.

It was full dark before Strom made his way back to Binnie Tuk's cookfire. The big man was something of a legend with camp food, and Strom was hungry. Cold water and hard cheese might keep you alive on the trail, but they were a poor substitute for Tuk's savory ministrations.

Turning the reins of his near exhausted mount over to Mol, he gratefully accepted a cup of steaming broth from Tuk.

"This'll warm ye, General, or my name's not Binnie Tuk. Which it is. So there ye are," the big man grinned.

Strom blew across the surface of the cup and sipped, letting the hot liquid slide down his throat and thaw the lump of ice that tried to take up permanent residence in his stomach.

"Good?" Tuk inquired.

"Good," Strom nodded.

That was all the encouragement Tuk needed. He hacked a chunk of meat off of a haunch of something, Strom had no idea what, that was roasting over the firepit, dug deep to hide the flames from anyone more than ten paces away, and offered it to Strom.

"It's not done as well as ye like it, General. I know you prefer your meat crunchy like those Southlanders do, but this'll fill an empty place, I tell you what."

Strom accepted the meat, nodding his thanks while volleying the smoking meat between his hands. Charred on the outside, the meat still oozed juices when it bit into it. Strom grimaced briefly, but only briefly. He did prefer his meat well done, some would say burnt. *I don't eat red meat,* he was fond of saying. *I eat my meat brown - all the way through.*

He rarely displayed such finickiness when he was in the field. Food was fuel and he consumed what was at hand with businesslike efficiency. He had eaten worse. Much worse.

"Your guests have already retired for the night," Tuk offered between mouthfuls of juicy meat washed down with a swig of broth. Wiping his chin with the back of his hand, he pointed to two tents in the center of the camp.

"Your friends, the more important one and the not so important one, they'll be in the little tent to the left. Hizzoner the Ambassador, now. Well, he moved right into your tent just like he owned it. *General's not going to like it, your honor,* I told him. *No, sir. General's not going to like it one little bit.* He just looks at me with them dead-black eyes of his and walks right on in. Closes the flaps behind him, he did, just like he owned it. I don't like that man, General. By the Five Faces of God I don't. He smells wrong."

Strom gave an almost imperceptible nod. He didn't like

the man, either. But he was given his charge whether he liked the man or not, and he would see him safe to White House, or die trying.

He finished chewing the half-cooked meat and welcomed the cup of hot tea the big Forrester offered. He didn't particularly like hot tea, but he loved the way the steaming liquid warmed the cup. He loved the way the hot cup warmed his hands and the way the steam carried the subtle scent of the tea to his nostrils.

"This is bad business, Binnie," he whispered. "Could get real bad before it's over. Might come to bloodshed or worse before it's over. You'll want to watch your back."

"Aye, sir," Tuk replied. "When has it not been bad business for the likes of us?"

Strom chuckled. "When indeed, Binnie Tuk? When, indeed?"

With a week's worth of weariness settling into his bones, Strom forced himself to his feet. He threw what remained of the tea into the fire and watched it transform into steam. He watched the fire quickly regain the territory it momentarily lost to the quenching liquid invader.

It had the feel of prophecy. Strom felt a shiver run up his spine that had nothing to do with the cold.

The impending storm finally broke with Helish fury; wind and thunder competed for dominance. The storm woke neither Strom nor Sencha, for Strom was already awake and Sencha seemed to have mastered the art of sleeping through anything, as evidenced by an impressive snore that threatened to do battle with the elements.

Battered by weariness and frustrated by a sense of unease he couldn't put his finger on, sleep evaded Strom more successfully than the agile barmaid at the Harp and Clover tavern. The harder he reached for it, the bolder it teased and the faster it ran from him. At last he surrendered to the inevitable and got up.

*If I can't sleep, I might as well work. I should check on the guards. It will keep them on their toes.*

Stamping his feet into his boots Strom hoped to make enough noise to wake the ambassador, just for spite. He was unsuccessful.

*No one knows we're here.*

*Oh, General. Someone knows. Someone always knows.*

The words haunted him.

*Knowledge is power.* Maxwell's Rule Six. Strom didn't like the thought of that power being used against him.

With a last grudging look at his blissfully slumbering tentmate, Strom Maxwell trudged into the storm, defying it to assert dominance over him.

He didn't even try to sneak up on the guards. Not exactly. He wasn't trying to catch them unawares, but neither did he go out of his way to make much noise. In his mind he was making enough racket to wake the dead. For Strom that was very little noise indeed. But he had trained these men. They should be able to detect the slightest unnatural disturbance, even in the midst of this storm.

So far they had lived up to his expectations. Less Olsson had threatened to skewer him with an arrow from fifty paces. Leek merely greeted him with a familiar grunt, recognizing his commander long before Strom saw him, half-buried in a snow bank.

So why wasn't he being challenged by Tomsyn? Liberty knew he was making enough noise.

*If Tomsyn is asleep I will skin him and use his hide for window curtains*, he swore under his breath.

Strom stopped dead still. If Tomsyn was asleep and awakened suddenly, he might strike out without taking time to find out if his disturber was friend or foe. Men had died from such encounters, and Strom didn't want to be the one dying, although at that moment the thought of throttling the derelict guard did cross his mind.

Finding a tall pine, thick enough to provide cover - just in case — Strom took up a defensive position.

"Tomsyn? Tomsyn! Report, damn it to Hel," Strom swore loud enough to carry over the howl of the wind.

The storm threw his words back in his face, swirled them around him and carried them off into the blackness of the night, but he knew it was enough for a well-trained sentry to hear. Tomsyn was well-trained.

Something was wrong. Bad wrong.

With a silent curse Strom dropped to his belly and low-crawled on his knees and elbows the last thirty paces through the snow to where he had left Tomsyn less than four hours before; where he was supposed to be awake, keeping watch over the camp.

With mixed relief and anger, Strom saw Tomsyn. He was in position, just like he had been trained, but was totally oblivious to Strom's approach.

*Asleep. Hel take him for real and true.*

Strom rose to his feet. He was still deciding between a public beating and a private execution when a rogue flash of lightning split the darkness, revealing the crossbow bolt protruding from Tomsyn's skull.

# CHAPTER 12

**Strom turned on** his heel and ran. He had been a soldier too long to be shocked into inaction.

*Charge an ambush — Maxwell's Rule Three.*

If you froze you died. Retracing his steps at a dead run he drew first Olsson and then Leek into his wake, assessing the situation as he ran. With his lips curled back in a snarl, Strom ticked off the facts in his mind. The camp was under attack, an attack that had to be planned and executed to perfection. Tomsyn was taken out with silent, deadly efficiency. That meant someone knew they were going to be at this precise location at this precise time.

*Somebody knows. And if somebody knows, then the wrong person can know. After all, everyone has a price.*

The howling wind and near continuous cracks of tree limbs collapsing under the combined weight of the snow and force of the wind made verbal communication impossible. But Strom's soldiers were battle-hardened vets. They knew instinctively what to do.

At the inner perimeter of the camp the three dropped to the ground, watching, waiting for the intermittent flashes of lightning to reveal their attackers.

*Patience. We are not here first with the most men.*

Strom gripped the hilt of his sword, wondering absently when it had come into his hand.

*Patience. When you can't get there first with the most men, make damned sure you get there undetected.*

Strom watched, his eyes shifting like a cat's to catch any movement in the darkness. But there was no movement. No sign of ambush. No sign of attack. No hint of danger. Nothing.

Low, near the middle of the camp, Strom could make out the cookfire, carefully hidden from prying eyes that might lie outside the camp, but visible from this proximity. He could see Mol Graumet warming her hands, and the small mountain that was Binnie Tuk keeping watch over the small tent that housed Alwyn and LaFranc.

*We got here first,* the thought brushed past Strom's subconscious. *But do we have the most men?*

Strom motioned Olsson and Leek to him.

"Rouse the camp, but quietly. Account for everyone. They may already be in the camp, so don't take anything for granted. Olsson to the right, Leek to the left. I'll take the center and secure the ambassador. Go."

*It's Sencha they're after,* he thought.

He gritted his teeth, ducked low, and scrambled toward the big tent in the center of the camp.

Thunder drummed in a continuous roll, muffling any sound he made as he slithered through the snow. He sensed the cold more than felt it, his energy concentrated on reaching the tent that housed the sleeping ambassador. Sweat beaded on his forehead despite the cold, squeezed out by the knowledge that unknown assailants could just as easily be waiting inside that tent.

Six more paces; three more paces; two more. Strom drew himself up, taking time to work feeling back into his near frozen fingers. Now was no time for a sword hand to go numb with the cold.

Sucking in a deep breath of frigid air, Strom threw back

the tent flap and rushed inside, only to find the Sencha fast asleep, snoring louder than ever, as if he were in a celestial competition with the thunder.

In three quick strides Strom was beside Sencha, covering his mouth with one hand while shaking him awake with the other. Sencha's eyes flew open, but Strom motioned him to silence. If the ambassador was flustered by his sudden rousal, he didn't show it.

"The camp is under attack," Strom hissed loud enough to be heard above the storm, but low enough to carry no further than Sencha's ears. "Keep quiet and come with me."

Unimpressed the ambassador rolled over, throwing Strom's hand from his mouth.

"General, go away, can't you see I'm sleeping. I have complete confidence in your ability to protect me right where I am. Besides, you've got Mol Graumet on your side," he sneered. "A soldier's soldier to be sure. How could you lose?"

"We could lose because I'm trying to protect a jackass instead for trying to protect the camp," Strom snorted before dragging Sencha to his feet by the scruff of his nightshirt. "It's you they want and I promised the Adam, Hel take him for real and true, that I'd get you to White House in one piece. Now get up. We're leaving."

Before Strom could finish his final curse, Sencha suddenly twisted, knocked the sword from Strom's grip, and held a dagger at his throat.

"Don't ever touch me again, General," Sencha spoke with aristocratic indifference that belied the deadly intention behind his word. "I don't like it when people touch me without my permission."

Strom gritted his teeth. He had been caught off-guard by a civilian court popinjay, and it rankled. He might be embarrassed, but he didn't move. Sencha's steel was razor sharp against his throat.

"Your Honor," Strom sounded like he was chewing

saddle leather, "I've already lost one guard. I've no intention of losing more on account of you. And I've no intention of losing you, either."

Strom shot a surreptitious glanced at the tent flap, and waited until Sencha's eyes flickered to see what the general was looking for. It was an old soldier's ploy, but that momentary break in Sencha's concentration was all the opening Strom needed. An elbow to the ribs and a firm grasp on the wrist, and Sencha was disarmed, suddenly finding his finely honed dagger at his own throat.

"Your Honor, if you please, this is the first place they will come," Strom did his best to keep his tone as level and dispassionate as Sencha. "Let's get you someplace safe, hmmm? Before you really get hurt."

Sencha chuckle, and then his chuckle became a full-throated laugh that never reached his dead-black eyes.

"You win, General. I am your willing prisoner. Take me where you will…but by Kennedy, Washington and Roosevelt you had better be right."

Strom stuck his head through the tent flaps and scanned the camp with a soldier's efficiency. Nothing appeared amiss. Mol Graumet and Binnie Tuk had already taken up defensive positions as if it were the most natural thing in the world.

Strom drew Sencha in his wake, and deposited him unceremoniously in Alwyn's tent. A brief explanation was all Strom had time for and then he was gone to organize the camp's defense, leaving the Adam's scavenger and the Chief Librarian to protect the Adam's ambassador.

The storm settled into a dull, steady, joint-numbing, freezing rain. The sky grayed toward morning twilight before Strom was finally convinced there was no enemy to fight; at least none that could be found within bowshot of the camp. Everyone was accounted for.

*Everyone except Tomsyn, Hel take him for real and true.*

Tomsyn's body and Tomsyn's mount were gone. No tracks in the snow. No markings of any kind. Nothing to indicate he had died there. Nothing to indicate he had ever been there. Just gone.

For once, Sencha's unflappable composure was broken. And for once, Strom wished that it wasn't.

"You are incompetent," the Adam's ambassador assailed Strom when he learned the results of the night's exercises.

"One of your legendary hand-picked Forresters deserts in the middle of the night and the only thing you can think to do is pretend there is an attack on the camp to cover it up."

Sencha cut off protest with a dismissive wave of his hand.

"I'll hear no more excuses. It is clear to me that you are not fit to command. I've no idea why the Adam entrusted you with this mission in the first place. Therefore, by the authority of the Adam, you are relieved of your duties. I assume command as of right now. You may tag along if you wish, *General*, as my second-in-command. Otherwise, you may go to Hel or the Gulf of Texas. It makes no difference to me."

Strom stood stone-faced. He endured the tongue-lashing because he deserved it. A grudging fist to heart and he turned to go.

"Oh, and General," Sencha's tongue resumed its mellifluous tones, as if it hadn't just been sharp enough to flay the hide off a mule, "have your man, Tuk, prepare me a cup of that hot tea he is apparently so famous for. Then I am going back to sleep — since there is unlikely to be a repeat of last night's assault."

Strom nodded curtly and started once more to exit from the tent.

"And have your men…and Graumet…strike camp and be prepared to move out by noon. And tell them to do it quietly. I do not wish to be disturbed. I assume you can at least manage that, hmmm?"

Strom pulled up just short of the tent flap, straining to contain his mingled rage and frustration, then stalked into the blessed cold outside. He found Binnie Tuk tending the fire and relayed the ambassador's request to the big man.

Tuk spit once in the fire, then nodded.

"I do not like that man, General," he grunted. "He smells wrong. But I'll fetch Hizzoner his tea, like a good dog."

Tuk cocked his head, looking for all the world like a mongrel dog Strom had as a child, as if a fresh idea had just popped into his mind.

"I could cut his liver out for ye, General. You just say the word. The men have been grumbling for some fresh meat. I can even make it look like an accident if ye like."

Tuk touched his finger to his nose as if that settled the matter, and went back to tending the fire.

"You're a good man, Binnie Tuk," Strom said with mock solemnity, fist to heart. "The honor is to serve."

"Aye. We each serve with the gifts we are given," Tuk replied, returning the ancient salute. "You taught me that. Not all's got the healing touch. Not all's got the gift of languages. Few there be that know how to lead men, and few there be that are worth following, I tell you what.

"And, well, we can't all be Mol Graumet, that's the Kennedy's own truth. Still, Liberty has given to each some small talent. I use mine in your service, General, and no civilian court popinjay is going to change that with a wave of his hand."

As if to emphasize his confession, Binnie Tuk once more put his fist to his heart.

"Give me Liberty or give me death. I regret I have but one life to give."

Strom nodded once, briefly, and placed his own hands over his heart.

"Life, Liberty, and the pursuit of happiness be to you and to your posterity," he replied with unfeigned solemnity. "Now, fetch the tea, Binnie. We wouldn't want to keep Hizzoner waiting."

Strom performed the rest of his duties efficiently and professionally - informing each member of his team that he was no longer in command, stifling objections, demanding obedience, stamping down threats of insubordination. They were soldiers. They would behave as soldiers

As the Forresters began the task of striking the camp, Strom strode to the little tent to the left of what used to be his tent, but now housed the new commander of the expedition — to the tent that housed Alwyn and LaFranc. He needed to settle his thoughts and he couldn't do it in front of his men.

"You do not knock," LaFranc charged, as Strom crawled into the tent. "You are a boor."

For once Strom didn't reply, merely nodded. The general's lack of a combative reply caught the big librarian off guard. LaFranc's eyes never left Strom's as he reached into his pouch and pulled out a wad of shredded leaf and shoved it into his mouth.

In a rare display of camaraderie, LaFranc extended his pouch toward Strom. In an equally rare display Strom reached his forefinger, index finger and thumb into the pouch and removed a generous amount of the aromatic leaf. He pondered it for a moment, then shoved it into his mouth.

Alwyn sat cross-legged on his sleeping bag. He watched and listened. Strom needed to talk — that much was obvious. He would ask if he wanted Alwyn's input; so Alwyn waited, silent, as Strom related the details of Tomsyn's death and the attack that never came.

"Tomsyn's no deserter," Strom muttered. It was evidence of his agitation that he accepted the proffered pouch of shredded leaf from LaFranc. He rarely chewed the leaf. Now he did so absently, as if it helped him think.

"Tomsyn has served well and faithfully for years; served when others turned back, when it could have gotten him killed. And he was too good to have someone sneak up behind him."

Strom's jaw stopped working in mid-chew. Jumping to his feet, he spat the half-chewed leaf to the ground and cursed himself for a fool. Alwyn and LaFranc eyed each other in quiet confusion, waiting for the general's self-flagellation to end so they could ask what it was that distressed him so.

"Don't you see," Strom explained through gritted teeth. "Tomsyn would not have allowed anyone to sneak up on him from behind. He was too good for that."

"But you said Tomsyn was dead, that he had a crossbow bolt stuck in his head. How do you account for that if they didn't sneak up on him," Alwyn asked.

"He was shot from behind because that crossbow bolt protruding from his skull had its point coming out of his forehead," Strom roared. "And they didn't sneak up on him. Tomsyn let them come close enough for the bolt to penetrate all the way through his head."

The light of recognition dawned in Alwyn's eyes.

"Liberty on high," he swore. "Tomsyn was taken out by someone he knew, and trusted. Someone from within the camp."

# CHAPTER 13

**Franklyn cursed himself** for a fool. It was a task he was growing accustomed to. His piebald pony picked its way with careful, confident steps up the mountain path with little need for Franklyn to intervene. Unencumbered by thoughts of obligation or worry the filly tossed her head and snorted with joy for the journey.

*Massad!* This is *madness; a fool's errand.*

The thought rose unbidden for the hundredth time, and for the hundredth time Franklyn pushed the thought from his mind. A fool's errand it might be, but it was Pepin's only chance; his grandfather's only hope of survival. Franklyn bit down the fear that threatened to creep from his belly into his throat and urged the pony to a trot.

*Massad!* Samildanach. Master of All Arts. The shiver that ran down Franklyn's spine had nothing to do with the icy wind than billowed his cloak behind him.

*Massad!* It was a name mothers used to frighten their little children into obedience.

*If you are not good, Massad with get you.*

*Massad eats little boys and girls who don't go right to sleep.*

Legend had it that when hail fell from a cloudless sky, Massad was beating his wife, although no one knew if Massad really had a wife. If the truth were told, Franklyn wasn't sure he had ever seen hail fall from a cloudless sky, but that did nothing to lessen his sense of foreboding.

This was the creature Dora wanted him to bring to his grandfather? Franklyn shook his head to clear his thoughts.

"It is written," he quoted to himself from his childhood lessons, *Have no fear. You have been given a sound mind.*"

A wry laugh dribbled from Franklyn's lips. Whoever had done the writing had obviously never encountered Massad. If he had, perhaps he would not have written such an admonition.

The quote calmed him, nonetheless, and as he began to deconstruct his grandmother's command it started to make sense. Of course Dora would send him to the Samildanach. Though forbidden, it was whispered that desperate people sought out the Master of All Arts for his miraculous cures. And Dora was desperate.

The ritual was set forth, confided in ghost stories told around fire pits on dark nights.

*Bring an offering to the mountain promontory overlooking the settlement; you know the one,* a knowing look and a finger to the nose said.

*Massad appears there every seventh day to hurl his cursed down on the people below. Do not seek the wizard. It is forbidden. Should he appear, do not speak to the wizard. It is forbidden. Build a fire, prepare a meal, but do not eat. Speak to the fire. Proclaim your need to the sky. You may be rewarded by a potion, poultice or elixir – and the Samildanach's cures always worked. If the Samildanach heard. If the Samildanach accepted your offering.*

*If...if...if...*

If not...

*If not there is no hope.*

Franklyn choked on the possibility that his offering would be rejected, that Massad would not appear, that he would fail and therefore be responsible for his grandfather's death.

*No. He will live. He will live!*

The sudden rumble in his stomach shook him from his train of thought.

*Fool.* He cursed himself again.

He seemed to be doing that a lot lately. In his haste to find the Samildanach he had taken no provisions. Two days of hard riding, and a night of keeping vigil by Pepin's sickbed were taking their toll.

No time to hunt and nothing but hard tack and a bit of jerky to fill his belly, and Mother, he was weary. More than once on this journey he had jerked awake, startled to find himself still in the saddle.

*Better to climb out of the saddle than to fall out*, he decided, unable to fight the hunger and weariness any longer.

Sliding to the ground, Franklyn hobbled his pony, and foraged for dead wood to start a fire. Flint and steel quickly produced the required sparks and in moments a small blaze served to leech the cold from his fingers. He retrieved the hard tack and jerky from his saddlebags, but decided he was too tired to eat.

He left his meager meal beside the fire, determined to eat after a brief nap.

*A few moments will make little difference. I'll just rest my eyes a bit.*

Wrapped in his cloak, Franklyn curled himself around the tiny fire.

*It is written: A few moments' rest. A little folding of the hands to sleep.* He couldn't remember the rest of the quote before sleep took him.

He was disturbed briefly by a small knot in his side. He sat up irritably, pulled his knife from its sheath on his belt dug the offending rock from the ground and tossed it aside.

Adjusting himself once more to rest, his thoughts went

to his family - or what was left of it. Reaching inside his shirt he closed his hand over the locket he always carried around his neck on a chain of metal links.

He pulled it from around his neck and examined it. It was crafted from a metal unlike any he had ever seen. Dora, his grandmother, told him his father had brought it from a great city, far to the North. It possessed a sheen like steel, but polishing with a soft cloth produced a luster that steel could not match.

It was delicately worked with characters that Dora told him were words. Written words. Though none of the Amarillo Nomes could say what they meant.

Franklyn drew in a deep breath, then blew it out. He wished he had known his father.

He deftly worked the catch, springing the locket open. It had been a gift from his father to his mother. Dora passed it on to him after they died, his only memento from parents he had never met. Inside was a portrait of his mother in miniature.

He was never sure how the artist had captured her likeness within that tiny chamber. She looked like his grandmother, Dora, but young. There were the same proud eyes, the same challenging stare, the same confident demeanor. She was every bit a Raek's daughter; born to rule.

Catharine.

*My mother.*

It was his last thought before weariness conquered him. The locket slipped from his fingers and lay beside the fire on the mountain promontory overlooking the settlement.

No dreams dared disturb his sleep.

It was the smells that first tickled Franklyn back to

consciousness — the delicious smell of roasting rabbit, potatoes, and carrots. The friendly sound of a crackling fire, popping and snapping, sizzling as juices dripped down onto hot coals filled his ears, beckoning him to wakefulness. But it was the full-throated laugh — his grandfather's laugh, he would swear to it — that finally goaded him awake.

Swimming through the inky blackness of an exhaustion-induced slumber, Franklyn finally managed to force his eyelids open. They felt like someone had rubbed sand under them.

The fire was larger than he remembered making it.

*Strange — it should be burned down to nothing by now.*

The smell of roasting game was unmistakable. Perhaps it had all just been a bad dream.

*Yes, it must have been a bad dream. Of course. I'm home. Dora has a meal prepared, and Pepin is laughing as he often does over something that no one else can find the humor in.*

Supporting himself on an elbow, Franklyn surveyed his surroundings. There was open sky above him, not a roof. There was a rabbit, spitted and roasting over a fire that was indeed larger than the one he had made, sizzling and dripping hot juices onto the coals. A cookpot hung suspended from a tripod over the fire, and from it issued forth the delicious smells of stewed vegetables.

Franklyn salivated, his stomach a black empty pit that yawned open like an unsatisfied grave. But before he could think of reaching for the roasting meat the realization that he was not in his home smacked him in the face. Franklyn felt a prickling of the hairs on the back of his neck, like a shadow sliding across his grave. Something was behind him, watching him. He could feel it.

*No sudden moves,* his Uncle Jon had taught him. *It is just as frightened of you as you are of it.*

Easy for his uncle Jon to say. *It* wasn't watching Uncle Jon.

*Move slowly, purposefully.*

Franklyn eased himself down from his elbow and cautiously rolled over to face the watcher. He wondered absently why his pony had not warned him of danger, and immediately dismissed the thought as irrelevant. He would worry about that after...if the pony was still alive. If *he* was still alive.

With an inbred patience native to the Amarillo Nomes, Franklyn turned until he could look behind him. His pony, placidly cropping the last vestiges of tough, hill country grass, was all he saw. He let out a relieved sigh, chiding himself for letting fancies take him, and pulled himself into a sitting position to ponder the source of the fire and the tantalizing scent of the roasting rabbit.

When he turned back toward the fire, he found himself staring straight into the face of the oldest man he had ever seen, and an unearthly, womanish scream pierced the quiet.

The face before him was deeply etched across the forehead with sequential furrows, evenly spaced, like rows of newly plowed earth. Snow-white, bushy brows accentuated the clear, brown eyes. The old man's feathery white hair, which was still stained with a hint of brown, receded from his forehead, and hung nearly to his waist in the back. Framing his sun-darkened face was a prodigious white beard that covered his chest.

Franklyn colored bright red as the old man laughed, and he realized the scream that rang in his ears came from his own mouth.

Neither spoke, but the look of mirth never left the old man's face. As they sat studying each other, the old man reached down and snatched the forgotten jerky and the locket from beside the firepit.

"Here, give that back," Franklyn wanted to demand, "It's mine!" Yet he couldn't manage to coax the words from his mouth.

The old man's laugh was full-throated and rich, so like his grandfather's that it caused an ache in Franklyn's heart. Those crystal brown eyes flashed — amusement or danger, perhaps a touch of madness; Franklyn was not sure which. He bit a generous chunk off the jerky, revealing perfectly-formed, straight, white teeth beneath full lips, and began to chew.

Nodding in seeming approval of the quality of the dried meat, the old man waved the remaining portion at Franklyn, then at the spitted rabbit and vegetable stew. The invitation to eat was unmistakable. Nodding and grinning the old man continued to chew while fingering the locket.

Abruptly the catch tripped and the locket sprang open. The old man bit off another chunk from the jerky, then shoved the remainder into his mouth, chewing with those impossibly white teeth while studying the image within. The look on his face never changed, but Franklyn was almost sure he caught a hint of recognition in the old man's eyes.

Franklyn wanted to grab the locket - *my locket!* - from the old man and then beat him within a hair's breadth of his life, but he found himself transfixed, unable to defend his property. Instead, he reached for the spitted rabbit and pulled it to him, blowing on the meat until it appeared cool enough to not scorch his tongue.

A cautious bite of the roasted flesh set his salivary glands flowing and his stomach let out an undignified yawl. He found himself helpless to resist and set about the task of devouring the rabbit. He never took his eyes off the old man, who sat nodding and smiling, until he realized there was not another morsel of meat on the spit. Even the rabbit's bones were gnawed clean.

The old man nodded approval, wiped his mouth with the back of his arm, rubbed his hands together and stood. Dropping the locket into a pouch that hung from the belt at his waist the old man assumed a ritualistic stance and intoned formally.

"You have come with fire and food. You have brought the oblation. Your offering is acceptable. I am unclean. Speak not to me. It is forbidden. I am unclean. Touch me not, lest you too become unclean. Speak to the fire. Proclaim your need to the sky. Perhaps old Frollo Massad may be able to minister to your problem."

The savory taste of rabbit turned to dust in Franklyn's mouth.

*Massad!*

He did not like the metallic taste of fear that rose in his throat. He hawked it up and spat it out. Still he could not force words to come out of his mouth.

Massad waited, apparently used to the reaction his presence evoked, and with his staff drew magic symbols in the dirt. With the fire between them Franklyn could not make out whatever it was the old man was drawing. Satisfied with the results of his labor, Massad covered the symbols with his foot and move closer to Franklyn.

Eying the boy hopefully, expectantly, he drew another magic symbol in the dirt at Franklyn's feet - a wide arc, nothing more — and then leaned on his staff studying the boy for a reaction.

Franklyn stared wide-eyed at the symbol, trying to puzzle out its meaning; hoping he wasn't being cursed by the Samildanach. He looked a question at Massad, but the old wizard merely spat in the dirt, covered the symbol over with his foot, shook the dust off his sandal and turned away, walking toward the edge of the promontory that overlooked the settlement.

As Franklyn watched, transfixed, the old wizard raised his staff above his head, lifting his eyes to the sky. Spreading his arms wide with grand, ominous gestures Massad began to chant, low at first, like the rumbling of a distant thunderstorm, then gaining strength and volume like the fierce whirlwinds that ripped roofs from homes and leveled ancient trees. His cloak, flapping and billowing in the wind, his long, white hair streaming behind him, endowed the wizened old man with the appearance of power, the image of authority.

It was a strangely beautiful language the Samildanach used, at odds with the curses he hurled like lightning down on the village below.

Franklyn thought briefly of killing the old man while his back was turned. He could do it. His uncle Jon had taught him how to walk so softly he could reach a deer without spooking it. A swift dagger between the ribs and it would be over in moments. He would be a hero to his people – the man who ended the curses.

He dismissed the idea almost before it was formed. He had never killed a man before, and this wasn't just a man. It was a Samildanach, a Master of all Arts.

He wasn't so sure he could catch the old wizard off-guard. Besides, it was probably best not to disturb a Master of All Arts when he was in the process of cursing. It might be bad luck. And he needed Massad's cure for his grandfather.

Franklin could not have committed the murder even if he had truly wished to. There was something curiously familiar about the wizard's hauntingly beautiful chanting that rendered him powerless to move. The words, like none he had ever heard, were beyond his comprehension, yet they wrapped themselves around his heart, caressed his mind like a lover, and filled him with a deep yearning and piercingly sweet sadness.

He could only watch and listen, oblivious to the tears that crept unbidden down his cheeks, settling with a salty residue in the corners of his mouth while his heart ached for an embrace he had never known.

Franklyn didn't know how long the Samildanach stood, arms outstretched, chanting his strange incantations, but the fire burned low, and the sun now hung a bare hand above the horizon. Time meant nothing. The boy stood transfixed, unsure he would be able to speak if he wanted to — unsure of what he would say if he could.

Massad made one last grand gesture, waving his staff in a wide arc that encompassed the whole village below. He raised and lowered the staff, brought it from side to side — none would escape the effects of his incantations. Finally finished, the ancient wizard stumbled exhausted back to the fire.

Laying his staff aside the old man sat on his haunches across the fire from Franklyn. He retrieved a second spit from beside the fire and began munching on the burnt meat that remained. He produced a flask from his belt and took a long swallow, then offered it to Franklyn. Franklyn shook his head.

Neither the Master of All Arts nor the boy who would be Raek spoke, but merely studied each other, each content for the other to begin.

At last Massad, refreshed by the meat, threw back his head and laughed a hearty, unfettered laugh. His eyes said he found the whole ritual a bit silly, yet his words, when he at last spoke, were deadly serious.

Turning his back on Franklyn, the Samildanach intoned formally to the air.

"I am Frollo Massad, called by some Samildanach. I am accursed; unclean; dead, yet undead; untouchable; forbidden fire and salt; forbidden water and shade. Few have sought me out these past fifty-seven dry seasons. Yet you have come with fire and food, and an offering of peace. Speak not to me. It is forbidden. Touch me not, lest you too become unclean. I would not have any share my fate by breaking the Raek Law.

"However, it is not forbidden to speak to the fire or to tell the wind what is on one's heart. Perhaps old Frollo *might* overhear. It is *possible* that old Frollo might be of some small help. If someone can find his tongue."

Franklyn swallowed hard, trying to work moisture back

into his mouth. Grateful for the out provided by the old wizard, he took a deep breath and, staring into the fire, began. At first halting, and then as if a dam had burst, the words came in a flood.

The wound, which was less than his grandfather had taken in many hunts, burned with a fire that could not be quenched. His leg was growing putrid. Neither Healers nor Holy men could staunch the infection. He was sent by his grandmother to seek the Samildanach and his cures. If the Samildanach would not help then his grandfather would die. If he was not dead already.

*He will not die!*

As quickly as the words had flowed, they dried up. Franklyn sat trembling, staring into the fire he had made his confessor. Neither Franklyn, Massad, nor the fire spoke another word for a long moment.

At last Massad picked up his staff and reaching across the fire, used it to lift Franklyn's head so their eyes met. Burned free of fear by his ordeal, Franklyn did not flinch.

"Who are you?" the old man demanded.

"I am Franklyn, son of Catherine who is dead," the boy told the Samildanach.

He did not speak to the fire. That time was past.

"Your father?"

"He is dead, too."

"His name," Massad demanded.

"He is dead," Franklyn answered a second time; his jaw set in rigid finality. "I never knew him."

Massad studied the boy for a time and then released the staff from under his chin. He turned away.

"There is nothing I can do," he said finally to the air.

Franklyn sat stunned. He had held his hope so closely that having it ripped from him left him breathless.

The Samildanach's magic always worked. All the stories said so. Why would he not give Franklyn some potion or elixir; some magic incantation? Massad had accepted his fire and food, and his offering, although Franklyn was unaware at the time that he had offered any of them. He *had* to help.

*My grandfather will not die!*

"Why?" was all the boy could manage.

Massad cleared his throat and spat into the fire, watching the spittle sizzle into nothingness.

"This is no simple wound. It is a deadly infection. The symptoms you describe are called in the old tongue, *gangrene*," he explained to the air. "The cure is beyond my skill. I am sorry. Your grandfather will die. Perhaps if you had summoned me sooner..."

"No! He will not die," Franklyn shouted at the fire. "You can heal him. You have to heal him. Dora said so."

Massad jerked his head up and stared at the boy, as if he saw something in his eyes he had not seen in many years. Once again he addressed the fire. This time there was no humor in the old man's voice.

"Who are you?"

"I don't understand," Franklyn stammered, shaken by the sudden change the Samildanach's demeanor. "I told you who I am. I am Franklyn, son of Catherine who is dead."

"Who is Catherine," the old man whispered to the flames.

"Catherine was the daughter of Theodora and Pepin, whom she chose to be Raek. It is Pepin who is my grandfather. It is he who dies. You must heal him. Dora said you would."

Silent laughter shook the old man's shoulders, then worked its way throughout his body until he convulsed with it, and it spilled from his mouth. It was not the kindly, familiar laughter Franklyn heard earlier.

"Pepin is your grandfather," he laughed. "Pepin, who was chosen of Theodora is your grandfather?"

Massad laughed until he fell off the rock he had been

sitting on. On hands and knees he laughed until fifty-seven years worth of bile and bitterness spewed out onto the ground.

Franklyn stared in amazement.

"Why do you laugh?" he demanded. "My grandfather dies, and you laugh? You must heal him, or tell me how."

Massad's laughter dried up. He fixed the boy with a hard stare.

"Pepin, who was chosen of Theodora, Raek of the Amarillo Nomes, cast me out fifty-seven years ago," Massad cried out. There was no hint of laughter now.

"Pepin, chosen of Theodora, cut me off from my people, forbade me fire and salt, water and shade; proclaimed me accursed; unclean; dead, yet undead; untouchable."

Rounding on the boy, Massad rose to the full height and stature of his authority, planted himself between Franklyn and the fire, stared the boy in the eyes and intoned with deadly formality, "I would not heal him if I could. May he find the embrace of Hel and rot there for all eternity."

Unable to meet the Samildanach's gaze, Franklyn turned his eyes to the ground, his sight blurred by the hot sting of womanish tears.

"Please," he whispered. "There is no other way."

Massad studied the boy for a moment.

"Even if I could, why should I heal the man who sent me into exile? Hmm? What wisdom is there in that? Pepin, who is chosen of Theodora, has his own healers, and his own gods. Let them heal him, if they can. For I will not."

Franklyn scrubbed the back of his hand across his eyes. He had no argument left; no words to turn the old wizard's heart. He had tasted the lust for revenge himself; fed on it and found it sweet. Would he lift a finger to help one of the White Sands Nomes?

*Never!*

Yet he couldn't accept Massad's answer.

"Please," was the only word he could manage.

His entreaty was met with harsh laughter, which was suddenly cut off. Massad cocked his head quizzically, as if listening to the wind. He shook his head, slowly at first and then more vehemently. The Samildanach raised first his eyes and then his fist to the sky and cried out.

"No, I cannot. I *will* not."

Franklyn's jaw dropped unnoticed to his chest as he watched the crazy old man battle the air, swinging his staff like a club, shouting defiance in that strange tongue he had used for cursing the village. Finally, as if exhausted from wrestling with an adversary too powerful for him, Massad sat back down.

Tears streamed down the old man's face and soaked into his beard. Running his hands through his hair, Massad raised his eyes from the fire and looked directly at the boy.

"I will go," he said.

# CHAPTER 14

**Long shadows stretched** across the path that led into the village, and the sun, which hung low on the horizon, gave but sparse warmth. Franklyn clutched his cloak tighter around his shoulders while he fought the continual urge to kick his mount to greater speed.

Massad had come, but he came at his own pace and he steadfastly refused to quicken it no matter how Franklyn pleaded. It made the boy want to chew saddle leather. He spat blood, realizing he had been chewing instead on the inside of his cheek.

"Unclean!"

The cry from the old man slapped into Franklyn's back like a leather strap, forcing an unaccustomed squeak from his lips. A man carrying wood let his burden fall to the ground, stumbled backward and turned to run blindly the other direction. Few of the Amarillo Nomes had ever seen the Samildanach, but all knew his reputation. None were eager to have his gaze fall upon them.

"Unclean," Massad cried out again to no one in particular.

This time Franklyn turned back to stare at the old wizard. The look on the boy's face caused Massad to burst out in bitter laughter.

"You see," he cackled, "I keep the Raek law. I am accursed; untouchable. Lest any touch me unaware, and be forced to share my fate, I am required to announce my presence."

"Unclean," he shouted again and looked at the boy with a wry smile. "It has a certain charm, don't you think?"

Massad threw back his head and roared, "Unclean!"

Franklyn hunched forward, trying to work the dagger-like feeling from between his shoulders. Only the sight of Pepin's home offered any relief.

Confusion clouded the faces of the men who stood guard at the home's entrance as the odd pair approached. Franklyn recognized them; Shyrman, tall and lanky, and Tyler, gnarled and tough as an old ironwood tree root; both good men who had stood with their Raek for more years than most in the village had been alive. Franklyn could sense their indecision, almost smell their fear. Caught between loyalty to their chief and dread of the Samildanach, they hesitated for a moment, but only a moment, before drawing sword.

Franklyn jumped between the guards and Massad, shouting "No!" at the same time a more feminine - yet more commanding - voice ordered, "Hold."

Theodora appeared from within, her presence brooking no dissent from the guards.

"The Samildanach holds guest-right in my home. He is accorded full honor, though fire and salt, water and shade are not permitted him. None may speak to him, nor touch him. You will turn your back as he passes and thus maintain your honor."

Shyrman, the younger of the two, made as if to protest, but was silenced by the force of Dora's countenance. Reluctantly, the two turned their backs and waited. Franklyn did not doubt the pair would have risked being declared unclean to protect their Raek.

Massad laughed as he walked past the still confused, grimacing guards. He stopped a pace in front of Dora, gazing into her face, studying, weighing. Nodding to himself, Massad inclined his head barely enough to satisfy decorum.

Dora matched his gaze with never a flinch, meeting stare for stare, weighing, considering, studying. More passed between the two through their gaze than Franklyn could comprehend. He stood transfixed by the whole ordeal.

Without allowing her gaze to drift from the Samildanach's face, Dora addressed Franklyn.

"Pepin is worse. He burns. He shivers. He talks of days gone thirty dry seasons past as if they were but yesterday. And there is the stench of the grave about him. I think he may die soon. Unless...," she left the comment unfinished.

Massad nodded, and taking great care to not accidentally brush against Dora, sauntered leisurely past her and into the darkness of the tent. Franklyn followed in his wake, drawn by the twin threads of dread and curiosity.

A brazier had been set up near Pepin's bed. Thin tendrils of incense-laced smoke danced lazily over the coals, twisting, contorting into fantastical shapes before drifting toward the roof to form a thick haze.

Franklyn shuddered at the sickly-sweet smell of the hwana, the herb the priests burned to ease the suffering of the dying. Inhaling too much of its smoke produced a pleasant euphoria, a relaxed disposition and eventually an incoherent stupor. Death came without pain. Franklyn clinched his teeth. Only the presence of his grandmother kept him from dashing the brazier to the ground.

*Pepin will not die!*

Jon, who had kept vigil since Franklyn's departure, stepped from his place at his father's side, dropped his hand to his belt knife and eyed Massad purposefully. Though no words were spoken, Franklyn was sure both men knew that if Pepin died, the old Raek would not be the only one to depart the land of the living. Jon inclined his head just low enough for decorum and stepped back. It was clear from his demeanor that he did not agree with his mother's decision to seek out the old wizard.

With slow, measured steps, Massad approached the dying chief. The easy, almost maniacally joyful smile that had graced the wizard's face since he had agreed to come and heal Pepin constricted into a rictus snarl as he bent over his old foe. However much he hated this man, it was clear that he loathed the disease that was claiming Pepin's life more.

Lowering himself to within a finger's width of Pepin's lips, Massad listened to the shallow, labored breathing. With a practiced eye he observed Pepin's flushed and fevered brow. He smelled the fetid, sickly-sweet odor of rotting flesh.

"I must see the wound," Massad spoke not to Dora, but to the smoking brazier. Dora immediately pulled back the coverings, but gently, so as not to cause her husband any more discomfort. Despite her caution, Pepin groaned as if a knife was being twisted in his guts.

Franklyn bit the inside of his cheek to keep from vomiting at the stench that rose from the uncovered wound. Others were not so successful. Several attendants barely managed to make it out through the entrance before the sound of retching floated back inside.

Massad took notice of nothing other than Pepin. He stretched forth his hand toward the wound, trying to feel it without actually touching Pepin.

"How long has he been thus," he asked the brazier.

"It has been many days since Pepin was gored," 'Dora spoke to Jon, not the wizard, but in a voice pitched to be overheard. "It looked bad, but Pepin has endured worse. It was the next day that the fever came. His breathing became rapid, like a dog panting in the sun. Pepin's mind began to wander and he lost all thought of food or drink. Any food or water we manage to get into him, he vomits up. He soils himself. Two days ago, the pain became more than he could bear. The priests burn the hwana to ease his suffering."

Jon nodded shallowly and paled visibly. He had seen death, but never like this. Franklyn cringed at the description of Pepin's decline, and sucked in his breath at the crackling sound that came from beneath Pepin's skin.

The wound where the boar's tusk had ripped open Pepin's leg was swollen and black. The color over the remainder of his leg ranged from a sickly greenish-bronze to dark brown. Angry red streaks radiated from the wound and the skin bubbled with foul-smelling brown pus leaking from dozens of burst pustules.

Massad studied the wound for long minutes. Reaching into a pouch at his side, he drew out an odd contraption – a tangle of thin metal that held two circular pieces of clear glass. Even in the midst of worry over his grandfather, Franklyn found himself intrigued with the device the Samildanach fitted over his nose and hooked around his ears.

*Oculars?*

Franklyn had heard rumors of these wonders that allowed the weak-eyed to see, but he thought them to be just another of the fanciful stories told around a fire pit late at night, along with tales of were-bears and... Franklyn swallowed the knot in his throat... and Massad.

Massad didn't stop examining the old chief until he had seen every inch of his body. Satisfied he had missed nothing, he stood up straight at last. Pulling the oculars from his face, Massad shook his head and let out a slow, deliberate breath. Franklyn thought his face betrayed some slight remorse at the words he was about to speak.

Gazing into the still smoldering brazier, the Samildanach, in slow and measured tones, explained his predicament to the ashes.

"Pepin can be healed," he began, and for the first time in days, Dora shuddered, fat tears leaking down her cheeks.

"But…" 'Dora choked back the tears at the caveat. "I cannot heal him without touching him. That would make him unclean. For a man like Pepin, that would be a fate worse than death. He would not thank me for it."

The Samildanach turned a sorrowful eye to Dora.

"He would not thank you for it. But the decision is not mine to make. I leave it to those who love him."

Dora now began to weep in earnest, silent shudders racking her chest as tears streamed unheeded down her face.

Franklyn shook his head in denial, backing away from his grandfather, mouthing a wordless, *No! Pepin will not die!*

"You are Samildanach," Franklyn cried at last, defying the Raek law by speaking directly to the old wizard. "Heal him!"

"I can only do what I am commanded," Massad, still mindful of the Raek law, replied to the fire, but it was clear that he did not take his commands from the Raek.

"Still…" He cocked his head as if listening to the wind, and a small grin turned up the corners of his mouth. "There might be a way," he muttered to himself.

Massad continued to listen, nodding wordlessly, as a child receiving instructions for a complex exercise; at last, he smiled openly.

"There is a way," he announced to the brazier. "I can use a conduit; a surrogate; a go-between. If one can be found with the courage to lay his hands on Pepin's wound, I can lay my hands on him, and the power to heal may be transmitted through him. In this way, it is possible to for me to heal Pepin without touching him."

Franklyn felt the silence that followed Massad's mad rambling grow palpable, and then oppressive. No one spoke. No one moved. The same thought paralyzed everyone in the tent.

*Pepin might be healed, but the go-between would be touched by Massad; Unclean, and therefore doomed to exile.*

Pepin shuddered once, and then lay still, breaking the reverie of those gathered around him. All eyes rested on the old chief. For long moments it appeared death had taken him, making the decision moot. At last Pepin drew a strained and shallow breath, marked by a strangled gurgling in his chest.

"Pepin is strong," the Samildanach whispered in grudging admiration. "But the infection is stronger. Come, you must choose. His time grows short."

Barely recognizing the movement of his feet Franklyn found himself kneeling beside his grandfather, his hands covering Pepin's putrid wounds, and being covered in turn by the hot, vile liquid that oozed from them.

"Heal him."

Franklyn spoke directly to the Samildanach.

Massad's smile was sad, acknowledging the sentence the boy had just pronounced upon himself. He nodded and, in the deepening silence, moved forward and knelt beside Franklyn, placing his hands on Franklyn's thigh, in the exact location of Pepin's wound.

Franklyn was surprised that the wizard's touch did not sear his flesh. His attention shifted as slowly, quietly at first and then with an increase of both volume and cadence, Massad began to chant in that private language of his. There was a confidence in the wizard's tone that contrasted sharply with the pleading, wheedling cries of the Nomish priests, Franklyn thought in the far corners of his mind.

He had no time to dwell on the thought, at it flitted away as within moments he felt a languorous warmth flow into him from Massad's hands. At first it was a tickle, a tingle, a trickle that was easily dismissed as a trick of the mind. But the trickle became a flow that was impossible to ignore; then the flow became a flood.

It started in Franklyn's thigh, filled his leg, his hips, his belly and chest with an incomprehensible warmth. It ran down his arms and into his fingers. It flowed like a waterfall out into Pepin's wound.

It was impossible to describe. Franklyn wanted to laugh, to cry, to shout, to sing! He wanted it to never stop. He wanted to be filled with it, immersed in it, to bathe in it, to drink it in. It thrilled him. It terrified him. And under it all, he could hear Massad chanting, laughing, singing in that strange, sweet, unearthly language. So majestic. So magnificent. So beautiful. Why had he ever thought it a fearsome thing? He couldn't remember.

The Samildanach began to laugh and Franklyn laughed with him. As he did, corruption began to ooze from Pepin's wound over his hands. The red streaks began to fade, chased by a superior power that now coursed through Pepin's veins. Putrid, infectious pus gushed out over Franklyn's hands and onto the floor. Baby pink skin appeared, replacing the crusted and decaying flesh that crumbled away.

Pepin's breathing grew stronger, heartier; the flush on his face from a healthy glow rather than a fevered rash.

Massad's chant gave way entirely to laughter, at first gentle, then fierce, and at last defiant. Franklyn matched him guffaw for guffaw until at last the Samildanach shouted, "It...is...finished!" and fell to the floor, breathing hard, but still chuckling softly.

Startled by the sudden ending, cut off from the life-giving flow, Franklyn wanted to weep for the memory of it. He thought the world a sad and lonely place without it.

Removing his hands from Pepin's thigh, Franklyn reached for a towel and wiped the pus and corruption from his own fingers. Then, with gentle, confident strokes he wiped the filth from his grandfather's leg.

He had felt the power from the Samildanach flow through him, yet he stood slack-jawed, staring at the perfectly whole leg that had moments before been a rotting wreak of a limb.

*Not even a scar.*

The knot in his throat would barely let him breathe, much less speak, but he felt he must thank Massad or his heart would burst. Turning to the wizard, Franklyn was surprised to see Massad's gaze on him, saddened by the recognition of what Franklyn had now become.

Dora and Jon, who had stood to the side during the ordeal, not daring to intervene, hardly daring to breathe, now moved tentatively forward, examining Pepin for signs that the witchcraft performed on him has indeed healed him.

Whimpering like a young girl, Dora ran her fingers over the thigh that had once been gored so savagely. The decaying flesh was gone. The leg was perfect. She listened to Pepin's regular breathing, felt his cool brow, and satisfied that the healing was both complete and real, stood to face the Samildanach.

"He will need to sleep, now." Massad instructed the brazier that still smoldered with the sickly sweet smell of the stupor-inducing hwana. "But get thee hence. He needs real sleep, not a drugged stupor. And bring him some food. When he awakes, he will be hungry".

Caught between laughing and whimpering, fat tears running openly down her cheeks, Dora turned from her husband to her grandson and took a step toward him to embrace him. She paused in horror as Franklyn stumbled backward. The full weight of his decision crashing down on him.

Franklyn held up his hands to ward off her embrace and cried out a single word in anguish.

"Unclean!"

# CHAPTER 15

**The two weeks** since Tomsyn's death − or desertion, if Sencha had his way - had everyone in camp walking on eggshells. Everyone except Sencha, who behaved as if nothing of significance had happened. Though he frequently reminded Strom who was in charge, giving him that look that said, *and you know the reason why,* Sencha seemed content to let Strom lead the contingent as he saw fit.

For his part, Strom had grown increasingly more irritable. Guards were doubled − no one was left alone for any reason, except Mol Graumet who demanded a certain amount of *girl time* as she put it. Strom knew to pick his battles, and this was one he would not win.

Strom was determined that there would be no repeat of the Tomsyn incident. The result was everyone got half as much sleep and everyone was twice as edgy.

Everyone except Sencha, who didn't loose sleep over anything.

Strom slept less than anyone. When he wasn't checking on his outposts, he was busy scouting ahead, choosing paths for the next day's ride - trails which were always less than direct. Most could not be called trails at all.

Avoiding settlements, solitary farms and anything else

that could remotely be considered a sign of civilization became an obsession with him, and he brooked no argument. Breaking new trails through the dense underbrush, then covering the tracks they left in the snow cost precious time. To compensate he pushed the company that much harder — up earlier; pitching camp later.

*Someone knows. And if someone knows, the wrong person can know.*

He was fit to chew saddle leather, and that was Kennedy's own truth.

When he did stop for a moment's rest it was usually in Alwyn's company, and even then he spent most of his time fuming about the need for haste vs. the need for security. Lack of sleep, combined with the smoldering resentment he harbored toward Sencha, crept up to the corners of his eyes giving him the look of a man on the edge of violence - though to Alwyn's way of thinking, Strom always looked like a man on the edge of violence.

"You're not and easy man to be around right now, you know that?"

Alwyn made the remark after Strom paced the length of the camp for the fourth time.

"What?"

Strom looked at his friend as if seeing him for the first time in days. He had just returned from scouting the next day's path, stopping only long enough to report to Sencha. The experience left him in a sour mood. A barely perceptible turning up of the corners of his mouth betrayed a momentary lightening of his mood.

"Oh. Sorry, Alwyn. I suppose I have been a bit preoccupied of late."

"Sit down, Strom," Alwyn encouraged. "Binnie's whipped up a batch of stew that's good for what ails you."

"Aye, General," the big Forrester added. "You're bound to wear yourself to a frazzle if you don't stop for more than a couple of hours a night. You eat this stew. Can't have you losing your strength before we even get to the battle, now can we?"

"What makes you think there will be a battle at the end of this parade, Binnie?" Strom demanded.

"There's always a battle at the end of the parade for the likes of us, General," Tuk replied, holding a steaming mug out to Strom with one hand while he held a knowing finger to the side of his nose with the other.

This time Strom allowed a genuine grin crease his face. He accepted the mug from Tuk and plopped down beside Alwyn.

"I think I will have a cup of tea while you're at it, Tuk," he said.

After all the years he had know the big Forrester, Strom was still amazed at his culinary abilities. Forresters were famed for their ability to live off the land, hunting while they traveled; cooking if time and situation permitted; more often than not settling for roots and nuts and the occasional raw egg rather than roasted meat.

Still, here was Binnie Tuk, preparing a stew of some kind of meat, with generous chunks of vegetables of questionable origin, all swamped together in a thick broth that smelled and tasted delicious. Strom grinned and slurped it down eagerly. It had, indeed, been a long time since he had eaten more two mouthfuls together of anything hot.

Washing it down with Tuk's famous hot tea, Strom allowed the small, well-hidden fire to leach away some of the cold that had settled into his bones.

"So, General," Binnie Tuk asked in a low-pitched voice. "When do we get to White House?"

Strom glared at him over his tea.

*Somebody knows...*

"Who said anything about White House, Binnie? If that civilian court popinjay doesn't know how to keep his mouth shut…"

*Someone knows.*

Tuk chuckled softly, producing a disconcerted look from Strom.

"No need to throttle Hizzoner, General. He hasn't said two words together to anyone, 'ceptin' you, of course, and I don't suppose those are the kind of words that bear repeating in mixed company.

"No, I just says to myself, I says, *Binnie, what is it that lies North by Northwest? And I answers myself, Why Binnie, the only thing between here and the Kingdom of Canada is a barbed-wire fence, and White House. Now Binnie, I says to myself, Goin' to Canada would likely just start up the war again, and there don't be no reason to start up no war with no fool Canadians. They pays their tribute to the President and their tithe to the Sons of Liberty, I reckon, else we'd have heard of it.*

"So, I says to myself, I says, *Binnie, what is it that lies North by Northwest? And I answers myself, Why, Binnie, the only thing between here and the Kingdom of Canada is a barbed-wire fence and White House. Now Binnie, I says to myself, Goin' to Canada would likely just start up the war again, and there don't be no need to start up no war with no fool Canadians. They pays their tribute to the President and their tithe to the Sons of Liberty, I reckon, else we'd have heard of it.*

"No, I says to myself, *we must be going to White House. But then I says to myself, I says, If we be going to White House, why are we going the back ways, as if we don't want Hizzoner, the President, to know we's comin'?*

"*Why, indeed? I asks myself.*"

"And what did you answer yourself," Strom said in a voice like cold steel sliding out of a leather scabbard.

"Well, as to that, General, I didn't answer myself. No sir, Binnie Tuk is a soldier, and he goes where he's told to go, and does what he's told to do…as long as the one what's doing the tellin' know what he's about."

A quick finger to the side of his nose left no doubt about his confidence in Strom Maxwell's leadership.

"You just get us where we're going, General. I figure you'll tell us what we needs to know when we needs to know it, or my name's not Binnie Tuk, which it is, so there ye are."

Strom grunted and threw the rest of his tea on the fire, watching the flames lick it up.

"Just make sure *yourself* is the only one you talk to, Tuk," he admonished. "I've got to check on the guards."

Without another word or a backward glance, Strom Maxwell melted into the darkness.

Alwyn watched his friend's back until it blended into the night, then let out an exasperated sigh. No, Strom Maxwell was certainly not an easy man to be around these days. And he couldn't shake that itching between his shoulders, as if he were waiting for someone to plunge a dagger, *right there.*

*LaFranc's not much better,* he mused.

There was something disconcerting about the way the big librarian chewed his leaf and spat — observing everything, and saying nothing; something disquieting in the way he practiced *balance* with that great claymore broadsword.

*Balance,* he always said. *Cool head, cold steel, fire in your eyes, but above all…balance.*

It was a mantra Alwyn was growing weary of hearing. In fact, the only thing he had not grown weary of on this Liberty-forsaken journey was his time talking with Binnie Tuk, the man-mountain Strom had apparently assigned as his personal bodyguard.

Tuk, he discovered, was a treasure-trove of stories both fantastical and humorous, and an amazing storehouse of the most obscure knowledge — an incongruous facet to a man who was adept at killing with any weapon Alwyn could conceive of, and quite a few that he could not.

"General's been in a taking ever since Tomsyn's death,"

Binnie stated as he handed Alwyn a second cup of tea. "He never was one to take losing a man lightly, but I've never seen him like this before."

"Binnie," Alwyn hesitate, trying to put a vague feeling into words. Wrapping his hands around the steaming cup, inhaling its pungent fragrance, he asked, "You don't believe Tomsyn deserted, do you?"

"Don't matter what I believe," Tuk snorted. "Won't change the truth, whatever it is."

Binnie turned back to the slowly dying fire and gave it a vicious poke, sending a few stray sparks spiraling skyward.

"Tomsyn was a good man. And a good friend."

For a moment Alwyn was sure the big man shivered, although he had never known the cold to affect Tuk.

"He saved my life once," Binnie's voice was soft, faraway, spoken through a distant haze of memory. A quick shake of his shaggy head and he was back in the present.

Turning back toward Alwyn he sword, "By the Fifth Face of God, Tomsyn saved all of our lives at least once. He was the best field alchemist I've ever known, and I've known more than a few in my day. He patched up the general more than a few times, too, I can tell ye that."

Tuk's voice turned to ice. "He *best* be dead."

The silence that followed Tuk's declaration was complete, save for the muffled pop from the tiny fire. Alwyn did not doubt the truth of Tuk's statement. It remained unsaid that if Tomsyn lived, if he simply deserted, Tuk would kill him. Probably in a most unpleasant fashion.

Both men stared at the stubborn flames clinging tenaciously to the few remaining twigs in the firepit. If either could read the future in the coals, neither revealed what he saw.

"Binnie," Alwyn blew across his tea, sipped and swallowed, struggling with an idea that tickled the corners of his mind and finally crawled instinctively, yet unbidden, from between his lips, "you seem to have obtained an inordinate amount of obscure information; for a man in your profession, I mean."

Tuk chuckled, flattered.

"Just stories mostly, with little enough of the truth to 'em, or my name's not Binnie Tuk..."

"Which it is, to be sure," Alwyn finished.

"Aye," Tuk agreed, shrugging. "Folks talk when they have a full belly. A good meal, a little after dinner leaf, perhaps a bit of Tuk's special tea with a bit of brandy and everyone, high born or low, talks freely enough. No one ever said Binnie Tuk didn't know how to listen. After all, Liberty himself gave us one mouth and two ears."

Tuk put his finger to the side of his nose as if that settled the matter, and chuckled softly again.

"Oh, aye — one mouth and two ears. I suppose I might have picked up a few interesting tidbits here and there."

"You know, Binnie, in my line of work I frequently come across obscure terms, strange stories, artifacts that we can't seem to decipher. Maybe with your vast experience at listening you could shed some light on a subject for me?"

"The honor is to serve," Tuk struck fist to heart with mock formality, bowing slightly at the waist. "And what subject would you like me to elucidate upon?"

"An obscure term; more myth than legend, really. Portents of the end of the world; dark prophecy; that sort of thing. It's called *Tyrfingr*. Heard of it?"

For a hairsbreadth Alwyn thought he saw a flash of...fear?...lightning across Binnie Tuk's eyes. One blink and it was gone. Alwyn wasn't sure whether it had ever been there at all.

Filling his mouth with stew, Tuk shook his head.

"No, can't say I've ever heard tell the word. *Tiefinger*, you say? No, I'm sure I've never heard of it. Perhaps you, being a learned scholar scavenger and all, could enlighten a poor, uneducated Forrester such as myself?"

Tuk continued shoveling the stew into his mouth with relentless gusto, all the while eying Alwyn expectantly.

"*Tyrfingr*," Alwyn corrected, failing to keep a lecturing tone from creeping into his voice. "Well, there's not much to go on, really. Old wives tales mostly, and a few odd references in some ancient manuscripts.

"Every culture seems to have similar myths about how the world ends — a great war filled with blood, and fire, and ice; and a ruler of unspeakable power who defies God himself.

"Kind of silly when you talk about it during the day," Alwyn gave a half-hearted chuckle. "But at night around a firepit, with the flames tossing strange shadows about, the stories seem…I don't know, almost plausible sometimes.

"Anyway, the stories all speak of a Sword of Power - or perhaps it is better translated a Sword of Light. Occasionally a Canadian crosses the border on a quest to find it. Their traditions say it will bring peace and harmony to the land.

"Tyrfingr is supposed to be such a sword — or maybe not a sword at all, none of the ancient texts really agree on that part — yet still a sword for all that — a great sword of Light.

"It is supposed to be guarded by the Fairies; locked away in an impenetrable vault of stone. Some say Tyrfingr refers to the *land* of the Fairies, or maybe their version of heaven."

Alwyn's voice took on a tone of hushed awe bordering on reverence. There was no reason for it. It just seemed…right.

"It is said that he who holds Tyrfingr — the one who pulls the great Sword of Light from its resting place in the stone vault - is the rightful King of the World."

When Alwyn stopped talking there was not another sound to be heard, save the muted popping of the fire. Tuk's spoon was held frozen between his cup and mouth. Abruptly, Alwyn barked an abrupt laugh.

"Silly legend. But still, it has weight...the feel of something more than a legend. More than..."

His voice trailed off and he found himself once more gazing into the coals, hoping for an answer to a question he didn't know how to ask.

Binnie Tuk let the spoon drop lightly back into the stew, following it with his eyes, contemplating. He chewed as if he couldn't remember where the mouthful he was eating had come from.

Staring into the fire, there was none of his accustomed humor on his face. Binnie Tuk looked haggard, tired. He spoke slowly in a voice pitched low and heavy with import.

*"Behold a white horse, and he that sat upon him was called Faithful and True. He had a name written, that no man knew, but he himself. And he was clothed with a vesture dipped in blood. And out of his mouth goes Tyrfingr, that he should smite the nations. He treads the winepress of the fierceness and wrath of Almighty God. And on his thigh a name is written – King of Kings and Lord of Lords.*

"Whatever this Tyrfingr is, if it still exists, if it *ever* existed at all, it is accursed." Turning his head, Tuk fixed Alwyn with a stare. "Leave it be, Master Scavenger, for it divides not only flesh from bone, and bone from marrow, but also soul from spirit. It is a power man was not meant to have."

Alwyn nodded mutely, stunned by the big Forrester's fiercely whispered outburst.

Tuk waited another long moment to make sure his warning was taken to heart, nodded, and rose, the old Binnie now firmly back in control.

"I must leave you now, Master Scavenger. Hizzoner has made it something of a ritual for me to bring him his evening tea each night before he retires. Mustn't keep so great a personage as he waiting, now must I?"

"No, I suppose not," Alwyn agreed with a wry smile.

"Binnie," he added almost as an afterthought. "You just quoted from Girard's *Legends of the Fall*. There are not two dozen copies of that scroll scattered across the entire United States. All are in Libraries and not readily accessible to one such as yourself. I didn't even know you could read."

"There are a great many things you don't know, Master Scavenger."

Binnie Tuk put a quick finger to the side of his nose as if that settled the matter, and disappeared into the night, carrying a cup of steaming liquid with him.

*There are a great many things that I don't know*, Alwyn mused. *Too many things that I don't know.*

He raised the mug to his lips and took a large swig of tea, grimacing as he swallowed.

*Cold. Bad enough when it's hot. Damned near intolerable when it's cold.*

He remembered the citizens of the Confederation of the Southlands drank their tea cold... and sweet. He couldn't fathom it.

Alwyn pitched the dregs into what was left of the fire, stood, and kicked dirt over the remaining coals. He started walking. He always did his best thinking when he was walking, and Liberty knew he needed to think clearly tonight.

He paced more than walked. Strom had guards posted, and after Tomsyn's demise, *or desertion*, the men were a bit testy and just as likely to slit your throat first and ask *who goes there* later. Alwyn made sure he never got close to the camp's perimeter.

*Forresters getting careless and getting themselves killed - or deserting; mercenaries quoting prophesy; court ambassadors relieving commanding generals; renegade scavengers unearthing artifacts of incalculable historical significance. Madness!*

Alwyn walked until he could no longer feel his feet in his boots. His mind was still a jumble of questions without answers, but he had performed this drill long enough to know that there were times the mind had to work at its own pace. Pushing it would only drive the answer further away.

By the time he decided to seek the relative warmth of the tent he shared with LaFranc, and now with Strom Maxwell as well, the waning moon had settled above the trees. Alwyn had never been able to decipher why the goddess of the night always appeared so much larger when she was closest to the ground.

"Where have you been?"

The challenge slapped him in the face as soon as he threw the flaps back on his tent.

"Well, it's nice to see you again, too, Strom," Alwyn retorted.

He was cold, tired, more than a bit anxious for this whole expedition to be over. He was in no mood for Strom's Mother Hen routine.

"You didn't answer my question."

"Nor do I intend to," Alwyn shot back. "I'm not one of your Forresters, and you're not the godalmighty Adam, so back away."

In two strides he was at his bedroll, trying with half-frozen fingers to pull the boots from his feet.

"Don't bother," Strom ordered.

"Why," Alwyn asked, suddenly aware that LaFranc was fully dressed and leaning on his claymore. "Another attack?"

"No," Strom replied. "Worse. Sencha is dead."

# CHAPTER 16

**Alwyn knew his** mouth was hanging open, but he felt powerless to close it. He let his still booted foot fall back to the ground and eventually found his tongue.

"When? How?"

"Within the hour," Strom answered, then shrugged. "As for how…" his voice trailed off. "Mol said he complained of a headache, walked into his tent, let out one muffled whimper and hit the ground. Mol called in to him to see if he was all right. When she got no answer she stuck her head through the tent flaps. She found him lying on the ground with his hands still pressed to his temples."

It took another moment for reality to sink in. Sencha was dead. He was the diplomat, the negotiator, the go-between. If anyone could have managed a tenuous peace between the Sons of Liberty and the President, it would have been Sencha. Without him the expedition could not succeed. The possibility of civil war, or worse, suddenly looked more than probable.

"No foul play?" Alwyn shook his head in amazement. "No attack? No accident? He just complained of a headache and died?"

Strom nodded, still staring Alwyn in the eye while

LaFranc stuck his head outside the tent flap and spat a prodigious amount of brown liquid onto the snow covered ground.

Quietly, but with infinite authority Strom added, "There is no one else."

Alwyn nodded. There was no one else. Sencha was dead. The mission was over. They had failed. Julian would take it hard, but there was nothing left to do but return home and try to hatch an alternative plan.

"You are the only one who can take Sencha's place as the Adam's mouthpiece."

Alwyn's mouth once again dropped open as he bounded to his feet, but this time it took only a moment for him to regain his composure — and only a moment more before a torrent of expletives exploded from his mouth.

"No! That was not part of the deal. Bad enough being Julian's spy. I will not be his ambassador. I'm a scavenger, not a diplomat," he shouted. "Burtyn I can deal with. I may have to wring his scrawny neck to make him talk, but I can do that. Willam is another matter. He'll have my head on a pike before I get a word out edgewise.

"No. That's it. I quit. I'm going to the Gulf of Texas coast to look for my wife. You wanted me to go, Strom. Remember? You begged me to go. Well, I'm going. I'm going. Tonight. Right now."

"All things change, Alwyn," Strom said softly, sadly.

The two friends stood staring each other in the eye; one filled with fury and fear, the other full of solemn resolution.

"There is no one else. Only you."

Alwyn's mouth worked wordlessly for a moment. When he did find his tongue he appealed to LaFranc.

"Would you talk some sense into him?"

The Chief Librarian only stood there, leaning on his claymore. He reminded Alwyn of nothing so much as a cow chewing its cud. At last LaFranc nodded, expectorated, spit the spent wad of leaf from his mouth, and answered.

"Balance," the LaFranc intoned. "Above all…balance. Of course the mission must go forward. The alternative is unthinkable. But how? Sencha is dead. We are three weeks gone from Omaha and at least that many more from White House. There is no time to send back for another diplomat, and there is none of the stature of Sencha, anyway. That leaves only the three of us to convey the Adam's words to the President."

Ticking off points on his fingers, LaFranc lectured to his captive audience.

"General Maxwell commands the respect of the military, but his, shall we say, *unorthodox* leadership style, has created many enemies. He has won as many victories by deceit has he has by might. And he has no breeding. He is not what one would call welcome in civilized company."

Strom snorted, but did not deny it. He had little enough use for *civilized* company.

"I may have earned some slight respect among my peers," LaFranc continued, "but among the powerful I am considered much too much of an academic to have any grounding in the real world."

Alwyn began to protest, but LaFranc held up his hand, ticking off his third point.

"Balance, Alwyn. Balance. Who better to convey the words of the Adam than the childhood friend and confidant of the Adam? Who better than the most respected scavenger in the United States of America; a man of learning and passion; a man of grand lineage; and one who can read Ancient American?

"Yes, Alwyn, I think it must be you. There is no one else. And the alternative…"

LaFranc let the words trail off. There was no need to speak them. The alternative was civil war; chaos; destruction.

LaFranc dug two fingers and a thumb back into his

pouch, pulled out a wad of the aromatic shredded leaf, shoved it into his mouth and promptly resumed chewing as if he had not just issued Alwyn's death warrant.

Alwyn looked from LaFranc to Strom Maxwell, his face pleading for a way out. Finding none, he dropped to his bed and lowered his head into his hands. After a shudder that shook his whole body, Alwyn inhaled deeply, raised his head to look each man in the eye.

"All right," he said.

The sigh that left Strom's chest suggested he was unsure Alwyn would come to that conclusion. LaFranc's contented chewing suggested he never had a doubt.

"So, what now," Alwyn demanded.

"First you must be properly commissioned," LaFranc assumed his lecturing posture once more. "General Maxwell may certainly get you to White House unmolested; may even get you into the Great Hall where anyone, high-born or low, may speak his piece. But without the commission, no one, least of all Willam Norman will accept your words as coming from the Adam.

"General, I assume you brought Sencha's papers and Adamic commission with you when you left Sencha's tent?"

Strom's jaws worked wordlessly for a moment before he shook his head. An unaccustomed sheepishness colored his cheeks as the mumbled something about setting Mol Graumet to guard Sencha's tent and rushing right over here.

LaFranc merely nodded as if he expected nothing else from a slightly incompetent student. He spit.

"Then we should go and retrieve them."

LaFranc started out of the tent, paused briefly to give the younger men a studied glance.

"Are you coming?"

It didn't take long for the three men to reach Sencha's tent.

*Strom's tent, again*, Alwyn thought.

Situated in the center of the camp, it was immune to a surprise attack. Seated outside, whittling on a piece of wood as if nothing in the world was wrong, Mol Graumet rose unhurried to her feet.

"He's still there," she told Strom as he walked past her to throw back the flap. He paused to give her a look that said he might skin her alive. She smiled back sweetly.

"Just thought you'd want to know his body hasn't disappeared. I mean, after Tomsyn got lost and all."

Strom ground his teeth, started to say something, but thought better of it. He plunged into the darkness and relative warmth of the tent that was once his, and was again now that Sencha was dead. Alwyn and LaFranc crowded in behind him.

Just as Mol said, Sencha was still there, exactly as Strom had found him, hands still pressed to his temples.

"I never liked that man," Alwyn began, "but I never wished death to take him. I wonder what he died of?"

"I wonder if it's catching," Strom added.

"I wonder where he kept his scrolls," said LaFranc, who did not bothered to even look at the corpse. He was to busy rifling through Sencha's belongings. "We will need to find his Adamic commission, and any instructions he may have received from the Adam personally before he left."

It wasn't long before the big librarian discovered a small, brass box, bound and locked, hidden inside Sencha's saddlebags.

"Ah. Perhaps this may contain something of interest? I could, of course, force it open, but where there is a lock, one would expect the owner to have a key. Knowing how trusting Sencha is…was…I should expect that he kept it on his person. General, if you please."

Relieved to be doing something of use, Strom started a

systematic search of Sencha's corpse. It took only moments before he discovered a small key on a chain around the dead man's neck.

With as much care as respect for the dead allowed, Strom lowered Sencha's now rigid hands from his temples in order to work the chain over his head. Strom held the key dangling from the necklace like a thief who had been caught for the last time. It swung in a rogue gust of wind that whistled through the tent flap and reminded them that winter still ruled this land.

LaFranc reached for the key, his big hand closing over it, warming it within the folds of his flesh, as if defying the winter to take possession of the tent's occupants. A frown creased his mouth as he glanced down at the rictus snarl on Sencha's cold, dead face. His dead black eyes, stared back at LaFranc like a challenge, unsettling him somehow, in a way he couldn't put his finger on.

"How did he die, I wonder," the big librarian muttered, the key all but forgotten in the wake of the reawakened mystery.

"Why?" Strom demanded. "He's dead. Nobody killed him. No one was near. He just died. People do just die, you know."

"I think *some* people *just die*. I do not think Master Sencha *just died*," LaFranc retorted. "Look here, at his eyes. Do you not see?"

Strom and Alwyn studied Sencha's eyes; those dead, black eyes; eyes that had missed nothing while he lived; eyes that could see the lie behind your own eyes. Strom shuddered in spite of himself. He would swear those eyes could still see into his soul. He had a sudden urge to cut them out.

"Do you not see?"

LaFranc badgered the two younger men as if they were dull-witted students who could not see the obvious answer to the simplest of questions.

"Look at his eyes, the whites of his eyes."

"They are tinged blue," Alwyn said. "I suppose the lack of air caused the blood in the eyeballs to lose its richness and turn blue?"

"You suppose wrong," LaFranc chided, "but at least you suppose something. Master General?"

Strom merely shook his head. He didn't feel like playing the student, or the fool.

"There is only one thing that affects the whites of the eyes like that at death. And the means we have a problem on our hands - a very serious problem."

Strom exploded to his feet and grabbed LaFranc by the front of his shirt.

"Out with it, you insufferable old goat. What is it that turns the eyes of the dead blue that is going to cause us such massive problems that you have to play guessing games?"

"Maxwell, you are a boor."

"LaFranc, one day I'm going to cut your liver out," Strom voiced a vicious whisper. "By the Five Faces of God I will."

"You have no patience. You have no balance. You are a boor."

By a sheer act of will Strom forced his fingers to release LaFranc. In an exaggerated show of mock contrition, he brushed the wrinkles he had created from the front of LaFranc's shirt, and in a deadly calm voice asked again, more politely this time.

"Master LaFranc, what is it that turns a dead man's eyes blue?"

LaFranc expelled the spent wad of leaf he had been chewing onto the floor of the tent, oblivious to the fact that Strom would reclaim the tent now that Sencha had no more use for it.

"Only one thing," he finally answered. "Whitesnake Root."

"Whitesnake Root?"

Alwyn looked back at the dead man's eyes, searching his memory for some reference point. He was one of the foremost authorities on ancient America, but the more recent past was a blur to him.

What little he remembered of the Whitesnake plant was that its flowering vines were said to entwine anything they came in contact with. Its pale blossoms were supposed to look like a white snake.

Then he recalled an obscure history text written more than three hundred years before called, *The Wars Between the States,* by the Librarian, Marc Shuulz. It was a dry and dusty tome he had read when he first came to study under LaFranc. It mostly contained names and dates of battles long forgotten. But it also included a section on less honorable, more covert methods the States used to gain advantage in the wars, including the use of assassination by poisoning.

"The juice from the Whitesnake plant's root was toxic. In the old days, they made poison from it. But that poison ahs been anathema for generations," Alwyn protested.

"Anathema, yes, for generations," LaFranc concurred. "Odorless, tasteless, colorless, lethal, it was too dangerous. The major houses nearly wiped each other out before they decided to exterminate the plant instead."

"But Whitesnake root no longer exists," Strom added. "It hasn't existed for a hundred years or more. Few still remember that it ever did; some keepers of ancient lore perhaps, such as yourself, Master LaFranc; some in the military might still know if it, and..." he trailed off.

"The H'ashishiyyin," LaFranc finished.

# CHAPTER 17

**"The H'ashishiyyin,"** **Strom** repeated, rolling each syllable slowly over his tongue as if tasting the word. Finding it bitter in his mouth, he spat.

The H'ashishiyyin was an outlawed sect, hunted nearly to extinction by every civilized government for the past four hundred years, but no one doubted they still existed. Indeed, it was rumored that most of the governors of most the United States kept a personal H'ashasine on their payroll, to handle *difficult* situations.

The cult believed the taking of human life to be a religious rite – one that guaranteed salvation. The promise of eternal life was, of course, necessary as most H'ashasine did their work in public, thereby forfeiting their earthly lives.

"The H'ashishiyyin. Here? Impossible," Strom denounced the idea. "No one could have gotten into the camp. No one is that good; not with double guards; not to the center of the Liberty-forsaken camp; not right under our noses."

"Think of Sencha's last moments, as reported by your ever-vigilant Mol Graumet," LaFranc pressed the matter. "The headache, the muffled cry, the final grasping of the head, the sudden death. I suppose it could have been a stroke. It looks like a stroke. But the eyes – the eyes tell all. They are after all, the windows to the soul, eh?

"Besides, no one needed to get past your guards. As you said yourself, the H'ashasine had already infiltrated your ranks, remember? How else did he approach Tomsyn and shoot him from behind?"

Alwyn could hear Strom's teeth grinding with denial. He searched his memory for details about the shadowy cult.

It was said they followed Sinan Salman, the legendary Old Man of the Mountain. Girard, he remembered, had written a brief, fanciful passage about them in his *Travels Beyond the Central Highlands* in the Fifth Century of the Common Era. Alwyn had been required to memorize that passage during his childhood training at the Library.

*"Sinan Salman had caused a certain valley between two mountains to be enclosed, and had turned it into a garden, the largest and most beautiful that ever was seen, flowing freely with milk and honey. He furnished it with numbers of the most beautiful damsels in the world, who could play on all manner of instruments and sing most sweetly, and dance in a manner that was intoxicating. For the Old Man desired to make his people believe that this was Paradise.*

*"No man was allowed to enter the Garden save those whom he intended to be his H'ashasine. There was a Fortress at the entrance, strong enough to resist the armies of whole world, and there was no other way to get in.*

*He kept at his court a number of youths from many countries, from 12 to 20 years of age. He would introduce them into the delights of his garden, having first made them drink a certain potion, which cast them into a deep sleep.*

*So when the Old Man would have any slain he would say to such a youth: 'Go thou and slay; and when thou returnest, my Angels shall bear thee into Paradise. And should'st thou die nevertheless even so, I will send my Angels to carry thee back into Paradise.'*

*And in this manner the Old One got his people to murder any one whom he desired.'*

A question, itching in the back of Alwyn's mind, wormed its way to the front and wriggled out of his mouth.

"Even if they could manage to infiltrate our company, why now? Why didn't they take Sencha out the night Tomsyn was murdered?"

"Not murdered," LaFranc corrected. "Assassinated. As to why, well, that part might be a little clearer if this key really does fit this box."

Setting the brass box on Sencha's cot, LaFranc slipped the key into the lock and gave a tentative twist; gently to not break its delicate mechanism. A soft *click* rewarded the Chief Librarian's efforts, and as LaFranc lifted the lid Alwyn and Strom gathered around him to see what answers the box might contain.

LaFranc reached in and delicately pulled out a small scroll, sealed in gold with the Adam's personal seal.

"Sencha's commission," he announced.

He pulled another scroll from the box, also bearing the Adamic seal, but in wax. LaFranc broke the seal, held it before the guttering lamp and whistled as he read Julian's ultimatum to Willam Norman.

"The Adam demands fealty on pain of excommunication not only for Willam, but for his posterity for all generations, and all his lands and property forfeit to the Sons of Liberty.

"Further, continued rebellion would result in excommunication for any who bore arms against the Adam's representatives, and finally the entire state would be declared anathema, its bordered closed to trade, its people outcast from every other state."

LaFranc paused, pursed his lips and read silently for a moment, as if to make sure of what he was reading.

"What else does it say," Strom demanded, when the big

librarian hesitated.

LaFranc blew out a sigh and seemed to deflate.

"If Willam refuses to repent, Sencha had orders to shake the dust from his feet in the sight of Willam's entire court."

Alwyn stared wide-eyed at the command. Strom stood tight-lipped, stone-faced. Julian was invoking the *Carnavon*, the Curse of the Dust.

It was possible, even likely, that the messenger would never leave White House alive, but the message was sufficient unto itself. Even if the messenger did not return, the Curse of the Dust would still be heralded in the judgment halls of each of the United States and all foreign governments with which the Adam had relations — and many which he didn't.

The state of North Iowa would be declared dissolved. Ownership of property would no longer be recognized. Contracts with citizens of North Iowa would no longer be recognized. All marriages in the rogue state would be declared dissolved. All debts, large and small, would be declared null and void. All slaves would be declared free of their masters - and free to repay stroke for stroke upon their masters - without fear reprisal under the law. Law, in fact, would cease to exist in North Iowa.

War would ensue, death would reign and the land that was once the flower of the United States of America would be consumed in a land grab like none since the Time of Madness.

LaFranc rolled the scroll up and set it aside, then examined the remaining contents of Sencha's box. There was a diminutive quill and stoppered ink bottle, a small sand box for blotting, and several tiny cylinders.

"I didn't think we carried any pigeons on this mission," Alwyn said as he examined the message writing paraphernalia. "All communication was supposed to be cut off. Too dangerous, you said."

Strom spat out a curse.

"That is true," LaFranc answered. "Perhaps Master

Sencha has been sending progress reports to the Adam. Perhaps the H'ashasine intercepted one of those messages, learned of our mission, our vulnerabilities. Perhaps the H'ashasine used that information to kill Tomsyn and assassinate Sencha."

"Perhaps the Adam dances naked on tabletops and bays at the moon when it is full," Strom retorted. "Perhaps Sencha always carries message writing materials. He is, or at least was, an ambassador, after all. I didn't see a bloody pigeon coop in that bloody box, and I know we didn't carry one with us, so unless Sencha conjured one out of thin air there have been no messages sent, to the Adam or anyone else."

"Someone must have discovered Sencha's mission," LaFranc insisted stubbornly. "Someone who didn't want the message delivered. It is possible that Willam sent his personal H'ashasine, as a precaution against just such a proclamation. If such an edict is never delivered, it can have no effect."

"Paval," Alwyn interrupted. "It is obvious the H'ashasine, if that's what he is, wanted Sencha's death to appear natural. Otherwise he would have used a crossbow, like he did on Tomsyn."

"That's likely," LaFranc agreed.

"Why? Why not just kill him and steal the box? No one would have been the wiser."

"A natural death could be seen as the retribution of Liberty," LaFranc replied. "If the Adam truly is the representative of the God of Five Faces, surely his ambassador would be delivered safe to his adversary. Since Sencha appears to have been struck down not by man, but by God Himself, the Adam must therefore, not be God's emissary."

"No one who knows Willam's thirst for power will believe that," Strom retorted.

"But the people don't know Willam's thirst for power," LaFranc replied. "And they *will* believe."

The big librarian nodded and put a finger to the side of

his nose as if that settled the matter.

# **CHAPTER 18**

**The wind whipped** Franklyn's cloak about his shoulders in a vain attempt to wrest it from the boy and send it flying to some unknown destination. He grasped it and pulled it more tightly around him. It was only the first hint of winter, with occasional blasts of frigid air mingling with the dying breath of autumn.

Stories told around campfires late at night spoke of lands far to the north where it was always winter, where great white bears ruled and the snow and ice never left.

Franklyn felt a shiver creep up his spine and he shuddered in spite of himself. It was not the cold that made him shudder.

Massad stood on the promontory where Franklyn had first encountered him, arms raised, hair wild in the wind, oblivious to anything save his mission. Massad chanted, muttered, cackled, laughed and sang, all in that private language of his.

*It is the seventh day.*

The thought twisted Franklyn's mouth into a grimace.

*Massad curses on the seventh day.*

He still found it odd that Massad used the same unknown tongue to chant the healing words over Pepin.

*Blessing and cursing from the same tongue. These things should not be. It is written, A well does not give forth both bitter water and sweet.*

Franklyn kick a stone in annoyance, turned and walked back to the mouth of the cave he now shared with the Samildanach, the Master of All Arts. Dropping to the ground he allowed himself a scant moment of self-pity.

He was unclean, had become unclean through a selfless act of love and mercy. His action saved the life of his grandfather, but there was no reprieve from the Raek Law. He had been touched by one who was unclean and he was therefore, by Raek Law, unclean.

*I wonder what they told Pepin about me?*

The thought flittered across his mind, but he squashed it like a dung beetle.

Franklyn barked a harsh laugh, then raged against any hint of regret. It was not fair, but then life was not fair...had never been fair. It was likely life never would be fair.

Very well. He was dead. At least all who loved him - and even those who didn't — considered him dead. It was the Law. His name was not to be spoken except as a curse, or as an admonition to those who might be foolish enough to consider breaking the Raek Law.

It was a bitter death.

*The dead don't cry.*

Franklyn brushed away the trace of a tear.

Still Massad chanted in that incomprehensible, reprehensible, powerful, strangely beautiful language.

Franklyn shook his head. Massad talked a lot, just not to him. He spoke to the fire, to the sky, to his book-rolls, to the village that had once been Franklyn's home. He spoke to his meals before he ate them. He spoke to his bed before he lay down on it and again when he left it. He muttered to himself.

*But when he talks to me, he talks to the air, or the fire, or the chair assuming I'll overhear.*

A stray thought wormed its way into Franklyn's mind.

*Perhaps the old wizard is just not accustomed to being able to speak to another human being. After all it's been more than fifty years since he was cast out.*

Franklyn snorted in frustration.

*Or maybe he just doesn't want to talk to another human being.*

The boy who would have been Raek among his people was now the Samildanach's apprentice. Franklyn laughed bitterly at the thought. Casting a last glance toward the old wizard, Franklyn heaved himself back to his feet. Massad would be finished with his ritual cursing soon. He would want a meal when he finished.

*After all,* he thought, a wry smile twisting the ends of his mouth, *cursing is hard work.*

Massad's chants buzzed lightly about Franklyn's ears like gnats around a day-old carcass. Gathering wood to build up the fire under the cookpot he chuckled, remembering his fear of ending up in that pot with vegetables and spices, and stewed until his meat fell from his bones.

For all his reputation, Massad had shown no inclination to devour human flesh. Indeed, though the old man was not squeamish about butchering and eating the animals he captured in his snares, he never caught more than they needed for a meal. He killed them quickly and butchered them efficiently. Massad never tortured the animals he caught. He never burned them alive in the fire as a sacrifice to the gods, neither did he try to read their entrails, as the Nomish priests did.

Franklyn found the old wizard an enigma wrapped in a mystery. He couldn't decipher why the old man had been cast out and proclaimed unclean. The legends of his people omitted that fact, Massad never spoke of it and Franklyn was still too afraid to ask.

*Not that he would answer me if I did.*

Shaking himself from his reverie, Franklyn noticed the scraps of wood still in his hands and bent to lay them on the fire. It was then that he realized the drone of the old man's voice had ceased.

Turning toward the place from which the sound of Massad's voice no longer came, Franklyn's breath caught in his throat. The Master of All Arts stood at the mouth of the cave, arms crossed, studying the boy.

"You are still here," Massad addressed Franklyn directly for the first time. "Why?"

With an effort that Franklyn worked moisture back into his mouth. After a few moments of silence that bordered on terror, he replied.

"It is time to prepare the meal."

"Yes. But why are you still *here*?"

Suddenly aware of the subtle inflection on the last word, Franklyn swallowed, and managed a question of his own.

"Where else would I go?"

"I am a monster. I gobble up bad little children who do not eat their vegetables. Or hadn't you heard?"

Franklyn tried to hold his gazed, failed and turned his eyes to the ground, answering nothing.

"The world is before you. True, you cannot go back, but you could go forward. You have chosen to remain here. I ask you again. Why?"

Franklyn kicked the dust at his feet, and spoke to the fire.

"I am outcast. Unclean. I accept that. I did so willingly. I would do so again. I have left my people, my position, my hopes, dreams and desires. All of my desires - except one.

"My father was murdered by the White Sands Nomes; my mother lived long enough to give me life."

Franklyn studied the dust at his feet and took a deep breath as if fearing his own words.

"You are Samildanach - Master of All Arts. I once

thought your powers to be merely legendary; your spells, your incantations, your potions and magic; merely the stuff of campfire stories. But I have seen with my eyes. You have the power."

Raising his eyes to meet the gaze of the old man, Franklyn said simply, "Teach me. I would learn your arts."

Massad stood unmoving. He studied the boy for a long moment.

"Why?"

"It is written, *I must be about my father's business.*"

Frollo Massad, Samildanach, shook his head, turned to go, then stopped as if listening to the wind. A shudder ran through his shoulders, then he turned and fixed Franklyn with a stare that made the icy wind seem warm.

"Come," he said as if inviting him to the grave. "We will begin."

# CHAPTER 19

**"Lyre," Glenferrin reached** for his betrothed, but she slipped from his grasp, hot tears draining from her cheeks to her diaphanous, delicately embroidered blouse.

"No," she protested through gritted teeth. "Don't touch me."

"Lyre..." Glenferrin stepped toward her.

"No!"

She pulled away from his outstretched arms once more and turned from him, only to encounter a mirror image of herself, cunningly woven into the tapestry that covered the bare rock wall. It was the only decoration in Glenferrin's otherwise austere quarters.

The doppelganger displayed the antithesis of every emotion she was feeling. It smiled; arms outstretched; joy mingled with desire dancing in its eyes.

She had presented it to Glenferrin less than fourteen candles past — a token of their betrothal. It seemed a lifetime ago.

"How can you throw it all away...for creatures that are not even men?"

Gwendelyre's shoulders shook. She turned to face him once more, her right hand clenched until the nails dug into her palms, her left hand brushing tears from her large, luminous green eyes.

"For creatures that are not even men," she repeated.

This time when Glenferrin reached for her she collapsed into his arms, buried her head in his chest and wept.

"Please," she whispered. "Repent."

"You know I cannot."

Glenferrin kissed her forehead, caressed her hair.

"I have done nothing worthy of repentance."

"Then hold your rebellion in your heart, and only say the words," she begged. "It will be enough. Timoth will intercede for you."

"*Rebellion is as the sin of witchcraft*," he quoted in the Holy tongue. "*You shall not suffer a witch to live*."

Gwendelyre did not understand the words. She looked to his eyes for the interpretation which did not come, and drew back from him, shaking her head.

"For me?"

"I cannot."

Nodding, she melted back into his arms. It was that same insufferable, unyielding integrity that had won her heart to begin with.

"Then hold me now, before…"

Neither moved when the knock came. Neither turned when the door opened. Neither responded to the embarrassed shuffling of feet, nor to the nervous cough. But both heard the words of the messenger from the Twenty-Four, and both knew their import.

"Glenferrin, Who Sits at the Feet of the Elder Timoth, is summoned now to appear before the Twenty-Four, to give answer to certain words that have come before them."

Letting go a deep sign, Glenferrin eased his embraced, but 'Lyre clutched him even tighter. Fiercely she crushed herself to his chest. He kissed the top of her head, and with an effort untangled her arms and gently pushed her back to arm's length.

The tears made Gwendelyre's eyes glow and sparkle in a way he had never seen before. He thought he might drown in them if he stared too long.

Holding her shoulders he bent down to kiss her lips. Gwendelyre deftly turned her head.

"It is not permitted," she reminded him. "We are betrothed, not married."

"What are they going to do," Glenferrin laughed softly, "exile me?"

Lifting her chin, he gently brushed her lips with their first, and what he feared might be their last, kiss.

"May I attend," she asked the messenger of the Twenty-Four, as Glenferrin backed away.

Gravely the messenger shook his head. 'Lyre nodded. She was not permitted in the shadow of the Sword - no woman was.

Raising herself to her full height of ten hands, tall for a woman, she looked full into Glenferrin's eyes, reached out and took his face in her hands, drew him down to her and kissed him roughly, fiercely on the mouth.

"Come back to me," she commanded as she released him.

Glenferrin nodded. His answer caught in his throat, but 'Lyre hear him in her mind in the way of friends and lovers.

*Somehow, my betrothed, I will find a way. One day, again.*

Following the messenger through the labyrinthine passageways, lit only by occasional candles set into carved niches in the stone walls, Glenferrin stared wistfully at the life that continued on about him, unabated. He was not startled that in the great hall, in the myriad marketplaces, dwellings and byways of the People, life continued as if nothing out of the ordinary had happened.

He failed to suppress a mirthless laugh, startling his escort.

*No one cares that a fragment of the sacred Sword is missing.*

Then he laughed out loud, drawing more than a few curious glances from people in the passageway.

*Of course they do not care. They do not even know.*

Little that happened in the Shadow of the Sword was known to the general populous. Life goes on. They work, they play. They raise families, and food. They love and die.

The Twenty-Four told the people - through the Speakers, of course - all they needed to know about how to live and how to die; and most importantly, about the One.

But no one, outside The Twenty-Four and the Sitters were permitted to read, and the knowledge of writing had long since passed into legend.

The Speakers only repeated what was uttered by The Twenty-Four, blessing the People in the Holy Tongue. It was rumored - rightly so, Glenferrin thought - that the Speakers themselves did not know the interpretation of the words they spoke. It was enough that the Words were spoken. Absolution was made; sins atoned; salvation assured.

The One was pleased to leave Tyrfingr in the keeping of The Twenty-Four, and the People were content to leave it so. For Tyrfingr was a mighty sword of light, it was said. The unrighteous could not look upon it, for it would blind the unworthy. It would cleave them in twain, dividing their soul from their spirit, leaving them eternally damned.

None but The Twenty-four, those who sat at their feet, and the Speakers were permitted to speak the Words, written in the Holy Tongue by Holy Men of old, before the Great and Terrible Day of The One.

Glenferrin smiled in spite of his circumstances. He loved the Words with all his heart. The Words were Truth. He knew that.

He had no quarrel with the Law that forbade the People to read. It was proper that the People not read, nor even speak the Sacred Words. Who but The Twenty-Four could begin to understand?

*But to deny men access to the Holy Words is wrong.*

He knew that in his heart; had been taught so from the time he was pledged by his mother to sit at old Timoth's feet. Old Timoth himself had taught him so.

*The Words I speak unto you, they are Spirit and they are Life,* Timoth had told the boy.

*Why then, do we deny The Words of The One to those who dwell Outside,* the child Glenferrin had asked repeatedly.

*Some things just are,* old Timoth had tried to explain.

*But why,* the child had persisted. *If The One loves all men, as the Sacred Words say, doesn't The One love those who remain outside?*

*They turned from The One before the Great and Terrible Day,* old Timoth patiently admonished. *Thus they were given over to a reprobate mind.*

*But, does not each man die for his own sins, Timoth,* the child inquired.

*They are no longer men,* Timoth replied.

*But, how can they stop being men?*

*Some things just are.*

*But...*

*No more 'buts'. Some things just are.*

It was as close as Glenferrin could remember old Timoth coming to getting angry with him.

The old man took a deep breath, and paused for a moment, as if battling some invisible war in his spirit. At last he turned to the boy, put his hands and his shoulders, and looked him in the eye.

*Glenferrin, one day, when I have shucked this mortal husk, you will be Timoth. Then you will understand. Today, it is enough to know that some things just are. It must be enough for you.*

But it had not been enough, and even as a child

Glenferrin knew it never would be. More than once he had made his way Outside, though it was forbidden.

He was still a boy the first time. It was amazing; brighter by far than his underground world, lit by an orb of indescribably beauty that hung so far overhead that he had stood for a quarter of a candle just staring at it.

Something unseen had moved across his face, rippling his hair, caressing his skin, causing him to laugh. It moved gently, then disappeared; then caressed him again.

He stared at his arms, watching the fine, pale hairs that covered them waving in time to the caress, and thought it must be the breath of The One.

Slowly the brilliant, beautiful orb descended and then disappeared altogether, leaving the Outside nearly as dark as Inside. It was then that he experienced the most painful lesson of his young life.

The air around him grew brighter by the moment, brighter than a hundred candles, a thousand candles; and warmer; hotter. Searching for the source of this new-found light, the boy cast his eyes all about him.

Then he saw it, and what he saw terrified him. He wanted to turn away. He wanted to stare at it forever.

The orb, which had disappeared completely, was rising again but from a different location, and it was a hundred times, a thousand times brighter than before. It was beyond comprehension.

He felt drawn to it; wanted to grasp it and hold it to his chest. He reached for it, yet it eluded his grasp. He stared at it until the orb was fully visible, though the sight of it stung his eyes.

Its touch on his skin at first warmed him, like the fires of his mother's cookstove. Then his skin began tingling, prickling, burning; the pain began as if he had held his whole body over an oven; its touch on his eyes, at first wondrous, was now painful, blinding.

Somehow he had groped his way back to the little opening that had let him Outside. He scrambled back Inside, relishing the cool darkness, trying madly to force his eyes to adjust to the pale, almost non-existent light of Inside. But everywhere he looked he saw the image of the orb, burned into his mind. He sat in the darkness, hugging his knees to his chest, whimpering.

Slowly, incrementally, his sight returned. He had not been sure that it would. He wept tears of gratitude and repentance.

He wanted to run straight to Timoth and confess his sin. Instead he covered his tracks lest any should discover he had been Outside, and stumbled to his mother's quarters, where she immediately put him to bed, calling of course for Old Timoth to come with oil for healing.

He had been ill for fourteen candles, his pale, luminous skin turning red, then peeling off in layers.

Glenferrin thought he must die. Old Timoth told him he would not, but the old man had not brought the healing oil, either. Timoth had no trouble guessing the cause of Glenferrin's mysterious malady, and determined it was a just punishment from The One.

*Perhaps now Glenferrin would learn to accept the prohibition against going Outside? The world Outside has been judged by The One. The world outside is accursed along those who dwelt there with it,* Timoth chided the suffering boy.

Glenferrin nodded. He trusted old Timoth's word, but wondered how he knew so much of the Outside. He ventured a question through parched lips.

*How was it Timoth knew of such things? Had he perhaps, in his youth, visited Outside?*

Old Timoth roared with laughter, then told the youth to sleep.

Glenferrin had slept. And just as the Elder had said, he did not die, though at times when he rolled over on his bed causing his skin to burn as if it was on fire, he had longed for death to ease the pain.

*Surely the fires of the Pit could not be worse than this*, the boy thought in fevered dreams. He determined then and there to have nothing to do with the accursed Outside.

His determination lasted exactly two-score candles after he was able to leave his bed. He was wiser for the experience, however. Wandering to the hidden opening, he watched until the relative darkness - still bright by Inside standards - fell Outside.

He observed the change from bright to unbearable, and before long he was able to track a pattern to the rise and fall of the orbs. Curiously, the pattern seemed to follow the cycle of life Inside — cool brightness for one candle followed by the terrifying, blinding light for one candle, which gradually gave way to the cool brightness again for another candle.

As he grew older, whenever he was free from his studies, and when Gwendelyre was too occupied with some womanly matter to pay him any mind — *What* did *women find to do all day, anyway?* — Glenferrin often found his feet leading him up the path that lead to his secret exit, and if the candle of cool brightness was burning, he would venture forth to explore the new world he had discovered.

Glenferrin found his reverie broken by the sudden halt before the doors that barred entrance to the Dome of the Rock, the great chamber of meeting which held Tyrfingr, the great and terrible Sword of Light.

He could never pass through those doors without the eager glow of anticipation that crept into his eyes. To stand, or kneel, in the Shadow of the Sword was more than generations of The People had ever dared hope for.

Yet the privilege was his.

He still felt the familiar rush of excitement, but this time it was tempered by a premonition that this might be the last time, for a very long time.

He stood for but a moment before the messenger of the Twenty-Four pushed the two massive doors apart and left him to walk under the Dome, alone. There was no need for ceremony; no announcement of his coming. None was necessary. No one entered the Dome who did not belong there; no one approached The Shadow of the Sword unbidden.

Glenferrin stopped after only a few steps inside the Chamber. The invisible hand that griped his stomach now clenched into a tight fist, and the knot in this throat that had made breathing difficult only moments before, now tried to choke off the air to his lungs completely.

The Chamber itself, with its vaulted domed ceiling resplendent in crystals that flashed like liquid fire at the hint of candlelight, and its majestic gold and red columns that flowed like solid water from roof to polished, obsidian black floor evoked such a sense of awe and reverence that no edict was required to maintain its dignity. This holy place was said to be carved out by the hand of The One himself.

If the surroundings were not enough, in the very center of the Chamber was the Rock, called the Corner Stone, and on the Corner Stone rested Tyrfingr — The Sword of God.

Glenferrin forced air into his lungs in long, slow breaths. Moisture popped out on his palms, but he made no move to wipe them on his blouse. Instead he stood for another moment, willing his heart to beat at a slower, more normal pace, then began a slow, measured walk to the Shadow of the Sword.

The Twenty-Four Elders, he noted somewhere in the back of his mind, were assembled in a semi-circle around Tyrfingr, each standing in their accustomed place. There were no chairs in the Chamber. Each Elder had a young man sitting at his feet.

All except Timoth.

It was Glenferrin's one true regret. In a thousand lives he would never have brought shame on old Timoth; yet he had, and the taste of it was bitter in his mouth.

Along with the Twenty-Four and their Sitters, a great number of the Speakers of the Word gathered in attendance. Glenferrin grimaced slightly at the sight. It would appear that whatever decision the Twenty-Four reached, news of it would be spread to all the People, bringing shame and pain to his family - and to Gwendelyre. It was a consequence he had not considered. Yet in his heart he claimed no sin, and so could not repent of his crime.

All eyes turned toward him the moment he stepped into the Chamber. They followed his slow progression as he knelt in the Shadow of the Sword, spread his arms wide and bowed formally. Rising, he turned and bowed likewise to the Twenty-Four, as was custom, then moved to take his seat at the feet of Timoth.

Glenferrin raised his eyes, hoping to catch a glimmer of hope in the old man's eyes. Timoth would not meet his gaze, but merely turned away.

He was barely seated before the quiet, authoritative voice of The James, First among the Twenty-Four, First among the Twenty-Four, filled the Dome of the Rock.

"Glenferrin, Who Sits at the Feet of Timoth," The James intoned formally, "you are summoned to give answer to certain words which have come before us."

Rising obediently, Glenferrin took his place before the Tyrfingr, the Sword of Light which dispels the darkness and reveals the truth. He knew the ritual. He had witnessed the justice of the Elders on more than one occasion.

"Certain words have come before us, Glenferrin. It has been spoken that you have been Outside."

Though no sign of surprise touched the faces of the Twenty-Four, a murmur filtered through the Speakers, and those who sat at the feet of the Elders stirred uncomfortably. Few ventured Outside, and those who did, did so only at the express orders of the Twenty-Four.

None had been accused of going Outside without permission in more than a generation. The last had been exiled for life.

"It has been spoken," The James continued, "that you have been Outside more than once; more than twice; more than three times."

The murmur became astonished chatter, and the stirring became a jittery rustling. The First among the Elders did not seem to notice the disturbance, but continued on with his accusations.

"This also has been spoken, that not only have you been Outside without permission more than three times, but that you have both seen and been seen by those who dwell Outside."

The Speakers were now openly talking to one another while the Sitters turned to their Elders with searching eyes.

"And it has been spoken as well, that you have spoken with those who dwell Outside — and that you have spoken the Sacred Words to those whom The One had judged accursed."

At this accusation all speech ceased.

All present stared at Glenferrin as if seeing an adversary from the Pit standing before them. To venture Outside might be considered daring by some, if somewhat reckless, not exactly forbidden, but rarely done and then only with permission and for a specific purpose.

But to speak to an Outsider was unheard of; and to speak the Sacred Words, to share a piece of the Tyrfingr with the Accursed, was blasphemous. Unforgivable.

"Speak the truth, Glenferrin," The James commanded, "for the Truth will set you free."

Glenferrin felt a cool chill slide through him from his head to his feet; not an uncomfortable chill, but as if he was suddenly washed clean by some unseen fountain. He swallowed to clear his throat, but found the knot that had been there was already gone. The sweat that had dampened his palms was dry, and he felt at peace with himself and The One.

He was a lover of the Truth and had never lied. He would not begin today, though he was sure his punishment would be severe.

Rising to his full height, Glenferrin strode confidently to within an arms-length of Tyrfingr, knelt and bowed, then rose again and turned to face the Assembly.

"Where are my accusers?"

He addressed The James directly, but allowed his eyes to flow over every face in the Chamber.

"You have been summoned to give answer, not to ask questions," The James replied.

"Is it not my right to face my accusers?"

"You have been summoned to give answer," The James replied once more.

Glenferrin nodded, but his mind would not give up the question. He had no enemies, at least none that he knew of. He had given no offense to any man. Who would betray him in such a way? It made no sense.

"I have been Outside," he said at last.

The collective intake of breath from the Sitters and the Speakers was palpable; the stark silence that followed was deafening.

"I have been Outside more than once; more than twice; more than three times. I have both seen and been seen by some who dwell Outside. I have twice spoken to one who dwells Outside. Once have I spoken the Words of Life to one who dwells Outside."

"Thus do you confess your sin before the Assembly," The James intoned formally.

"I confess no sin," Glenferrin cut the Elder off before he could speak either judgment or absolution.

The eyes of each of the Twenty-Four Elders widened, while the Speakers exploded with exclamations of disbelief bordering on outrage. Accusations of B*lasphemy*! rang out, punctuated by demands for banishment.

Raising is voice to be heard over the din, The James said, "You have answered that you have been Outside more than three times without permission; that you have seen and been seen by those whom The One has judged accursed; that you have spoken the Sacred Words in their presence."

"I have."

"Then you confess…"

"I confess to the acts – not to the sin."

"They are the same."

"They are not."

This time the exclamations burst from the lips of the Sitters as well as the Speakers of the Word. Glenferrin was speaking blasphemy in the very Shadow of the Sword.

"How is it that The One did not strike him dead for his rebellion, Elder Joshua?" Glenferrin heard Aengus who Sits at the Feet of Joshua whisper. "Is not rebellion as the sin of witchcrafts? You shall not suffer a witch to live."

Glenferrin nodded to himself. Not so long ago he might have agreed.

The James raised his right hand above his head. When the Assembly quieted enough for him to be heard, The James commanded simply, "Explain."

Glenferrin took advantage of the lull in the Chamber and launched calmly into his defense.

"Tyrfingr has no prohibition against going Outside. It is a law of man, not of The One. Tyrfingr has no prohibition against seeing, or being seen of those who dwell Outside. It is a law of man, not of The One. Tyrfingr has no prohibition against speaking the Sacred Words to any man. It is a law of man, not of The One."

"The One has entrusted The Twenty-Four with The Sword of Light," The James thundered back. There was the heat-lightning of righteous indignation in his voice. No longer the soft-spoken First among the Elders, he was now the image of the Holy Prophet, ready to dash any idol to pieces with his staff.

"The Twenty-Four rightly interpret the Words, therefore the words of The Twenty-Four have the weight of Tyrfingr."

"They do not," Glenferrin insisted. "They are the words of man, not of The One."

"The One has judged the world according to His Holy Word, as The Mal'chi does say, *The day comes, that shall burn like an oven; and all the proud, yes, and all who do wickedly, shall be stubble: and the Great and Terrible Day that comes shall burn them up, says The One. It shall leave neither root nor stubble,*" The Elder quoted.

"You, Glenferrin, who sat at the feet of The Timoth from your youth; you know the Law better than any save The Twenty-Four. You have been Outside, not once; not twice; but more than three times. Have you not felt the burning with which The One still judges the world? Has it not consumed your flesh and burned your eyes? Are you not already marked by the judgment? Will you repent?"

Glenferrin stood silent for a moment, meeting the eyes of The James.

"I have done nothing worthy of repentance."

"You do not repent."

"I do not repent."

"By your own words, you are judged," The James intoned formally, sadly, the heat gone from his voice.

Gripping the neck of his robe, his gnarled hands began tugging at the material until a tiny rip appeared. Gaining strength, he pulled harder until the sound of his robe ripping filled the hall. He pulled until his garment was rent from top to bottom, then with formal finality he turned his back on Glenferrin.

The Marc rose to his feet, ripped his robe and turned

away. The Jude followed immediately after, then the Mal'chi. One by one, each of the Twenty-Four Elders stood, rent his garments from top to bottom, and turn his face away. The last, old Timoth, allowed a single tear to fall as his aged fingers ripped his robe, and he too, turned his back on his disciple.

Glenferrin stood alone, stoic. He had suspected it might come to this. There would be no concern for why; no mitigating circumstances; no pleas for clemency.

No one had challenged the authority of the Twenty-Four in nearly three hundred years. The Elders would not allow a challenge now. Their way of life depended on their absolute authority.

In their eyes there was no justification. There was only guilt of high treason, and only one punishment, though it has not been executed in nearly three hundred years.

The James motioned a Speaker of the Words, who promptly made his way to the Elder. Glenferrin did not need to hear the Speaker formally announce the verdict to know his punishment.

There were tears in the Speaker's eyes, but his voice was strong and steady, as befitted his station.

"Glenferrin, who Sits at the Feet of Timoth, having confessed to the crimes of willful and knowing disobedience, is judged guilty of treason. It is the will of The Twenty-Four Elders that Glenferrin be no longer known as He Who Sits at the Feet of Timoth. His name is to be blotted from the Book of Life, and he is now banished from the realm of men.

"He will be cast Outside, where there is wailing and gnashing of teeth. He will bear chains for his blasphemy. He will not die, but will live the remains of his life Outside, in hopes that he may one day repent.

"Food and water shall we provide each week on The Sab. Yet because he has spoken to those Outside, no one - not even the one who brings him food and drink - shall ever speak to him again."

# CHAPTER 20

**The grotto was** small, barely tall enough for Glenferrin to stand upright, barely wide enough for the mat that served as his bed to stretch from side to side, barely deep enough to allow him to escape the burning rays of the great orb that ruled the day.

There were no other furnishings, save the dull, metal chain that linked Glenferrin's ankle to a "U" shaped peg that had been driven deep into the rock wall of his prison.

Bitter laughter crawled up Glenferrin's throat threatening to choke him until he swallowed it back down; laughter at the irony of it all. He had risked his freedom once, to set a man free from such chains.

*Man should be free, not bound.*

He had, in fact, brought him to this very grotto to nurse him back to health.

*He was a man, no matter that the Twenty-Four consigned all who dwelt Outside to non-human status. He was a man!*

Glenferrin cringed at the sound of the chain, slithering behind him as he walked, like a cave serpent coiled about his ankle, bruising his heal, injecting him with its poison, binding him to his prison, reminding him of his sentence.

*Am I a thief, beyond trust?* he demanded of the two

officers who made fast his fetter.

Two pairs of pale eyes met his without pity. No answer was given. The ringing of the great hammer that drove the final link into the rock wall filled his ears, and despair gripped his heart.

*Is my honor not sufficient to hold me here?*

The pale eyed stare was all the reply he received.

*I have been judged and found wanting by the Twenty-Four,* he had declared. *I will bear their condemnation though my soul is guiltless. But this chain is an abomination to my honor. I am Glenferrin, who Sits at the Feet of Timoth!*

*No one sits at the feet of Timoth.*

The response, though spoken softly, without recrimination, lashed Glenferrin's soul with its whip-crack honesty, and froze the air in his lungs. He fell to his knees, dropped his head into his hands, and said no more.

Twelve candles, six days, had passed since he had been exiled from Inside. Not that he had candles to mark the passing of time. He had learned long ago that the changing of the darkness and the brightness accounted for one candle each; a morning and an evening.

*The Evening and the Morning were the first day. A Day,* Glenferrin mused.

He had learned the words at the feet of Timoth. Though he was permitted to memorize the first books - that task went to Abel, who Sits at the Feet of Dutronomy - but he knew some of the Words.

*Six days.*

It was spoken that the One had created all in six days.

*Were they days like these,* he wondered.

It did not seem possible.

*Perhaps the One uses a longer candle to mark time,* he mused and the thought creased his lips with a brief smile.

Gazing into the deepening darkness, Glenferrin's large eyes gathered in the starlight, like a million candles. The great

Orb that ruled the day blinded him with its glare, forcing him deep into his grotto. But when it descended, Glenferrin found himself drawn back to the mouth of the cave where he stared into the darkness, watching the paler orb rise and rule.

He found could see more clearly here than he ever could Inside. Colors were sharper, shapes more well defined. It seemed he could see forever, with nothing to obstruct his vision. And there was so much to see. So much to learn and no one to tell him it was forbidden.

Except for the links of gray that bound him to the wall.

It was the colors that convinced him that The One must not have abandoned the Outside altogether. The overhead that changed from almost black to sparkling blue to hazy azure and then deepened to darkness again. The ground that varied from dull browns, to brilliant greens, marked by things that grew, he was sure of it, some to incredible heights, some low to the ground.

There was an abundance of animal life as well. Glenferrin found himself spending half-a-candle or more watching small, mole-like creatures capering around the mouth of his cave. Livelier than the furry rodents that the People hunted for their pelts and meat, these little fellows seemed to use their eyes, as well as their ears and noses.

Most amazing of all the creatures Glenferrin had observed, were strange animals that floated in the air, like smoke. They worked their arms in a strange, swimming motion that seemed to keep them aloft, and they appeared to be covered with a substance that was neither flesh nor fur.

Since they were most active when the great Orb appeared, Glenferrin did not have much time to study these creatures, but he had determined there was a large one that must live somewhere up above his cave.

Glenferrin took delight in the small stream that meandered past the cave's mouth. He loved the slight, gurgling sound it made as it stumbled over rocks and fell laughing on itself, and the glittering reflection of the sky lights on its surface during the darkness. Its taste was sweeter than the water Inside; a wild, unfiltered sweetness; rich with life and freedom.

He envied the stream for that freedom. No one altered its course, or dammed it up. It ran from high in the mountains and fell with abandon to the lowlands, slowing at times to linger in small pools before continuing its descent.

It was free.

*Not so free*, Glenferrin pondered at last. *It is confined to its banks, and it must run down; never up. We are all prisoners of sorts. You hem me in behind and before; You have laid your hand upon me. Perhaps The One hems us all in. Perhaps when I did not wear this chain, I was a prisoner still. Strange. I did not consider myself so, before.*

Beyond providing plenty of fresh water, the stream was an unending mystery to him. It abounded with small insects that danced across its surface. He couldn't fathom how they did that.

Then there were the fish, astounding in their shimmering, multi-colored scales; gracefully segueing from shades of red and blue to green and violet, a hundred hues, colors he had never encountered and couldn't put a name to — so unlike the pure white, eyeless fish his father, Padrag, taught him to catch when he was a child, Inside.

Those fish were a staple of the diet of the People.

He was sure these fish must be poison. The streaks of red and blue that ran the length of the fish too spectacular, too vivid for healthfulness.

But then, the whole world Outside was full of colors that had only been hinted at Inside. Was all of the Outside poisonous, too? It did not appear so.

Sound was different Outside, too; thinner, yet somehow traveling farther. He was sure if he shouted he would be heard forever.

During the darkness he heard sounds that were awe-inspiring, and strange; small skitterings, as of tiny feet; wild screams, like a woman in travail, inhuman, fearsome; whispers and whistlings as something invisible rushed, or strolled, past the cave's entrance.

It was a sound that broke him from his reverie — the sound of something walking on two legs. Footsteps, treading lightly across the ground, moving toward him, but haltingly, as if unsure of the footing, or perhaps distracted.

*It is the Sab, the day of rest. They are bringing me food.*

His stomach responded to the thought with a rude grumbling, reminding him that he had dined on the last of the stale bread the two officers had left more than two candles ago. The thought of fresh bread, and perhaps a bit of mushroom, set his mouth to watering.

But all thoughts of food melted from his mind when she appeared at the edge of his vision, carefully picking her way around the rocks that lay strewn down the hillside.

"'Lyre," he whispered, doubting his eyes.

"'Lyre!" he shouted, laughing while tears crept down his cheeks.

He started to run to her, forgetting his fetter until reaching its limit he found his feet jerked out from under him. The world exploded before his eyes. His breath abandoned him as he smacked down hard, face-first on the ground.

He lay there, clutching for air, willing his lungs to breathe, but they refused to cooperate. He thought he might die. At last he managed to wheeze a thin stream of air between his lips.

Rolling to his back he forced himself to be satisfied with the tiny bits of air that trickled with excruciating slowness into his lungs. As the panic receded his breath came easier. At length he was able to drink in large gulps of air, and the sea of flashing whiteness that flooded is vision faded to pinprick dots.

He forced himself to one elbow, then raised an exploratory hand to his forehead and gingerly caressed the already rising lump. Shaking the last of the cobwebs from his head, he sat up to find Gwendelyre staring down at him, her eyes, so large, so dazzling, leaking tears down onto her gossamer gown, her waist-length white hair cascading over her shoulders, framing her face as she reached down to touch his wound.

Glenferrin felt the sensation of hot liquid trickling down his own cheeks as he stared at her, saying nothing. It had not occurred to him that the Twenty-Four would allow his Betrothed to bring his provisions.

Rising to his feet, he tentatively reached out his hand to brush a tear from her face.

"No tears, 'Lyre," he begged in a hushed whisper. "Please, no tears."

Gwendelyre nodded, taking his hand in hers and drawing it to her cheek. Turning her head, she kissed his palm. It was a thing lovers did – a part of the betrothal ceremony.

Glenferrin reached for her, wanting nothing more than to crush her to his chest; to smell the sent of her hair; to hold her forever. The sound of someone clearing his throat brought him up short.

"My lady, if I may remind you, it is not permitted that any should speak to the condemned."

The fat, little man stared into Glenferrin's eyes as he spoke to Gwendelyre, pressing the matter home.

"I need no reminder."

Gwendelyre's voice was music, soft and low, but it was a cold requiem. She spoke to the fat, little man behind her, but her eyes never left Glenferrin's.

"I bring provision, as the Elders decreed, and nothing more, Master Geofmorin."

"Yes," Geofmorin agreed, a hint of skepticism tweaking the corners of his mouth. "So I see. Well...the provisions have been brought, and I have ascertained the condemned still lives, as the Elders required. We must return. I don't like being in this accursed Outside any longer than I must."

"The condemned has a name."

Gwendelyre's voice was music, a strong, swelling symphony. Her fingers traced Glenferrin's lips, brushed the hair from his forehead, the backs of her finger lightly stroked his cheek in a lover's caress.

"It is Glenferrin, son of Padrag and Eithne, known as He Who Sits at the Feet of Timoth."

There was pride in her voice, though it cracked with emotion.

"The condemned has no name that is spoken Inside," Geofmorin chided.

"We are not Inside."

Turning, Gwendelyre addressed Geofmorin directly for the first time.

"We are not Inside, Master Jailer."

Her voice was ice; her stare was daggers.

"As my lady wishes," Geofmorin bowed as low as his girth would permit him. "But as my lady says, we are not Inside. We are Outside. And Outside is cursed by the One; a refuge for demons, imps, and banshees, prepared for the devil and his angels — and condemned sinners. I must insist, my lady, by the word and authority of the Elders, that we return before we are tainted by this cursed land."

There was no hint of submission in his voice, now; no doubt who commanded of this expedition.

"You can bring provisions to this...man...next Sab, if you wish. But for now, we will go."

A curt nod was all the response Gwendelyre made to the fat, little man before she turned back to Glenferrin. Her eyes locked on his and the tears he forbade streamed down her face again, a dam broken that could not contain the overflow of emotions.

She melted into his arms, holding him more fiercely for the shortness of the moment. Glenferrin held her as if she were his last breath, fearing to exhale lest there never be another.

Gently, with painful tenderness, Glenferrin untangled 'Lyre's arms, stroked her face, and whispered, "Go, my heart. No Tears. Please."

"My lady, if you wish to be permitted to return I must insist…"

"I…am…coming, Master Jailer," 'Lyre managed through clinched teeth, her voice cracked and parched.

She stood for a moment more, resting her palms on Glenferrin's chest, gazing into his ice blue eyes, before burying her head in his breast and shuddering a last sob.

The knot in Glenferrin's throat threatened to cut off his breath as Gwendelyre inched backward. At arms length she raised her hand to him, and he stretched his out to hers, meeting palm with palm.

Turning, Gwendelyre walked away, head high, shoulders back. Glenferrin stood rooted, watching her as she picked her way carefully down the hillside, until the pale luminescence of her skin faded into the endless darkness of the Outside.

Only then did he collapse to his knees, impaled by the sudden knowledge of all that he had thrown away in his pride. For the first time he begged the One to take his life.

Candles passed with monotonous regularity. Glenferrin noted the time the great Orb inhabited the sky growing a bit less each day; the relative darkness increasingly ruling the cycle. The thin clothing that sufficed Inside where the temperature varied little, offered scant comfort the Outside environment that went from scorching heat in the light to shivering cold in the dark.

'Lyre returned each Sab, accompanied by the ubiquitous Geofmorin, bringing fresh food, solemn eyes and no hope. It was the torture he dreaded and desired the most. The sight of her filled his senses, giving him the will to live another seven days.

Yet it also filled him with despair. Since her first visit she had been faithful to his admonition to shed no tears. Unable to address him with her lips, lest she be forbidden to accompany the jailer when he brought provisions each Sab, she expressed her love and devotion through her eyes, which appeared more vibrantly emerald in the brilliant light of the lesser Orb.

His own eyes reflected Gwendelyre's emotions, yet there was more to his gaze, an unrepentant defiance that stabbed at her heart.

Faithfully, Sab after Sab, as 'Lyre appeared, it became clear to Glenferrin that she would return each Sab until he was dead. Each visit weighed more heavily on him, as he realized both the burden and the shame he had brought on his beloved.

He wasn't sure when he decided to grant Gwendelyre her freedom.

It was the great, floating creature that finally convinced him. With an arm-span twice the length of Glenferrin's body, covered all over with something that was neither flesh nor fur, the creature's head was white and its body was golden brown. At times it walked, or hopped about, on taloned feet that looked capable of disemboweling a man.

Daily now the creature flapped its way down to the entrance of his cave and stood there eying him as if it would like to rip out his liver and feed it to her young.

The creature's sheer size and ferocious appearance had frightened Glenferrin at first, but when he cried out in terror the creature flapped away into the air. Of late it seemed to sense the powerlessness of its prey, and merely cocked its head to get a better look at this tasty morsel. Glenferrin gathered a stock of good-sized rocks, scrounged from the back of the grotto, to heave at the predator.

Some nights he dreamed of the animal; its razor sharp talons clawing open his belly; its fierce hooked beak tearing out his liver.

Some nights he awoke screaming.

Some nights he awoke disappointed.

*There must be an end to this!*

# CHAPTER 21

**Alwyn lay awake**, staring at the canvas roof of his tent, listening to the gentle snoring that marked LaFranc's sleep. In all the years Alwyn had known LaFranc, he had never known the Chief Librarian to miss a night's sleep. How the man managed to clear his mind of the events of the day, no matter how momentous, and fall into a deep slumber escaped him.

The ragged, stuttering sound of old cloth ripping, followed by the rushing wind of a prodigious exhale, repeated without variation, wasn't as irritating as the root that dug into his hip, or the grave-cold wind that crept under the tent flaps and into his bedroll. For a time Alwyn allowed the rhythmic cadence of LaFranc's snoring to lull him to near unconsciousness.

But every time he almost dropped off a stray thought would jerk him back awake. Foreboding lay on him like harlot after a three-day festival; cold and unresponsive. He stared at the canvas roof, undulating in the wind, rife with brooding shadows that coalesced into fantastic shapes, bidding his imagination to run free with them.

The wind whispered to him between LaFranc's snores, but its message was beyond his comprehension. Still he strained to hear whatever, or whoever, might be hiding in the shifting shadows. Nothing was as it seemed. Alwyn smelled the sour stench of fear, and knew that it oozed from his own pores.

*H'ashasine, within the camp.*

*Impossible!*

*Undeniable.*

*Whose side is he on? Willam's? Julian's? Does it matter? Once we get to White House with that message we're all dead men anyway.*

With slow, measured movements he reached for the only object he had that he knew was exactly what it appeared to be. His finger closed around the hilt of a dagger. Delicately, almost reverently, he traced the three cords that wrapped the hilt, drawing strength from them.

*Cold steel, cool head, fire in the eyes, but above all, balance.*

His fingers traced the cold steel of the slightly curved, razor sharp blade, noting the delicate etchings of twisting knots and fanciful animals that decorated it. Gripping the hilt of his Marriage Knife in one hand, he instinctively raised his other hand and rubbed the scar on his chest; three hair-thin lines of white scar tissue that stood out against his tanned chest, slightly raised; the Marriage scar that sealed him to Catharine, his wife.

The sense of loss that washed over him forced all other thoughts and emotions out of his head, as he knew it would. He allowed the moment to work its magic. He embraced the pain of loss, and used it to clear his mind.

*Cold steel, cool head, fire in the eyes, but above all, balance.*

Slowly, almost imperceptibly, Alwyn slowed his breathing, ruling over his emotions and conquering his fear.

*Cold steel, cool head...*

He allowed his thoughts to draw inward, to feed on themselves. It was what he always did when confronted by a puzzle that seemed to have no solution. It was the same cold resolve that drove him to distant lands and hostile environments, to dig through the ruins of long dead civilizations.

*Cold steel…*

His thoughts whirled, leaves caught in a dust devil on the Amarillo plains, tossed about with no agenda but the need to run.

*They killed my parents…and perhaps my wife.*

The thought drifted through his mind, but failed to settle and was swiftly dismissed, brushed away like a stray fruit gnat. He allowed his thoughts to drift randomly, without conscious direction. He drifted.

*Brush away the dust, gently.*

He recognized the voice as belonging to Malcolme, his father. It echoed in his head, reverberated with import.

*Brush away the dust, gently, one layer at a time.*

He was a boy on his first collection, Malcolme's hand rested on his own, guiding the boar's hair brush in his hand as he swept a layer of dust from the bones of some long dead animal.

*Again.*

Another layer of dust.

*Again.*

Another layer of dust.

*They don't match,* the boy observed, while continuing to brush the dust away.

*It is a mystery, Alwyn, wrapped in an enigma. But Liberty gave us brains to solve any mystery. The secret is in the bones, and the bones will answer if we will only ask the right questions.*

*This animal has been dead for years, perhaps centuries. It might have died before the Time of Madness; before the Great Burning. Much has changed in those years.*

*No, the bones don't always match, but they will eventually fit. Brush away the dust, one layer at a time.*

*Brush away the dust, gently, one layer at a time.*

Alwyn brushed the cobwebs that had fallen over his mind.

Sencha – dead.

Tomsyn – dead.

Both from within the camp. Who was capable? Who had a reason? What did they have to gain?

*Brush the dust away, one layer at a time.*

Sencha was the Adam's ambassador and trusted advisor, a negotiator of rare and compelling skill. But he was a man of secrets as well.

*Brush away the dust…*

Sencha was a man who loved his comfort, his position and prestige, his wealth. He was also incredibly astute, observant and of unequaled intelligence. He must have known the Adam's demands. He had probably helped draft the letter.

He also would have known the death sentence that would accrue to the bearer of such tidings. Would he be willing to die for such a mission?

No, of course not.

*…one layer at a time.*

And the vials for carrier pigeons, but no pigeons. How was Sencha sending messages without pigeons? And to whom? Or were the vials for something else? What would be small enough and valuable enough to be stored in the tiny vials?

Poison?

Whitesnake Root, perhaps?

It made no sense. There were more questions than answers.

Exhaustion finally overtook him while these thoughts played handball inside his head. He knew better than to force it. Sleep would allow his brain to work at its own pace without the stress of demanding an answer. Too many times, he knew, he had lost a solution by pushing too hard.

The long sought after sleep finally closed his eyes as a single thought drifted past.

*Brush away the dust, one layer at a time.*

There was no doubt they were dreams. Sencha *was* dead,

after all; as was Tomsyn - the crossbow bolt protruding from his head proved that. That the two dead men conversed like old friends, or business partners, while Tuk served them hot tea did not concern Alwyn in the least.

The image of Catharine, great with child, sweating in the throes of labor, gritting her teeth but refusing to cry out in pain, caused him to whimper in his sleep and try to force his mind to try to shut out that dream. Catharine stared at him wild-eyed, begging for something, he wasn't quite sure what. Her eyes grew wider, her skin paler. All he could see were her eyes, so large…

He lay on his back, bound about the wrists and tied like an animal to a post. Two unnaturally large eyes peered at him out of the darkness. The face, so pale it appeared to glow in the rising moonlight, would have been frightening had it not been for the sense of benevolence that emanated from it. It held up a knife and reached for him…

That face, so pale it glowed, faded into the background as the raucous laughter of Binnie Tuk filled his mind. Tuk walking like a snowslide down the side of a mountain — slow, inexorable, devouring everything in its path. He threw back his great head and laughed, holding a finger to the side of his nose, indicating that everybody should get the joke. In the next instant Tuk loomed over him, a knife in his massive fist held before him.

*Leave it be, Master Scavenger,"* the phantom Tuk warned, *"for it divides not only flesh from bone, and bone from marrow, but also soul from spirit. It is a power man was not meant to have.*

Tuk whirled about and threw the knife.

The ambassador sat with a Tuk's knife buried to the hilt in his forehead, drinking tea with Tomsyn, the latter with the point of a crossbow bolt protruding from the front of his skull.

They did not seem concerned that they were dead.

Tomsyn stood, put his fist to his chest, and withdrew,

fading into nothing as he walked into the night.

Seeming to suddenly realize he had a knife between his eyes Sencha sat bolt upright, screamed, grabbed his head and died.

*Brush away the dust, gently, one layer at a time.*

Malcolme guided his hand, whisking the boar's hair brush as he flicked layer after layer of dust from Sencha's body.

It was LaFranc guiding his hand.

It was LaFranc holding the brush.

LaFranc was anything but gentle. Each sweep of the brush peeled back the diplomat's skin to reveal another layer, shifting from light to darkness — smeared, bloodied, blackened.

LaFranc would not stop. Each layer revealed more truth about the man, but each layer was a lie.

*Only in the heart will you find the truth, young scavenger,* the phantom LaFranc lectured. *But it requires patience to uncover the heart. Discipline. Dedication. Practice.*

*Cold steel, cool head, fire in your eyes, but above all, balance!*

LaFranc brushed another layer from Sencha's rapidly decaying body.

No honor — only corruption, greed, stealth.

*...one layer at a time.*

Sencha's body began to dry out, to break apart, to turn to dust under LaFranc's incessant brushing until finally there was nothing left but dust, caught in a whirlwind, and blown away.

*Nothing fits,* the boy said.

*The bones don't always match, but they will fit, if you ask them the right questions.*

Strom reached out to shake Alwyn awake, but the scavenger was already staring at the canvas roof.

"I'm awake," he whispered, noting that LaFranc stood by Strom's side.

"Tuk is gone," Strom announced through tight lips.

Alwyn nodded, the bones inside his head snapping into place.

# CHAPTER 22

**In the ten** days since Tuk's disappearance Strom Maxwell had driven the team hard, even for him. Sleep became a luxury, grabbed a few hours at a time when there was no alternative except to fall out of the saddle.

Strom ground his teeth at every delay, but experience taught him that an exhausted soldier was a worthless soldier. Pushed too hard even the best-trained men started making mistakes, and he had made far too many mistakes on this mission already.

If Strom pushed his team hard, he pushed himself all the harder. Where before he had relied on the reports of scouts, now he scouted ahead himself. He doubled back to cover their tracks, and scouted ahead again. He was seldom seen unless he was giving directions, or chewing someone out for carelessness.

Deep within The Ohios, and already compromised to Strom's way of thinking, he took no chances. They rode at night and made use of the thick Ohioan forests for cover, avoiding the thinly populated farming settlements that dotted the region.

Tall pines that may have stood for a century or more dominated the forest, although occasionally a rare and stately oak managed to assert itself. The trees threatened to blot out what little of the sun that managed to peek through the clouds, though they did little to keep the snow from building layer upon layer on the ground.

On the one occasion a grizzled old woodsman noticed the travelers. Strom whispered something to Less Olsyn, and the man had simply disappeared.

Of the twelve remaining riders, eight were always on guard. Sleep rotated in three-hour shifts. Fire was permitted long enough to heat water for tea, then immediately doused.

On the eleventh day, Strom halted the team an hour before the sun rose. More than a few eyebrows raised, but no one raised a complaint. The Forresters methodically set up camp.

Mol Graumet hopped lightly from her horse and knuckled her back before scurrying to the task of building a fire for tea. LaFranc pulled the two canvas shelter-halves from behind his saddle. Within minutes he erected a tent, unrolled his bedroll and was snoring contentedly.

Alwyn unsaddled and hobbled his horse, then made his way to the small fire Mol had started. A cup of hot tea to warm his belly and a moment with fingers outstretched to the fire to warm his hands would help leach some of the perpetual cold from his bones before he sought sleep in the tent he shared with LaFranc.

Mild surprise lifted his left eyebrow when he saw Strom Maxwell squatting on the other side of the fire, pouring steaming liquid from the teapot into a metal cup. He had spoken less than half a dozen words together to Alwyn since Tuk's desertion.

"Thought you'd be out checking the guards," Alwyn grunted as he settled himself beside his friend.

"Thought you'd be sawing logs beside the librarian," Strom shot back with only a slight upturn at the corner of his mouth to offer any hint of amusement. He blew across the surface of his tea and stared at the fire.

"They're good men, Alwyn. They are here because I

asked them to come, and they might all be dead tomorrow. I at least owe them one good night's sleep."

"Does that mean you are only posting single guard tonight, and everyone gets six whole hours sleep?"

A genuine grin split Strom's face, and he chuckled softly.

"Oh, I'm not that lenient. There will be double guards, but we'll pass daylight here, and tonight as well. Everyone will have a chance to get some serious rest and a bit of warm food in his..." noticing a slight bristling from Mol Graumet, who had sidled up between them, he added "or her... belly."

"You've pushed us like a slave-trader for the past ten days, Strom. Why the sudden wave of humanity?"

"I *am* a slave-trader, Alwyn," Strom shot back.

While few in the United States disparaged the practice of slavery — indeed, most agreed their economy depended on it — many in polite society looked down their noses at those who made their living as slavers. Strom had been known to fight duels over a slighting remark about his first profession.

"Bad choice of words," Alwyn apologized.

"Bad choice," Strom agreed, mollified.

"And what do you mean, 'they might all be dead tomorrow?' What makes tomorrow any different from the past month?"

"Tomorrow we enter White House."

Alwyn paused with his cup halfway to his lips, blew across the surface of his tea, and then sipped it slowly, savoring the feel of the hot liquid streaming down his throat.

"Eat, drink and be merry for tomorrow, well... Are you sure? We should still be four days ride from White House?"

"That's what I'm hoping Willam thinks," Strom replied. "You think I've been riding us this hard for my health? We crossed into North Iowa two days ago."

Alwyn nodded and the pair sat in silence for a few moments.

"Did you have to kill the woodsman," Alwyn asked, as if the thought took him by surprise and forced its way through his lips before he had time to retrieve it. "There's no way he could have known who we were or why we were here."

Strom held his cup by the rim in one hand, and swirled the remaining tea around, staring into the fire.

"No way? Are your sure? You are a scavenger, Alwyn. You make your living by making assumptions. You find two stones on top of each other and assume a house was there a hundred years ago, or a thousand. You see what appears to be four faces carved into the side of a mountain in Dakota and you assume it is an ancient holy place of worship, and you wonder why the Fifth Face of God is missing. Did the ancients not know of the Fifth Face? Did they perhaps offend God by not including his Fifth Face? Did he destroy their world for their blasphemous presumption that he has only Four Faces?"

Strom paused, pitched another branch onto the fire and watched the flames lick it, first tentatively, then hungrily.

"Does it never occur to you that maybe the original assumption might be wrong?"

Alwyn's lips twisted in a wry smile. Strom may be overly sensitive about his own profession, but he certainly didn't mind denigrating Alwyn's.

"I assume you're getting at something, Strom, but I need to buy a vowel."

"What's a vowel?"

"A vowel is a kind of letter the ancients used in their written language."

"Right. Of course. How foolish of me. What's a letter?"

A smile creased Alwyn's face.

"As you know, Modern Americans use glyphs for our written language. Every word has a unique glyph. It is a very precise system, though it can be unwieldy. Ancient American, however, used a remarkable system of letters, symbols that were divided into vowels and consonants that could be rearranged into an infinite number of combinations to represent every word in their language. *Buying a vowel* was a method of filling in the blank spaces in a word."

"I have no idea what you just said."

"Sorry. It's just an old saying - something my mother used to say. It means I need some help to understand what you mean."

"Oh."

Strom sipped the last of his tea, still pondering how one buys a vowel, and if one did somehow manage to purchase the letter how that helped him understand anything. He set the thought aside and sat quietly for a moment watching the fire consume the last of the wood.

At last Strom explained, slowly and reverently, as a man talks about his religion.

"In your world, Alwyn, you make assumptions. You have nothing else to go on, nothing to compare your discoveries to. You take something that is completely alien and try to explain it by using something that is familiar."

Alwyn nodded. How else would you interpret such findings?

"In my world assumptions get you killed. Few things are as they appear."

He stared into the dying flames as if studying an object lesson from a master.

"We call that *fire,* but we don't really know what it *is.* Is it good, or evil? It is both, and it is neither. It provides heat; it burns your house down. It cooks your meat; it burns your hand. Does it have a mind of its own? Is it alive? We don't know. Even in appearance it constantly changes; flickering softly; roaring brightly; glowing like a bride on her wedding night with a beckoning warmth."

Alwyn nodded.

"In my world, everything is fire," Strom said.

He tossed the dregs from his cup into the flames and

watched them sizzle, turn to steam and disappear like a phantom, or a H'ashasine, into the blackness of the pre-dawn.

"In my world nothing is as it seems, and if I want to stay alive, I have to remember that.

"Just a woodsman who couldn't possibly know who we were and why we were there? Sencha was *just* an ambassador. Tuk was *just* a soldier. Tomsyn was *just* dead.

"There is more at stake here than *just* a woodsman's life."

Alwyn nodded in the sudden silence, aware that Mol Graumet had disappeared into the night. That Strom was right, he had no doubt. He didn't have to like it.

Alwyn rose and emptied his cup into the fire. The sun started peeking through the trees, and he wanted to be asleep before it got any lighter. He nodded and turned toward his tent, then paused and turned back to the fire.

"Strom, do we have any chance of coming out of this alive?"

"Two chances," Strom grinned. "Slim and none."

It was an old soldier's joke, though Alwyn couldn't find the humor in it.

"Actually, only one chance," Strom said as he poured the last of the tea into his cup.

"If we can reach the High Court without being recognized, Willam will be compelled to receive us, to uphold his own law. Anyone, high born or low, has the right to appear before Willam in the High Court. If we are discovered before that, we're as good as dead."

"How do you know Willam will uphold the law?"

"I know," Strom replied, sipping contentedly.

He watched the embers shift from orange to dull gray as if looking for something constant. Not finding it, his lips curled up in a smile that never touched his eyes.

Alwyn nodded, ducked inside the tent, and crawled into his bedroll. Sleep was a long time coming.

# CHAPTER 23

**Alwyn waited, studying** the city gate, looking for… well, truth be told, he didn't know what he was looking for. Something out of the ordinary. The itch between his shoulder blades, like a dagger waiting to be driven home, made him squirm as he waited.

White House was well named. The thick stone blocks that made up the city walls gleamed brilliant in the morning sun. Those walls rose seven times taller than a man, perhaps 75 to 80 hands high, and were capped by defensive turrets at regular intervals. The top of the walls were thick enough to drive two ox carts on, side by side. Men in armor that shone brighter than the walls patrolled the top of those walls and more took up position at their bottom.

The guards at the gate were tense, and thorough, but no more thorough or tense than the guards at Omaha. People passed through, coming and going, the rich in carriages and palanquins, merchants on wagons, soldiers on horseback, common folk on foot. All were subject to the open scrutiny of the gatekeepers, but none was detained for longer than a few moments. This was after all, America. Citizens of any United State were free to come and go as they pleased. As long as they obeyed the laws of the United State they were in. If not, things could get ugly.

Alwyn wiped his palms on his ragged tunic, swallowed the hesitation that crawled up his throat, thrust himself from his hiding place in the tree line, and joined the steady stream of humanity that occupied the road to White House.

He remembered to hunch over at the shoulders, and walk with a limp. A slight grin played at the corners of his mouth as he considered the beggar's rags he wore.

Outlander fighting men and diplomats from the Adam would definitely draw the attention of the Republican Guard. A poor beggar, one of the great unwashed, seeking a handout from his betters might bring contempt, but little notice.

*Don't do nothin' dumb? Strom Maxwell, you are a genius.*

Strom had it all worked out before they even left Omaha, of course. But that was before Sencha got involved. And now that Sencha was no longer involved the plan had come full circle. The Forresters would remain outside, waiting. They were too few to help in a fight, and too many to try to smuggle inside. Only Strom, LaFranc and Alwyn would enter the city; one at a time, disguised as beggars

The horses would remain with the Forresters. Paupers did not ride. They would reclaim their mounts when, Liberty willing, they returned.

If they returned.

If they did not return, the Forresters had orders to return to the Adam and tell him to prepare for war. Liberty willing, one of them would live to deliver the message.

Strom and LaFranc were already in the city, having left at one-hour intervals. Once inside they would meet at The Oaks, a disreputable tavern on the poor side of town, and from there, on to the High Court.

*Strom does seem to know where the seedier business establishments of any city are located,* Alwyn mused, recalling their earlier rendezvous at The Cap and Gown where Strom had tried to talk him out of coming.

Doing his best to slouch, Alwyn melted into the midst of

the merchants and soldiers, the farmers and the riff-raff, the people who constantly did business in the great capitol city of North Iowa.

Alwyn barely set foot inside the city walls when a fist the size of a small ham closed around his cloak, and jerked him from his feet. The fist's owner, a gap-toothed monster with a three-day growth of beard, a nose that must have been broken a half-dozen times, and breath like stale wine, peered down at Alwyn where he lay flat on his back.

The man's dented helmet and stitched leather jerkin marked him as a soldier, a veteran of more than one battle. Dark slashes on his sleeve had not yet faded, indicating he once held a higher rank than now.

"We don't like beggars in White House," he rasped, hawked, then spat beside Alwyn's head.

Rage colored Alwyn's cheeks. He bit the inside of his lip to keep from cursing the half-drunk soldier and clutched his cloak with both hands to keep from reaching for the Marriage Knife he had tucked inside his shirt.

*Don't do nuthin' dumb.*

Stumbling to his knees, Alwyn bowed before the guard with all the humility he could muster.

*Liberty on high, let it look like humility.*

"Pardon, master," he wheedled. "I was once a soldier like yourself. Oh, not a *great* soldier like yourself, but a soldier, nonetheless.

"I served with President William when he won the Battle of Thousand Lakes. I was wounded, good master. Grievous wounded to the point that I could no longer act as husband to my good wife. She left me, good master. Said she needed a whole man, a *real* man. Fortune has been harsh to me since. I've come because I heard of the President's bounty, given freely to such as myself.

"If you please, good master, could you tell me in which part of the city I might find the President's bounty?"

Alwyn wrung his hat in his hands with such passion that several in the crowd tossed copper rings to him.

"Let him go, Griggs," a voice from the gate commanded. A younger guard with a bright red crest of horsehair flashing from atop his helmet, one who was obviously used to being obeyed, strode up to Alwyn, looked him over and dismissed him as a non-issue.

"And get yourself to the Sergeant at Arms. Tell him I want him to cure you of your hangover."

Griggs blanched, his mouth working but producing no sound. He slapped his fist to chest and disappeared at a quick trot inside the gates.

Staring after the haggard guard, the young officer spoke to Alwyn without looking at him.

"So, you were with the President at Thousand Lakes. Under whose command?"

Alwyn's stared at the man's back, his mind racing to try to remember something, anything, Strom had mentioned about the battle. There wasn't much.

The young officer turned and stared directly into Alwyn's eyes.

"Well?"

"Uh, begging your worship's pardon," Alwyn licked his lips and hoped he wasn't signing his death warrant, "I served under Strom Maxwell. Mad Max, we called him. Oh, aye, he was a fine captain. Not that one such as myself had any intercourse with one such as he, but there was not a man among us who would not have followed Mad Max straight into the embrace of Hel herself."

"Mad Max, indeed," the young officer mused with a chuckle. "On your way, my good man. The President's bounty is to be had at the Dog Gate on the East side of town. You've got a long walk ahead of you, but with luck you can reach it by sundown."

Turning back the way he came, the young officer

admonished the remaining guards to remember discipline, then stopped and looked back.

"They say Maxwell saved the President's life at Thousand Lakes."

"I've heard that, good master," Alwyn replied. "I can't say as I saw it myself, but I have heard it said."

The young officer nodded, then disappeared around the gate, walking swiftly in the direction Griggs had taken.

*So much for not attracting any attention,* Alwyn thought.

A wry grin twisted his mouth. Hunching forward, he bent to pick up the few coppers that lay strewn at his feet, and then limped through the gate.

He found the first shadow-filled alley that presented itself and ducked into it. Once inside far enough to conceal himself from passersby, he stopped to catch his breath and steady his senses. Pressing his back against the wall, he allowed himself to slide down until his bottom rested on his heels.

Little sun reached this ground, and the perpetual shadows kept the snow thick. There were no prints on the white carpet save his own, and some that looked as if they belonged to a stray dog.

*Waiting was an acquired taste,* his father had told him when he was but a lad. Alwyn had cultivated a taste for it, and it had served him well over the years. Now he waited. Time would remove everyone that had witnessed his altercation with Griggs. When he decided to leave the relative safety of the alley, he didn't want anyone to recognize him.

So he waited, and watched the mouth of the alley.

The people who ventured out into the cold and the snow mostly kept to the main roads, which were swept clean by the President's road gangs; prisoners of minor crimes who served their sentences by doing menial labor.

*These Iowans pride themselves on being able to negotiate the snow and ice, and delight in deriding Southerners for their lack of similar ability.*

Alwyn grinned in smug vindication as more than one found their feet swept from under them, landing roughly on their backsides.

*Ice,* he thought, *is the great equalizer of us all.*

The uncertain footing kept people from the secondary thoroughfares, and the wind kept their heads down. If anyone had noticed him at the city gate, they didn't seem intent on keeping an eye on him.

Still Alwyn waited. Impatience could kill a man, and he was facing death soon enough.

*One more moment,* he whispered to himself as he blew on his fingers, still staring intently at the mouth of the alley.

He was just starting to rise when a small mountain of a man strolled past the alley. Gone were the forest-colored cloak and trousers that helped even a man of his size disappear into the gloaming, replaced by North Iowan silk that seemed incongruous on the man's bulk. There was no doubt as to his identity.

Alwyn's jaw dropped to his chest.

*Tuk.*

Trusting the snow to muffle his steps, Alwyn ran with as much stealth as he could manage to the end of the alley. He pressed himself against the wall and peered around the corner just in time to see the renegade Forrester's back disappear into a side street.

Alwyn took a quick glance both directions, then darted after Tuk, all pretense at hunching over and limping forgotten.

*What's Tuk doing here? If he assassinated Sencha, then surely his work is done. H'ashasine don't kill arbitrarily — they are paid for their skill, and paid well. Why would he come to White House unless…*

*Willam.*

It was rumored that many who held power used the

Shadowmen to stay in power. But how Willam had come to the knowledge of their mission with enough advance warning to have his personal H'ashasine infiltrate the team was more than Alwyn could puzzle out.

Distracted by these thoughts, Alwyn rounded the corner of the tiny street that Tuk had entered without slowing down, and ran headlong into the big man.

The impact knocked him down, but had no affect on Tuk at all. Tuk stood like a mountain, implacable, immovable, as if he were waiting for Alwyn to follow.

Reaching down with methodical precision, Tuk grasped the front of Alwyn's shirt with both hands and effortlessly lifted him off the ground until the two were eye to eye.

Tuk glanced down at the snow-covered ground, and Alwyn followed his gaze. With his foot Tuk traced a wide arc in the snow, then looked back into Alwyn's eyes for any sign of recognition. Finding none, he looked back to the ground and scraped a second arc in the snow, inverted, intersecting the first at one end and joining it at the other.

Once more the renegade Forrester looked Alwyn in the eye.

"Find it," he whispered, his breath stained with fear. "Find it and destroy it...before it destroys us all."

Moving with the grace and power of a striking snake, Tuk gave Alwyn a vicious head butt, dropped the stunned scavenger to the ground and faded into the gathering shadows.

# CHAPTER 24

**Something pungent and** altogether unpleasant wriggled its way through Alwyn's nostrils, grabbed the sensitive nerve endings at the base of his brain and yanked him back to consciousness. He tried to jerk upright, fighting to get away from the vile odor, struggling to regain some sense of where he was and why, but found his head snapped back down.

"Quit fighting it and sit still," Mol Graumet commanded. She had a handful of hair from the back of his head in one hand and a tiny glass vial in the other that she jammed under his nose.

Alwyn managed to slap the hand with the offending aroma away, though he was less successful in disentangling Mol's fingers from his hair.

"Go easy on the hair, Mol," he managed between gritted teeth. "I don't have that much left to spare."

Mol gave a soft, ladylike snort and loosed her grip on his scalp.

"Just wanted to make sure you didn't run into a wall or something. This is potent stuff. Been known to make people do crazy thing until they come to their senses."

Alwyn shook his head, still trying to clear away the cobwebs, when the reality of her presence broke over him.

"What are you doing here, Mol?" he exploded as he

scrabbled to his feet.

The instant he managed to rise to his full height he realized the sudden movement was a grave mistake. He went down on one knee, gulping the frigid air to keep from emptying the contents of his stomach onto the alley floor.

Mol chuckled and offered the vial, which he promptly declined.

"You don't know me well, Master Scavenger, but Strom Maxwell should have told you enough to know that I only obey orders that make sense. When they don't I obey my own set of rules.

"Trust you three in White House, to do Liberty alone knows what, while I wait in the snow for a signal that may never come? I don't think so. Besides, you've already proved you can't get along without me. If you'd laid there much longer you would have frozen to death."

Spitting out the sour bile that collected at the back of his throat, Alwyn was at last able to gain his feet without the world dancing a jig around him, and the pounding in his head was starting to recede. He stood bent over, his hands on his knees, breathing deeply.

"Strom's not going to like this."

"I don't give a Tinker's dam whether Strom likes it our not. Strom doesn't have any say in it," Mol replied, too sweetly. "But speaking of Strom, perhaps we had better start making our way toward The Oaks. He doesn't like to be kept waiting."

Alwyn looked at her like a sideways, and slowly straightened to his full height.

"No one knew where we were meeting," he said.

Suspicion coiled around his spine and began to tighten. *Someone knows.*

"Strom didn't make the decision to meet at The Oaks until after we left camp. And how did you know where to find me, just in time, before I froze to death?"

Mol took a quick step backward, but Alwyn reached out and caught her wrist in his grip. A moment later he found himself face down in the alley floor, his arm twisted painfully behind his back and Mol Graumet's knee planted squarely on the base of his neck. With deliberate slowness, Mol bent over until he could feel her hot breath on his ear as she whispered in a throaty, seductive voice,

"Don't ever try that again, Master Scavenger. You're Strom's friend, so I've let you live. This time. But if you ever again so much as touch me without my permission I'll gut you like deer — Strom's friend or no."

Bending even closer she licked Alwyn's earlobe, and then nipped it with her teeth. Alwyn suppressed a yelp that was more surprise than pain, and just as abruptly felt the weight of his captor rise from his back.

Rubbing his ear, he rolled onto his back and stared into a face that seemed carved of ice. There was no hint of pity, remorse or anything resembling feminine charm.

"You don't have to like me," Mol said. "You don't have to trust me. I don't care. I don't give a pitcher of warm spit for your mission, or your God of Five Faces, your precious Adam or your Tyrfingr — whatever that is.

"But I do care about Strom Maxwell, and I make it my business to know where he is. Now, if you want to stay alive I suggest you stop thinking like a man and listen to reason for a change."

Alwyn gritted it teeth and struggled to his feet again. His head was splitting and the churning in his stomach was threatening to overflow, but he swallowed and managed to remain in an upright posture.

"How did you know about The Oaks?"

A hint of a sly smile played around the corners of Mol Graumet's mouth, giving her the appearance of cat that had just discovered a nest of baby rabbits.

"I know," was all the reply she offered. "Now, if you

wish to continue freezing to death you may remain here. I'm going to The Oaks, with you or without you."

She raised an eyebrow at his hesitation, and then turned toward the mouth of the alley.

"Wait," Alwyn muttered, and shuffled after her.

Mol turned back and stood with one hand on her hip, smiling triumphantly. She looked radiant, even beautiful, Alwyn thought.

"I could have taken you if my head wasn't hurting so bad," he said as he walked past her.

"Remember to stoop," she shot back with a tinkling laugh. "And limp."

They made a strange pair as they worked their way across town. Mol took the lead, dragging him down narrow alleys as often as along broad avenues. A couple of times he was sure they traversed the same intersection and told her so.

"Someone cracked your skull for you before you got half a league into the city," she answered. "Someone knows you are here. If that someone is following us I want to know it before we get to The Oaks."

Alwyn nodded his head in grudging admiration. He hadn't thought of that. He wasn't thinking of much of anything, for that matter. His head still felt like it might explode, and nodding his assent had only added to the pain.

Long shadows stretched across the cobblestone road before they reached their destination. Mol led them down a trash-strewn alley that emptied into an unpaved road across from a seedy tavern. A large wooden sign that bore a faded painting of an oak tree swung in the light breeze above the entrance. Common working-class men, farmers and laborers by the look of them, occasionally sauntered in or stumbled out.

Hidden in the shadows, Mol refused to budge further.

"What are you looking for, Mol," Alwyn whispered.

"Something."

"Something what?"

"Something," she hissed, exasperated. "Something not...normal."

"Something...not normal."

"I'll know it when I see it. *If* I see it."

"I freezing and my head hurts."

"Tough."

"I'm going in."

"Move and I'll break your arm."

Alwyn considered going anyway, but a flash from Mol's eyes told him she meant her threat - literally. It wasn't that he was afraid of her. It was just that his head hurt, and a struggle with Mol would only call unwanted attention to them. A few more minutes wouldn't make any difference anyway. He wasn't all that cold.

Alwyn found a discarded wine cask, dusted the snow from it, and sat down to wait while the sun began its slow descent and disappeared behind the city walls. Huddled in his beggar's cloak, and still fighting the affects of Tuk's vicious head butt, Alwyn's mind drifted toward drowsiness.

"Alright, you can go now."

Mol's voice, spoken at her normal volume, jostled him back to full alertness.

"Are you sure," he whispered.

"What are you whispering for," Mol shot back. "We're here. If you wait out here much longer you'll freeze to death."

Alwyn thought of a clever retort but swallowed it before it could creep out of his mouth. Nodding, he started across the street, holding his cloak closed against the wind. Walking as if expecting a blow at every step Alwyn finally made it across the snowpacked street. No doubt about it, Mol Graumet had him spooked.

He looked up and down the seedy looking street, but saw not another living soul. Even the slat-ribbed alley dogs, so prevalent where refuse was as likely to be thrown in the street as hauled to the dung port, had given up the hunt and sought warmer quarters for the night.

The sign above his head creaked wearily in the wind, as if it wished it too could go inside and warm up by the fire. Alwyn tugged at the handle and pulled the door open. He peered cautiously into dimly lit common room.

"Come in or get out, but close that door and do it now."

*The fat little man behind the bar won't win any personality contests*, Alwyn thought.

But hearing additional grumbling from other patrons scattered around the room convinced him that closing the door might be the best way to avoid undue attention. He took a step into the room, but before he could pull the door closed, Mol Graumet shoved past him and slammed the door behind her, cursing the wind and snow loudly and with gusto as she strode over to the fireplace.

"I thought we were trying to avoid attention," he muttered to her under his breath.

If Mol heard him, she gave no indication, but made a grand show of backing up to the fireplace in the middle of the room, making satisfied noises as her fingers and backside started to thaw.

The fat little barkeeper ignored Mol. Dressed in her traveling garb, she looked for all the world like just another working man – scrawny perhaps, but well-dressed enough to look like she could afford the price of a glass of ale.

Alwyn, however, didn't look like he had a ring to his name, and the barkeeper did not appear to be the charitable sort. He kept eying Alwyn as he polished a pewter mug.

Alwyn stood just inside the doorway, wrapping his arms around himself in an effort to ward off the cold. He gazed around the room to find Strom and LaFranc.

It took a few moments for his sight to adjust to the dim light. Scattered, mismatched tables and chairs, occupied by scattered and mismatched men populated the room. Some laughed loudly; some drank alone. Few made eye contact with anyone other than the men at their own table and the serving girls who danced their familiar dance between the bar and its patrons.

Alwyn eventually spotted Strom at a corner table, his back to the wall. He was busy ogling an amply endowed serving girl with long legs, and equally long blonde hair. LaFranc was sitting across the room from Strom, studiously ignoring him and everyone in the room.

Managing a weak grin for his tardiness, Alwyn started across the room toward LaFranc, remembering to stoop and limp. At that moment Strom rose and tossed a ring to the long-legged serving girl, accompanied by a grin and a sly wink.

Strom turned his back to Alwyn, gave the giggling girl a grand bow, then turned and crashed squarely into Alwyn, knocking him to the ground.

"A thousand pardons, good master," Strom apologized loudly.

His breath was so saturated with ale that Alwyn was surprised he could walk. Reaching down, Strom grasped him by his shirt and hauled him to his feet, stumbling into him as he did so, requiring Alwyn to hang on to keep from falling back down.

"Buy a drink, and then ask the barkeeper for a room," Strom whispered into Alwyn's ear. Then more loudly, "Indeed, a thousand pardons. Inexcusable. Insufferable," he slurred badly.

"Here, little father," Strom continued. "Let me make it up to you. A drink. That's what it calls for. No... I insist. Barkeep! A mug of that fine ale for my friend. Sit him close to the fire, you hear? And when that's gone, here... have another. On me."

Strom made a grand show of dropping a handful of gold and silver rings into Alwyn's hand before pushing himself away and stumbling up the stairs to his room.

Mug in hand, the barkeeper motioned for Alwyn to follow. The display of gold and silver transformed the man's countenance from dark and scowling to beaming and eager to serve.

Alwyn limped to a table close to the fire that the fat little barkeeper indicated. He sat, savoring the warmth of the fire, and the pleasant, bitter flavor of the dark, brown ale. He had almost forgotten the pleasure of being somewhere warm.

He gestured to the giggling serving girl that had captured Strom's attention to fetch him another round.

She had sea-green eyes.

The twin influences of the fire and the ale caused his mind to drift, and he found himself recalling another pair of sea-green eyes. He closed his own eyes and for a moment, and the rundown common room in this Liberty-forsaken town was gone. He was back on the plains with the wind sweeping through his hair, looking down on the girl with sea-green eyes who had just become his wife.

He wasn't sure how long he was lost in the memory, but there were four empty pewter mugs in front of him when he finally noticed that neither Mol Graumet nor LaFranc were still in the room. He swore under his breath as the realization brought him back to his senses.

He rose slowly, and none to steadily, as the ale was as potent as any he had ever drunk. Focusing on the bar, Alwyn walked stiffly toward the fat little barkeeper, intent on making it without falling flat on his face.

Alwyn grunted in surprise when his hands made contact with the bar, only slightly downwind from his original target. With exaggerated slowness, resulting from his intense desire to stay in an upright position, Alwyn motioned the barkeeper to him.

"I would like a room, for as long as that will keep me," he slurred as he laid a golden ring on the counter. "And a bath. A hot bath."

The ring disappeared faster than Alwyn's eye could follow. The fat little man gestured to the giggling, long-legged serving girl who promptly took Alwyn by the hand and led him up the stairs and past a series of doors before opening one halfway down the hall.

Still giggling, she fastened her sea-green eyes on his and pointed to the end of the hall.

"The baths are in there. The water is hot. There are plenty of towels." Her voice took on a sultry tone as she asked, "Are you sure you can manage to undress yourself?"

Alwyn nodded his head, then immediately repented as his equilibrium threatened to desert him.

"I'm sure I can manage. Thank you. Maybe I'll just rest for a few minutes before I bathe."

"As you wish," she giggled.

Alwyn managed a lop-sided grin, nodded again as she turned to go, then opened the door to his room and stumbled in. The room was sparsely furnished with a fireplace against one wall, a narrow bed against another, and a pair of ladder backed chairs with woven seats for guest. An earthenware water pitcher and basin sat on a wooden stand in the corner.

Alwyn ignored everything except the bed, and headed straight for it, aching to fall onto it without thought of getting out of his clothes or under the blanket.

No sooner had Alwyn's head hit the pillow than the door burst open. Strom, LaFranc and Mol Graumet rushed in, closing the door quickly and quietly behind them. Still in a half-stupor, Alwyn rose on one elbow and grinned stupidly at his friends as if it were a wonderful surprise that they should all be there together. What were the odd?

"Oh, merciful Liberty," Mol muttered. "I hate it when men can't hold their liquor."

"Hello, Mol," Alwyn managed to slur. "Strom, did you know Mol was here? She tried to kill me."

The stupid grin came back to his face and Alwyn

laughed as if it were the funniest thing he had ever heard.

The next instant he found himself yanked off the bed and thrust face first into a basin full of icy water. He thrashed about wildly, desperate for a breath, when suddenly the hand that had forced his head beneath the water now jerked him back up.

Sputtering and swearing, Alwyn lashed out at his captors, but to no avail. He had time for a couple of quick breaths before his head was once again forced under the water. A second and third time the ritual was repeated before Strom at last allowed him to drop to the floor, gasping for air.

"I said *a* drink, Alwyn. I didn't tell you to drain the whole keg," Strom chided.

"Balance, Alwyn," Paval LaFranc's booming bass voice drew his attention. "Cool head, fire in your eyes, but above all – balance. A man should know his limits and not exceed them, particularly in matters of wine and women."

Alwyn shook the water from his eyes, still coughing up some that he had inhaled. He might still be drunk, but he was now a wide-awake drunk. His thinking might not be entirely clear, but at least he could think.

"Now, what's this about Mol trying to kill you?"

Strom pulled one of the ladder backed chairs to him, turned it around backward and sat straddle-legged with his head resting on the back of his hands on the back of the chair. From this vantage point he was able to look Alwyn in the eye.

"I told her to look after you."

"You told her what!?"

"Don't get your small clothes in a wad, Alwyn. You're not used to this sort of thing, and I just wanted to make sure you got here in one piece. You weren't supposed to see her, and I'm still waiting for an explanation about that."

Strom directed that remark at Mol Graumet, who ignored it completely.

As memories seeped back through the ale-induced fog,

Alwyn related his meeting with Binnie Tuk, gingerly rubbing the knot on his head where Tuk had butted him to unconsciousness.

"These kinds of blows to the head can be most dangerous," LaFranc warned.

He grasped Alwyn's head between his massive hands and examine the bump.

"This stupor may be as much a result of the blow as the ale."

LaFranc looked into Alwyn's eyes, and directed him to look at the light, observing the contraction and dilation of the pupils.

"Either you are very lucky, or our friend Tuk is an expert," he said. "If he had hit you any harder you would be dead, or your brain would be so damaged you would never think again. As it is, you will have a very bad headache, but not much more."

"Tuk *is* an expert," Strom answered. "If he wanted Alwyn dead, Alwyn would be dead – Mol Graumet or no Mol Graumet."

Mol sniffed derisively.

"He obviously wants Alwyn alive. But why?"

Strom stood and paced the room like a caged mountain cat.

"The H'ashasine doesn't give warnings, and they never reveal themselves. Tuk has done both. It makes no sense."

Strom strode back to Alwyn, and grasping him by the shoulders, stood him on his feet. Slapping him gently on the cheeks he asked him, "Other than knocking you senseless, did Tuk do anything... say anything that might shed a little light on the subject?"

Alwyn put up his hands, trying vainly to ward off the irritating blows, and finally convinced his friend that he was sober enough to think without outside stimuli.

"He said, *Find it. Destroy it. Before it destroys us all.* He was afraid, Strom."

"I've never known Binnie Tuk to be afraid of anything," Strom answered doubtfully.

"He was afraid," Alwyn shot back. "And he drew something in the snow with his boot, a symbol of some kind. I think he expected me to know what it meant."

Alwyn's eyes widened suddenly at the memory of a night when another man he knew, who never showed fear, was afraid. That man had drawn the same symbol in the dust.

"He drew an arc," Alwyn fixed Strom with an unflinching stare. "Then he waited for me to do something. I didn't know what to do, so I just stood there with a dumb look on my face. Then he drew another arc, inverted, joining the first at one end — intersecting it at the other. *Find it,* he said. *Destroy it. Before it destroys us all.*"

Alwyn's eyes passed from Strom to LaFranc to Mol. A brief flash of recognition lit LaFranc's eyes, but Mol looked both bewildered and bored, as if it meant nothing to her.

Strom lowered his eyes.

"I told you not to come," he muttered.

"What is it, Strom? What could make someone like Binnie Tuk...and you...afraid?"

Strom exhaled deeply, rose from the chair, walked to the basin and splashed icy water on his face. Resting his elbows on the washstand, he allowed the water to drip from his face back into the basin, each drop distorting his reflection in concentric waves of doubt and certainty. He studied his wavering reflection for a moment, allowing the memories to filter back into his consciousness; and then he began.

"I road with Willam during the Canadian Wars. That was ten years ago. Willam was young, not yet twenty, but he carried himself like a king. He was big — head and shoulders taller than anyone else — and he was born to the sword. He found more pure joy in battle than any veteran of a hundred campaigns that I had ever known.

"He was fierce; implacable. He offered no quarter and asked none. He led his troops with confidence and determination. They would have followed him to the gates of Hel if he just gave them the word. He never lost. Never. Until…"

Strom reached for a towel, patted his face, and turned to face his companions. His eyes misted over with a faraway gaze.

"The battle of Kaibec. Willam was never one to hold back. *You can't lead from the rear,* he would laugh at anyone who said he was too valuable for front line battle. He charged into the thick of of the fight, hacking at anything in his path with that great broadsword of his, driving the Canadians before him, forcing them to retreat.

"Some threw down their weapons and ran. He pursued after them, cutting them down whether they were armed or not, and all the while laughing like a man on a picnic with a pretty girl by his side. Like fools we followed right behind him.

"We pursued too far, too fast. We outstripped our support and found ourselves cut off from our foot soldiers, and out of range of our archers. There were thirteen of us. We ended up atop a hill fighting back to back when the Canadians regrouped and counter-attacked.

"We were going to die. There was no doubt in my mind. But Willam just laughed; not hysterically like those taken by the berserk, but joyfully. If they had attacked us en masse they would have gutted us, but you know how the Canuks love their glory. They fought us man to man, and even as we cut one down, they fought over who would get to go next.

"Suddenly their ranks parted and this giant Canadian - I swear he stood two hands taller than Willam - strode toward us, and he was laughing too. The giant had six fingers on each hand. You could see them wrapped around the hilt of his battleaxe."

Strom shook his head.

"Odd thing to remember after all these years. Willam just sat on his horse, waiting. The big Canuk stopped laughing. He snarled, let out a bloodcurdling scream and ran right at us.

The giant took a swing at Willam with that oversized battleaxe. Willam met the blow with his broadsword. The force of that blow shattered Willam's sword and took the head off Willam's horse, clean through the armor. Willam hit the ground, hard, stunned. He just laid there, an easy target.

"The big Canadian, carried away with the berserk, jerked his ax free and leapt for Willam. I stepped between them and somehow got my sword underneath his axe. I buried it to the hilt in his belly.

"He smiled as he died. They call it the Beautiful Death, to die in battle against a worthy adversary. Something about being carried to some great drinking hall in the sky with their Canadian gods and dead heroes. Crazy Canuk. I never found anything beautiful about death. He fought well, though. Sometimes I'm surprised he didn't kill us all."

Strom licked his lips, and shook himself as if shaking the past off. The light of the present returned to his eyes, and he gave a self-conscious laugh.

"By that time our foot soldiers had caught up with us. With their champion down the Canadians turned tail and ran. Our foot soldiers ran after them and continued to rout the Canadians. They never bothered to see who it was that was wounded on the hilltop.

"Good thing, too. If they saw Willam down, it would have broken their will, I think. There wasn't one of us who wasn't wounded and bleeding from a dozen places. We somehow managed to get Willam on my horse and lead him back down to the camp, to the healers — although I didn't see much point in it."

LaFranc fished into his leaf pouch, pulled out three

fingers full of the aromatic mulch and shoved it into his mouth.

"No point? Why?"

"Because he was dead already – or as good as," Strom fixed the big librarian with a stare, daring him to argue.

LaFranc stopped in mid-chew, levelly returning Strom's gaze, then calmly began working the leaf between his teeth in a slow, grinding motion.

"So you carried him down to the healers for what purpose? To prepare the body for burial?"

Strom nodded.

"He deserved that honor. I wouldn't leave him for the birds."

"You said he was dead," Alwyn sat on the bed, elbows on knees, completely sober now. "Are you saying the man at White House is not Willam?"

"I said he was as good as...dead," Strom replied, the heels of his hands pressed tight against his eyes.

The faraway look returned to his eyes. He saw it as if he were still there.

"That Canuk's blow, the one that shattered his sword? It caught Willam on the side of the head. Willam's sword turned the blade, so the flat of the axe crashed against his skull. He just crumpled to the ground like all his bones had turned to water. No man could recover from such a blow."

LaFranc snorted.

Strom's eyes cleared.

"I've seen death, old man. Plenty of it. I know what it looks like. I know what it smells like. Willam was breathing, but that was all. The left side of his skull was crushed. I thought the healers might be able to make him comfortable. That's all. I left him there with the healers, then I went back to my tent and passed out. It was morning before I came back to my senses. By then the battle was all but over.

"The Canadians retreated back beyond their borders.

Their king agreed to pay tribute, and the Americans declared themselves the victors — if you can call losing a third of your army a victory.

"I went back to the healers' tent to prepare Willam's body for the burial pyre. As I said, he deserved that. But when I got there, he was sitting up, eating and drinking, pinching unwary female attendants on the backside and laughing like he was still cutting down Canadians with his broadsword."

Mol snorted over the pinching part, but other than that there was not a sound in the room. LaFranc paused in his chewing long enough to spit a prodigious amount of brown liquid into a brass bowl. Alwyn just stared.

"Willam didn't have a scratch," Strom continued. "He complained of a mild headache, and couldn't remember anything past the big Canuk swinging at him. When I told him I thought he was going to die, he just laughed and said it would take more than one Canadian with an axe to take him down.

"The healer who tended him called me over to talk privately. He was completely baffled. He told me Willam had died the night before. No breath. No heartbeat. Nothing. Dead. Then this morning he was roaring for his breakfast and demanding to know where his sword was."

LaFranc chewed his wad of leaf slowly, considering.

"Who else knows of this," he asked.

"Only me, the healer, and the twelve other men who were with us on the hilltop. You might know some of them. The healer's name was Tomsyn."

LaFranc nodded as if he had already guessed, and spit again into the brass bowl.

"Would another of those have been Binnie Tuk?"

Strom nodded.

"Bigger and Les Olsyn?"

Strom nodded again.

"We were all there. All except Mol. Mol came later."

Mol Graumet folded her arms beneath her breasts and stared unblinking, as if daring anyone to challenge her right to be there.

"The war was over," Strom continued. "We rode back to White House to a hero's welcome. Willam offered me command of his Republican Guards, and more wealth than I thought existed. I turned him down.

"Alwyn, I've been all over this country and I've seen a lot of things I can't explain. But I've never seen anything that made me afraid just because it *is*. I'm not a man who is easily spooked. But this...this was not natural. I don't know who, or what, Willam Norman was or had become...but he scared me spitless. He made me fear for my soul. I rode back to my estates in Omaha and offered my services to the Sons of Liberty."

Kneeling, Strom Maxwell used his finger to draw in the dust on the floor — one wide arc, followed by another, inverted, joining the first at one end, intersecting the other.

Alwyn and LaFranc stared down at the emblem in the dust, nodding almost imperceptibly. Mol Graumet feigned indifference.

Strom stood, brushing his hands against each other as if trying to wipe away an unseen filth in addition to the dust that clung to his hands.

"On the road to White House, Willam told me he had a dream that night when we brought him down from the hilltop. Only he said it wasn't a dream — it was something...more.

"He said everything was black. Blacker than you could imagine, but in the distance there was a light, flickering, pulling him to it. He was moving toward the light. He said he was moving faster than possible, faster than thought. He didn't know how he knew. Nothing changed around him. He just knew, he said.

"Then he stopped. Before him was the source of the light

that drew him. He said it filled his vision, it was burning but not being consumed. Two arcs, one inverted, joining at one end, intersecting at the other.

"He told me he heard a voice. He said it filled his ears like the vision before him filled his eyes. *You are my son*, the voice told him. *This day I have begotten you. Under this sign you will conquer.*

"As swiftly has he arrived, he started to move away from the light, until all around him was darkness and the stench of death. Then he woke up and was lying on a cot in the healers' tent."

No one said a word. LaFranc and Alwyn alternated stares between the sign on the floor, and Strom. Mol Graumet just stared at Strom open-mouthed.

"By the Fifth Face, Strom," Alwyn finally managed to whisper. "Willam is claiming to be the Son of God?"

Strom nodded.

"And what does this have to do with it?" Alwyn pointed to the symbol on the floor. "I've traveled all over the known world and I've never seen any thing like it. What is it? What does it mean?"

Strom heaved a deep sigh, and lowered his eyes.

"Tyrfingr," he said at last. "It is the sign of Tyrfingr. It is the sign under which Willam was 'called' to conquer. He hasn't made his claim public before now because he didn't know what the symbol was, or what it meant. He was convinced that when the time was right his *Father* would reveal it to him."

"And now he knows what it means," Alwyn said. "Now he will stop at nothing to obtain it so he can conquer...what?"

"Everything. The whole world."

Alwyn nodded.

"*And the kings of the earth, the mighty men and the generals, the rich and the poor, free and slave shall hide in caves and cry to the mountains and say, 'Fall on us and hide us from the face of him who sits on the throne,*" LaFranc quoted the dark prophecy from the Hervararkvida, then spat the spent ball of chewed leaf into the brass bowl.

Mol still stood unmoving, but her face was now ashen, and her lips trembled as she spoke.

"Strom, is he really...I mean is it possible that he is the..."

"I don't know who he is, or what he is, Mol," Strom replied. "But I do know this – whatever he is, Willam Norman is not the Son of God."

# CHAPTER 25

**Alwyn sat on** his bed for a long time after his companions left his room. His headache grew increasingly painful, whether from the ale or the blow he received from Binnie Tuk, he did not know. Nor did he care to ponder. It hurt bad enough thinking about their planned encounter with Willam without the added pounding from a hangover.

Bending over to tug his boots off sent shards of pain through his brain, but he managed to pull off one and then the other, dropping both boots to the floor with a dull thud. He considered crawling into bed and letting oblivion take over, but the stray thought of a hot bath promised by a giggling, blonde-haired serving girl proved an overpowering temptation.

Although he was sobered by the evening's conversation, or perhaps the repeated dunking in icy water, Alwyn still felt the effects of his head injury. He staggered to the door, opened it and surreptitiously stuck his head outside the doorway. Determining the hall was empty, Alwyn padded in stocking feet toward the bath chamber at the end of the hall.

Inside, the chamber's elegance belied the inn's shoddy exterior. Alwyn's jaw dropped as he scanned the room's marble floor, mirrored walls, and elegant statuary. A single attendant, an old woman, dozing on a corner stool, kept careless watch over the six copper tubs, each of which was big enough to hold four grown men. The atmosphere was thick and moist, and smelled of lilac and cedar.

White House was famous for its hot springs, and an ingenious system of pipes funneled the aromatic, faintly pungent spring waters to inns and public baths throughout the city.

Each of the bath chamber's six tubs was filled to within a hand's breadth of the top with steaming water. Only one tub was occupied, and that by a single bather, sunk to the neck in the fragrant water, face covered by a steaming white towel.

Alwyn pulled his beggar's tunic over his head and let it drop to the floor. Balancing on one leg, he hopped like a wounded frog as he tugged off his mud-crusted wool stockings and dropped them on top of the tunic.

A quick yank at the fasteners of his breeches and they joined the pile of rags at his feet. He kicked them to the side toward the refuse bin. He would need them no longer, for tomorrow he would dress in all the finery expected of an ambassador from the Adam's court, smuggled in by LaFranc in his guise as a merchant.

Standing in his smallclothes, Alwyn cleared his throat, rousing the drowsy attendant from her nap.

"Pardon, good master," the old woman yawned. "It's late, and we don't get many calls for the baths at this time. Still, honored to be at your service. My name's Sofie, but most folks just call me Mother."

Fully awake now and conscientious of her duties, Sofie hasted to fetch oil and a strigil from the cabinetry built for such utensils. Although her face was etched with lines and framed by downy white hair pulled back in a severe, matronly bun, Sofie was still a handsome woman; might even have been considered lovely in her early years, Alwyn thought. The old woman still had her girlish figure, though she limped as she hastened about her duties, as if the bones in her knees ground against each other.

"Lie ye down here," she commanded in a grandmotherly voice, indicating a padded table, "and we'll sluice the dirt from your pores."

Alwyn complied gratefully. Washing in the field was not an easy process when you rode all day and froze all night. There had been little time to boil water for cooking and none at all for personal hygiene, beyond a quick spit-bath before crawling into his bedroll. His last real bath had been in Omaha, nearly a month before.

Face down on the table Alwyn felt the tension slide from his shoulders as Sofie poured the warm, pleasantly scented oil on his back. Practiced fingers that were both amazingly strong and surprisingly soft kneaded his muscles, coaxing the knots out and chasing the stiffness away.

The old woman knew her craft. She started at his neck, just behind his ears, and worked her way down. By the time she reached his lower back, Alwyn was so relaxed he wasn't sure he would be able to move.

"You'll have to lose this if you expect me to do my job properly," Sofie declared, indelicately tugging at the waistband of his smallclothes.

"Pardon me?" Alwyn started, and felt the blood rush to his face.

"Ah…I see. You're not from around here. I should have guessed from your accent. A thousand pardons, sir. Old Sofie sometimes forgets that outlanders have a misguided sense of modesty. Here, I'll fetch a towel to cover your privates…not that you've got that much to cover."

The old woman chuckled softly to herself while Alwyn sputtered and a darker shade of crimson stained his cheeks. Sofie swatted Alwyn on his backside on her way the get the towel.

"I must have made that comment to a few thousand men in the years I've been here." She laughed generously now.

"I never get tired of the reaction it causes in you men."

Sofie returned with the towel, and gave a cluck of mild exasperation when Alwyn made her turn around before he shucked his smallclothes and covered himself with the towel.

Back on the table and decently covered - well, as decently as the towel allowed - Alwyn's embarrassment faded and he found himself once more relaxing as the old woman continued to anoint him will the soothing oil. Sofie proved to be both thorough and professional. By the time she finished, he felt like a bowl of thick, gooey porridge.

"Now, off to the sweat room with you," Sofie commanded, pointing toward a door to Alwyn's right. "It will draw the impurities from your pores."

She handed him the strigil and raised an eyebrow as if questioning his ability to use it.

"Thank you, Mother," Alwyn held the towel about his loins with one hand and raised the curved iron scraper with other. "I believe I can manage."

"I suppose you can at that," she laughed. "I'll fetch you in a few moments. You'll still need me to scrape your back for you. I've never met a man yet who could scrape his own back. Nor woman either, for that matter."

Alwyn followed Sofie's pointing finger to the next room. Ladling a generous amount of water from the bucket in the middle of the room onto the heated rocks in a pit on the floor, Alwyn inhaled the steam it created. Easing onto a hot wooden bench, he marveled at the prodigious amount of sweat that oozed from his pores.

He pulled the strigil gingerly across his flesh, sweat and grim surrendering to the dull blade. Stroke by stroke Alwyn scraped away the filth of the journey. Hot, fragrant water spurted from the mouth of a stone fish and disappeared through a drain in the floor. Alwyn rinsed the strigil in the fountain, scraped, and rinsed again. He had almost forgotten what it felt like to be clean.

"Cover yourself if you must," Sofie called out. "I'm coming in to scrape your back."

Laying the towel across his loins, Alwyn called back, "Come on in, little Mother. I'm decent enough, I suppose."

The old woman strode in as if she owned the inn, took the proffered strigil and began her professional ministrations. With practiced strokes, Sofie dug the embedded filth from Alwyn's back, pausing briefly to examine her handiwork, then ordered him to duck his head under the fish's mouth.

She pulled a vial from her apron pocket and poured a small amount of viscous fluid into her palm. Rubbing her hands together, Sofie produced a modest lather and then began working the suds into Alwyn's scalp.

"Not much here to work with," Sofie chuckled as she massaged the soap into Alwyn's hair. "My Hodwyn, when he was alive, had more hair than this - and he was 77 years from his naming day when Liberty took him."

"Well," Alwyn sputtered under the flow from the stone fish's mouth, "grass don't grow on a busy street."

Sofie's fingers stopped working his scalp for a moment, as she considered his comment.

"Pardon, good master, but what does the condition of a road have to do with my Hodwyn having more hair than you?"

Alwyn grinned in spite of the soap that ran from his scalp into his eyes.

"Nothing,        little      Mother.      Just      something my…Mother…used to say."

"Oh, you're a good boy to keep your mother's sayings — even if they make no sense. Now, back under the water. We'll get the soap from what little hair you do have."

After a final inspection, Sofie finally decided Alwyn was clean enough to climb into one of the baths. Clutching the sweat-saturated towel about his waist, Alwyn dutifully followed her back to the main room.

"In you go," Sofie pointed toward the tub with the single occupant. "A nice soak, and you'll sleep like the dead tonight. But you can't go in with that."

The old woman snatched the towel from Alwyn's waist so rapidly that he didn't have time to react. The next instant he felt a whip crack on his bare backside as Sofie playfully popped him with the towel.

"I said, in you go. You don't want to make me tell you again," she cackled.

Alwyn complied as quickly as he could, as much to preserve what was left of him modesty as to avoid another smack from Sofie's towel.

Satisfied that her charge was at last settled comfortably in the tub, Sofie settled down on her stool in the corner, and almost immediately began snoring rhythmically.

Alwyn eased further down into the hot, swirling water and allowed it to work its magic. His muscles, already limbered from the massage and the sweat room, now surrendered all control and relaxed completely.

*I could stay here forever,* he sighed to no one in particular.

Casting a fond glance at the old woman, snoring peacefully in the corner, brought a smile to his eyes and a chuckle to his lips.

"Old woman rules this place with an iron fist," he said to his companion, across the tub from him.

Mol Graumet pulled the towel from in front of her face.

"Yes, she does."

Without another word Mol stood and stepped out of the tub. She stretched leisurely, then walked unhurriedly across the room, touching Sofie gently on the shoulder, rousing her from her drowse.

As Sofie rose and disappeared around the corner, Mol turned and stared at Alwyn, whose jaw had dropped almost below the water line.

Alwyn knew he should avert his eyes. After all, he

hadn't been born in a barn. But he was taken by such surprise that in truth he was far from successful in his quest. He couldn't help noticing that Mol's near-perfect body was marred by an ugly scar around her neck. He wondered what could have caused it, and he wondered why he had never noticed it before.

In less than a moment Sofie returned with a thick, white robe and deftly draped it around Mol's shoulders. With practiced fingers she wrapped and tied a belt around Mol's waist.

Mol bent down and whispered something into the old woman's ear and they both laughed; Sofie with great glee and Mol with a gentle, almost girlish quality. They both looked at Alwyn and stifling another chuckle, turned away.

Sofie fetched Mol's garments, and Mol fishing into a pocket, pulled out a silver ring and passed it over to the keeper of the baths. Sofie bowed and smiled as if she were serving royalty.

Alwyn finally managed to lower his gaze, now that there was no reason to. He frowned sourly, suddenly realizing he had nothing left with which to pay the attendant. He doubted the money he had paid the innkeeper would make its way into the old woman's pocket.

When he looked back up, Mol was no where to be seen.

# CHAPTER 26

**Maddye sat on** the edge of the massive bed she shared with her husband when he called for her, her legs gathered under her, her left hand gingerly rubbing the rising welt on her cheek. Tears welled up behind her startling violet eyes, but she refused to let them fall. She stifled the sob that tried to shake her bare shoulders, and instead held her head high; her gaze level.

In the twelve years of their marriage, Willam had never lifted his hand to her...until now.

The President of the United States stalked back and forth between his desk and the bed, clenching and unclenching his fists, his face a thundercloud. His eyes never left his wife as he continued to berate her.

*"Give me the time, I will give you the names,"* he mocked her. "Well, I've given you the time, and what have you given me in return? I'll tell you what you've given me. Nothing!" he roared.

He flung his hand back, saw her flinch almost imperceptibly, then let his fist fall back to his side. He paced once more, a wolf in front of his lair. Seven paces to his massive rolltop desk. Seven paces back to the foot of his bed.

"No word," he grumbled to himself - then as if remembering his wife was in the room, he spoke aloud through clenched teeth, hurling the words at her like daggers.

"No word. *The Adam's envoy craves audience*...and I don't even know who they are!"

Seven paces back to his desk. Willam snatched up the single, tiny, vellum scroll with the five cryptic words, *A delegation. Twelve. Perhaps more.* He studied it, turned it toward the light, tried to will meaning into it. He crumpled the scrap of vellum in his fist and threw it at his wife.

"No word!"

It only took Willam four paces to reach the bed where Maddye sat, nursing her cheek. He clutched her by her arms and pulled her close.

"Where are your informants, Maddye? For all your boasts of high intrigue, you have accomplished *nothing*. I would have my highest ranking commander hanged if he failed me as miserably."

"Then hang me," Maddye said with a deadly calm that belied the turmoil she felt in her belly. "If I have done so much worse than you, hang me. It was my sources, not yours, that revealed that Sencha was no longer in Omaha. With that information you could have formulated a strategy. But, no. You dismissed it. You believed that ridiculous story of the Adam sending him to the Calif of Orange. I've given you a name. That's more than you've gotten on your own. So hang me if I displease you; but never strike me again."

Maddye's eyes flashed with a smoldering fire that appeared ready to explode into a raging inferno. The fire in her eyes held Willam's gaze and melted the ice in his veins.

Laughing, he pushed her back down on the bed. She stirred him like no woman he had ever known. She exasperated him, frustrated him, and confounded him as often as not. But she also exhilarated him; drove him to exceed every expectation he had ever had for himself. Sometimes he thought she wanted him to be emperor more than he did.

He held her gaze with his own, equally volcanic stare.

He climbed onto the bed, clutched her to him and crushed his mouth to hers.

The Adam's envoy would have to wait.

*The Adam's envoy craves audience with His Highness, the President of the United States.*

The message still rang in Willam's ears as he strode down the wide stone corridor, two Republican Guards flanking his heels and liveried servants scattering or bowing at his approach. It was the message that had driven him to strike his wife for the first time in his life.

The messenger had fared worse. Much worse.

Willam shook his head at the memory. He would have money sent to the man's family, and pay a personal visit to him while he recovered. It was bad business to abuse ones servants, particularly when all they had done was their duty.

*No word!*

The thought burrowed into his mind and refused to be dislodged. He hated being outmaneuvered, especially when the stakes were this high.

A single message from Maddye's informant a week after the envoy left, then nothing. Nothing more from Maddye's informant, and nothing at all from his network of spies. For weeks there had been no word of the envoy, no word of Julian's plan, no word of Sencha's famed double-talk.

No word!

Until now.

Now, when the Adam's envoy craved audience with His Highness, the President of the United States.

*Liberty on High, how did they manage to get across the border and past the city gates without being seen? How did they manage to get past my guards, my spies, my seers and soothsayers?*

A snap of his fingers and the Republican Guard on his right quickened his step.

"My lord?"

"I want a list of the gate guards and the officers over them for the past seven days. I want it on my desk before the sun marks high."

A quick fist to chest and the Guard disappeared without a word. Willam gave him not another thought. By high he would have the information he requested. There was no question about it.

Servants and courtiers alike scattered at Willam's approach, praying to Liberty that the scowl on his face was not directed at them. But Willam Norman had no eyes for them. His eyes were fixed on the door to the High Court, where he held audience with both high born and low, meting out justice with an even hand.

It was there that he would hear the Adam's reply to his demand. It was there that the Adam's envoy waited, refusing refreshment or hospitality until they could deliver the Adam's reply into the hands of His Highness, the President of the United States.

For all the rage in his eyes, Willam had to chuckle at their audacity. They knew the law he upheld for high-born and low. It was his law. He had hanged nobles and upheld the poor thereby. He would not break his law, not even for his own convenience.

He knew it, and apparently they knew it as well. They obviously knew more about him than he did of them. Willam laughed at the thought. His laugh was not pleasant.

Willam burst through the doors of the High Court without waiting for the herald to announce him. The Adam's envoy, four figures dressed alike in black robes which reached the floor and accented with chevrons of pale blue on the sleeves, turned as one to face him. Willam's eyes widened slightly as they passed over the smooth, feminine features of one of the four, and realized it was a woman. Three of the four were unknown to him, but as his eyes rested on the fourth his visage changed from feral anger, to one of genuine amazement bordering on delight.

Ignoring the bows and obeisance of the citizens occupying the Great Hall, the President of the United States ran across the floor with astonishing speed, and to a chorus of amazed gasps, grabbed Strom Maxwell in a bearhug and spun the man around, laughing.

"Only you," Willam laughed. "I should have known."

At last Willam released his hold on Strom. Stepping back a pace, he threw back his head and roared with laughter.

"Your Excellency," Strom bowed formally.

"My Excellency?" Willam chuckled. "That must have curdled your tongue."

His shoulders still shaking with laughter, Willam mounted the dais that led to the Throne of Judgment and took his place, ceremonially signaling he was ready to hear all petitioners.

"Oyez, oyez. Let all who have matters of judgment and justice approach and be heard," a bailiff in court finery intoned formally, tapping his staff three times on the polished marble floor.

There was little in the world that caused Alwyn much nervousness, but he found his palms dampening of their own accord. The trappings of the Great Hall were austere in comparison to the Adam's Chamber of Judgment. Plain red tapestries hung ceiling to floor, insulating the bare granite walls. Ten great, polished stone columns, so large that two men together could not reach around them, supported the vaulted ceiling, thirty feet above. The floor before Willam's throne was of inlaid marble, depicting a pair of scales indicating the equality of justice meted out in this room.

There was a dignity in the simple austerity that suggested neither wealth nor power would be considered here;

only truth and justice.

Wearing Sencha's medallion of office, Alwyn stepped forward.

"May your Excellency live forever."

Alwyn amazed himself by not stumbling over his tongue as he spoke. Somewhere in the back of his mind he registered the audible gasp that rose from the assembled nobility. He had addressed the President of the United States without first bowing, as custom decreed, proving his allegiance to the office of the President.

The move was calculated. As an official envoy from the Adam, Alwyn assumed not only equal, but superior authority to the President. He met the President's gaze levelly, and watched a grin play around the corners of Willam's mouth. Willam did not order his guards to bend the knees of the Adam's envoy, Alwyn was relieved to note. But neither did Willam bow in obeisance to the authority of the Adam.

Stepping forward Alwyn reached into the voluminous sleeve of Sencha's ceremonial robe - how Strom managed to smuggle the garment into the city was still a mystery to him - and retrieved the scroll that contained the Adam's response to Willam's ultimatum.

Before he could take a second step, Alwyn found himself face down with a booted foot on his neck and a long, pointed blade at his throat.

"Hold," Willam commanded.

Alwyn was convinced the blade that left his throat did so with reluctance, but at least it left. The boot on the back of his neck pressed a bit more heavily before it lifted. Heavily muscled fingers grasped his arms and jerked him unceremoniously to his feet, allowing him a clear view the six Republican Guards that had taken such a dim view of him putting his hands where they could not be seen.

Garbed in spotless, ceremonial uniforms, clean shaven, with close-cropped hair, the Republicans reminded Alwyn of the Adam's Libertarian Guards. They might look like a feast-day accoutrement, but these were hard men, accustomed to killing.

Alwyn doubted they needed much of an excuse.

Though the blade had left his throat, it did not make its way back into its owner's scabbard. Indeed, it was joined by five others, each gripped by hands that looked ready to strike without remorse.

One of the six, a young man with a scar that ran from his left eye to his chin, reached into Alwyn's sleeve to discover the weapon he assumed was hidden there. He appeared genuinely disappointed when all he found was a scroll, sealed with the signet of the Julian, by the grace of Liberty, Adam.

The scar-faced young man pointed a warning finger at Alwyn before turning and handing the scroll to Willam.

Other than preventing his guards from slitting Alwyn's throat, Willam merely watched the incident with mild amusement. He took the scroll without looking at it; more interested in studying the messenger before him.

"I would have thought the great Sencha would have known to carry nothing concealed into the presence of the President of the United States," he mused aloud.

"May your Excellency live forever," Alwyn grated formally. "Perhaps the great Sencha did know of such protocol. I, however, am not the great Sencha. I am unaccustomed to such formalities. I humbly beg your Excellency's pardon."

The fire blazing in Alwyn's eyes indicated anything but humility, and he enjoyed the slight widening of Willam's eyes on learning of his mistaken identity.

"Indeed," Willam replied, still more intent on Alwyn than on the Adam's scroll. "Perhaps your traveling companion should have given you some pointers before letting you attempt to beard the lion his den."

A glance at Strom revealed a slight shrug of his

shoulders, but otherwise no indication of remorse. LaFranc looked as if he were fighting to keep from shoving more of his leaf into his mouth.

"Each day brings its own challenge," Alwyn replied. "If we are wise, we learn."

A smile played with the corners of the President's mouth, and he now took the time to examine the scroll more closely.

"You have taken great pains to bring this to me."

It was more statement than question.

"The way from Omaha to White House is hard this time of year. The weather is harsh and the highwaymen cruel. Please accept the thanks of a grateful nation."

Once more Alwyn bowed formally.

"The honor is to serve, your Excellency. But we did not find the way unpleasant and encountered no brigands on the way. Your Excellency's soldiers are adept at keeping the peace."

"And so may you go in peace," Willam replied, allowing his fingers to play lightly over the Adam's seal. With a wave of his free hand he dismissed the Adam's envoy.

"Begging your Excellency's pardon, but we are here at the bidding of Julian, by the grace of Liberty, Adam; the First Man of the Faith. We are commanded to bring a reply to the Adam with all haste."

"Indeed."

The half-smile did not leave Willam's face, but neither did it reach to his eyes. Alwyn began to doubt whether they would leave the room alive, Willam's decree or not.

In a single, swift motion Willam broke the Adamic Seal and allowed the vellum to unroll in his hands. His eyes darted over the glyphs as if they were of no import. He chuckled as casually rolled the scroll back up.

"The great Sencha would have no doubt been made privy to the contents of this dispatch, that he might intelligently discuss the finer points of diplomacy. Since the Adam has conferred on you this honor, I must assume you are aware of what your Adam has demanded."

This time it was Alwyn's turn to grin.

"Your Excellency, if the Adam discussed the matter with the great Sencha, that information died with him. Sencha was indeed with us, but he suffered a stroke on the road to White House, and alas, we had to lay him in the embrace of Hel without the pomp and ceremony he so richly loved. I appear before you simply as a messenger, not as a diplomat. Next time, I promise, I will peek."

Willam nodded, as if it were of no consequence.

"How are you called?"

"My parents named by Alwyn."

Willam pursed his lips, obviously deep in thought.

"Alwyn. I've heard the name. Your calling?"

"By the grace of Liberty I am a scavenger, as was my father, and my father's father."

"Of course, Alwyn Malcolmesson," Willam snapped his fingers, the memory returning like a flood. "Obtainer of rare antiquities, master of languages, interpreter of the ancient tongue...and friend and confidant of Julian, by the grace of Liberty, Adam."

Willam's grin reached the corners of his eyes this time.

"More than a messenger, I think. Perhaps while you visit with us we can find something of interest to occupy your time."

Alwyn grimaced, but nodded his acquiescence. Before he could speak a sudden collective intake of breath forced him to follow the eyes of the President to the back of the Great Hall.

Without fanfare, The First Lady Madeline swung through the doors and casually strolled down the center aisle, graciously acknowledging the bows extended toward her from the nobles gathered in the Hall. The breathless hush that fell over the room was indication enough of the effect she had on this congregation.

Her gown of golden silk fell in soft folds from her bare, milky-white shoulders, gathered about her tiny waist and flowed to the floor in a cascade of frothed lace. Her mane of auburn hair was gathered in a net of spun gold and held in place with an amethyst broach. A faded patch of red beneath her eye spoiled the perfection of her looks, though none but those within two paces could see it beneath the layer of flesh colored power she had applied.

Maddye played the moment for all it was worth, allowing the moment to extend itself as all eyes fastened on her. Reaching the foot of the dais, Maddye curtsied deeply, bowing low before Willam with downcast eyes. Rising, she met his eye with a sly grin.

"My husband, our guests have not been refreshed," she said, her voice a bell of mellifluous tones that rang pleasantly through the hall. "Surely the laws of hospitality extend the representatives of the Adam. And though the Adam has, at times, seemed inhospitable to your Excellency's envoys, that is no reason for us to deny our visitors guest-right."

For the slightest of moments, Willam looked as confused as Alwyn felt. But in less than a heartbeat he was concurring heartily with his wife.

"With your permission," Maddye cooed demurely, "I have ordered rooms prepared, baths drawn and meals delivered to their rooms. Their journey from Omaha has been swift, and difficult, I think, with little time for such amenities."

With a glance from her husband that was at once approving and dismissing, Maddye turned to leave. Casting a meaningful glance toward Strom, she stopped.

"It has been a long time, Strom Maxwell. We must talk of old times."

Strom inclined his head slightly.

"Hello, Maddye," he said familiarly, without the

formality due her station.

Maddye's eyes widened at the use of her familiar name, then she smiled, a cat with a cornered mouse.

"Audacious as ever, I see."

Her look grazed over Alwyn and LaFranc before settling momentarily on Mol. The smile that had crossed her lips broadened and she put a delicate hand before her face as if stifling a laugh. Gathering her skirts, the First Lady left the Great Hall without another word.

Mol stared daggers at Maddye's retreating back and Alwyn would have sworn Mol looked ready to stick her tongue out at her. The cool gaze she turned on Strom would have frozen Lake Omaha, but Strom didn't seem to notice. His eyes remained fixed on Maddye's retreat.

Willam rubbed his chin, as he also watched his wife depart.

"Yes," he said, whether to Strom or himself, even he did not know. "We must talk of old times."

# CHAPTER 27

**Alwyn fell in** behind Strom, LaFranc and Mol Graumet as a tall, scar-faced guardsman that had recently held a sword to his throat, led them from the Great Hall. He was mildly surprised that only two of the Republican guards were detailed to accompany them. He was pretty sure that, even unarmed, Strom Maxwell could kill both guards before they could even draw steel.

Not that Strom had any intention of killing anyone. At least, not right now.

"I am called Jasyn," their sandy-haired guide announced, "Jasyn Grey. First Lady Madeline asked me to show you to your rooms, and to make sure you have anything you require. You have only to ask. The honor is to serve."

Jasyn looked ready to cut Alwyn's liver out, honor to serve or no. Still, the Republican Guard took his duty seriously, talking non-stop as he led the Adam's envoy through the labyrinthine corridors of Willam's palace. He described the history of the wall hangings, the quality of the porcelain vases that sat on polished rosewood stands, and the rarity of the flowers they displayed - grown in houses of green glass, so that even in the dead of winter, First Lady Madeline could have the flowers she so dearly loved.

Alwyn schooled his face to stillness. The glassmaker's art

was highly prized, and highly compensated. A master glazier could demand, and get, exorbitant rates for his skill. One who knew the craft of injecting color into the glass rose to an entirely new level in the eyes of the wealthy. That Willam would engage such a craftsman to create an entire house out of green glass, just so his wife could have flowers in the winter was...astounding.

Alwyn turned his thoughts to his present situation, trying to glean what he could from their escort's lecture.

Jasyn Grey knew, and was happy to detail, the history of each of the Presidents whose portraits hung on the walls. Often he turned backwards as he walked, to make eye contact with his charges, but he never missed a step, or a turn at a crossing hallway.

Alwyn tried to keep track of the number and direction of turns they made. You never knew when you might have to backtrack quickly. He learned that from his father, and found it to be true on a number of his collections. But Jasyn's incessant chatter distracted him, as did the grim and silent Republican Guard who brought up the rear.

Just as he was beginning to believe they were going in circles, Jasyn announced, "Here we are," and thrust open a pair of double doors to reveal a sumptuous suite of rooms.

The common area revealed a woman's touch. It was large and airy, yet the richly brocaded chairs and occasional tables, polished to a gleaming luster, were arranged for intimate conversation. The great stone fireplace had already been laid and lit, providing a pleasant warmth that contrasted sharply with the cold that radiate from the thick granite walls. Thick carpets muffled the sound of their footsteps.

"If you need anything, anything at all, just pull this cord."

Jasyn demonstrated by tugging on a heavily brocaded length of linen that hung from the ceiling, next to the door.

"A bell will ring in the servants' hall and someone will

attend to you immediately. There is a pull-cord in each of your rooms next to the door."

Before Jasyn finished his explanation, a maid servant appeared. Dressed in the pearl grey livery of the White House staff, she blended into the background of the granite walls. Like all servants, she would be nearly invisible unless required.

"You have need?" she inquired.

"These are honored guests of the First Lady. They have traveled long. See to them."

"The honor is to serve," she replied with downcast eyes and a perfunctory curtsy.

"Indeed," Jasyn sniffed.

Turning again to his charges, Jasyn bowed formally, low at the waist, and covered his heart with his hands. "Give me Liberty, or give me death. I regret I have but one life to give."

"This nation was conceived by Liberty. Life, Liberty, and the pursuit of happiness be to you and your posterity," Alwyn responded with equal formality.

Jasyn Grey straightened, gave a sharp eye to the maid, an appreciative smile to Mol Graumet that accentuated the scar on his face, a curt nod to Alwyn, purposefully ignored both LaFranc and Strom, turned on his heel and was gone.

"How are you called," Alwyn asked the serving girl with the downcast eyes.

"My parents named me Gynnea, sir, if it please you. Gynnea Owyn."

She curtsied again without raising her eyes.

"A lovely name," Alwyn replied. "Gynnea. The mythical fire rose that is supposed to grow only on the peaks of the Central Highlands and bloom only in the coldest of winters. It is said to be a flower of such breathtaking beauty that even strong men weep to behold it; of such potent perfume that a whiff renders a man hopelessly in love."

"Yes, sir."

Gynnea keep her eyes lowered. The shudder in her shoulders said she had borne ridicule for such a splendid name. She was a handsome girl with a strong face and golden hair pulled back from her face with a gray ribbon.

*Pretty even in a rustic sort of way*, Alwyn thought, *though few would consider her a great beauty.*

That she had suffered for her name was obvious. She waited silently for the ridicule to begin.

"A fitting name for one with such obvious beauty of spirit."

Gynnea at last raised her eyes, widened in surprise to hear a feminine voice among her guests. Mol Graumet nudged her companions aside and planted herself in front of the startled servant.

"Gynnea, why don't you see if you can find us some light repast; perhaps some fruit and cheese? And then we will need some privacy. We have indeed had a long journey and would like to rest."

"Of course, mistress," Gynnea curtsied deeply, a glimmer of a smile creasing her face at the small compliment, and she was gone, pulling the door closed behind her.

In one smooth motion, Mol pivoted on the ball of her left foot, and caught Strom off-guard with a roundhouse, open-palmed slap that almost knocked him off his feet.

"And just how is it you know *Maddye*, and what are these *old times* that she wishes to discuss with you," she stormed, shaking her finger under his nose the whole time.

Nursing his nearly dislocated jaw with one hand, Strom tried to wave her away with the other. Alwyn joined in with his own observation.

"It would have been nice to know that you were old friends with the First Lady."

The interrogation was interrupted by a sharp knock at the door, followed by a train of servants laden with trays of fruits and cheeses, breads and sweetmeats, along with pitchers that beaded condensation, holding iced citrus, and pitchers that steamed, holding hot, tangy-scented, mulled wine.

Gynnea chivvied the servants along, directing them to set their wares on strategically located tables scattered around the suite, then prodded them out the door just in time for a second wave of servants to enter carrying hot, moist towels for their hands and faces.

It was an amenity that Alwyn would have been grateful for at any other time, but at the moment his attention was still on the Strom's answers.

"Will there be anything else, M'lady?" Gynnea address Mol as if she were obviously the one in charge.

"Not now, Gynnea," Mol answered, with only a slight smirk at the men.

Crossing the room she stood before the girl, who now looked at her with adoring eyes, and pressed a silver ring into her palm.

"You have done well. Will you please see that we are not disturbed until I ring for you?"

A crimson flush rose from Gynnea's chest up to her face. Alwyn didn't think she often heard the word, *please*. With her deepest curtsy yet, Gynnea answered breathlessly, "Yes, M'lady," and backed out of the door without ever again raising her eyes.

Mol turned back to Strom who had strategically backed away, putting a tray of cheeses between himself and the enemy. Crossing her arms beneath her breasts, Mol stood implacably, her right foot, planted slightly in front of her left, was tapping irritably.

"Well?" she demanded.

Holding up his hands in mock surrender, Strom allowed a sheepish grin to play across his face.

"We were…lovers."

Strom lowered his eyes to the tray of cheeses and made a grand show of choosing a small chunk that was white and aromatic, flecked with red and green. He popped it into his mouth, savoring the pungent bite it produced on his tongue. The twinkle in his eye said he was thoroughly enjoying the stunned look on Mol Graumet's face.

*Paybacks are sweet, if fleeting,* he thought.

LaFranc, who had been sampling a chunk of cut fruit that was pale orange and fleshy, licked his fingers and chided the younger man.

"And you did not think this important enough to discuss with us before we arrived? You are worse than a boor. You are a stupid boor."

LaFranc turned his attention back to a plump red berry, ignoring the growing stillness in the room. When Strom Maxwell broke the silence it was with a dead, flat voice.

"Few men have called me stupid to my face and lived, Master LaFranc."

LaFranc popped the berry into his mouth and rolled it across his tongue before he bit into it, letting the juices excite his tastebuds, seemingly oblivious to the threat. He swallowed, then replied.

"And I have called few men stupid who did not deserve it. I am at your convenience."

Stepping between the two, Mol Graumet fix Strom and then LaFranc with the kind of icy stare schoolmarms usually reserved for foolish boys.

"This is an *inconvenient* time to be having this discussion," she declared, stamping her foot for emphasis. "Men and their Liberty-forsaken pride," she added under her breath.

Strom's shallow nod was followed by an equally shallow one from LaFranc, and Alwyn discovered he was able to breathe once again.

Clearing his throat he said, "Strom, perhaps now would be a good time to tell us about your ...relationship...with the First Lady."

Strom poured a pewter mug full of steaming mulled wine and took a long draught. Intentionally wiping his mouth on his sleeve - an act which brought a derisive snort from LaFranc, and an equally disapproving 'tsk' from Mol - Strom grabbed a handful of the red and green flecked cheese, plopped down on an overstuffed chair facing the fireplace and threw one leg over the arm of the chair. Between bites of cheese and swallows of mulled wine, he recalled the events from his youth.

"It was a long time ago, before the Canadian Wars. I was in North Iowa conducting negotiations with the Government for the import of some commodity or other..."

"Slaves, most likely," LaFranc interrupted under his breath.

"...or other," Strom repeated. "The Governor was giving a ball and I was invited. Everyone of importance in North Iowa was there, including the President and his bastard son, Willam. We struck up an acquaintance that night. I knew even then that he would be a man of great importance.

"There really isn't much more to tell. I met Maddye at the ball and we were immediately attracted to each other. The affair was brief, though passionate. She is a woman of rare...giftings."

A slight smile crossed his lips at the memory, but quickly faded as Mol cleared her throat.

"Unfortunately, her husband appeared at an exceedingly inopportune moment and tried to kill me. I managed to kill him first, purely in self-defense of course. I swear by the Fifth Face of God, I didn't know she was married."

"Did you bother to ask," Mol demanded.

Again the grin played across Strom's mouth.

"No," he admitted. "But neither did she volunteer that information. Anyway, as you can imagine, I had to find my clothes and leave pretty quickly."

"You said it was self-defense," Alwyn said.

"Yes, well, it was, and I wanted to stay and clear my name," Strom explained. "But Maddye's husband happened to be the Governor of North Iowa. Maddye convinced me that I didn't really have much chance of a fair trial, given the circumstances. And to stay would have besmirched her name, branding her an adulteress, a crime punishable by both banishment and literal branding. So, to make a short story even shorter, I left. I haven't seen her since."

Strom stretched out his legs, crossing them at the ankles. Lacing his fingers behind his head, he concluded, "As I said, it all happened a long time ago. I'm sure she has forgotten all about it."

A sudden banging at the door interrupted Strom's reverie. The door opened without waiting for an attendant, and a Captain of the Republican Guard strode unceremoniously in followed by four rather ominous looking soldiers.

"The First Lady Madeline craves audience with General Strom Maxwell," the Captain announced. "She requests he attend her at his earliest convenience."

Strom cast a glance at the others. Nodding, they indicated their understanding.

*At his earliest convenience*, meant, *Now*.

# CHAPTER 28

**Franklyn bit his** tongue in concentration as he drew the metal tipped stylus down the vellum. A blue-black line trailed the stylus, staining the prepared goatskin with a permanent blemish.

Massad had shown Franklyn how to soak the untanned goatskin in water and treat it with lime to loosen the hair. He had instructed, demonstrated and instructed again before allowing Franklyn to scrape, wash, stretch and dry the goatskin, and then to rub it down with chalk and pumice stone.

*Measure twice, cut once,* the old wizard often repeated, although Franklyn could make no sense of the proverb. He wasn't cutting anything, and he wasn't measuring anything. Sometimes the Samildanach could be downright incomprehensible.

Once Franklyn completed the process Massad examined the resulting vellum with the eye of a master craftsman, looking for something to complain about in the work of his apprentice. Franklyn had already noticed a pair of obvious blemishes on the hide. Massad merely sniffed and tossed the vellum back onto the table.

"It is a beginning," he said at length. "For all things there is a first time. And now, you shall learn *alchiber*, the making of *deyo*. The paper guild of the Kanetuck wilderness call it *ink*, and they would kill you if they suspected you knew the process."

The old wizard put his finger alongside his nose and winked at Franklyn, as if the boy who would have been Raek had any idea what a *paper guild* was or where the *Kanetuck wilderness* was.

Alchiber, it turned out, was a complex process and it took Franklyn several attempts before he managed a batch that met Massad's approval.

Massad showed him how to select wood from the aromatic gum tree, how to burn it slowly and how to collect the residue the smoke from the rosin produced. The blackened rosin was then commingled with honey and isinglass, the gelatin from goatskin, and pressed into a small wafer. A few drops of water applied to the wafer produced *deyo*, ink that could not be washed away.

Massad spent days instructing the youth in the making of symbols. The old wizard taught with unexpected patience, and Franklyn learn impatiently, soaking up the old man's every word and yearning for more.

Massad taught meticulously, requiring the lad to practice drawing with a stick in the sand, again and again, until every jot and tittle was exact.

*Sand is transient,* Massad told him. *Sand wipes away all mistakes. In time, sand wiped away memory. The dead bury their dead in sand, and in time the dead turn into sand and the sand becomes one with the earth. Even the great monuments of stone in the Dakota and Atlantis are eventually worn down by the sand, until they too become sand.*

Franklyn nodded, as if he had any idea what a stone monument was, or where Dakota and Atlantis were.

*But sand also kept secrets.* Massad lectured. *One day, if you are still here, I will show you some of the secrets of the sand.*

But today was not that day. Today Franklyn sat in the

cave of the Samildanach. Today Franklyn sat at the wizard's table. Today Franklyn drew symbols on the vellum — for the first time. Any mark he made today would not, could not, be wiped away.

With meticulous care Franklyn lifted the stylus, taking care not to drip ink from its nib onto the book roll. Placing the nib back at the top of the previous mark, he made a diagonal line, lifted the stylus and the made another mark straight down, joining the diagonal line at its bottom.

Carefully wiping the stylus tip on a cloth set aside for that purpose, he had laid the instrument on the table beside the vellum, let out a deep breath and looked over his shoulder at Massad for approval.

The Samildanach reached into the pouch by his side and pulled out his oculars. Slipping the curved pieces of metal over his ears, Massad settled the circular bits of glass in front of his eyes, then reached for the vellum roll.

Franklyn held his breath, waiting for some indication from his master that his work was either acceptable, or rubbish.

The old man shot a surreptitious glance at his apprentice, then returned his attention to the vellum, spending more time examining Franklyn's markings than was strictly necessary, comparing it to his own copy. Tossing the roll back onto the table in front of Franklyn, Massad took his time removing his oculars and stowing them safely back in his pouch.

"Well?" Franklyn demanded, realizing he had been biting his lip while waiting for the old man to speak.

"Well?" Massad repeated.

"Well, is it all right?" Franklyn demanded.

Massad paused, studying the youth.

"Read it to me," the old wizard commanded.

Now it was Franklyn's turn to study Massad.

*Read?*

A frown creased Franklyn's brow. It was not a thing Massad had mentioned before.

Massad merely waited, silent, with arms folded. After a moment Franklyn nodded, turned back to the vellum roll and cradled it in his hands as if it were beyond precious. Massad had taught him the sounds each symbol represented. He hesitantly sounded out the gathering of symbols he had just created on the vellum, stammering words from a culture long dead, speaking words whose meanings he did not know and could only guess at.

Massad had taught him the symbols, their names and sounds, and Franklyn suspected they represented more than their names and sounds. He just didn't know what.

Gently laying the roll back on the table, the boy who would have been Raek let his fingers linger on the roll for a moment more, then raised his eyes to Frollo Massad.

"Well?" Franklyn asked.

"Well," Massad repeated once more, holding Franklyn's gaze without a sign of approval or rejection.

"You have read well, yet without understanding, have you not?"

Franklyn nodded, his brow knotted.

"Have I? Read well, I mean?"

"The symbols you have inscribed in your bookroll are old...old beyond time. The ancients called them *letters* and there are twenty-six in all. Alone, individually, they possess little power - much like men. But they can be combined, rearranged into an infinite number of combinations, each with its own meaning. And combinations of combinations can be made, recording thoughts, ideas, history, poetry, science. It is the power to change the world — for good or for ill.

"What you have done, lad, is called reading and writing, a skill known by few. It is perhaps the most powerful force in the world."

Franklyn knew his mouth was hanging open, and with

an effort managed to close it. His eyes wandered back to the vellum, his fingers caressing the markings he had made.

*Writing. He had performed writing?*

Working moisture back into his mouth he finally managed to ask, "What did I write?"

"*It is written*," the Samildanach answered. Appropriate, don't you think? It has been a talisman of your people for generations, has it not?"

Franklyn dropped his gaze to his feet for a moment, took a deep breath and then returned Massad's stare.

"I have no people."

Massad nodded, the hint of a sad, knowing smile curled the edges of his mouth.

"No, I suppose not," he agreed, then continued. "*It is written*. Yes, a powerful talisman for your...for the Amarillo Nomes; a powerful talisman for any people, whether they realize it or not. The only problem is, like most peoples, the Amarillo Nomes have *nothing* that is written. And if they did there is no one among them that would know how to read it."

Franklyn once again dropped his jaw while Massad threw back his head and roared with laughter.

Every rule, every word of wisdom, every Raek Law was proceeded by, *It is written*, therefore something must *be* written. And *someone* must be able to read that which has been written.

"But...the priests, the griols..." Franklyn stammered.

"The griols are family historians for the wealthy among the Nomes," Massad replied. He laughed no longer. "They memorized and tell the tales of each generation to the next. But man can only remember so much, and much is lost.

"The priests? The priests would personally gut anyone who claimed to read. Reading is forbidden to all except the priests, and they do not read for they lost the knowledge generations ago, if they ever had it. That is a secret they would not have any learn, and would kill to preserve.

"You are the first of the Amarillo Nomes to write or read a word in at least twelve generations. It is therefore fitting that your first written words should be, *It... Is... Written!*"

"How can these things be," Franklyn asked.

Confusion seemed to be his constant companion since he had been exiled from his home and people.

Massad only laughed that wild, contagious laugh and shook his great head.

"Too many questions for an empty stomach, lad. Come. It is time for the evening meal. Once we have eaten, we will talk. You wish to know much. Well, lad, It is written, *to whom much is given, much is required*. And right now, I require food."

Massad laughed again, and this time, though he could not say why, Franklyn laughed with him.

The next few weeks passed quickly for Franklyn. Since writing his first halting words on the vellum, he had spent his days pestering the Samildanach for more knowledge. Frollo Massad indulged the boy, pouring a lifetime of experience into a thirsty, bottomless vessel, while Franklyn sucked up every lesson like a leech on dog's neck.

Unlike the Nomish priests who taught with a rod to the back, Massad coaxed knowledge into Franklyn by asking him questions, and then questioning his answers. Most of the time Franklyn left these sessions more confused than when they began. But on occasion a spark of understanding caught in his mind and he found himself delighted by a scrape of knowledge that he didn't know existed. At other times the answer to a long pondered question would pop into his mind when he least expected it.

Every occasion Franklyn was with Massad became an

opportunity for learning. Gathering nuts and berries might carry a lesson on the habits of animals, and how those habits could be applied to life among humans. Building the evening fire might spark questions about the elements of earth, fire, water and wind. Washing their eating utensils fostered discussions on hygiene and its relation to health.

"The first thing you must do," Massad demanded, "is to forget everything, every opinion you have ever held that passes for knowledge. Hold nothing back; not your most cherished beliefs nor the most commonly held opinions of your...the Nomes. If you would learn anything, you must first understand that you know nothing.

"Do not believe your eyes," the Samildanach admonished. "What you think you see is the most untrustworthy of your senses. Do not believe what you have been told. False knowledge is still false, regardless of who teaches it. Do not believe even what you read. Lies can be written as easily as truth, and gain much power for the permanence of the writing.

"Only that which has been examined in the light can qualify as knowledge," Massad insisted. "The power of wisdom is to penetrate behind the world of appearances. And not just the world of physical appearance, but emotional and perceptual appearance as well."

"How can you not trust your eyes?" Franklyn countered. "That which is, is."

"Is it?"

The Samildanach paused to allow his apprentice time to answer.

"Of course," Franklyn replied. "What else would a thing be if it is not what it is?"

"A thing is what it is," Massad agreed. "But a thing is not always what it appears to be."

Franklyn frowned, considering the idea. He did not like the way it tasted in his mind.

"I don't understand."

"The world of emotional appearance, the world as I like it or as I dislike it, the world as I perceive it to be may be the way the world is. But is it just as possible that it is not?"

Franklyn shook his head again, not capturing the old man's meaning.

"You see a man do good to another. Would you say this outward appearance of goodness is a sign of inward goodness?"

"Of course," Franklyn answered. "It is written, *by their fruits you will know them.*"

"Have you ever cut into a potato and found it hollow, rotted from within?"

"Yes, many times."

"But you examined the potato before you cooked it?"

"Yes."

"The potato looked good. To all appearance it was a good potato. You believed it was a good potato. Everything in your experience taught you this was a good potato."

"Yes."

"It wasn't until you cut open the potato that you discovered it was not good."

"Yes."

"Outward appearance of goodness in a man is the same. The outward appearance of goodness obviously might be a sign of inward goodness, but it is just as possible that it is not. Experience is a remarkably poor teacher, as attested by your experience with the rotten potatoes. Even so a man may *do* good and not *be* good."

Franklyn nodded, a hint of understanding gnawing at the edges of his confusion.

"But, if we do not trust our senses, how do we know anything?"

"We don't," the old man replied.

Franklyn expected Massad to burst forth with his

customary laugh, as he did so often when he said something intended to confuse his student. Massad only looked at him expectantly. Franklyn kept silent instead.

"To penetrate beyond the curtain of perception means to transform our opinions, our certainties, our beliefs," the Samildanach explained, "not only about the world we see, but about the world we construct with our knowledge. We must learn to see through what is held forth as knowledge, and recognize the possibility that it may be a mistake.

"Wisdom begins when you learn to doubt," Massad fixed his eyes on Franklyn, willing him to understand. "Learn to doubt your cherished beliefs, your dogma, your axioms. Ask, how did they come to be so? Are they true? Or are they only some ancient ruler's secret desire, clothed in the dress of thought?

"If your beliefs are true, they will withstand the examination of your mind," Massad declared. "If they are false, they will shatter like a clay pot struck by a rod of iron."

The old man laid his hand on Franklyn's shoulder, and smiled.

"Do not be afraid. We live in an already constructed world, one in which we base our beliefs on presuppositions, and our habits on an understanding of the world which might or might not be true. If we would be wise, we must choose to allow our beliefs to be challenged. Indeed, we must seek to challenge our own beliefs, even in the face of the fear that what we have always believed to be true...might be false.

"To know that we know nothing, is the beginning of wisdom."

Massad paused to let his words take root in the boy's mind.

"Bank the fire, then it is time for sleep," the Samildanach commanded his apprentice, then disappeared into the night, leaving Franklyn to obey, and to ponder the beginning of wisdom.

Each day Massad taught Franklyn something new, or demolished some bit of knowledge that Franklyn had been sure was true only the day before. That he was grudgingly beginning to accept that the way he had always perceived his world was likely false no longer troubled him. It was just one more tie to his old life that had been cut.

The first tie was severed when he allowed Massad to use him as a surrogate conduit to heal Pepin. Never mind that his intervention had saved his grandfather's life; Massad had touched him and by Raek Law he was unclean and outcast, his name a curse and a byword.

If he was dead to the Amarillo Nomes, they were dead to him as well. When thoughts of his grandmother, Theodora, or his uncle Jon, or any of the dozens of his councilors, teachers, and friends floated across his consciousness he squashed them like a dung beetle.

*Death works both ways*, he thought.

And if he banished memories of the Amarillo Nomes from his mind, he cherished his hatred of the White Sands Nomes in his heart. It had been his choice to become unclean to his people. He had done so willingly; would do so again. But the White Sands Nomes had stolen the lives of his father and mother. He nourished his loathing, feeding it daily, watching it grow like a stunted thorn tree on the Amarillo plains.

One day, when his hatred was mature, it would blossom with blood-red thorns and scourge the clan that had taken his parents from him before he even had the chance to know them.

*It is written*, he quoted to himself, *revenge is a dish best served cold.*

His reverie was broken by Massad calling him to his

chores. The Samildanach worked him tirelessly, and every chore came with another lesson. Gathering firewood meant instruction into the nature of trees; how they grew, how old they were, how to read the past from the rings within the wood, which kind burned hottest, which burned longest, which was strongest for fashioning furniture or weapons, which kind produced fruit that was good for food; which kind produced fruit that was poisonous.

It was the poisonous varieties that held the most fascination for the boy. And the ones best suited for fashioning weapons.

Franklyn never complained. He had never feared work, and never shrank from a challenge. He performed his tasks in silence, but attacked his lessons ravenously, asking question after question.

Massad answered each question with another question, prodding him, cajoling him, forcing him to order his thinking.

"Answers mean nothing," Massad told him whenever he got frustrated. "To question is everything."

More often than not, Franklyn found that by answering Massad's questions, he answered his own questions. He suspected that was Massad's intent all along, though the old wizard never gave any indication of his motives.

For six days Massad drilled Franklyn, driving him toward reason. On the seventh day Massad did not require Franklyn to perform any physical labor beyond what was necessary to prepare meals. He was free to wander the hills and valleys, to fish the brooks and streams without concern for whether or not he caught anything. If he so desired, he could lay on his back all day and ponder the fantastical shapes in the clouds.

On the seventh day, Franklyn could always find the Samildanach standing on his promontory, casting down his cursed on the village below in that strange, wild, powerful, beautiful language of his.

During the other six days, physical labor was interspersed with what Massad called, *teachable moments*. Mealtime provided the only respite from Massad's incessant activity. The Samildanach kept Franklyn busy from sun-up to sundown, but when the sun dropped below the horizon, physical activity ceased. It was then that the real learning began.

Massad had developed a sophisticated arrangement of reflecting devices that magnified the lamplight within his cave. Far from being a savage environment, Franklyn found the Samildanach's abode comfortable, even sumptuous by Nomish standards, which were the only standards he knew.

After sundown, after the cooking utensils were cleaned and stored following the evening meal, it was then that Massad would pull out a book roll and give it to Franklyn. Opening the roll lovingly on the table, Franklyn carefully removed the lid from the clay jar that contained his cake of deyo. He added a few drops of water to produce ink, dipped the metal nib of his stylus into the ink and painstakingly copied the markings, *the letters*, from Massad's book roll into his own.

After each passage he would read the words he had written aloud to Massad, and Massad would pass judgment whether they were acceptable or not.

"Samildanach," Franklyn asked, "why do we write in the old tongue, and not in our own?"

"We have no symbols of our own to convey this knowledge," Massad answered. "There are other peoples in other lands who have writings for their tongues. The Americans, far to the North have one symbol for each word or idea; thousands of symbols that few can remember. Those who can make these symbols are called *clarks*, and they are highly valued. But their writing is unwieldy."

The old wizard reached over and laid his fingers lovingly on Franklyn's vellum.

"This system of writing, developed by the ancients, is genius. A people who learned this could record their history, their philosophy, their science and folklore. It is a thing most desperately to be desired."

"It is a thing the priests would never allow," Franklyn said.

The Samildanach allowed a smile to crease the corners of his mouth. He touched his finger to the side of his nose, then turned away to his bed.

# CHAPTER 29

**Willam sat motionless** behind his desk, his lips pursed behind steepled fingers. A slight flickering of his eyes was the only sign that he was intently studying the tall, slender man who sat across the desk from him. Though the President's face remained granite, there was a hint of a smile that creased the edges of his mouth, as if amused at his guest's intensity.

Burtyn, clad in the cowl and cassock that marked him as a member of the Guild of Scavengers, a small, exclusive sect of the Librarians, pored over the Adam's letter for the seventh time.

"Well," the President of the United States asked.

"Patience, Excellency."

Burtyn lifted a finger as if to forestall further interruption of his concentration. He leaned forward, intent, his eyes never leaving the vellum scroll he studied.

"Patience?" Willam's voice was emotionless, dead.

"Patience," Burtyn repeated without looking up.

Willam's open palm slammed the desktop with enough force to crack a walnut. Burtyn let out an exasperated sigh, as if he were dealing with a petulant child, and finally raised his eyes to meet Willam's gaze.

"I am…impatient," Willam said in the same flat voice.

Burtyn had heard that tone in the President's voice

before, and it usually meant someone's head was about to be separated from his body. If the thought crossed Burtyn's mind that the implied threat was directed at him, he didn't show it.

"There is a code of some kind here, your Excellency," Burtyn replied.

Willam, he knew, liked strong men who spoke their minds. Weakness he would not tolerate.

"I only need time to find it. Give me the time, and I will give you the answers you seek."

Irony and rage wrestled behind Willam's eyes as he remembered a similar conversation he had had with his wife many weeks before. That conversation had led to a physical expression of his displeasure. The memory forced a brief grimace. He thought of wrapping his fingers around Burtyn's neck, but shook his head as if to himself. Only the thought that Burtyn might be right stayed his hand.

"What makes you think there is a code," Willam asked, forcing himself to sit back into his chair. "The message is straightforward enough. A blind man can see there is no duplicity. Julian has rejected my authority. Simple enough."

Burtyn smiled a toothy, ingratiating smile, the kind he used when instructing the child of a wealthy patron who failed to adequately grasp a simple lesson.

"The Adam may be many things, but he is not simple," Burtyn replied.

"The Adam is a worthy adversary who holds a position of enormous power with both the will and authority to use it," Willam countered. "He needs employ neither guile nor stealth. He issues a command and does not doubt it will be obeyed. He shows no hint of weakness. I like that in an enemy."

The smile that turned the corners of Willam's mouth touched his eyes with an almost boyish eagerness. Willam relished open confrontation, and if death were the end, so much the better. Subterfuge and intrigue irritated him, though he was not above engaging in them. He used guile and deceit, misinformation and carefully placed rumors whenever the need arose without a qualm.

But while such tactics could be effective, might even be necessary, there was no honor in it, and it left the taste of bile in his mouth. He much preferred a direct combat. There was honor it battle, even if you lost.

Not that he had any intention of losing.

Burtyn schooled his feature to stillness and nodded in acquiescence.

"Indeed, Julian, the Adam - or should I say Julian the Apostate - expects his word to be counted as law," Burtyn replied. "He is after all a man under authority, much as yourself. He tells a man to go, and he goes. He tells another to come, and he comes. He tells yet another to do something, and he does it. But he loves his power too much, which is why Liberty in His wisdom has torn the mantel of Adam from him and given it to you."

Willam nodded once, then waited for the scavenger to continue.

"Julian knows his time is short," Burtyn continued. "Therefore he plays the ravening lion. He replies in such a manner as to *appear* straightforward and simple. He must save face. He could not reasonably be expected to acknowledge your claim publicly, yet with the evidence we have supplied he cannot hope to deny your claim privately. Hence, there must be a code.

"Believe me, your Excellency," Burtyn reasoned, tapping the letter with an impatient forefinger, "there is a hidden meaning here and I will find it. It is in the way the characters are arranged, or perhaps the position of the seal. It could even be hidden in the title, or the signature.

"I need not remind your Excellency that I *am* a scavenger, trained to find things long hidden. There is a code here somewhere. I will find it."

"In the ferreting out of secrets you have no equal,"

Willam admitted. "I do not doubt your ability. It is what you do best. But I didn't call you here to discuss the Adam's commands, nor to find any hidden code. For the time being I'll take Julian's word at face value, and deal with it at the appropriate time."

A scowl crossed Burtyn's face.

"If not for my expertise with words, then of what use can I be, your Excellency?"

Willam rose from his chair and crossed to where Burtyn was still seated. He plucked the scroll from the scavenger's fingers and tossed it carelessly on his desk. Settling himself on the edge of his desk, Willam crossed his legs at the ankles and laced his fingers together before him at his waist.

"There is something that troubles me, Burtyn," the President of the United States began. "A mystery, something I do not understand. I don't like things I don't understand."

Burtyn's smile slipped momentarily, but he swallowed hard and pasted the smile back on his face.

"If there is any way I can be of service, I am at your Excellency's disposal. The honor is to serve."

"To be sure," Willam smiled. "To be sure."

Kicking back to his feet Willam began pacing, lost in thought and barely acknowledging the presence of his scavenger. He could have been talking to himself, but only a fool would make the mistake of not paying attention to every word, every inflection.

Burtyn was many things, but he was no fool.

"Julian's envoy," he mused aloud as he paced, "a strange delegation. Strom Maxwell I can understand. He is the commander of Julian's forces, and the finest military mind of our age. Brilliant in battle, fearless in single combat, a swift and sure strategist. But he is also a master of stealth and deception. He can do more damage with a handful of men than most generals could do with an army. There was no better choice to penetrate my borders and get the delegation to White House undetected."

"Indeed, your Excellency…"

Willam cut Burtyn off with the flick of a finger, and the scavenger clamped his mouth shut and waited.

"Paval LaFranc is one of the most learned men in America, the Chief Librarian of the Book Depository at Omaha. Julian no doubt sent him to intimidate my court. Few beyond my clarks can read or write, and the presence of one so adept at both lends a certain awe and dignity to the delegation."

Before Burtyn could open his mouth to interrupt Willam silenced him with a glance. Burtyn wisely snapped his mouth shut and sat listening.

"The girl is inconsequential. She is only a woman after all, and probably brought along to keep Maxwell amused. But it is the fourth member of the envoy that troubles me, this Alwyn. He is an enigma."

"Alwyn, Excellency?" Burtyn squeaked.

"Yes, Alwyn, he called himself. He has a reputation of sorts among your kind, I think, but he is no ambassador. He lacks any courtly manners and very nearly got himself killed in the Great Hall by concealing his hands. He obviously knows nothing of protocol. He said Sencha, the Apostate's chief diplomat, died on the journey, a victim of a stroke."

"This Alwyn troubles me. He is a mystery. Why would Julian entrust this mission to one so obviously ill-prepared?"

Willam stopped pacing and fixed Burtyn with a stare.

"I need to know who this Alwyn is. I need for you to find out. That is why I've called you here."

The smile that crept across Burtyn's face was broad, genuine and wicked.

"This Alwyn," he asked, his fingers steepled before his face. "Is he about of a height with me, bald on the top yet with a fringe of dark hair around the edges, with a snow white beard?"

Willam raised his left eyebrow a fraction, and nodded.

"You know of this man?"

The smile never left Burtyn's face. If anything it turned colder, with a hint of cruelty around the corners.

"I know of him," Burtyn answered, a faraway look in his eyes as if he were remembering unfinished business from a long time ago.

"Yes, I know him well."

# CHAPTER 30

**The door had** barely closed behind Strom Maxwell and his "honor guard" before it opened again to admit a vehemently arguing Gynnea Owyn and a mildly amused, vaguely aristocratic man dressed in the plain, brown cowl and cassock of the Librarian caste. A mixture of anger and chagrin colored Gynnea's face as she turned to Mol Graumet.

"I told him you were not to be disturbed, M'lady," she cried, tears of frustration leaking down her cheeks. "I told him you were First Lady Madeline's honored guests and he could not enter, but he would not listen. He..."

"It's all right, Gynnea," Mol tried to pacify the distraught serving girl. "Few men have the manners of a goat. Most have considerably less. You have done well. Be at peace."

Turning to the intruder she assumed command and began to upbraid him.

"You are either someone very important or someone very stupid. I hope you are important. I hate killing stupid people."

The man ignored Mol, waving her away as he would a troublesome gnat. The sardonic smile never left his face, nor rose to his eyes, as he sauntered to a tray of exotic cheeses and selected a dark yellow chuck with veins of red running through it. He popped the morsel into his mouth, reached for the pitcher of chilled citrus and poured the golden liquor into a silver chalice that stood beside it. When it was full, he raised the cup in salute to Mol.

"M'lady," he said, then took a long drink.

Mol stood for a moment in confused silence as she observed the effect the man's presence had on both LaFranc and Alwyn. LaFranc stood stock still, his eyes flickering between Alwyn and the intruder, waiting...watching.

Alwyn moved as if in a dream, if a man in a dream could be said to move like the wind. Before the interloper could lower his cup Alwyn had his fists twisted into the fabric of his cassock. He lifted him off the floor as he thrust him up against the wall. Long suppressed fury seethed between Alwyn's teeth, forced hot tears from the corners of his eyes and caught in painful spasms in his chest.

"I should have killed you a long time ago," Alwyn choked between clinched teeth.

He shoved the newcomer against the wall once more for emphasis, then threw him to the floor, pulling his marriage knife from a hidden pocket inside his robes the Republican Guards had thankfully missed.

"I should kill you now."

The intruder appeared only mildly surprised at his savage reception, and struggled not at all. Flat on his back, with Alwyn's knife poised to plunge into his heart, he laughed.

Baring his teeth in a rictus snarl he spat out, "Do it."

Alwyn gripped the hilt of his knife until his knuckles turn white. He had no compunction against killing. He had killed men before, and probably would again. But there was something vile to him about killing an unarmed opponent.

At last the rage drained from him, taking his strength with it. He stood and let the knife drop unnoticed from his fingers. Turning his back on the intruder, the scavenger who was now the Adam's ambassador walked silently across the room to a plain wooden chair and sat, staring at nothing.

LaFranc moved to the table with a grace that belied his bulk, poured a mug full of the steaming mulled wine, carried it to Alwyn and placed it tenderly into his hand. The younger man looked up into LaFranc's face, then down at the mug. He swirled it gently, watching the dark purple liquid slosh placidly inside the mug, staring as if trying to divine the future, or obscure the past.

"Do you know what they did to me, because of you," Alwyn's voice came out as a low whisper that somehow filled the room. "Do you know?"

"There was nothing I could have done, Alwyn," the stranger whispered back.

The tremor in his voice could have been pity or remorse, but Mol thought it had the sour stench of self-justification.

"I could not have saved you if I tried."

The stranger had not risen from his prone position on the floor. He stared at the ceiling as if the same memory joined his mind with Alwyn's.

"If I *had* tried they would have killed me."

"You brought them down on us," Alwyn's voice cracked. "You, with your arrogant pride, your damnable desire to know."

"You knew the risks," Burtyn whispered back. "No one held a knife at your throat. You wanted to go with me."

"They're all dead."

Alwyn raised the cup to his lips and forced himself to swallow a tentative sip of the steaming wine. He licked his lips, forcing them through a sheer act of will to refrain from trembling.

"They are all...dead. Malcolme. Brianna. Catharine. Our child. They are all dead. Except me."

Alwyn's eyes, glazed over with a fog of memory, narrowed to focused slits as he studied the man on the floor. He took a purposeful swallow from the cup in his hand, though he did not taste the sweetness of the wine.

"And you."

The cup slipped unnoticed from Alwyn's grip and bounced with a hollow ring on the flagstone floor.

"I should have killed you," he whispered again.

"Alwyn."

Alwyn heard his name through the haze of memory that clouded his mind, and raised his eyes to meet LaFranc's compassionate gaze.

"Alwyn, remember the traditions of the scavengers; the law of hospitality," the older man said with quiet dignity.

Alwyn stared at LaFranc for a long moment, then shook his head as if trying to clear away the cobwebs.

"Remember the traditions," LaFranc repeated.

A laugh rang out as Burtyn pulled himself to a sitting position on the floor.

"Of course. The traditions. They are everything, are they not? Where would we be without our traditions?"

With an easy grace Burtyn regained his feet and made a grand show of brushing the dust from his backside. He winked mischievously at Mol Graumet, popped another piece of the red-veined cheese into his mouth and chewed, content to let another have the next word.

His gaze alternated between Alwyn and LaFranc, but neither appeared ready to speak. Pulling a slat-backed chair from the table, Burtyn abruptly turned it backward and sat straddled with his arms resting on the chair back.

"Gynnea," he called over his shoulder, never taking his eyes from Alwyn and LaFranc, "be a sweetheart and pour me another cup of Citrus. I seem to have spilled mine."

The serving girl glanced at Mol, who nodded a grudging permission, then moved quickly to obey, placing the cup in Burtyn's outstretched hand.

"You may go now, Gynnea," Burtyn ordered, never doubting he would be obeyed. "You have done your duty."

Gynnea stood her ground with her eyes downcast, afraid she would be punished severely for disobeying the President's scavenger, yet fiercely determined that Mol Graumet stood higher.

Mol nodded slightly and indicated the door with her eyes. The girl curtsied and met Mol's eyes with smoldering devotion before she turned for the door.

"I'll be just outside should you need anything, *My Lady*," she emphasized before closing he door behind her.

Once more a palpable silence hung over the room, Burtyn's nervous rocking of the chair the only movement.

"So," Burtyn said at last, his smile taking on a gleeful gleam. "Do you want to see it?"

Alwyn and LaFranc exchanged a startled glance while Mol stood open jawed. Burtyn threw back his head, laughing with a joy that could only be described as childlike.

"Come," be beckoned as he rose to his feet. "Come, and prepare to be amazed."

# EPILOGUE

**Glenferrin picked up** a stone that was the size of his fist. He walked to the edge of the grotto that had been his prison for more candles than he cared to count. He might have walked farther had his ankle not been fettered with a dull, metal shackle that was attached to a chain, that was fastened to a U-shaped bolt, which had been driven into the rock at the back of the grotto. In a single, smooth motion he threw the stone far out over the mountainside and watched it continue to bounce until it was out of sight.

He walked back to the pile of stones he had gathered. They were his only defense against the creature that floated in the air and appeared daily now at the mouth of his prison. The creature would spread its arms wide, wider than a man was tall, and cry out as it eyed Glenferrin fearlessly, hungrily. Covered with something that was neither flesh nor fur, the creature hopped on taloned feet; talons that looked capable of rending his flesh and tearing out his liver.

Glenferrin picked up another stone from the pile, carried it to the edge of the grotto and threw it away Twenty-eight times Glenferrin, who once sat at the feet of Timoth, repeated the ritual. The last stone was larger than the rest. Glenferrin set it on the edge of his grotto, nudged it over with his foot, and watched it bound away - free.

The lesser orb had descended from the sky. It was dark now, thought still far brighter than Inside. Soon the greater orb would rise with its burning, blinding light. As a boy Glenferrin had felt its power to burn and to blind. Today, he was determined to feel it again. He would watch the orb rise until it burned him sightless. Then he would wait for the creature to come and end his captivity. Then, at last, he would be free. Then, at last, Gwendelyre, his love, would be free of him.

Glenferrin sat cross-legged at the mouth of his grotto and waited. The now familiar sounds of the world stirring to wakefulness cheered his spirit. Small scurrying sounds, the floating creatures singing to each other, the whistle of something unseen dancing among the rocks, tickling the fine hairs on his arms.

*It is the Sab. It is was a good day to die.*

The great orb peeked over the edge of the world, and Glenferrin opened his eyes wide to drink it in. Shadows fled from the valley below as the orb ascended, now one-third of its circle visible above the horizon.

Still Glenferrin watched.

The brightness reached the mouth of the grotto that was his prison, warming his flesh, burning his flesh.

Still Glenferrin forced his eyes to observe.

At last the great orb that ruled the morning was full. Glenferrin's eyes drank in the light. His sight began to fade. Colors melted into a dull red with the image of the great orb floating before him. He could see nothing else.

He smiled. He waited.

*Soon.*

The familiar flapping noise greeted him like an old friend. He welcomed the scratching sound of talons hopping toward him; welcomed the life-ending slice of those talons, the piercing of the fierce, hard-looking mouth. He feared neither the pain nor the shadow of death. He was in the hands of The

One.

A sudden thud startled him, and the sound of something falling down the mountainside. The soft footsteps approaching bewildered him. It could not be 'Lyre and Geofmorin. They would not come until the great orb set. None other knew he was there.

Strong, calloused hands grasped his face. Glenferrin tried to bat them away. He could not see and fear tried to grip his heart. The strong hands brushed Glenferrin's hands away. He heard a soothing, *'Shhh,'* like a mother might say to a crying child who had skinned his knee.

The hands drew Glenferrin back into the shade, to the small bed in the back of the grotto, and sat him upon it. They drew open his eyelids and he heard and exasperated, 'Tsk.'

The hands went away for a moment, then returned. One hand opened an eyelid, and the other gently slathered a soothing ointment onto Glenferrin's eye. The hands repeated their ministrations on his other eye, then some kind of material was wrapped about his head, forcing his eyes to stay shut.

The hands pressed a waterskin into Glenferrin's hands and he lifted it to his lips. The liquid inside was not water. It burned his mouth, but it warmed Glenferrin inside in a way he had never experienced before.

Glenferrin felt a sharp blow beside his ankle and stifled a yelp of pain. The he felt the fetter that had held him fast fall away.

"Who are you?" Glenferrin tried to make himself understood. He spoke slowly, enunciating each word distinctly, as if to a dimwitted child.

"What do you want? Why did you help me?"

Though no words were spoken, Glenferrin heard the words form in his mind.

*I am called Catharine, who was once daughter of Theodora and Pepin, Raek of the Amarillo Nomes. I seek a man called…Alwyn.*

*So Ends*

# The Scavengers
Book I of the Tyrfingr Chronicles

*Coming Soon*

# Treasures of Darkness
Book II of the Tyrfingr Chronicles

# GLOSSARY

**Abel** - One of the People. He who Sits at the Feet of Dutronomy

**Alchiber** - The process of making ink.

**Alycia** - Alwyn's twin sister. Julian's wife.

**Amarillo Nomes** - A wandering people indigenous to the Amarillo Waste.

**Amarillo Waste** - Nomish territory in the south central part of the Continent.

**Ancient American** - The language of the people of the United States before the Time of Madness.

**Angleesh** - An obscure dialect predating Ancient American.

**Baldwyn** - A Nome. Cup-bearer to Pepin, Raek of the Amarillo Nomes.

**Battle of Kaibec** - A battle in the Canadian Wars.

**Battle of Thousand Lakes** - A decisive battle in the Canadian

Wars.

**Bigger Olsson** - A Forrester.

**Binnie Tuk** - A Forrester.

**Brianna** - Alwyn's mother.

**Burtyn** - A scavenger. Alwyn's older brother.

**Calif of Orange** - Ruler of the Califorangians.

**Califate of Orange** - Island nation to the west of the Central Highlands.

**Candlemas** - A two-week celebration marking the shortest days of the year.

**Canada** - Barbaric nation to the north of the United States.

**Canuk** - Derogatory reference to Canadians.

**Capital Building** - Seat of power of the Adam and the Sons of Liberty.

**Catharine** - Daughter of Pepin and Theodora. Alwyn's wife. Franklyn's mother.

**Common Era** - Calendar measuring time since the Time of Madness.

**Confederation of the Southlands** - Loose alliance of southern city-states. Once thought to be a part of the United States, now fiercely independent.
**Corner Stone** - Resting place of Tyrfingr.

**Dakota** - A United State.

**Deyo** - A dry substance which, when mixed with water, produced ink.

**Dome of the Rock** - The great chamber of meeting which holds Tyrfingr.

**Donation of Constantine** - Oath taken by all United States Presidents acknowledging the supremacy of the Adam's authority.

**Dutronomy** - One of the Twenty-Four Elders of the People.

**Eithne** -  One of the People. Glenferrin's mother.

**Fair Folk** - A mythical race. Said to dwell underground. They refer to themselves as The People.

**Frollo Massad** - A Nome. Exiled, but reputed to have great powers.

**Franklyn** - A Nome. Alwyn and Catharine's son.

**Glenferrin** - One of the People. He who Sits at the Feet of Timoth.

**Geofmorin** - One of the People. An enforcer of the Law.

**Great Burning** - The cataclysmic, undefined event which marked the end of one era, and the beginning of another.

**Griggs** - A soldier in the Republican Guard.
**Grimoire** - A book of evil magic.

**Guild of the Librarians** - A learned class of citizens. Keepers of knowledge and the written word.

**Gulf of Texas** - Body of water separating the continent from the Califate of Orange.

**Gwendelyre** - One of the People. Glenferrin's betrothed.

**Gynnea Owyn** - A serving girl in the Presidential palace in White House.

**Hand** - Standard unit of measure. The width of a man's hand. Five fingers make one hand.

**Handball** - A children's game where contestants slap a ball over a net, back and forth between them. The ball cannot be grasped, but must be hit with an open hand or closed fist. The side that allows the ball to touch the ground loses a point.

**H'ashasine** - Adherent of the cult of H'ashishiyyin.

**H'ashishiyyin** - An outlawed religious sect that exalts the taking of human life. Thought to be extinct.

**Hel** - The goddess of the dead and the underworld. Often depicted in contemporary art as a beautiful young woman from the waist up, but a skeletal figure from the waist down.

**Henbane** - A sleep inducing drug.

**High** - Midday.

**Highlanders** - Clannish tribes who inhabit the Central Highlands.

**Holy Medallions** - Ancient relics used to mark rank among the Sons of Liberty. Each Holy Medallion depicts one of the Five Faces of God.

**Hwana** - An herb. Burned to produce a smoke that is used to alleviate the suffering of the dying. Some inhale the smoke recreationally for its euphoric effects.

**James** - First among the Twenty-Four Elders of the People.

**Jasyn Grey** - One of the Republican Guards.

**Jon** - A Nome. Catharine's brother. Franklyn's Uncle.

**Jude** - One of the Twenty-Four Elders of the People.

**Julian** - The Adam. The First Man of the Faith. Head of the priestly caste of the Sons of Liberty.

**Justice** - The name of Willam Norman's great sword; a symbol of his power and justice.

**Kanetuck Wilderness** - Wild, wooded area in the eastern part of the continent. Known for producing paper and leaf.

**Kennedy** - One of the five incarnations of God.

**Library** - The repository for all learning in the United States of America.

**Leaf** - An aromatic plant prized for the euphoric, relaxed mood it produces when chewed.

**Leek** - A Forrester.

**Less Olsson** - A Forrester.

**Libertarian Guards** - Elite bodyguards of the Adam.

**Liberty** - The name of the God of the United States of America; the God of Five Faces.

**Loch-Lann** - Ancient kings of the White Sands Nomes.

**Madeline** - Wife of Willam Norman. First Lady of the United States of American.

**Mal'chi** - One of the Twenty-Four Elders of the People.

**Malcolme** - A renowned scavenger. Alwyn's father.

**Marc** - One of the Twenty-Four Elders of the People.

**Marriage Knife** - A ceremonial knife used in the marriage ritual of the Nomes.

**Modern American** - The written language of the United States of America.

**Mol Graumet** - A Forrester.

**Mother** - One of the many gods and goddesses worshiped by the Nomes.

**Never-Dimming Flame** - Symbol of the Librarians.

**North Iowa** - A United State.

**Occam** - Late President of the United States. Willam

Norman's father.

**Oculars** - A device of wire and glass used to help weak-eyed people see more clearly.

**Omaha** - A United State.

**Omaha** - The capital city of the United State of Omaha. The Seat of Liberty.

**Padrag** - One of the People. Glenferrin's father.

**Paper Guild** - A secretive guild of craftsmen who possess the knowledge of making paper.

**Paval LaFranc** - The Chief Librarian.

**Pepin** - Raek of the Amarillo Nomes. Catherine's father. Franklyn's grandfather.

**Powyl Mac** - Governor of the United State of Atlantis.

**President** - The figurehead political leader of the United States of America.

**Puhl-Lichter** - A comet.

**Raek** - Title of the Clan Chief of the Amarillo Nomes.

**Raek Law** - Unchanging law of the Amarillo Nomes.

**Republican Guards** - Willam Norman's elite personal guards.

**Rings** - Unite of money in the United States. Made of gold, silver, copper or baser metals.

**Rule 3** - Charge an ambush.

**Rule 6** - Knowledge is power.

**Rule 7** - He who gets there first with the most men, wins.

**Rule 8** - When you can't get there first with the most men, make damned sure you get there undetected.

**Rule 14** - Don't do nuthin' dumb.

**Sab** - The holy day of the People.

**Samildanach** - The title given to men of great learning and power. In the old tongue it means, 'Master of all arts.'

**Scavengers** - An adventurous sect of the Librarians who search for artifacts from ancient civilizations.

**Scylla** - One of Julian's four wives.

**Sencha** - The Adam's personal ambassador.

**Shadowmen** - Slang name for the H'ashasine.

**Shyrman** - A Nome.

**Sinan Salman** - The Old Man of the Mountain. Founder of the H'ashishiyyin.

**Sitter** - Apprentice who sits at the feet of one of the Twenty-Four Elders of the People.

**Smit Mikalsson** - A scavenger of great renown. Alwyn's

grandfather.

**Sofie** - A citizen of White House. A tender of the baths.

**Sons of Liberty** - The religious leaders of the United States of America.

**South Iowa** - A United State.

**Southlanders** - Citizens of the Confederacy of the Southlands.

**Speakers of the Word** - Those who hear the words of the Twenty-Four and speak them to the People.

**Stone Wall** - A holy place of worship in Atlantis.

**Strom Maxwell** - A solder, smuggler, founder of the Forresters, and closer personal friend of Julian.

**Sun Festival** - A two-week celebration marking the longest days of the year.

**Texas** - Mythical land at the end of the world. Some compare it to paradise; others compare it to hell.

**The Ohios** - A United State.

**The One** - The God of the People.

**The People** - The name the Fair Folk refer to themselves by.

**The Pol** - An ancient prophet of the People.

**The Stone** - The legendary resting place of Tyrfingr.
**The Twenty-Four** - The ruling body of the People.

**Theodora** - A Nome. Pepin's wife. Catharine's mother. Franklyn's grandmother.

**Tomsyn** - A Forrester.

**Timoth** - One of the Twenty-Four Elders of the People.

**Time of Madness** - A period of approximately 300 years between the Great Burning and the rise of Modern America.

**Tyler** - A Nome.

**Tyrfingr** - A portent of the end of the world.

**Washington** - One of the five incarnations of God.

**White House** - Capital city of the United State of North Iowa. Home to the President.

**White Sands Nomes** - A wandering people indigenous to the White Sands Waste.

**White Sands Waste** - Nome territory in the southwest part of the continent, adjacent to the Central Highlands.

**Whitesnake Root** - A particularly deadly poison.

**Willam Norman** - President of the United States of America.

# ACKNOWLEDGEMENTS

Writing a novel is a bit like conceiving a baby - its requires a lot of energy, it's a lot of fun and nobody does it all by themselves. Here's a brief Thank You to all those who participated in breathing life into **The Scavengers.**

To my big brother, Rick, who was the first storyteller I ever knew, and whetted my appetite for masters of the craft like Poe, Verne, Howard and Burroughs. Thanks.

To my little brother, Chris, who showed more courage in the face of adversity than I can imagine. Thanks.

To my Mom and Dad, who are the definition of the word, Steadfast. Thanks.

To fellow authors and friends, Chris Coppernoll, Melanie Wells, Andrew Peterson, Bonnie Keen, and GP Taylor, who have walked this road before and encouraged me to come along. Thanks.

To the family at SWAC (you know who you are) for the freedom to express creativity as an act of worship. Thanks.

To David Warren for your amazing design skills, and for your unwavering friendship. Thanks.

To Robert and Tracy Sugg for your incredible talent and enduring friendship. Thanks.

To Helen Jones for always believing. Thanks.

To Rachael, Anna, Nathan, Joshua, Bethany, Billy Mary and Isabella. You all ROCK! Thanks.

To Paula, the wife of my youth, for everything good in my life. Thanks.

To The One. Thank you.